KEEP YOUR
FRIENDS
CLOSE

ALSO BY JANELLE HARRIS

KEEP YOUR FRIENDS CLOSE

JANELLE HARRIS

LAKE UNION
PUBLISHING

Text copyright © 2020 by Janelle Harris
All rights reserved.

Published by Lake Union Publishing, Seattle

www.apub.com

Amazon, the Amazon logo, and Lake Union Publishing are trademarks of Amazon.com, Inc., or its affiliates.

ISBN-13: 9781542004954
ISBN-10: 1542004950

Cover design by Dominic Forbes

Printed in the United States of America

Beware of jealousy for verily it destroys good deeds
the way fire destroys wood

—*Muhammad*

Prologue

THE IRISH INFORMER
13TH MAY 2000
MISSING TEENAGER IN DUBLIN

Gardaí in Westrow are appealing for the public's help in locating a missing 18-year-old. Gillian Buckley is a 6th-year student at St Peter's boarding school. She is the daughter of the renowned businessman and philanthropist, Andrew Buckley.

Gillian is described as 5'6" and of slim build, with green eyes and strawberry-blonde hair. Gillian was last seen in the school library yesterday afternoon and she was wearing her St Peter's school uniform: a navy jumper with crest, white blouse and a navy and grey tartan skirt.

Principal at St Peter's, Mr Martin McEvoy, said: 'We have serious concerns for Gillian's welfare. Gillian is a popular and happy pupil in our school. It is most unlike her to miss class or not to phone home regularly.'

Gardaí ask anyone with information to please contact Westrow Garda Station on 01 64737266 or the Garda Confidential Telephone Line on 0807 888 111, or call into any Garda station.

Chapter One

Darcy

Monday 10 June 2019

Jinx, my fluffy white Bichon Frise, is tucked under my arm. My other hand is curled around my husband's – my fingers knitted between his – as we stand outside a large, revolving door at the television studio. The grey-brick building is the biggest among many others set in private and secure grounds. Every building bears the national broadcaster's logo above the door and there's little to differentiate one building from the other, except for size. After a couple of false starts I hope we've finally found the main reception.

'A penny for them?' Luke asks.

'Hmm?' I say, distracted.

'What are you thinking, honey?'

'Oh erm . . .'

'I know you're nervous,' Luke says.

'Is it that obvious?' I ask, stroking my thumb under Jinx's ear, just the way he likes it. His tail wags.

Luke laughs. 'Well, if you hold my hand any tighter, I think you're going to cut off my circulation.'

'Oh.' I glance at my hand wrapped tightly around my husband's. My knuckles are white and shaking. 'Sorry,' I say, as I let go and realise how clammy my palm is when the cool air hits it. 'I'm just feeling the pressure a little. We need this to go well so badly. Airtime like this is invaluable. Especially at the moment. And—'

'And you've got this,' Luke says, reaching for my hand again and slipping his fingers between mine. 'Do you remember when you were Rizzo in our school play?'

'It's hard to believe that was twenty years ago. I remember it so well,' I say.

'You stole the whole show,' Luke says. 'Everyone in St Peter's was asking "Sandy who?"'

I blush. 'That's not quite how I remember it.'

'You were amazing,' he says. 'And you're going to be amazing again today. People are going to love you as much as I do.'

'Thanks,' I say, smiling as I finally pluck up enough courage to lead us through the doors and into the main reception.

I introduce myself at the desk. 'Good morning. I'm Darcy Hogan. I'm a guest on *Good Morning, Ireland* today.'

'Go through the doors behind me.' The receptionist points over her shoulder without turning her head. 'I'll buzz you in now.'

'Thank you,' I say, as the security door makes a loud clinking sound and I cross my fingers behind my back and hope this all goes as well as Luke and I desperately need it to.

The hustle and bustle on the other side of the door is a stark contrast to the calm and silent reception.

'Oh good, you're here,' a young woman with a clipboard and headset says, draping her arm over my shoulder and guiding me down a long corridor. 'Oh. And a puppy too,' she adds, seeming less excited to see Jinx. 'We were beginning to worry you'd got cold feet.'

'I'm so sorry we're late,' I say. 'We got a little lost.' I leave out the part about having to pull over on the side of the motorway – twice – so I could be sick, and then it was almost impossible to pull back into the manic morning traffic.

'No worries. You're here now,' she says, as we step into a brightly lit dressing room. 'I don't think people realise that although the show starts at 8 a.m. everyone has been here for hours beforehand prepping.'

'I don't mind,' I say. 'I like mornings.'

It's true. I am an early bird. Always have been. I get up most mornings at 6, sometimes 5.30. I like to get a walk in before work. I'm usually just arriving home after 8 kilometres when Luke is getting up, and we drive to the factory together. We're always in our office or on the floor by 8 a.m. at the latest. But for the last couple of months, Luke has usually left for work before I even manage to open my eyes.

'Is that something important?' the clipboard lady asks, pointing at the book tucked under Luke's arm.

'It's my new recipe book,' I say, excitedly. 'It's not out for a couple of months yet—'

'And you don't want to miss an opportunity to plug it. I getcha,' she says, winking. 'C'mon.' She places a hand on Luke's shoulder as she guides him towards the door. 'I'll show you where to leave it.'

I'm alone only for a matter of seconds when there's a gentle knock on the door, followed by a cheery voice. 'Hello, hello, hello. Is it okay to come in?'

'Yes. Of course,' I say, recognising the distinctive lilt. 'Come on in.'

The door creaks open and Lindsay St Claire's head appears in the gap. Her golden hair is in curlers and she isn't wearing a scrap of make-up, but she is still stunning. And I wonder if my inner fangirling over my favourite TV presenter is noticeable.

5

'Welcome to *Good Morning, Ireland*. I'm so glad you're here, Darcy.' She smiles, flashing her dazzlingly white teeth.

'Thank you,' I say, bubbles of nervous excitement fizzing in my veins. 'I'm glad to be here, at last.'

'And you're welcome too, Mr Fluffy,' Lindsay says, stroking a sleepy Jinx's head. Without opening his eyes he nuzzles into her hand, letting her know he loves her gentle touch.

I introduce my beloved puppy. 'This is Jinx.'

'Gosh, you're just gorgeous, aren't you?' Lindsay says, putting on that squeaky voice that people use sometimes when they're talking to animals or babies. 'Aren't you a good boy? You are. Yes, you are.'

'Thank you for having me on the show,' I say, but I don't think Lindsay is listening. She's petting Jinx and smiling and cooing.

Lindsay's team has been inviting me on air for months – ever since I won Businesswoman of the Year. And for months I have politely declined. Marketing and publicity is my top concern, but we're an eco-friendly business – flashy awards and morning television shows aren't exactly in keeping with our carbon-footprint-conscious image. Besides, it's almost impossible to sing the praises of Darcy's Dishes without sounding as if I think I'm special. I don't. I work damn hard and I've been lucky, too. That's all. But Lindsay has made no effort to hide her disappointment at my reluctance.

'I'm not giving up, you know,' she joked each time.

And she didn't. When Lindsay called last week, her confidence radiated down the phone. There was no doubt that she'd finally come up with an offer I couldn't refuse.

'Please be my guest and talk about how hard this pregnancy has been for you. Help other women know they're not alone,' she said, sincerely.

As soon as I sighed and said I'd think about it, Lindsay knew she had me.

I'd foolishly used my condition to wriggle out of her previous invite. Hyperemesis Gravidarum is torture. I've been in and out of hospital like a yo-yo. Lindsay was sympathetic and understanding. Too understanding, because now she wants me to comfort other women in the same boat.

Hanging up the phone, I was as dubious as ever, but Luke, on the other hand, couldn't contain his excitement when I told him.

'Do it for me . . . I've always wanted to sleep with a celebrity.' He laughed, but I know it's not a joke. My husband has an unhealthy obsession with Reese Witherspoon. He's fancied the pants off her since we were teenagers. I think that's what he fancies about me. Everyone says I'm a dead ringer for her.

But, Reese's looks or not, the timing has never been right for a TV appearance. Not until now.

'It's publicity that money can't buy,' Luke said.

I explained that money was my concern. Darcy's Dishes is up to its neck in debt. Staffing cost are ever increasing, but orders are down. We're struggling like never before.

'How can I go on national television and pretend everything is fine? I'm not an actress. Or a liar. The public will see straight through me,' I said, terrified.

'You're a star, honey,' Luke said. 'Businesswoman of the Year.'

His words ring in my ears now as I get a sinking feeling in the pit of my stomach. I don't deserve to be Businesswoman of the Year. Not when my business is failing.

Lindsay must notice my jitters as she finally pulls her attention away from Jinx and says, 'Someone will be in to you shortly to do your hair and make-up.' She points to her own hair.

'Oh. I didn't realise.' I glance at the mirror, taking in my full face of make-up and my hair that I spent ages straightening this morning at silly o'clock when I could barely keep my eyes open.

'You look great,' Lindsay says, 'but studio lights are no one's friend. We usually go a couple of shades darker than normal. Even the male presenters wear bronzer. Don't worry if you feel a bit over made-up. It will look fab on camera, I promise.'

'Erm, okay.'

'And Berta from fashion will be around to you shortly. She is a genius. I just know you're going to love the dress she's chosen for you.'

'Oh that's okay,' I say, running my hands over the black, maternity business suit I've been itching for a chance to wear. 'I'm very comfortable in this.'

I can see Lindsay taking a deep breath, and she hums before speaking. 'And you look a-*ma*-zing in that chic suit. Every inch the businesswoman, which of course you are. But we're hoping for something a little more fitted. Show off that precious belly.'

'Belly,' I say.

'Absolutely. Viewers love to see a glowing mama-to-be.'

I shake my head. 'I'm not sure—'

'Don't be shy,' Lindsay cuts across me. 'You're all bump, not a pick of pregnancy weight on you. It must be the vegan diet. You'll have to give me some tips after the show.'

'I *do* have some recipes to share.' I smile. 'My husband has actually just gone to give them to your research assistant.'

'Very exciting,' Lindsay says, but she doesn't sound excited. 'Now, I just want to check if there are any personal questions you'd like me to avoid.'

The question catches me off guard and I wonder if my expression tells Lindsay as much.

'Some people don't like talking about their childhood,' she explains. 'Or relationships and marriages can sometimes—'

I gather my thoughts and interrupt her. 'I'd rather not discuss my personal life at all.'

'Ah,' Lindsay nods. 'Gotcha. Say no more. It can't be easy working and living together. We'll keep all questions focused on the baby.'

I'm about to reiterate that I don't want to discuss anything personal when Luke walks in. 'Excuse me, Ms St Claire, the lady with the clipboard and headset is looking for you,' he says.

Lindsay rolls her eyes and exhales loudly. 'Excuse me, won't you.'

'She's amazing, isn't she?' Luke says, when she's walked out.

'Um . . .' I sigh. 'I have a bad feeling about today. Maybe this was all a terrible idea.'

'That's just the nerves talking,' Luke reassures me. 'You are going to be great. And some day our little girl will watch this back and be as proud of you as I am.'

Chapter Two

Tina

Monday 10 June 2019

The curtains are drawn as I sit on the bed flicking through television stations, not particularly paying attention to what's on. My compact bedsit always seems even smaller with the curtains closed. They're top-quality blackout ones. Floral, in autumn colours, and certainly not my taste. But the landlord was chuffed with himself when he arrived with them tucked under his arm a couple of months ago.

'They'll give you a little extra privacy,' Vinny said. 'And they'll keep the heat in. They're thick, they are.'

'Great. Thank you,' I said, humouring him.

This place is a sweet deal and we both know it. The rent is a steal and in return Vinny knows I'll take care of the place and not cause any trouble. It's nestled in an old part of town; a linear stream of rundown bungalows with some recently refurbished and divided into bedsits. This area of Dublin once had community spirit and hard-working people at its core. Now, less so. There's a bunch of twenty-something lads crammed into the bungalow to my left. Their souped-up cars and tracksuit bottoms do little to disguise their drug-dealing habits. But, it's small-time peddling – they use more than they sell. It's the couple at the end of the road with the fancy Mercedes and *friends* stopping by at all hours whom I'm wary of.

An elderly couple live on my right. The Simmons. A kind man and his ailing wife. I try to help them out once in a while. Carry some groceries in, pop in for a chat and a cup of tea, that sort of thing. But nonetheless, it's hard to fit in in a place where it's obvious I don't belong.

I hit mute on the TV remote and cock my ear towards the door, thinking I hear the doorbell. It dings again. I pull myself off my bed, and pins and needles attack my toes after spending too long curled up with my feet tucked under me.

'Just a minute,' I say, panicked.

I grab the cash, piled high on the kitchen table, and shove it down the side of the couch. The lady in the bank looked at me as if I had two heads when I withdrew it all in a single lump sum last week, pretty much clearing out my account.

'And can I ask why such a large transaction today?'

I glared at her.

'For security reasons,' the nosey cow added.

Stating the obvious, I said, 'I'm buying something.'

'Right.' She smiled and gave me my money. Highlighting how stupid the whole conversation was in the first place.

The doorbell rings again.

'Hello. Heeelllooo. Tina, I know you're in there. I heard the telly.'

'I'm coming. I said I'm coming.'

I glance over my shoulder and give my pokey living space the once-over. Convinced everything looks as it should, I open the door.

'Good morning,' I say, unsurprised to find my landlord on my doorstep.

'Um. Yeah,' he says, stepping past me without an invite. 'Good morning.'

'Eh, would you like to come in?' I groan sarcastically, as I close the door behind us.

'Don't pull that crap with me,' he says. 'I still own this place.'

I watch as he paces around the tiny living space. His eyes sweep over every piece of furniture. His body language is tense and jumpy. 'Right. Where is it?' he asks.

'Where is what?'

'The money?'

My throat tightens. 'What money?'

Vinny shakes his head. 'I've no time for games, Tina. I know you've gotten yourself mixed up in something. Drugs most likely, eh? You've always been a bit odd but I've tried to give you the benefit of the doubt. I thought you were just lonely, if I'm honest.'

I am lonely.

'I'm not doing anything illegal,' I say. 'I promise.'

'Well that's not what your neighbours say. Apparently, you've a stack of cash hiding in here somewhere. They've seen it through the window.'

'My neighbours said this? Ironic since they're the ones up to no good.'

Vinny jams his hands on his hips and puffs out. 'That lovely elderly couple. I don't think so.'

I shake my head. 'Hang on. Mr and Mrs Simmons? I've been nothing but nice to them.'

'Oh I know,' Vinny says. 'I've had them in my ear plenty about you.'

I shake my head and look at Vinny with an expression that asks, *What have they said?*

'You can't keep turning up on their doorstep unannounced.'

'But I just want to help,' I say.

'They have grown-up children of their own. They don't need you. It's bad enough that you call me at all hours of the day and night but now you're pestering the neighbours too. It's not on.'

I try not to let Vinny see how much his words hurt, but my eyes are glossing over.

'Look, Tina,' he says, clearly losing patience. 'You're not a bad kid. Maybe you got dealt a lousy hand in life or whatever but I can't have trouble. You're going to have to move out. I'm sorry.'

'No, please,' I say. 'I've just been let go from work. That's why I've so much free time. It's where the money came from too. It's a redundancy payment.'

'Oh.' Vinny sighs, and his stiff shoulders relax.

'I'm going to set up my own business,' I say. 'I just need a little time.'

'Good for you.'

'Thank you,' I say, smiling. 'Here, let me show you.' I hurry over to the countertop next to the cooker and fetch my scrapbook. I flick through the pages excitedly showing him pictures of elaborate cakes and muffins that I've cut out from baking magazines to create beautiful collages. 'This one is lemon drizzle.' I point. 'Oh, and my favourite, a chocolate biscuit here. See?'

Vinny exhales and pulls a face. 'These are all very nice, love, but there's more to running a successful business than sticking pictures in some old scrapbook.'

'I know. I know.' I can't curb my enthusiasm. 'This is just the start. I have loads more ideas.'

'Do you want my advice?' he asks.

'Sure.' I shrug, closing my scrapbook, deflated that he's not showing an interest.

'Use the cash to buy yourself some decent clothes.' He glances at my pyjamas where the seam on one side of my top is unravelling up to my ribcage and a long thread hangs loose. 'Find a new job. And a new flat.'

'A new flat?' I echo.

'In a better area, eh?' he says.

'You want me to move out?' I say.

Vinny nods and his eyes are focused on the ground. 'You have until the end of the month. Good luck, love.'

I watch as Vinny walks himself to the door. He doesn't turn around, not even to say goodbye. I wait until he's turned the corner at the end of the road before I slam the door behind him. I don't realise I've been holding my breath until I press my back against the door and breathe out, exhausted. Bending my knees, I slide slowly to the floor, my eyes staring into the distance. I don't even notice I'm staring at the TV – not until her face comes on.

Her!

It's really her.

After all these years it's Darcy Hogan. I don't believe it.

Chapter Three

DARCY

Monday 10 June 2019

Luke kisses the top of my head. 'I'd say good luck, but you don't need it, honey.'

I raise my head to meet my husband's loving gaze. I don't tell him that my stomach is heaving and my palms are sticky. 'Thank you,' I say.

Luke takes a step back, drinking me in with his eyes the way he always does when he wants to make me feel special. The way he has done since we were just a couple of kids.

'Can you watch?' I ask. 'Does the waiting room have a live stream or anything . . .' I trail off.

'I'm not going anywhere.' Luke is grinning and his excitement is palpable. 'I'll be at the side of the set. Out of camera shot, of course,' he adds.

'Oh.'

'I mean, I had to ask,' Luke says, running his hand through his dark hair that's greying at the sides. 'But they didn't seem to mind, and I thought you'd like the support.'

It's uncomfortable to fold my arms above my large bump but I do it anyway as I nod and say, 'I'm glad you're here.'

'Me too.' Luke smiles. 'Do you think many people will be watching? I really think it's going to be so good for business.'

'Yeah. Everyone watches the show, don't they? Parents before the school run. *Us* when we're getting ready for work. And it's on the telly in every waiting room in the country. Every single appointment I've had at the maternity hospital has *Good Morning, Ireland* playing in the background.' I take a moment to realise the enormity of what I've just said. 'Oh God, Luke. So many people will be watching.'

Before Luke has a chance to reply, the girl with the clipboard comes to find us.

'Ready?' she asks, peeking her head around the door.

I wince, twitching nervously. I wish she'd introduced herself, or I had thought to ask her name earlier. It all feels awkward not knowing what to call her.

'Oh God,' I say, freaking out.

'C'mon, honey. You can do this,' Luke says. 'I'm so proud of you.'

I feel Luke's hand on my knee, squeezing gently. Jinx barks loudly and suddenly, clearly objecting to Luke's arm reaching across him.

'Bloody dog,' Luke grunts. 'I swear he thinks no one should touch you except him.'

'He's just a puppy,' I say, rubbing under Jinx's ear to calm him. 'Shh. Shh, boy.'

'I know you don't want to hear it, Darcy, but we might have to get rid of him once the baby arrives. If he's this snappy around me if I get too close to you, can you imagine what he'll be like around the baby?'

I pull a face. 'Take him, please. I gotta go.'

I pass Jinx over, and after his initial silly protest he snuggles against Luke's chest.

'Can we leave the dog here, please?' the clipboard lady asks. 'It's just, we can't have barking in the background while we're rolling.'

I look at Luke with a pleading expression.

'Fine,' he sighs, rolling his eyes. 'I'll wait here with him.'

'Thank you,' I mouth as I'm ushered away.

Reaching the set, I'm surprised at how different it seems now to what you see on TV. The area is sparse and overly bright. There's a single armchair for Lindsay on one side and a couch for her guests opposite. Cameras seem to take up the bulk of the area in front. And people in dark clothing and headsets far outnumber those in front of the camera.

Lindsay totters into position effortlessly in high, spindly heels. Her hair bounces on her shoulders and her make-up is subtle yet flattering. She notices me out of the corner of her eye and turns to beckon me, smiling.

Slowly, I take my seat opposite her on a couch big enough to fit four adults comfortably. I feel a little lost, all alone in the middle. My hair is equally as perfect as Lindsay's, my make-up flawless, and I'm glad I wore my suit and not that horrible polka-dot dress. I look professional and calm – for now, at least.

Silence descends suddenly and my palms sweat as I realise we're rolling.

'Gooooood morning, Ireland,' Lindsay chirps in the familiar sing-song voice she uses every morning to introduce the show.

I watch as she announces yesterday's competition winner and reads today's newspaper headlines with enthusiasm and vigour. And her toothy smile never falters. Finally, she turns away from the camera and towards me.

'Good morning, Darcy,' she says. 'I'm so happy you're here.'

'I'm delighted to be here,' I reply as we repeat the pleasantries from the dressing room, almost word for word.

It isn't long before I begin to relax, almost forgetting that there is a nation of viewers on the far side of the camera, watching. Lindsay introduces me and my business with ease. She talks up Darcy's Dishes' savoury line first before moving on to the desserts, chatting with the vocabulary of an experienced chef. All I need to do is nod and smile. *Luke was so right*, I think, grinning as I stare into the camera. *This interview will be so good for business.*

'And now, moving on to more serious matters,' Lindsay says, sliding to the edge of her seat so she can reach me and take my hands in hers. 'Have you heard of Hyperemesis Gravidarum, ladies and gentlemen? Probably not. And that's because although the condition is estimated to affect point five to two per cent of pregnant women, it is very rarely talked about. Darcy is currently experiencing this serious condition and she is here to tell us all about it in her own words.' Lindsay squeezes my hand gently. 'Whenever you're ready, Darcy, tell us . . . how are you feeling?'

I take a deep breath. I knew this question was coming. It's the whole reason I'm on the show, but somehow forcing the words *I'm struggling* to pass my lips is incredibly difficult.

'It's been hard,' I finally say.

'I can imagine,' Lindsay says, sympathetically.

I straighten my back and with confidence I say, 'People think they understand. I've had countless women tell me about their pregnancies and their experience with morning sickness. They mean well, I don't doubt. But comparing Hyperemesis to morning sickness is like comparing a summer breeze to a tropical hurricane.'

'So, tea and dry crackers aren't going to help?' Lindsay jokes.

I laugh. 'Unfortunately not. I've been hospitalised several times over the last seven months. Sometimes the condition eases in the second trimester. And sometimes it doesn't.'

'And for you it didn't?' Lindsay says.

'No. No, it didn't,' I say.

Lindsay's lips curl into a sympathetic smile as she nods with her head slightly cocked to one side. 'And it's taken a massive toll on your business too, hasn't it?'

I wince, unsure how to answer. I am the face of Darcy's Dishes. The vibrant, healthy vegan. My body is my brand. I've spent as many years honing my image as I have perfecting my products. And being ill and gaunt is bad for business. No one wants to buy a vegan cheesecake from Dracula's first cousin. Luke has done his best, taking the reins of the company, but my absence has cost us a couple of huge clients in recent months and we are heading into the red.

'It's fair to say this condition has turned your life upside down,' Lindsay says.

I smile, grateful that Lindsay has sensed my distress and changed direction.

'Yes.' I swallow. 'It has really been very, very hard.'

'Okay,' Lindsay chirps, letting go of my hand and sitting up straight. 'It's time for a break, but when we come back we'll be taking some of your calls.' Lindsay waits for the cue from the director and says, 'The lines are open now.'

Someone dressed all in black rushes over with a coffee for Lindsay. They ask me if I need water or anything, but I raise my hand and shake my head. The smell wafting from Lindsay's flask is already making me queasy.

'You're doing great,' Lindsay says between mouthfuls. 'The calls should be a fabulous way to talk about your product line. Is there anything in particular you'd like us to plug?'

'Oh.' I smile, delighted. 'The lasagne would be great? It's all meat free, of course, but impossible to tell. And maybe the cheesecake, that's new.'

'Super,' Lindsay says, passing the flask back to the assistant who then quickly touches up Lindsay's lipstick before dashing away.

'And we're back in three . . . two . . . one . . .' someone announces.

'Hello, and welcome back,' Lindsay says, her enthusiasm punctuated with a single clap of her hands and a beaming grin.

I follow her lead and smile too, but my nerves are back to square one after the short repose off air and I find myself fidgeting with a button on my blazer.

Lindsay presses her finger subtly to her ear and says, 'I think we have our first caller. Good morning, who do we have on the line?'

'Eh . . . hi . . . hello,' a nervous voice replies. 'I'm Sarah.'

'Hi Sarah, what is your question for Darcy please?'

'Um . . .' Sarah gulps and it sounds oddly loud as it echoes around the studio. 'I love Darcy's Dishes' ready meals, but um . . . eh . . . my local supermarket has stopped stocking them and they said there's a problem with the supplier. Erm, I'm just wondering if you know when they'll be back in stock.'

'Hi Sarah,' I say, smiling brightly as I pretend to be calm and not completely shocked by Sarah's revelation that there are blank shelves in supermarkets where my product line should be. 'I'm sorry you haven't been able to get Darcy's Dishes for a while. But I'll personally see to it that they are back in stock very soon.'

I mean it. I'm already itching to call the office to see what on earth is going on. *I wonder if Luke knew about this.*

'Great. Thank you,' Sarah says.

'Thanks so much for your call. Bye-bye,' Lindsay says, before adding, 'and who do we have on the next line?'

'Hello, Darcy.' A low hum rattles down the line.

'Hello,' I reply, squinting as I stare into the camera. As if I might find the owner of the strange voice hiding inside.

'Hello there. You're live on *Good Morning, Ireland*. What's your name, caller?' Lindsay asks, facing the camera.

There's silence.

Lindsay tilts her head to one side, waiting, and the cameraman rolls his eyes.

'Don't be shy,' Lindsay says.

Still nothing. I wonder if the line has dropped. I find myself hoping it has.

'Hello. Are you still with us?' Lindsay probes, gently.

'Yeah,' says a voice.

Lindsay smiles. It's the same way she smiled at me when I joined her on set still wearing my suit and not a polka-dot dress.

More silence. *This is torture.* It may be silent on set but inside my head it's blaring.

'I'm afraid I really am going to have to push you for your question,' Lindsay says, firmly.

Finally, sound ripples around the studio. It's coughing at first followed by a raspy voice. 'I have a question.'

'Yes,' Lindsay nods. 'Go ahead.'

'My question is . . .' There's a deep inhale on the end of the line, and my heart is racing. 'Does Darcy remember me?'

It's my turn to inhale sharply as the fine hairs on the back of my neck stand on end. I'm petrified that the answer, a resounding yes, is etched in the corners of my fake smile. My eyes flick to the side of the set, wishing I could find Luke standing there. And when I look back, Lindsay is watching me with a measured expression that seems to ask, *Well, do you know her?*

'I'm afraid we didn't catch your name,' Lindsay says.

'Darcy knows it,' the voice says. 'Don't you, Darcy?'

Tina. Her name is Tina.

The floor manager holds up his hand with his fingers spaced wide apart. I'm not sure if he's trying to sign five seconds or five minutes. *God, I hope it's the former.*

'Do you have a question?' Lindsay asks.

'I need a job,' Tina says.

'Oh.' Lindsay smirks, choking back a snort. 'Well this is certainly a unique approach. While I love a good interview, I don't think I'm qualified to do any hiring, I'm afraid.'

Lindsey laughs and she looks at me to follow. I do, but it's hard to find anything funny about Tina's call.

'I'm sure if you look up Darcy's Dishes' website you'll find all the job application info you need there. Am I right, Darcy?' Lindsay says.

I nod.

'I applied but I was told there was a hiring freeze,' Tina says. 'Cost-cutting, they told me.'

Lindsay looks at me sympathetically. She didn't know, I realise. She truly had no idea that Darcy's Dishes is struggling so badly at the moment. I suspect she wouldn't have pestered me so hard to come on the show had she known.

'I'm sorry,' I say.

'Bullshit.'

Lindsay gasps and the cameraman's eyes widen.

'This is a family show,' she says sternly with her eyes suddenly narrow. 'I am going to have to ask you to refrain from using such language.'

Tina's voice cracks and her desperation is palpable. 'I went to your husband. I begged him for work. He told me he couldn't afford to take me on.'

My stomach somersaults.

Tina sighs. 'He didn't tell you, did he?'

'I . . . I . . .'

22

'Don't bothering answering,' Tina says. 'It's written all over your face.'

I suddenly feel so exposed, sitting here all alone in the centre of this too-big couch as a ghost from my past reappears to haunt me.

'As I said at the start of this interview, I have been very ill and the company has had to adapt,' I say, a tremor creeping into my words. 'We're currently in uncharted waters and we won't be hiring any new staff until I am back to work full-time.'

'Okay,' Tina says, dramatically calm all of a sudden. 'Then I'd like to invest.'

Lindsay's eyes are wide with disbelief. This is car-crash TV and the whole studio knows it. Lindsay is pressing her finger subtly to her ear as she listens, clearly getting instructions on how to handle this mess. But no one is whispering in my ear. I have no help and no idea how to handle Tina. I never had.

'I have money,' Tina says. 'It will be just like old times. We can be friends again.'

'Thank you.' I nod. 'It's a lovely offer. But we have a potential investor coming on board and . . .'

'Who?' Tina gasps.

Lindsay cuts in. 'Well, thank you for your call but I'm afraid that's all we have time for today.'

'Who the hell is it—?'

The line goes dead as Tina is mid-screech and Lindsay's cheery voice fills the void. 'Thank you for watching, folks. From me and everyone in the studio all that is left to say is, good morning, Ireland. Have a great day!'

Chapter Four

DARCY

Monday 10 June 2019

Upbeat theme-tune music fills the air. Lindsay stands up and untangles herself from her mike pack and drops it into her chair as I get to my feet.

'Who on earth was that?' she asks.

Before I have time to answer, Luke races towards us with Jinx tucked under his arm.

'What the hell is going on?' Luke shouts, taking large strides as he races over. 'Don't you screen your goddamn calls?'

Lindsay's smile widens. Calm and poised, she says, 'I think we can say with some confidence that caught us all off guard this morning. But you handled yourself brilliantly, Darcy.'

My knees are shaking.

'Are you okay?' Lindsay asks. 'Can I get you some water?'

I don't have time to reply before Luke says, 'Of course she's not all right. How could she be?'

I run my hands through my hair. My fingers catch in the hair-spray holding my perfectly styled curly blow-dry. 'How live is this?' I ask. 'I mean, is there a delay?'

'Three seconds,' Lindsay says. 'To be honest, it's rarely even long enough to bleep out a swear word. But don't worry. There's no such thing as bad publicity. This morning's show is guaranteed to get the country talking.'

'You should have cut that crazy bitch off air the minute she said hello,' Luke says. He's animated and angry and he startles me and Jinx. Jinx barks and I grab my belly instinctively, protecting the baby as if she is somehow aware of what's happening. And I pause, realising that these maternal moments are somehow sneaking unintentionally into my psyche more and more often.

Luke puffs out his breath. 'We could sue, you know. That crazy cow told the whole country Darcy's Dishes is broke. That kind of crap being broadcast to a whole nation isn't right. It isn't.'

Lindsay St Claire's eyes round like two shiny pennies. She pretends to be surprised by Luke's ridiculous outburst, but the bright studio lights emphasise the glisten of tiredness in her eyes, and I can only imagine that she wants to retreat to the sanctuary of her dressing room and forget all about this morning.

Jinx squirms and tries to wrestle his way out from under Luke's arm. I reach over to take him and I ask, 'Is it true? Did she really come to you for a job?'

'Oh God, Darcy. I don't know,' Luke says, calming down. 'Half the girls who follow you on Instagram want to come work for us. I can't keep track of them all.'

'Didn't you recognise her?' I ask, surprised.

Luke shrugs. 'Should I have?'

'Yes,' I say. 'It's Tina.'

Luke stares at me blankly.

'Tina Summers.'

He's shaking his head.

'From school.'

'Oh.' Luke pulls a face. 'That nutter. I wonder what's dragged her out of the woodwork after all these years.'

A shiver trickles down my spine as Luke's words resonate. I *do* wonder. 'Tina is trouble,' I say.

Luke snorts. 'No, she's just weird. It must be twenty years since school and she's still thinking about you.'

'She was obsessed with *you*, actually,' I correct.

'Whatever.' Luke shrugs. 'You've got to feel sorry for her, really. Who doesn't move on after school?'

I sigh, still shaky. 'It was a disaster, wasn't it?'

'Darcy, I promise viewers will empathise with you,' Lindsay cuts across me. 'Honestly, even the best PR people can't make this stuff up. Now, if you'll please excuse me, I have a meeting. It was sooooooo lovely to meet you both.' Lindsay's sing-song voice is back as she shakes our hands, kicks off her heels and hurries away.

◆ ◆ ◆

Luke and I see ourselves out of the studio. We sit in our car in silence, both a little shell-shocked. Jinx is quiet too, as he lies on the back seat. He's never usually this content in the car. It's as if he can sense something is wrong. As if he, too, can't believe that Tina is in touch after all these years. It was never going to be easy to hear from her again. I guess part of me thought, or hoped at least, that we never would. But on live television, of all the bloody ways. It's just so typically her. To be honest, I'm even more shocked that Luke seems to barely remember her. Or at least that's what he's saying.

Luke tries to strike up a conversation on the drive home but my mind is elsewhere. Friends text to tell me I looked great, or that the show was really interesting. Unsurprisingly they avoid any mention of the crazy call. The rest of the country is not so considerate. Lindsay was right when she said that everyone would be talking

26

about us. We've barely left the studio car park when #DarcysDishes is trending on Twitter. And not in a good way. My phone is hopping as notification after notification lights up the screen.

'Listen to this,' I say, reading a tweet with hundreds of likes already. '@LoudMouth says, *Something fishy about that Darcy woman.*'

I glance at Luke but his eyes are on the road.

'Oh brilliant.' I cringe, scrolling on. 'They've tagged Lindsay too.'

'Ignore it,' Luke says. 'They're just trolls.'

'Someone else has replied,' I add. I scrunch my nose and mimic, '*Something fishy going on? Isn't she a vegan!*'

Replies are coming in as fast as I can read them. There is a string of tasteless memes. And finally, I read a comment I was expecting – a mirror of my own thoughts. '*Car crash interview. Is perfect Darcy really walking away from that one?*'

A car horn honks and startles me. The irony pinches.

'Keep in your own lane! White lines are there for a reason, mate!' Luke shouts, honking the horn again. 'Look at this guy,' he says. 'He's all over the road.'

I look up. A stream of traffic stretches out in front of me. I sigh, accustomed to city mornings, and look back to my phone.

'They think they're hilarious adding a million laughing emojis,' I say. 'Oh God this is bad, isn't it?'

'Honey, don't let it upset you,' Luke says.

'Yeah.' I lift my head to look out of the window as we sit in the bumper-to-bumper chaos.

I feel Luke's hand on my knee. 'Darcy's Dishes is today's news. Some other poor sod will be on the receiving end of their hate tomorrow. That's the internet for you.'

'Mmm. You're right,' I say, wishing I found it as easy as my husband to zone out.

I close my eyes and try not to think about how much of a spectacular fail this morning was. I'm napping when my ringing phone wakes me.

'It's Mildred,' I say, jolting.

'Leave it.' Luke shakes his head. But he knows a call from the production manager at the factory isn't something I can ignore.

'Hello,' I say, flicking my phone on to loudspeaker.

'Hi. Hello, Darcy. Can you talk?' Mildred's voice fills the car.

Familiar cherry-blossom trees come into view as Luke turns on to our road. But the feeling of relief at almost being home is marred by the sense of urgency in Mildred's tone.

'Yeah, of course,' I say. 'Is everything okay?'

'Erm, someone has found a photo online of you in a fur coat and . . .'

'Bloody Instagram,' I cut across Mildred immediately, knowing the photo she's talking about. Darcy's Dishes donated some goodies for the bands playing at a charity rock concert in the Phoenix Park last year. It was one of the last PR events I attended before I became pregnant. I got as many photos as I could of various artistes munching on a Darcy's Dishes brownie or muffin and bombarded social media with them. People went crazy for them all. But the stand-out shot, with countless comments and likes, was me with all four members of the headline act backstage.

'It's the photo of me with The Polar Kings, isn't it?' I say.

'Yeah,' Mildred says.

'It's not real fur,' I say. 'I checked with their manager. You know how I feel about fur.'

'Of course, I know. But I don't think the general public gets that.'

'I don't even know whose coat it was,' I say, becoming teary. 'The bass guitarist's, I think.'

'I don't think it matters,' Mildred says. 'Some goody two-shoes has printed the photo off and stuck it to a placard. A small group have been marching outside the factory for twenty minutes now.'

'What does it say?' I ask.

'Oh Darcy.'

'What does the placard say, Mildred?'

Mildred takes a breath and pauses before she says, 'It says *THE ONLY FAKE THING IS DARCY.*'

My heart aches. I can't count the number of interviews I've given over the years condemning fur and begging people not to buy or wear it. How can people not believe me?

Mildred sighs. 'If it helps, passers-by aren't paying them much attention. And if we keep the windows and doors closed, we can't hear the chanting inside.'

'There's chanting too?' I gasp.

'It's stupid, Darcy. They're shouting that you're a fraud. Shows what they know.'

'I'm sorry, Mildred,' I say. 'You shouldn't have to deal with this.'

'Don't be daft.' Mildred laughs. 'I'm sure they'll get bored soon and bugger off.'

'Do you want me to come down? Luke and I are nearly home but we can turn around and swing by the factory.'

'Absolutely not. It's nothing to worry about. I just wanted to give you the heads up, that's all,' Mildred says, and realising she's on loudspeaker she raises her voice and adds, 'Luke, you take care of her. I'll take care of everything here.'

'Thanks, Mildred. Speak soon.' I flop my phone on to my knees and look at Luke as we pull into our driveway.

'Right. Let's get you inside,' he says.

'Inside?' I say as Luke turns off the engine, ready to get out. 'You heard Mildred. This is a mess. We need to go into work.'

Luke exhales slowly. 'No. We need to get you inside. You need some rest.'

I shake my head.

'C'mon, honey. Lindsay is right. People who had never even heard of Darcy's Dishes before are talking about us now.'

'But they're saying terrible things.'

Luke smiles. 'But they *are* talking.'

'What if Andrew Buckley saw the show? He'll know we're in trouble. We told him we need his backing to expand, not to save us from going under.'

'I think someone like Mr Buckley is a little too busy to sit around watching morning telly.' Luke chuckles.

'What if he doesn't want to invest any more? We're screwed without that money.'

'Look,' Luke says, becoming serious. 'I have that Buckley & Co meeting this weekend. I am going to charm the pants off Andrew Buckley. He'll be throwing money at us.'

'I wish I could go with you,' I say.

'I know.' Luke sighs. 'I wish you could too. But you're going to have to trust me. I can do this.'

Exhausted, I open my door and swing my legs out. The rest of me takes a lot more effort to follow. I feel like such a blob. Luke appears at my door with Jinx under his arm, and when he reaches out to me I grab his hand tight.

'I trust *you*,' I say. 'It's Tina I don't trust. I never have.'

Chapter Five

TINA

I carry a loaf of bread tucked under one arm and a carton of milk under the other. The milk is uncomfortable as the cold bites into my bare skin. I regret my decisions to wear a sleeveless summer dress and to not pick up a basket, but I don't move the milk. I need my hands free to reach into the floor-to-ceiling fridge at the back of the shop. The shelf is marked 'Lasagne – Darcy's Dishes' but the space is bare.

'They're sold out,' a voice behind me says.

'Oh.' I turn around expecting to find a helpful staff member.

'There's only shepherd's pie left and I don't fancy that,' says a lady in a bright, loose-fitting tracksuit, who clearly isn't staff. 'Have you tried them before?'

I shake my head.

'Me neither,' she says. 'But I saw that pregnant woman on the television, and I thought, if eating this stuff makes her look that great even when she's about to pop a baby, I'm going to give it a go, what harm can it do?'

I don't know what to say.

'I'm just not sure if it tastes all that nice, you know?' she continues. 'I'm telling myself it mustn't be too bad if the lasagne is sold out, eh?'

'I guess not,' I say.

She laughs. 'Ah, I can see you're as disappointed as I am.'

I don't reply. I can't tell if she's being sarcastic, but I think not.

She reaches across me and picks up a small rectangular tray of shepherd's pie. The packaging is minimal: a pale-brown, egg-carton-type box and a small yellowish label with green writing. Earthy colours. Unsurprising. Ugly, but no doubt biodegradable. I resist the urge to roll my eyes. Darcy has really thought of the best way to market her product. And I must admit it's impressive, if not a little clichéd.

'Are you going to buy that?' I ask, as the lady reads the label, probably checking out the ingredients.

'Ah sure, 'tis worth a try, isn't it?' she says. 'Although I think I need more than fake meat to work a miracle on my thunder thighs.'

The woman isn't overweight. She looks perfectly healthy, actually. But compared to Darcy she is unattractive. Compared to Darcy most women are. I've felt it. And now, a stranger who has only seen Darcy through a television screen feels it. *Typical Darcy, making other people feel inferior without even trying.*

'But, don't you think she's completely full of herself?' I want to put my hands on my hips, but the ever-warming milk under my arm makes it too tricky.

She looks at me as if I have ten heads and she points to the vegan logo printed clearly on the bottom of the label. 'She's a vegan concerned about her carbon footprint. I can't say I'm as selfless. Can you?'

'She was horrible to her friend in that phone-in,' I say. 'The woman just needed some work.'

'Oh gosh yes, that was awful,' she says, dropping the shepherd's pie into her shopping basket. 'What a crazy woman.'

I exhale. 'But you're still going to buy her shepherd's pie?'

'Oh no, love,' she shakes her head as she reaches into the fridge and ironically takes out some pork sausages. 'I don't think Darcy is the problem. It's that other woman. Clearly looking for her five minutes of fame. Who on earth rings up a morning show looking for a job? Madness. I thought Darcy handled the situation so well. What a lady. It must be so hard living in the public eye and have all these people wanting favours all the time. To be honest, I blame Lindsay St Claire. That crazy woman should never have made it on air.'

'It wasn't Lindsay's fault,' I say, snapping the fridge closed.

I follow Ms Bright Tracksuit to the counter. She chats to the girl on the till as if they are old friends as she checks out.

'So, I said to my husband, I'm not a vegan but I'll give it a go,' she says as the cashier scans Darcy's Dishes shepherd's pie.

'Oh, I saw that Darcy woman on TV,' the cashier says, pointing at the label. 'God, she's gorgeous, isn't she?'

'And so down to earth,' tracksuit lady says.

'Did you hear that weird caller?' the cashier asks, hovering a tin of beans over the scanner.

Tracksuit lady sighs as if talking about this for a second time exhausts her. 'Crazy. Just crazy.'

The cashier pauses before reaching for the next item. 'You have to wonder what is wrong with those kinds of people, don't you? Just apply for a job like a normal person does.' She points to a sign above the till that reads 'Staff Wanted' in large bold font.

My back teeth snap.

'Ugh yeah,' tracksuit lady says. 'Hopefully she'll crawl back under her rock and never be heard of again.'

The back of my neck is hot and it's hard to even draw breath. I want to drop my milk and bread and wrap my hands around this woman's thick neck. But, of course I don't. I'm in public. I follow her into the car park instead.

Fortunately for her a tall man steps out of a nearby car to meet her. He kisses her on the cheek and helps her put the shopping into the boot. Lucky lady – today!

Chapter Six

DARCY

Friday 14 June 2019

I sit at my dressing table and stare at my reflection. My face is brighter than usual as the street light across the road shines through the window, casting an orangey hue over everything while dusk falls. I don't remember opening the curtains this morning, but they're wide open now exposing me in my underwear to the row of tall and thin red-brick houses across the street. Blushing, I slip my arms into my dressing gown waiting on the back of my chair and shake my head as the dark circles under my eyes in the mirror remind me that I'm exhausted and not thinking straight.

It's been a strange week. The social-media storm blew itself out almost as quickly as it began. On Tuesday I was so distressed and ill that Luke called the doctor. On Wednesday Luke reluctantly left me alone to go into work for a couple of hours. And by Thursday people were bored, as if it had never happened. For everyone except me, that is, because I can't seem to get Tina out of my head. I can't understand why she called in to the show. She purposely embarrassed me and it was almost as if she enjoyed it. But why? I was only ever nice to her. I felt sorry for her. People warned me to stay away from her. God, I wish I'd listened.

I stand up and snap the curtains closed. Darkness engulfs the room and I instinctively reach my arms out in front of me as I feel my way towards the light switch. The floorboards of my Georgian house creak underfoot and I freeze, reminding me that I'm a thirty-seven-year-old woman who's still afraid of the dark when she's alone. Flicking on the light switch, I groan at my messy bed I didn't have the energy to make this morning. The sheet twitches suddenly and my breath catches.

'Jinx, you naughty boy,' I say, calming as I pull back the bedding to find him chewing on the diamanté strip at the end of my elaborate duvet. 'Stop that. Stop that now,' I add, tapping him on the nose.

He yelps as if I've hurt him, and jumps off the bed to scurry out of the bedroom, his paws slipping on the highly polished walnut floor.

'Silly boy,' I say, making my way into my en suite bathroom to check on the bath I've left running.

I keep the door slightly ajar so I can listen for Jinx downstairs. Water cascades noisily into the almost-too-full tub. I hurry, and turn off the tap. It's instantly silent, apart from the odd crackle and pop of luxurious, waiting bubbles. The bathroom window and mirrors are fogged as steam dances in the air. It's a relief to sit on the edge of the bath, and I take care not to get my dressing gown wet and reach behind my neck to fiddle with my mother's pearls.

Jinx begins barking downstairs and I wonder if he needs to go out for a wee. *Typical.*

'In a minute,' I shout. 'I'll let you out in a minute.'

Unhooking the finicky clasp, I close my eyes and smile with satisfaction. I wait for the familiar clink as I drop my favourite necklace into the china soap tray next to the taps. But there's no sound. I open my eyes to find the pearls have fallen on to the bath mat. I bend awkwardly, my back objecting with an audible crack as I pick up my necklace that thankfully hasn't broken. Standing upright again isn't easy as my enormous pregnant belly gets in my way, and I grab on to the side of the bath for assistance. I'm standing, rubbing my back and mumbling curse words, when I notice the soap tray is missing.

Jinx's barking grows louder and a door downstairs creaks open. I hold my breath as I wait for the next sound. Jinx is muffled when another door closes, trapping him in the kitchen, or the sitting room, I imagine. Someone is on the stairs; I can hear the old oak groan under a person's weight. *Step. Creak. Step.* They're coming. My grip on the pearls tightens and my heart beats furiously. The walnut bedroom floor creaks and I step back until my spine collides with the sink behind me. It hurts, but I don't take my eyes off the door.

'Jinx, come here, boy,' I call, as if my little dog can rescue me.

The bathroom door handle rattles. Terrified and desperate to steady myself, I grab the sink edge behind me. Something pinches my hand. There's a sharp, sudden sting in the fleshy part below my thumb and I drop the pearls. I hear them hit the tiles with a bang and I know this time they've broken but I can't pull my eyes away from the door to check.

The door swings open and I scream. 'Who's there?'

'Hey. Hey. What's wrong?' I hear Luke's voice.

'Oh God,' I puff out, light-headed. 'You scared me half to death.' Steam separates us and I squint, trying to see my husband. 'What are you doing here?'

'I live here, remember.' He laughs, stepping forward and coming into view. 'Are you okay? You look as if you've seen a ghost.'

'I'm fine,' I say, so glad he's here.

Luke smiles. 'I brought you a little something. Don't worry, it's non-alcoholic.'

He's carrying a bottle of open champagne in one hand, and a pair of crystal champagne flutes dangle upside down in his other hand.

'But you're not supposed to be home until tomorrow,' I say, letting go of the sink to bend down and gather up the pearls that are scattered around my feet like shiny little marbles.

'Your mother's pearls,' Luke says, and he sounds as disappointed as I am to see them broken. He crouches beside me to help. 'I'm sorry, I didn't mean to startle you. I missed you.'

'But the pitch. You're supposed to be talking to Andrew Buckley.' I pause to catch my breath. My hand is throbbing and my heart is still beating uncomfortably fast. 'The meeting is tomorrow morning. We need that money or—'

'He moved it forward,' Luke says, grinning. 'He just couldn't wait any longer to hear our plans.'

'And . . . ?' My heart beats faster than ever, as I hang on his every word.

Luke raises the champagne bottle above his head with a triumphant air punch. Some champagne spills on his hair and he chuckles. 'He loved it, honey. He's going to give us the money. Darcy's Dishes is safe. Everything is going to be okay.'

'Really?' I squeak, ecstatic, suddenly dying for champagne. But not the crappy glorified grape juice Luke has bought. I'd love to pop open the good stuff that we've been keeping in the liquor cabinet for a time like this. 'He really liked us?'

'Yes.' Luke smiles, nudging closer. 'He loved everything about the pitch. He liked my accent. Told me all about his grandparents. They were from Kent too. Not far from where I grew up, actually.'

38

'Small world,' I say, hating the feeling that washes over me. I wanted to be at the meeting. I wanted to hear a story about Mr Buckley's English grandparents.

'Mostly he loved you,' Luke continues. 'He loved your ethnic-minority-inclusive work environment. Your constant efforts to reduce your carbon footprint. He even loved those silly little labels you insist must be made from recycled paper.'

I drop my handful of loose pearls into my dressing-gown pocket and sigh. 'I wish I could have been there.'

'I know. But you're supposed to be taking it easy. You know what the doctor said. Please tell me you spent today relaxing?' Luke stands up. He sets the champagne and glasses down on the vanity unit behind me and reaches his hand out to help me up. On my feet again, he gathers me into his arms, taking care not to crush my enormous belly between us.

'What about the gala dinner tonight?' I say, realising for the first time that Luke is wearing his tuxedo.

'I made an appearance, and then I hopped in a taxi home. It was painfully boring; a bunch of stuffy middle-aged men congratulating themselves on being millionaires. And once the deal was done with Buckley . . .'

I shake my head. 'It's not done until he signs on the dotted line, Luke. You really should have stayed at the party. It's important to network.'

'C'mon, Darcy, you know you're the charming one – not me.' Luke smiles. 'Besides, I missed you. I was worried about you.'

'And worried about the baby,' I add, hating that it comes out snappy.

'My amazing wife and soon-to-be amazing mother.' Luke dots a kiss on the top of my head.

I grimace, not wanting to talk about the baby again and have another argument about maternity leave. Luke seems to think I need months off to look after our child. I've told him countless times, that, all going well, I could be back at work a week after the baby is born. He laughed, and I took that as an insult. I told him he could take time off to look after the baby. He laughed more and it really pissed me off. I didn't tell him that Darcy's Dishes is *my* business, my baby – the only baby I'm really interested in. I didn't say it because Luke would be horrified to know how I really feel.

'I popped into work for a little while today,' I admit, knowing if I don't mention it that one of the staff will probably let it slip anyway.

'Darcy,' Luke groans.

'It was just for a couple of hours. I've been fine today. No dizzy spells, I promise.'

'And the baby?' Luke asks.

'Kicking up a storm.'

'Okay.' Luke smiles, and I feel his tense arms relax. 'But tomorrow is all about chilling out. No work. For either of us. Netflix and bed. All day. The new series of—' Luke pauses dramatically and pulls away. There's sudden panic in his eyes. 'You're bleeding,' he gasps, pointing at a patch of bright-red blood on my dressing gown. 'Oh Darcy. Sit down, honey. You need to sit.'

I shake my head. 'It's okay. It's just my hand,' I say, turning my palm over to show him. 'I cut it on a broken tile on the sink. I think. It stings a bit but I'm fine. And the baby is fine.'

I turn to investigate where the broken tile must be. I hope the sink bowl isn't chipped – that could be expensive to fix and without the investment from Mr Buckley we are so far in the red we are not only in danger of losing the business, we could lose our house too.

'Just your hand,' Luke says.

I nod.

Luke reaches for me again. 'Okay, let me see. If it's deep it might need stitches.'

'It's not deep, it's just . . .' I gulp, looking into the sink.

'What? What is it?' Luke says.

'Oh God. Oh God,' I exhale.

'Darcy, you're freaking me out. Will you just sit down?' Luke cups my elbow in his hand. 'Here, let me help you.'

'Look,' I say, trembling as I shake him off and point into the sink. 'It's the soap tray. It's broken.'

Luke nods, looking. 'Okay. No worries. I never liked that thing anyway. We can get a new one.'

'I . . . I—'

'Is that how you cut your hand?' Luke asks, reaching for me again.

'It wasn't broken earlier,' I say, staring at the shards of sharp, colourful china in the sink. 'It was beside the taps when I started running a bath.'

'Darcy.' Luke uses the same tone every time he tries to pacify me.

'I'm serious this time, Luke. I ran a bath and the tray was there. I saw it. Then I went back into our room to undress and Jinx—'

'There you go.' Luke nods. 'That bloody dog probably knocked it.'

I exhale. 'That's your answer for everything. The dog. Blame the dog.'

'He hates me, Darcy. Didn't you hear him barking his head off when I came home?'

'Yeah, but I thought—'

'You thought it was someone breaking in to murder you.' Luke rolls his eyes. 'I know. We've been over this. Things moving by themselves. Thinking someone is creeping around the house in the middle of the night. Now, the soap tray. This is why I came home early. To take care of you. The doctor says it's the stress. Your blood pressure is low, it's making you light-headed and paranoid. I hate seeing you so worked up . . . if you'd just take it easy—'

'My blood pressure didn't move the goddamn soap tray, Luke!' I snap, fed up that my husband's answer for everything lately is blaming my difficult pregnancy. It's been seven months of hell: chronic sickness that was supposed to go away after the first trimester, but I'm still puking at least once most days. Low iron, extreme fatigue and random dizzy spells and all the while trying to maintain a glowing outer image.

'Do you hear that?' I ask, as a loud bang sounds downstairs – a door closing.

'It's just Jinx,' Luke says. 'Listen. He's scratching at the door. He probably needs to pee, again. I really don't know how that bloody puppy pees so often.'

I loosen my dressing gown around me, the steam becoming irritating as it clings to my skin and hair, making me feel damp and clammy. I'm dizzy as I reach into the sink to gather up the broken china. *Maybe I really did drop the tray into the sink. I've had a lot on my mind today, I was worried about Luke's pitch and I'm always so on edge in this creepy old house when I'm alone. And with Tina on my mind . . .*

'Leave that, honey,' Luke says. 'I'll tidy up. Let's just get you into the bath, eh?'

Chapter Seven

Tina

Saturday 15 June 2019

Frank Sinatra's 'My Way' plays in the background of the hotel bar. I sit in a comfortable armchair swirling dark-burgundy merlot that I don't intend to finish around my glass. I smirk, listening to the lyrics that seem to sum up my life. *I do what I have to do.*

It's hard to believe that in less than fifty minutes by car I've left the hustle and bustle of Dublin behind and swapped it for this tranquil spot at the foothills of the Wicklow Mountains. I haven't been somewhere this luxurious in years.

I really need to get out more, I decide. After this I'm definitely going to take up a hobby. I've recently signed up for Pilates. It wasn't intentional. Last week at the gym, an overzealous staff member asked if she could help me. I was staring through the slender glass panels in the door watching the pregnancy Pilates class and she caught me off guard.

'Are you looking to join this class?' she asked as if people peeping into the studio happened all the time. 'Are you a member?'

When I couldn't think fast enough, she found words for me.

'First baby?' she said. 'Everyone is always a little nervous about their first.'

I smiled.

She took my name and number and said she'd give me a call once she'd checked in with the instructor. It was only as I walked away that I wished I'd given her my real name. Pilates might be enjoyable. It's such a convenient location – just around the corner from Luke and Darcy Hogan's house. And since I'm going to be in the area plenty soon . . .

I'm dragged back to the here and now by my obsession with that man at the bar. He's in his early sixties, I know; tall, charismatic and with a full head of silver hair. His tailored suit is offset by a dazzlingly white shirt, and he adjusts his polka-dot dicky bow every so often – I can only imagine it's uncomfortably tight. *Do people really wear dicky bows any more*, I wonder. The man at the bar is certainly alone in wearing one tonight. But somehow, instead of appearing the odd one out, every other man seems underdressed in comparison. He laughs among friends, or colleagues – I'm not sure which they are, and they all guzzle gin much too quickly.

He doesn't notice me watching. At one point a blonde woman in his circle glances my way and I stiffen, mistaking her for Darcy Hogan for a moment. But I quickly realise I'm wrong. The woman at the bar isn't pregnant. She also doesn't pay me any attention. To her I'm just another inconsequential woman, in an expensive dress, attending the evening's event.

The man at the bar didn't notice me watching him yesterday either in the lobby. He sat opposite Luke Hogan for over an hour. They both had their laptops open in front of them and even though there was minimal paper being shared it was obvious, to anyone glancing their way, that they were in the middle of a business meeting.

It was easy to study him in the lobby. I could hide behind my own laptop, sipping coffee as I cast my eyes over the screen to scrutinise him. It's harder to maintain a view of him now. The offensively upmarket bar is heaving with people. Each more glamorous than the next in their expensive suits and elegant dresses. It's the type of place Darcy belongs and I don't. The hotel decor is equally over the top, with huge leafy green plants dotted sporadically throughout in oversized gold pots. No doubt they cost a fortune, but to me they are vulgar and cheap, and a bloody nuisance.

Every so often the man moves, just a fraction, tossing his head back to laugh perhaps or twisting at an angle to catch the bartender's attention. And for a moment I lose him, as my line of vision is obscured by a large Grecian statue next to the bar.

'Can I get you anything else?' someone asks over my shoulder.

I shake my head without looking to see who's speaking to me. It's probably the annoying person who asked me the same question an hour ago. I gave her my attention then and I lost sight of the man. I had to hurry into the lobby, teetering on high heels that I'm not used to wearing. Thankfully I caught sight of him coming out of the loos, but I'm not risking taking my eyes off him again.

'Are you a guest of the hotel, miss?' she asks.

Oh for God's sake.

'Yes,' I say, waving my hand to dismiss her. 'Now please . . .'

She doesn't say anything else and soon I can no longer feel her shadow hovering over me.

Finally, the man at the bar glances my way and smiles. He's noticed me at last. I sit a little straighter, making sure the plunging neckline of my dress is given optimum exposure, and I smile back. But he's quickly distracted again by the blonde woman. I try to read her lips, but it's not a skill I possess.

I'm sniggering to myself – misreading something to do with baked potatoes and wellington boots – when the voice from earlier interrupts me.

'Sorry to disturb you,' she says, and there's a noticeable wobble in her tone as if I make her uncomfortable. I'm disappointed. The last thing I want to seem this evening is unapproachable. I probably shouldn't have grunted at her earlier. I try harder now.

'Yes,' I say, turning my head towards the sound of her voice and very reluctantly flicking my eyes off the man and the blonde and on to her.

She's carrying a single glass of red wine in the centre of a very shiny silver tray. The glass is different to the one already in front of me. Its stem is narrower and taller and the glass is finer and rounder. *This isn't house wine*, I think, it's the expensive stuff from the subtly lit, golden shelf behind the bar.

'It's from the gentleman at the bar,' she says, pointing.

I glance back at the man. The blonde woman is gone, at last. He's alone, swirling some lonely ice around the bottom of an almost-empty glass. He's watching me nearly as intently as I've watched him for the past goodness knows how long.

'Hmm,' I say, flicking my hair back, off my shoulders. 'I don't usually accept drinks from strange men.'

'Oh Mr Buckley isn't a creep,' she says quickly, as if it's in her job description to defend him – or to reassure me. 'He's the owner of the hotel. He's a lovely man. A really nice boss too.'

'The owner. Wow,' I say, my eyes wide as if I didn't already know.

'Yup. He bought this place a few years ago. It was a real tip before then. Now it's a five-star.'

'Hmm.'

She reaches for the glass while looking at me and I nod, letting her know it's fine to set it down on my table.

'Can I tell Mr Buckley it's okay to join you so?' she asks.

'Does Mr Buckley usually join women, on their own, and buy them wine?'

She shuffles awkwardly. 'He never does this,' she says. 'I think you're just lucky.'

I swallow and try to hide my disgust at her idea of luck. Doesn't she see that Mr Buckley is old enough to be my father?

'I should probably warn you . . .' Her eyes narrow and she lowers her voice. 'He's a little bit tipsy.'

I smile. *Perfect.*

I watch as he clicks his fingers and within seconds the barman replaces the empty glass in his hand with a new one, a slice of lime wedged among chunky ice cubes. He takes a large mouthful and walks towards me.

The girl beside me bends, and whispers in my ear. 'He's Andrew by the way. His name is Andrew Buckley.'

I suppress a smile. *I know.*

I uncross my legs as he walks closer. The girl winks at me, and leaves. And I know she wishes she was in my shoes. *Silly girl.* I cross my legs again, switching the one on top, and the slit in my dress gapes, exposing my tanned calves and lower thigh. I don't miss Andrew's gaze dropping to the parted material before he shakes his head as he disapproves and looks away.

'Do you mind if I join you?' he asks, placing his hand on the back of the chair opposite me, and I notice he's not wearing his wedding ring. I wonder when he stopped.

'Be my guest,' I say, enjoying the irony – this is *his* hotel, after all.

He places his drink on the table and drunkenly helps himself to the seat opposite me. His misty eyes are on me, waiting for me to introduce myself.

I cough gently and say, 'I'm—'

'Lonely,' he cuts across me.

Disconcerted, I stiffen and jut my chin forward, my confidence suddenly rattled. I worked so hard on my hair and make-up, getting the look just right. I used old photos to guide me. Although her hair was longer then than mine is now. But people change their hair all the time, don't they? I look so much like her. But obviously not enough. It's taken a single word from Andrew to remind me that I'm still me, and still inferior. I roll my shoulders back and push my self-pity aside. I've managed to pique Andrew's attention enough to bring him to my table. Now, I just have to keep him here.

'My name is Tina,' I say, leaning forward and extending my hand across the table. He shakes it. 'It's a pleasure to meet you.'

'Andrew. Andrew Buckley,' he replies. 'The pleasure is all mine. Where are you from? Not local – I'm guessing.'

'Kent,' I lie.

'Really?' He sounds surprised and I hope I'm getting the accent right. My thick Belfast twang is a hard one to disguise even though I've been practising. 'You're the second person I've met tonight from that neck of the woods,' he says.

An awkward silence falls over us. It's unsurprising. Is it ever easy for two strangers to strike up conversation in a bar? I let it hang in the air for a moment, waiting to see if he will make the first move. When he doesn't, I slowly lose patience.

I count backwards from three in my head, so I don't seem too eager, and I say, 'Thank you for the wine.'

'You're very welcome.' He looks at the wine he's bought that I haven't yet touched and then at the glass I already have, which is at least a third full. 'You're not much of a drinker.'

Andrew seems compelled to tell people what they are not. *Not a drinker. Not a local.* Let's hope he has no idea what I *really am*.

I giggle, acting shy or embarrassed while I try to decide what the best way to play this is. Should I admit I *do* drink? Regularly, actually. Spirits, mostly. A couple of neat doubles is usually sufficient to numb the mind. Wine, on the other hand, I rarely bother with. It's bitter and I can't bear the hangover the next morning. But I need Andrew to like me and a headache tomorrow is a small price to pay.

'It's been quite a couple of days,' I say, settling on a response. 'I'm still not quite right after the party last night. I drank much, much too much. It was embarrassing, really.'

'You were here last night?' He doesn't believe me.

'I was. Or at least I meant to be. But I met someone and well, we got a little carried away.'

'Oh.' His eyes widen as he catches on. I've shocked him. I hold my breath, not sure what way this will go. 'I suppose you're only young once. It was a bit different in my day,' he says. 'I knew my Margret a year before we . . . before . . .'

He's talking about his wife and there's such fondness in his voice. It's almost believable that he actually loved her. Or loved her at one point, at least.

'Well, I guess times are different now, eh?' he sighs.

I don't reply. I've nothing to say to something so obvious.

'So where is the lucky fella now?' he asks, looking around as if he would recognise him if he saw him.

His stupidity irks me. I know to blame the gin and I remind myself that I will be glad of his intoxicated state later. I reach for the glass of wine he bought me and ignore the plonk in the other glass. I raise it and smile. 'Cheers.'

'Cheers,' he echoes, crashing his gin glass against mine clumsily. 'To the lovely couple.' He slugs another mouthful of gin before banging the glass back down on the table.

I shake my head and tears gather in my eyes. I've no idea where they've come from. It must be the stress of everything. 'He's stood me up.'

'Oh, he hasn't?'

'I was supposed to meet him in the bar. But I've been sitting here alone for hours and there's no sign of him.'

'He's a damn fool.' He takes another mouthful of gin.

'No,' I sigh, letting the tears fall. 'The fool is me. I guess Luke Hogan just isn't the man for me. If that was even his real name.'

Andrew sits straighter, suddenly the colour of barley water. He slips off the bow tie that I know has been bothering him all night and pops the top button on his shirt effortlessly, and I wonder if he's really as drunk as I thought. His neck is as thick as his accent. It's almost impossible to believe this farmer from West Wicklow has made enough money out of pigs and cows to become one of Ireland's wealthiest businessmen.

'Luke Hogan?' he says, looking shocked.

'You know him?'

'I do.' Andrew's voice has deepened. 'He slipped out of the party early last night – told me he was going home to his pregnant wife. And I believed him. It would seem he made a fool of me too.'

'His wife?' I say. 'He's married. Oh my God.'

Andrew exhales, and the stench of alcohol-soaked breath claws its way through the air. 'How could you have known?'

Of course I knew. I know everything about Luke Hogan. I know how he likes his tea. How he's grumpy in the mornings and how he stays up too late most nights. I know he hates coriander and loves being the centre of attention. I also know that he likes his wife to be perfect, a trophy to hang on his arm, and he can't wait to be a father.

'You're not in the wholefood business, are you?' Andrew says softly as he reaches across the table, and it takes me a second to realise he wants to take my hands in his. I let him. 'You're not here for the conference?'

'Hiking,' I say. 'Fresh air and scenery. But it's a lonely sport. That's why I was so glad when I met Luke. He even said he'd come walking with me sometime. God, I'm such a fool.'

Andrew gazes at me with pity and I decide to elaborate. I have his attention. I might as well dig Luke a deeper hole.

'I was exhausted after trekking fifteen miles yesterday afternoon. I bumped into Luke in the lobby. Literally. I was mortified, of course. He was done up all nice in a fancy tuxedo and there I was, red-faced and sweating.'

Andrew lets go of my hands, thankfully, and eases himself back further into the armchair to sip his gin casually. He's relaxed. I can tell he's a man who enjoys a good story. I continue.

'I offered to buy Luke a drink by way of an apology. He suggested the bar but I felt horribly underdressed.'

'So, it was your idea?' Andrew says, tilting his head to one side, curious.

'Yes.' I swallow. 'I guess it was. Or at least a drink was.'

The story is effortless to tell. Because it is true. Mostly true. Except the hill-walking part. I can think of countless ways to exercise and none of it involves nature or blisters. Luke didn't remember me, unsurprisingly. More surprisingly he refused my offer of a drink, which pissed me off after all the effort I had put in. I was wearing khaki shorts with oversized pockets for God's sake and my tanned, toned legs go on for miles. I've spent the last few years getting into peak physical shape. I told him I was lonely after walking for hours. How much more of a hint did he need? Either Luke Hogan doesn't like getting laid. Or he really does love his wife. Either way I was an inconvenience, and when he told me he was married and on his way home, I had no more cards to play.

I followed him, of course, making sure he wasn't just blowing me off. In an unexpected turn of events I reached his house before he did, discovering later that he stopped off to buy champagne for that bitch. I wasn't planning to go inside – not at first, but when I watched her through the window flaunting her round belly I couldn't help myself. But I wish I'd known they had a dog. I got such a fright when I realised, I broke something in the bathroom. Thankfully, by the time the stupid furball noticed me, I was leaving anyway. But that didn't stop the little shit barking and nipping at my ankles. *The puppy will be the first thing to go.*

'And, what happened then?' Andrew asks, his words slurred and his eyes heavy as his voice slices into my thoughts.

The gin is making him sleepy. We need to wrap this up. I couldn't seduce Luke Hogan, so I will have to make do with the next best thing: convincing Andrew Buckley that Luke seduced me. One way or another, Luke and Darcy are not getting their hands on Andrew's money.

'I had a bottle of whiskey in my room,' I continue. 'I like a night cap. It helps me sleep. Anyway, I thought we could have a drink. One. Just one.'

'Whiskey.' Andrew shakes his head. 'It can make good men do bad deeds.'

Good men? Luke Hogan isn't a good man.

'And good women,' I add, keeping calm. 'And here I am sitting in an expensive hotel in a dress I bought last minute, that truthfully I can't afford, waiting for a man who will never turn up.'

'It's a beautiful dress,' Andrew says, as if I need to hear it. 'But you don't have to do this, you know.' He eyes drop to the slit in my dress and he shakes his head, disgusted. 'If that's all a man sees, then he's the wrong man.'

'You sound like my father.' I smile, adjusting my dress so my leg is no longer on show.

'I'm sure he's very proud,' Andrew says, draining his glass.

I don't reply. Partially because there is nothing to say about my father. Mostly because I notice the way Andrew is looking at me now. Father-like. Nostalgic. *Perfect!* He's thinking about her, I can tell. He's thinking about how my strawberry-blonde hair, parted a little off centre, is so like hers. He's thinking about her green eyes and button nose – her features similar, but more petite than mine. My eyes are a little darker too, more hazel than green, but they're close enough. I didn't have to bother with contacts. I don't have freckles that sprinkle across my nose like cinnamon. But I'm wearing so much make-up now that freckles would be impossible to see anyway. He's thinking about how much he misses her, I can see it in his eyes.

And then I see the tears, the subtle ones that sweep across his gaze, and he says, 'You remind me of someone.'

I don't ask who. Instead I say, 'Is there somewhere private we could talk some more? You can tell me all about them.'

He stands up. 'Gillian was the apple of my eye.' Unsteady on his feet, he grabs his drink, the ice cubes rattling as he waddles forward, mumbling. 'My office. We can talk more there. You'd have liked her, you know. Everyone liked her.'

Not everyone.

I leave the wine on the table and I follow him.

Chapter Eight

GILLIAN

Sunday 16 June 2019

I wake with a horrendous headache and my mouth is gaping and dry as I suck in filtered air. Above me is a slightly off-white ceiling and it's spinning, as if I'm on the waltzer at the funfair. Only there is nothing fun about this feeling. The bed beneath me is soft and comfortable. I just wish it was my bed. I rub my eyes and sit up, yielding to a crippling headache. This is the second time in my life that I've woken up with my mind on fire like this – my conscience is burning and guilt swirls in the pit of my stomach. *I've done it again. Something terrible. Really, really terrible.*

I slide out of bed and my legs are shaking as I throw back the curtains and stare outside. It's blisteringly bright – the sun shines high in a cloudless sky. Green fields stretch for miles. It couldn't be more different to the view when I open the curtains at home and the neon light of the Chinese takeaway across the street glares back at me. Steadying, I realise I'm staring out at a golf course. A glance left tells me I'm overlooking the twelfth hole. A glance right reveals a pair of shocked golfers open-mouthed and shaking their heads. I gasp, realising I'm standing in my underwear, and grab the curtains. Shutting them roughly, I plunge myself into near darkness.

I feel around for clothes. Finally, squinting, I make out a dress draped over the back of a chair. It's not the jeans and T-shirt I was hoping for but it will have to do. It's crumpled and smells like smoke. *Cigars*, I think as I shake it out. It's fitted and formal, and much too fancy for day wear, but I quickly slip it on because all I want right now is to get the hell out of this room.

I can't find shoes and I don't want to spend time searching. I also know there's no point looking for my bag, wallet or phone. They'll be waiting at home for me. The same way they were the last time I did this.

I hurry out of the door, slamming it behind me.

'Excuse me? Excuse me.' A woman with an American accent appears from a room directly opposite me and flags my attention. She's frazzled with a toddler on her hip and an older child holds her hand. 'Is the air con working in your room? Ours isn't and it's awfully stuffy.'

I shrug. My hands are clammy and my cheeks are flushed but air conditioning is the last thing on my mind.

'We weren't expecting it to be so hot, even in summer,' she adds.

A door opens at the end of the corridor and a man and a woman walk towards us. I drop my head.

'Morning,' they chirp.

'Good morning,' the American lady says.

'Morning,' I whisper, keeping my head low.

My heart is pounding. *I need to get out of here before someone recognises me.*

'It's our first time in Dublin,' the lady says as the couple pass by. 'Everyone told us Ireland is cold and wet.'

I force a smile.

'I want to go to the pool,' the older child demands, swinging his mother's arm back and forth impatiently. 'I want to go noooowwww.'

'In a minute.' She grits her teeth.

'I'm going to reception,' I say, beads of perspiration beginning to gather at the nape of my neck. 'I can mention your air con, if you like.' I lean to one side so I can read the room number on the door behind her. 'Room one-one-two, right?'

'Reception,' she says, nodding. 'Good idea. I'll come with you.'

'No. No,' I snap. The child steps back until his body is half hidden behind his mother's. 'I mean, no need for us both to go. You head on for a swim. Hopefully maintenance will have it fixed by the time you get back.'

'Okay. Thank you,' she says, jutting her hip out further to keep the toddler from slipping. 'That would be great. You Irish are all just so helpful. We're having such a lovely holiday.'

'It's no problem,' I say, sweating really starting to become a problem as I feel anxious beads trickle down my spine.

'That lady had no shoes.' I hear the child laugh as they walk away. 'And her dress was all dirty.'

'Shh,' his mother scolds. 'Don't be rude.'

I hurry.

Reception is spacious but chilly. The air con is most certainly turned on down here and I'm overly conscious of my bare feet and fancy red dress with a contrasting burgundy stain spattered across the front. I fold my arms, trying to hide the speckles, as I wait in line to speak to someone on the desk. The couple in front of me are having trouble with their room key and someone else wants to leave luggage for collection later. It's all so normal, mundane even. It's driving me crazy.

Finally, it's my turn and after rehearsing what I was going to say over in my head, when I open my mouth to speak, it's difficult to force words out.

'Hello,' says a pretty woman in a teal-and-grey uniform that matches the wallpaper behind her a little too well. 'How can I help you this afternoon?'

Afternoon? It couldn't possibly be. *Bloody hell!*

'I . . . I . . .' I swallow. I don't know what to say. The receptionist is smiling but her eyes are judging me in my crumpled dress and shoeless feet. I can't say I blame her. On another day I'd judge myself.

'Erm. The air con in room one-one-two is broken,' I say, remembering.

'Oh. I'm sorry,' she says, tapping something into her computer. 'I'll have someone look at it right away for you. You don't need to wait in your room. Maintenance can let themselves in, if that's okay?'

I don't correct her and explain it's not my room.

I'm distracted by whispering behind me. I can hear a couple of teenage boys and I wait for them to make fun of my bare feet or matted hair.

'That's her. It's definitely her,' one of them giggles. 'The one in the red dress.'

'Oh yeah,' says the other. 'She was so hot. Is that the same dress? What's all over it? Gross.'

'Looks like bl—'

'Excuse me.' I turn around and cut across them, and as much as it pains me to ask, I add, 'Did you see me last night? Here, wearing this dress?'

They look me up and down.

'Did you see me?' I raise my voice. They don't answer and I shout, 'Did you?'

One of them grabs the other by the arm and they leave together, turning their heads over their shoulders to glare at me.

Feeling the eyes of everyone dotted around the lobby on me, I turn back to face the girl on reception.

'Don't mind them,' she says. 'From what I hear, the party got pretty wild last night. I'm sure their parents were just as tipsy and feeling equally as bad today.'

She thinks I'm hungover. I don't know whether to be relieved or embarrassed.

'Did you see me here last night?' I ask, my face burning, and I've no doubt it's as red as my dress. 'Was I with someone? A man?'

'Wow, it really was a wild night, eh?' She smiles, trying so hard to be kind. 'I didn't see any of it, I'm afraid. My shift only just started.'

'Oh.' I sigh. 'Was someone else here? Did anyone else see me?' My head is spinning. I feel as groggy and hungover as she thinks I am.

'I'm sorry,' she says. 'Reception closes at midnight. I don't think anyone would have seen you last night? Is there anything I can help you with?'

I shake my head.

'Is everything okay?' She lowers her voice to a barely audible whisper. 'You're suddenly very pale. Has something happened?'

I choke back tears. *Something happened nearly twenty years ago.*

'Is it a noise issue? I know we had a lot of complaints about noise on that corridor last night. I can assure you that's not usual and the hotel takes the safety of its guests very seriously.'

I straighten, suddenly very serious. 'What kind of noise?'

'Would you like to speak to the owner?' she asks. 'He was at the party last night. I might still catch him if I call now.'

'I . . . eh . . .' I will my brain to think faster.

'I'm sure Mr Buckley will be happy to help you.'

My eyes widen. 'You know Mr Buckley.'

'Yes. Of course.' She nods. 'He gets to know all the staff personally. He has a meeting this evening. He'll be here any minute, I think. I'm sure he'd be more than happy to speak to you. He prides himself on quality service.'

It's suddenly hard to breathe. 'You're expecting Andrew Buckley? Here.' I point to the spot where I'm standing. 'Right here, any minute.'

The girl looks at me with confusion. 'Yes. He owns the place, after all.'

Oh God. 'I have to go,' I pant. 'I have to go.'

I run.

Chapter Nine

DARCY

Monday 17 June 2019

Jinx barks just before the doorbell rings.

'Can you get that?' I shout from upstairs, hoping Luke will hear me as he potters about in the kitchen.

The doorbell rings again.

'Luke,' I say, stepping on to the landing in my dressing gown and face masque. 'Luke, the door please.'

Ding. Dong.

I roll my eyes. 'Luke?'

Nothing. I venture further on to the landing.

'Where are you?' I say, the kitchen suddenly still.

'Jinx?'

Silence.

Downstairs is eerily still, exaggerating the age of my old house. The only sound is the groan of the floorboards beneath me as I step closer to the banister and look over to view the front door.

The doorbell doesn't ring again, but through the stained glass on each side of the door I can see a shadow on the porch. They're not moving.

I wait for the bell to ring again or for whoever is out there to leave. Neither happens.

'Luke,' I whisper.

The silence is all-consuming.

The door handle twists slowly and my heart races. The keys aren't hanging in the lock the way they usually are, keeping the outside world sealed away. The door will open with a fraction of a twist more. My eyes are watering and stinging but I don't blink.

I shriek as there's a sudden rattle and the heavy double doors of the sitting room part suddenly.

'Hey, there you are,' Luke says, carrying a very mucky Jinx under his arm. 'This little devil crawled under the decking. He's bloomin' filthy. It's taken me twenty minutes to coax him out.'

'Someone's at the door,' I say, pointing.

Luke cranes his neck as Jinx growls and yelps, demanding to be put down.

He shakes his head. 'I don't see anyone.'

'They were there. They were turning the handle. They were going to come in. The keys aren't in the lock.'

'Darcy, honey, it's probably just a sales rep or someone looking for directions. Nothing to worry about.'

My face is hot and I imagine that under my thick white face masque my cheeks are pink with frustration. I know how ridiculous I sound, but I can't help feeling something isn't right recently. Luke hasn't said it, but I know he thinks I'm a paranoid mess since Lindsay's show. Maybe he's right.

'You're tired, honey,' Luke says. 'Why don't you have a lie-down. I'll clean Jinx up and then I'll bring you up a cup of tea or something. I think you need it.'

'Um,' I say, having no intention of getting into bed. 'Yeah, okay. Thanks. Put the kettle on.'

Luke crosses the hall and walks into the kitchen wrestling to keep Jinx in his arms. I wait until I hear him running the tap before I hurry down the stairs. I press my face close to the front door and stare through the peephole. The row of red-brick houses across the street stare back at me like tall, stiff soldiers. I strain my eyes left and right, taking in as much of the street as the tiny hole will allow. There's no one out there. Not even a neighbour walking by. It's like a still from a movie set. At any moment the director will yell 'Action!' and everything will come to life.

Jinx begins howling – Luke must be attempting to wash him. A car drives past and the woman across the street opens her front door and walks down the steps on to the footpath. It's noisy again. Noisy and familiar and, without over-thinking it, my fingers curl around the handle and I try to open the door. It doesn't budge. *Luke must have locked it after all.* I shake my head at my silliness as I grab the keys off the low sideboard next to me and finally open the door.

I give a sigh of relief. A brown cardboard box with a white card on top waits on the porch mat.

A delivery, I think, realising how foolish I've been.

'Hello, Darcy,' my neighbour shouts and waves from across the street.

'Hey,' I shout back.

'I was just coming to take that in for you. I thought no one was home,' she says.

'Oh.' I cringe. 'I was napping.'

She makes a face, and I remember my anti-ageing masque. *God, I'm a terrible liar.*

Thankfully she doesn't dwell and her face lights up and she points to my bump. 'Not long to go now, eh?'

'No. Not too long.'

'I bet you can't wait. It's the best feeling in the world, Darcy. Nothing will ever be the same again.'

I smile. And I don't tell my lovely neighbour that that's exactly what I'm afraid of.

'Do you want a hand with that?' she asks, getting a little closer. 'Looks like it could be heavy.'

'No thanks. Luke's here,' I say.

'Okay. See you soon,' she chirps, walking away.

'Bye.'

I struggle to bend down, and it's even harder to get back up. I take a moment to curse my new body shape. The box isn't heavy and I close the door and shuffle backwards into the house with it. I suspect it's something Luke has ordered online for the baby. He's obsessed with buying stuff for the nursery. All neutral colours, of course, because he doesn't want to know if it's a boy or girl.

'Let's keep it a surprise,' he said at our first scan, deciding for both of us.

I hope whatever he's ordered this time isn't expensive. Our credit card is nearly maxed out. Luke keeps telling me not to worry, but until Mr Buckley signs on the dotted line I can't relax.

I set the box down on the sideboard and read the card on top. 'Darcy's Dishes' is clearly written in large swirly handwriting. Exhaling, I realise whatever is inside is most likely work related. I ordered some new labels for our lasagne last week but I usually direct that kind of stuff to the factory. I read the card again, confused when I find no address anywhere on the box. *How did the delivery person know where to find me?*

I crane my neck towards the kitchen. It sounds as if Luke and Jinx are locked in a battle of wits, going by the odd noises they are making. And it would seem my husband is losing. *Poor Luke*, I think as I lift the card and peel back some wide brown tape sealing each side of the lid.

I gasp excitedly when I part both sides and I'm met with a mound of raffia paper. Blue and pink shreds battle for space. It's the first gift I've received for the baby and I guess it's from the staff at the factory. My heart pinches a little as I allow myself a moment to miss my days in the factory and a staff who are the first family I have known for years. I decide it doesn't matter how much Luke protests; I *am* going into work tomorrow, even just for a couple of hours.

I tuck into the huge mound of paper. It separates and a few stray pieces scatter as I dig deep to find what's inside. Nothing! I dig deeper, scattering paper on to the ground, and finally the light catches something silver in the corner of the box. Smiling, I reach for the bracelet. *Oh Luke*, I think, torn between loving the thoughtful gesture and wishing he wouldn't spend money right now. The delicate bangle is slightly tarnished and warped as if it's spent years lovingly wrapped around someone's wrist. An antique. I flinch, afraid to even guess what it cost. I'm about to slip it over my hand when a bolt of recognition charges up my spine like an electric shock. I squeal and drop the bracelet. It stubbornly spins like a dreidel on the hall tiles before flopping on to its side, staring up at me. My eyes are wide with disbelief as I run towards the kitchen.

Luke meets me at the kitchen door with a wet and soapy Jinx in his arms. 'What is it? Are you in pain? Is it the baby?'

'I . . . I . . .' Words won't come out. The sudden movement has upset my stomach and I throw up on the floor.

'Oh God, Darcy.' Luke drapes his arm over my shoulder and guides me towards the kitchen table, ignoring the mess I've just made.

I'm light-headed as he pulls out a chair and I sit. Jinx escapes Luke's grip and scurries into my arms. I'm barely functioning enough to catch him as he whimpers and licks my face, trying to take care of me.

'I'll get you some water,' Luke says, steadying me on the chair before he turns to the sink. 'Do we need to go to the hospital? Does it hurt?'

'I told you someone was at the door,' I say, finally catching my breath.

'Oh. There really was someone there,' Luke says, running the tap. 'Yeah.'

Luke doesn't say anything more as he sidesteps a puddle on the floor in front of a sudsy sink where he's been washing Jinx. He fills a glass of water and places it on the table in front of me and watches me with trepidation. I know he wants to ask if the baby is okay. He can't take his eyes off my bump and when he does, he flicks them to the glass of water, hoping I'll drink it.

'I thought it was a gift at first,' I explain.

'At the door?'

I nod.

'Then why did you scream?' Luke folds his arms and I can see irritation sweep over him despite how hard he tries to hide it. 'I really thought you were hurt.'

'I thought it was from you,' I say. 'The bracelet.'

'What bracelet?' Luke exhales sharply. 'Darcy, what's going on? You haven't been yourself for a while. And you really scared me just now. I thought the baby—'

'It's from her,' I say, cutting him off.

Luke leans his head to one side as if he's suddenly too tired to hold it up straight. 'I know I'm going to regret asking this . . . but who? Who has been so awful they've sent you a bracelet?'

'Luke I'm serious,' I snap, frustration replacing shock. 'It's from Tina.'

Luke stands straighter. 'Oh.'

'Exactly. Oh.'

'That *is* a bit odd, in fairness.'

'Oh, it gets weirder,' I add. 'It's not just any bracelet.'

'Is it expensive?' Luke asks. 'Maybe it's a peace offering. Hopefully she's realised she was way out of line that other day.'

65

'Peace offering. Ha!' I roll my eyes. 'That bracelet is twenty years old,' I say. 'I didn't recognise it at first but it's definitely the one we gave her.'

Luke snorts. 'When did we give her a bracelet?'

'Christmas. Our final year.'

Luke stares at me blankly.

'A silver bangle. Delicate little thing. Remember?'

Luke's gaze softens and he says, 'If I say no, am I going to be in your bad books for weeks?'

I shake my head. 'Don't you remember anything from our schooldays? Were you even there at all?'

'I remember that it's where I met and fell in love with you. Nothing else is important.'

'Nice try,' I say. 'Well, even if you don't remember it, I do. And she knew I would, that's why she sent it. It's weird.'

'It *is* weird,' Luke says. 'But so is going on television and inadvertently letting the whole country know you're insane.'

'What do you think she wants?' I say. 'I mean, why now? Why come back after all this time?'

'We know what she wants,' Luke says. 'She's broke and she thinks you can fix her problems for her the way you did in school. Ignore her, honey. She's a waste of space.'

'You really don't remember the bracelet?' It's hard to hide my disappointment as I shoo Jinx off my knees and stand up. 'It had a sort of swirly, Celtic font carved into it.'

I look at my husband and wait for that light-bulb moment. When it doesn't come, I say, 'Right, come on.' I take him by the hand and lead him into the hall. Jinx follows us with his tail wagging excitedly.

'Look,' I say as we reach the sideboard.

'At what?' Luke asks.

My eyes are wide with disbelief. 'It was there. Just a minute ago. I swear. I dropped it right there.' I point to the floor.

'Darcy.' Luke stands behind me, rubbing my back in circles as Jinx barks at his ankles. 'Let me take a look. Maybe it fell back into the box.'

I nod, humouring him, but I know what I saw.

The box is still on the sideboard next to the front door. I can see the pink-and-blue raffia paper inside. Luke edges forward, warily. I keep a comfortable distance. I notice his shoulders rise as he takes a deep breath and reaches into the box. His shoulders relax and he sighs as he turns around with a beautiful, silver bracelet dangling around his fingers.

'That's not it,' I stutter, stepping back. 'That's a different bracelet. The other one was . . .'

Luke's forehead crunches. 'Darcy . . . honey . . .'

'That bracelet wasn't in the box a minute ago,' I say, my eyes darting to the front door. 'Someone switched them. Someone's here. Someone is in the house.'

'Darcy, please. Calm down,' Luke says, stepping towards me. 'Stress isn't good for you. For the baby. Take a deep breath.'

My heart is racing.

'Come on. Come on.' Luke breathes in slowly and out even slower, encouraging me to copy him.

Christ.

I turn on the spot. Scanning my house. My eyes can't search fast enough. 'Someone was here,' I say. 'Maybe they're still here.'

Luke exhales again, sharper now. 'Darcy, please. You're scaring me.'

Jinx is chasing his tail next to me. He finally catches it, yelping as he bites.

'Lie down, boy,' Luke commands sternly. 'Lie bloody down!'

Jinx crouches on to his belly and lowers his head.

I steady myself and stare at my husband. 'You think I'm losing it, don't you?'

Luke takes another step forward and his shoulders round, drained. 'No. I think you're tired, stressed out and feeling sick.'

'But I'm not.'

'The pregnancy has been hard and now with the TV stuff last week.' Luke sighs and places his hand on my shoulder. 'It's my fault. I never should have let you go on the show.'

I shrug his hand off me.

Luke doesn't say anything. But he follows my gaze to the front door.

Silence hangs in the strained air between us. I ignore it and tilt my ear towards the ceiling, trying to hear if someone is in my home. Upstairs, maybe. Nothing. My beautiful, old house doesn't moan or groan or hint that anyone is here.

'Look,' Luke says, and I feel him shove a card into my hand. 'Don't you want to see who the bracelet is really from?'

I close my eyes. All I want is for everything to stop. This pregnancy from hell. My business hanging by a thread. Stupid Tina back after all this time. *I want everything to go back to the way it was before.*

'Darcy, look,' Luke says, his tone laced with frustration.

I open my eyes to find Luke turning the cardboard box upside down as he shakes it. Shredded raffia paper rains down on the floor. But nothing else. Luke sets the empty box back on the sideboard and drops to his knees. He pats his hands all over the floor and slowly stands back up.

'See. There really is nothing to be afraid of. It was just your mind playing tricks on you.'

I stare at my husband with hooded eyes. *I am not paranoid.*

'Look at the card,' Luke says.

My hands are trembling and it makes something as simple as uncurling my fingers a monstrous task. But I finally unlock my hand and stare at the shiny gold card resting on my palm.

'Read it,' he says.

I run my finger over the embossed gold lettering. 'Buckley & Co.'

Luke's eyebrows raise dramatically. 'You're right, honey. The bracelet is a gift. It's for the baby.'

My head is spinning.

'Go on. Turn it over. Read it.'

I flip the card and read aloud: 'Many congratulations on your impending arrival. Warm wishes, Andrew.'

'How thoughtful,' Luke says. 'He asked all about the baby when I met him. I get the impression he likes kids.'

I stare at the card. 'Does Andrew Buckley have our home address?'

'Hey, do you think this means he's going to send the payment through?' Luke says. 'I think this means we'll be hearing something soon. It's been a long week waiting, hasn't it?'

'Someone dropped this to the door,' I say, thinking out loud. 'They knew where we lived.'

'I doubt Buckley delivered it himself.' Luke sniggers. 'Courier, I'm sure. Or maybe he has people for that sort of thing.'

'But how does he know where we live?'

'Our address is on all the investment paperwork, Darcy. Stick it in Google maps and it will bring you right to the door.'

'That's the factory address, Luke,' I say, shaking more than ever. 'Not our home. Andrew doesn't have our home address.'

Luke drags a hand around his face and exhales loudly as if he's exhausted. 'Well maybe he asked someone. I don't know.'

I want to remind Luke that most of the staff at Darcy's Dishes wouldn't have a clue about our home address. And none of them know Andrew Buckley is investing. We plan to make an announcement when the deal is done. To them, Andrew Buckley is a stranger, and no one there would give our address to a stranger.

I bite my tongue. Luke already thinks I'm some kind of pregnant porcelain doll, too fragile for the real world right now. No matter how I phrase it, arguing about addresses makes me sound paranoid and delicate and he will only try even harder to wrap me in cotton wool and insist on bed rest or something.

'Can't we just accept the lovely gift and be happy that Andrew went to so much trouble?' Luke says, smiling brightly. 'He likes us, honey. He must really like us.'

I say nothing.

'Why don't you go watch some TV or have a lie-down. You're still pale,' Luke says. 'I'll clean up all this mess.'

'Yeah. Okay,' I say, my mind wandering to the mound of paperwork on my dressing table. It's copies of all our correspondence with Buckley & Co. Maybe our home address really is on something.

Chapter Ten

GILLIAN

Tuesday 18 June 2019

I drag myself out of bed and shuffle sleepily into the kitchen in my bare feet and oversized T-shirt that I've had for years. Mornings have never really been my thing, but I appear to struggle with them more as I get older. Every morning it seems to take me a little longer to peel myself off the bed. And since I can rarely remember flopping into bed the night before after far too much supermarket own-brand vodka, I often can't make head or tail of what day it is. Thankfully, I usually wake up to find painfully efficient notes – dotted haphazardly around the flat. 'Pick your stuff up, lazy.' Or 'You were drunk again last night, stupid.' That one usually comes with a frowning, hand-drawn emoji.

Today, I check the fridge first, and unsurprisingly find an oversized magnet securing today's memo in place. This morning's piece of paper is cut precisely into the shape of a Hoover and I know it's a not-so-subtle hint to clean up.

I run my fingers over the neat, cursive handwriting: black ink on ivory paper as I've come to expect. I read aloud – as if anyone other than me is listening. 'Moving day. Clean and pack. Don't leave a trace.'

I groan inwardly. As if I could forget it's moving day. I often worry about how expensive the new place is in comparison to this little steal, but I'm wasting my time. Besides, the new place is lovely. All these gorgeous, Georgian red-brick houses converted into flats line both sides of the street. Two up, one down – usually. Some lucky feckers own the odd whole house but they're few and far between, the disgustingly wealthy. Rich and famous, and all that. A ground-floor flat with a purple front door will have to do. And very snazzy it is too.

I pull off the magnet and set the irritatingly Hoover-shaped paper on the counter. My tummy rumbles, reminding me it's God knows when since I last ate, and my chicken-drumstick-like legs are a hint that it's been a while. I wasn't always this thin. Just recently.

I open the fridge door and sigh despondently as I stare inside. The shelves are laden with numerous brown boxes of equal size. I pull out the nearest one and read the label. 'Darcy's Dishes Shepherd's Pie'. I groan at the sight of a generic, unappetising ready meal. I reach for the next. 'Darcy's Dishes Shepherd's Pie'. The next is the same and the next. As I empty the fridge and realise there is nothing else in here, I long for some fresh vegetables and meat. I really, really miss meat. I slowly put everything back in the fridge as I found it.

Still hungry, I glance at the cardboard boxes littered around the kitchen tiles. I wonder how often cardboard boxes sum up lives. Deciding I best get on with packing, I grab some newspaper off the shelf nearest to me and open the cupboard to fetch a glass. I start wrapping when a headline in the paper catches my eye: 'No Teeth. No Fingertips. No Face'.

I unwrap the glass, spread out the newspaper and read on . . .

Further to recent reports, the body of an unidentified male found earlier this week in Glenmallow, Co. Wicklow, remains under investigation. The man, believed to be in his late 50s or early 60s, was wearing a dark suit and white shirt. A bow-tie was found in his pocket. 'The man was not carrying any identification, was not wearing any distinctive jewellery and he does not have any identifiable tattoos or piercings,' a detective on the case said. 'He was however missing all teeth and fingerprints.'

The state pathologist is yet to issue a report. Gardaí have renewed their appeal for anyone with information to contact their local Gardaí station.

'Oh God,' I puff out. 'Oh. My. God.'

Chapter Eleven

DARCY

Tuesday 18 June 2019

The sun is glorious as it shines on my face. It's that not-too-hot, not-too-cold kind of weather that even my pregnant self can't complain about. Although I know if I'm enjoying temperatures this much so early in the morning, my feet will be a swollen mess by the time I get home later. I sigh and try not to think about how much I can't wait to feel normal again.

I got up before Luke this morning; I left a note on the bedside table, reminding him to let Jinx out for a wee, and then letting him know that if he's looking for me I've set out for the local coffee shop. I'm hoping to bump into my friend Rose. I know she usually stops in for a coffee before going to pregnancy Pilates class. I want to ask her advice about Tina. Rose is a Garda. She's quite high up. *Detective*, I think. I'm wondering if I should get a barring order or if I'm just a paranoid mess. And if anyone will tell me honestly, I know Rose will.

I've left the car for Luke and suggested he join me later. I quite fancy the walk. The trees have lost their delicate pink blossoms, but they are nonetheless aesthetic – all green and leafy and smelling of summer. They line the streets in beautiful contrast to the red-brick houses behind them like a watercolour painting. I'm enjoying the fresh air after spending much too much time cooped up in the house recently.

A removals van pulls into the house at the end of our road. The driver honks the horn as if he hasn't just cut across me on the footpath, almost taking my toes with him. I walk on, ignoring how he glares out of the window at me. *I hope our new neighbours have kids*, I think as I instinctively reach for my bump. There aren't many children living locally. Our neighbours are mostly retired couples with grown-up children who come and go independently. Or young, renting couples. And people generally keep to themselves.

I glance over my shoulder, hoping to get a clue about who's moving in as I walk past the largest house on our road. The van parks in the driveway and the driver hops out to open the shutter at the back, revealing neatly stacked and sealed cardboard boxes. There are so few boxes I wonder why they bothered with a van at all. The driver and the guy helping him begin to unload the van. The driver's eyes shift towards me as he says something I can't hear to the other man. They're both looking at me now and the driver is smirking and laughing. I look away and pick up pace. I'm about to cross the road when brakes screech and a passing car swerves and scarcely avoids colliding with the tree closest to me. I scream and jump out of the way, and losing my footing on the kerb I fall backwards and hit my coccyx. Pain shoots up my spine as I try to see into the car. I can't see much of the driver except red hair and hands gripping the steering wheel tightly as the car straightens again and is driven away speedily. It's all over in the blink of an eye. An accident narrowly dodged.

'You all right?' the van driver shouts, hurrying past the gate.

My heart is pounding and I can't form words but I manage to nod. His gaze drops to my round bump and he's suddenly ashen.

'Oh God,' he says. 'Can you stand?'

Tears stream down my cheeks but I'm not crying. At least, I don't think I am. Is this what shock feels like, I wonder? There's loud ringing in my ears and I have to concentrate hard not to faint. He places his hand on my shoulder and I think he's going to try to help me to my feet. I'm not ready. Thankfully, a familiar voice provides a positive distraction.

'Darcy. Oh my goodness, Darcy.' My elderly neighbour, Mr Robinson, crosses the street to come to my aid.

Between them they help me up.

'Oh Darcy you're shaking like a leaf, you are,' Mr Robinson says as he slips off his cardigan and drapes it over my shoulders.

'Thank you,' I whisper, slowly steadying myself on my feet.

'Did you see that?' the van driver asks.

I'm about to answer when I realise he's talking to my neighbour.

'I did. Crazy driving. Much too fast for a residential area,' Mr Robinson says.

'I swear it looked as if the car was aiming straight for her,' the van driver says. 'I really thought it was gonna hit her.'

'Did you get the registration number?' Mr Robinson asks.

'Couldn't,' the van driver says. 'They drove away so bloody fast.'

'Pity,' Mr Robinson says. 'That sort of driving needs to be reported before they kill someone.'

The van driver places his hands on his hips and shakes his head as he says, 'You wouldn't believe some of the lethal eejits I see on the roads day in, day out. No wonder there are so many accidents. Usually texting or something like that. Madness.'

When I'm less shaky Mr Robinson thanks the van driver for his help and suggests I go around to his house for a cup of tea.

'I'll call Luke, then,' he says, as he places his arm around me in a fatherly way.

'That was yer wan off the telly,' I hear the van driver tell his colleague as we walk away.

'The vegan one,' the other man says. 'Phwoah, she's even hotter in real life, isn't she?'

Chapter Twelve

Tina

Wednesday 19 June 2019

The new flat is smaller than I thought it would be. It was advertised as a spacious two-bedroomed home in a sought-after area. When in reality it is a cramped, dimly lit ground-floor flat with two narrow rooms masquerading as bedrooms to make space for a stupid open-plan kitchen and living area. Still, I can't argue with the location. It is very much sought-after, although probably not sought by anyone else quite as much as me. I can't believe my luck. Not only is this house in Darcy Hogan's neighbourhood, it's at the end of her road. Of course, it's crazy expensive like all accommodation so close to the city. I just about have enough to cover the first three months' rent, but hopefully I won't be here long.

I've been unpacking for hours. Some of the stuff in the boxes I'd forgotten I had. Like a scrapbook of old newspaper articles. I used to love collaging when I was younger. *Maybe I should take that up again*, I think, opening the scrapbook to read the first article.

Gardaí in Westrow, Dublin renew their appeal for missing 18-year-old Gillian Buckley. Gillian has not been seen by friends and family for eleven days.

Updated sightings suggest Gillian may still have been on the school grounds as late as 10.30 p.m. on the day she went missing. Gardaí are following all leads, and they appeal for anyone who may have been in or around the area at the rear of the school building on 12th May to come forward for questioning.

'We believe Gillian left the grounds with someone she knew,' a leading detective on the case said today. Gardaí are also particularly anxious to speak to a group of youths who appear to have been drinking at the extremity of the property.

I shake my head as I skip the rest of the article and flick through the scrapbook. There are some photos of St Peter's. The grounds, mostly. Or the grand, alluring building with its sandstone walls and latticed windows, like a giant gingerbread house. Only there was nothing ever sweet about St Peter's.

There are more articles and more photos. But I close the scrapbook before I can flick through them all. Besides, I know how this story goes. Renewed appeals for information became less frequent as time passed. They dwindled to a mention on an anniversary, and after a few years there was nothing at all. It was almost as if everyone forgot about her. Even I was guilty of forgetting, until recently.

The sound of the microwave pinging in the kitchen reminds me that it's time for dinner. I take a deep breath and exhale with satisfaction as the smell of shepherd's pie wafts towards me. I haven't quite finished sticking all my photos and posters to the wall yet, but my stomach growls and I know I need a break. I glance around at my handiwork. My bedroom is wallpapered with the life of Darcy Hogan. Her radiant skin sparkles at me from a shiny magazine interview that I've cut out and hung above my bed. Her blue eyes pop in a photo I took on my phone a few weeks ago while I was watching her and Luke in the park. She even manages to shine in the black-and-white newspaper article from last year. 'Businesswoman of the Year' is printed in dark, bold font above a photo of Darcy holding her chunky, crystal award. On each side of the article I've hung a page torn out of our yearbook. Darcy is on page seventeen. Even with her flat, sandy-brown hair that she hadn't yet bleached, she was still voted 'Most Likely to Succeed as an Entrepreneur'. The font is less assertive and has faded over the years, but nonetheless the title resides above her ever-perfect face. On the opposite page is a photo of me. Or the old me. I look nothing like that helpless nerd any more. Above my shiny, greasy face and equally flat hair it reads 'Most Likely to Be Alone'.

It used to bother me every time I read those words. But it doesn't any more. Mostly because I know they're mixed up. Wrong. Reversed. Because I will succeed and Darcy will die alone. And as the microwave beeps again, nagging me not to forget my dinner, I decide to leave the space next to my bedroom window blank for now. I'll need it for the most important article of all. The one not printed *yet*. Darcy's obituary.

Chapter Thirteen

DARCY

Thursday 20 June 2019

Luke is pottering about in the kitchen when I wake up. I can smell coffee and pastry. My stomach rumbles loudly and reminds me that I'm famished. I haven't been able to eat much recently. I was so shaken after the incident outside our new neighbour's house. Every time I close my eyes I see the car swerving towards me, and I keep thinking about what could have been.

Even worse, when I told Luke about what happened he said it proved his point that I shouldn't be out and about, and he reminded me that the doctor suggested bed rest as much as possible for the remainder of the pregnancy. But with just a few more weeks until my due date, going into labour can only be a positive thing. Like getting a sentence reduced for good behaviour. And I have been well behaved. *My God, I miss soft cheese and red wine.*

It's a mammoth task to roll out of bed, and I groan audibly when I find a note on the bedside table from Luke.

Honey,

Jinx is outside. He was sick again last night. Everything clean now, but house stinks of puke and antibac. All windows open. Have a good rest today. See you after work.

    Love,

    L x

My poor boy. I think of Jinx being sick in the utility room last night and I feel so guilty that he was all alone. Luke says we have to train him to sleep downstairs for when the baby comes but I'd much rather have him in our room with us. I pull something comfortable on and hurry downstairs just in time to hear the rumble of car tyres driving over the neat pebble-like stones in our driveway. I peer through the glass in the front door and I sigh with disappointment as Luke's car pulls on to the road.

'Here, Jinx, here, boy,' I call, turning away from the door and clicking my fingers.

Jinx bounds into the hall. He's clean, dry and smells okay. He's not the vomit monster I was expecting. Downstairs smells fine too. It's a little cold as the morning breeze whips through the open windows, but I'm not getting the smell of anything other than coffee. I hurry around, closing all the windows, and restore order to the flying curtains. The house is calmer – silent. I make my way into the kitchen.

There are freshly made croissants waiting on the table with jam and cream. Albeit they're the frozen variety bunged in the oven for ten minutes. But Luke still gets sex tonight for effort, I decide. I pause and exhale, realising how long it's been since I made love with my husband. A month. Two, maybe. And overall, we've only been intimate a handful of times since I've been pregnant. But Luke never complains. I think he's too excited about the baby to think about much else.

With Jinx nestled contentedly at my feet I sit at the table and enjoy peppermint tea and a croissant. I am so hungry. I polish off both the tea and pastry before I take my phone out of the pocket of my oversized and comfortable tracksuit, ready to call my husband. There's a missed call flashing on-screen and, assuming it's Luke checking in, I listen to the waiting voicemail.

'Darcy, hi. It's Lindsay here. Lindsay St Claire. How are you?'

I roll my eyes and groan loudly. Jinx is on his feet instantly and nudging his nose into my hip. 'I'm okay, boy,' I say, stroking him between the ears. 'It's just somebody I don't want to hear from.'

Jinx lies back down as if he understands.

'I just wanted to touch base with you after your visit to the studio,' Lindsay continues. 'Things got a little wild, didn't they? I thought you'd like to know we're following up on that call. We pride ourselves on providing the best experience for our guests and our audience and calls like that are totally unacceptable. Rest assured, I'm personally making sure nothing like that happens on air again.'

I sigh, wishing it were that simple, as Lindsay continues.

'I would also like to extend an invitation to come back on the show any time you like. Honestly, Darcy. Any time. Any product. You have our full support. Do have a think about it. Call the studio any time and someone on reception will be able to sort you out. Byeeee.'

'Sort me out,' I echo, as if Lindsay can hear me while I try not to take offence. 'I'm perfectly capable of sorting things out for myself, thank you. Aren't I, Jinx?'

Jinx whimpers, my irritable tone obviously upsetting him. I take a deep breath and try to calm down. I toss my plate and cup into the sink and let Jinx into the garden. If I grab a quick shower

I'll make the 9.30 a.m. bus and I'll be in the office in fifteen minutes. Luke won't approve, but I'm not spending another minute hiding from my life.

I'm just about to walk upstairs when the doorbell rings. I'm not expecting anyone. I glance through the peephole half expecting to find an overzealous Lindsay St Claire on the porch, but of course I don't. Although I can't help but feel that the red-haired woman with pretty green eyes and cherry lips waiting on the other side of the door is familiar.

I surprise myself when I open the door and say, 'Good morning, can I help you?'

She smiles and says, 'I really hope so.'

Chapter Fourteen

GILLIAN

Friday 21 June 2019

The smell of freshly cut grass and summer flowers wafts towards me as I sit in the garden. There are dogs barking in the distance and I can hear the odd cat too. The sounds and smells seem to sum up life in Cherryway so precisely. Perfect gardens, perfect pets and perfect people. I wonder if I stand out. I can feel anxiety heating the back of my neck as if the timid morning sun, shining down on me, has burnt me. Every time I think over yesterday, my stomach flips. But the wheels are in motion now and all I can do is hang on for the ride.

I don't actually know what possessed me to knock on Darcy Hogan's front door yesterday morning. I don't even remember walking up the somewhat-intimidating granite steps towards her front door, but somehow I found myself, dressed head to toe in a fancy business suit, ringing her bell.

'Can I help you?' Darcy said, unsure and almost nervous – it seemed so unlike her.

I smiled and pretended not to be intimidated by her and said, 'I'm Gillian Buckley.'

'Oh,' she said, her eyes wide with recognition. I knew, of course, that it was my name and not my face that was familiar to her. And while I never expected her to remember me, I must admit it hurt more than I thought it would to be so forgettable.

I had a whole speech prepared about my father and our troubled relationship and how nineteen years after I ran away we were trying to make amends, but Darcy looked so awkward and frail on the doorstep I decided to save my story for another time.

Instead, I asked her if she had received the gift from Buckley & Co. 'Something small for the baby,' I said, when she baulked as if I had said something awful.

Silence followed and Darcy was so pale I thought she might faint.

'The bracelet,' I reminded her.

She nodded and kept her hand firmly on the door handle as if she were seeing a ghost. I guess in some ways, she was.

The conversation was stilted from there. I thought, considering the eye-watering sum she's hoping to wrangle from Buckley & Co, that she might invite me in, but she never moved out of the doorway. At one stage a horrible, snow-white puppy arrived at her feet, his teeth bared and his tail rigid, warning me that I was not welcome inside.

That's when I stupidly invited Darcy to come here. 'I've just moved in . . . stop by . . . tea, biscuits . . .' I rambled on.

She didn't reply but she smiled. And when I suggested 10 a.m. today she nodded and said, 'Goodbye.'

It's 10.15 now and there is no sign of Darcy, and I gave her my number but there's no text or call to say she's running late.

Rude.

Another fifteen minutes pass before Darcy rounds the corner of the house, as I suggested she do. She's wearing a fitted red summer dress, her golden curls bouncing against the tips of her shoulders.

A beige wicker basket dangles from her arm, resting at her hip, and her face is bright and fresh. She looks like a real-life Goldilocks and for a moment she takes my breath away.

I inhale sharply and, light-headed, I stand up as she gets closer. 'Welcome.'

'Thank you for inviting me,' she smiles, stopping in front of me. She air-kisses one side of my face and then the other before she adds, 'You have a very beautiful house. This one is the talk of the whole street. It has the biggest garden. I didn't know it was for sale.'

I ignore Darcy's property envy. And I certainly don't add that it's not mine and I'm renting a minuscule flat with very little natural light. Thankfully, the people living above my flat are all at work. There is no one to disturb us, or dent Darcy's perception of me. Today, at least.

'I can't quite believe we're neighbours. It's such a coincidence, isn't it?' she says, her eyes sweeping over the house again.

'Yes,' I say, leaving it at that.

'I'm so sorry I'm late,' she says. 'I was a little under the weather this morning.'

'Oh,' I say, trying to sound surprised and concerned. 'I did notice you were a little pale.'

Darcy scrunches her nose. 'I'm sorry,' she says. 'You caught me by surprise. I didn't realise you were . . . erm, well, I didn't realise you were—'

'Alive,' I say boldly.

Darcy's eyes widen and she studies me for a moment, probably checking if it's okay to smile. 'I was going to say I didn't realise you were working with your father.'

'It's a recent thing,' I say, and I know with Darcy's impeccable manners that she'll leave it there.

'Um, I've brought some treats,' Darcy says, cheerily. She slides the basket off her arm and shows me inside. 'They're all from the

87

Darcy's Dishes freezer-to-fresh range. I thought you might like to sample some.'

'Freezer to fresh,' I repeat. 'I like that.'

'It's the range we're hoping to expand with the help of your father's investment. Croissants, scones, *pain au chocolat*, that sort of thing. Microwaveable and so good it's hard to believe they're not fresh. It's taken us quite a while to get the recipes right but we're very pleased with the results.'

'Sweet to complement the savoury,' I say, already more familiar than I want to be with Darcy's shepherd's pie.

'Yes.' She smiles. 'We want to be a leader in all areas of the market.'

Leader, I think. The word sticking to my brain like glue. Darcy has always wanted to be a leader. I guess some things never change.

'Tea?' I ask, guiding my arm through the air to direct her attention to the table.

'Will your father be joining us?' Darcy asks.

'No,' I say firmly.

Darcy's smile grows ever wider despite the awkwardness. She has an ability to make you feel special, as if every word coming out of my mouth is wildly interesting and she is soaking me up. On the other hand, every word Darcy utters *is* interesting and I hang on to her every nod, or smile or giggle the way I used to.

The sound on my phone is off but that doesn't stop it from vibrating against the patio table as it lights up receiving a call.

'Do you need to get that?' Darcy asks.

I slam my hand on to the screen to steady the dancing phone, and more importantly to hide the name flashing up. 'No. No it's fine,' I say. 'It's nothing important. I'll call them back later.'

Darcy looks at me with cautious eyes. I suddenly feel small and inhibited. I remember this feeling from our schooldays. Darcy can instigate it with just a blink of her crystal-blue eyes.

I count backwards from three in my head and say, 'Do tell me more about frozen to fresh, won't you?'

Like flicking a switch, Darcy's mind is back on work and she chats effortlessly.

Finally, the sun shines high above us, and without sunglasses we are both squinting and Darcy becomes restless.

'I hope it's okay to ask . . .' she says, pausing as if trying to find the right words. 'But, do you think I can count on your father's investment?'

I place my hand above my eyes to act like a visor so I can straighten my face and see her better. 'You can most certainly count on your life changing from here on, Darcy. I promise.'

'Thank you.' Darcy beams. 'I'm excited.'

'Oh. Me too,' I gush, not telling a word of a lie. 'This is going to be huge.'

Chapter Fifteen

Tina

Saturday 22 June 2019

'And hold. Hold. Hold. And breathe,' the Pilates instructor says as her gentle voice washes over the gym like a wave of calm.

My arms burn and wobble as I hold a side plank.

'And, three, two, one. Relax,' the instructor says.

I flop on to my side and smile.

'Great class, guys. See you next week,' she says, glancing around the hall as everyone gets to their feet and gathers their mats. 'Well, those of you still with us. And anyone who pops in the meantime, congratulations.'

There's lots of cheering and clapping and everyone looks at a woman in the middle of the room. Her bump is ginormous and she hasn't a hope of bending to pick up her mat so the lady beside her helps.

'She's going in for a section tomorrow,' the girl beside me says, her belly almost as big, and I can't seem to take my eyes off it.

'Ah.' I nod, not sure what else to say.

'You're new,' she says.

I nod. 'Is it that obvious?'

'How far along are you?'

'Erm. Four months,' I say, picking the first number that pops into my head.

'Really?' Her eyebrows shoot up as her eyes burn into my flat stomach. 'You're not showing at all, you lucky thing. I was a beached whale at your stage.'

'I've been really sick,' I add quickly, wishing I'd picked a smaller number.

'Oh, you didn't have that Hyperemesis Gravidarum thing, did you?'

'That what?'

'Horribly sick in early pregnancy. It's dangerous. One of the girls from this class had it. It was Darcy Hogan, actually. You know, of Darcy's Dishes.'

I nod.

She smiles and I can only imagine how much she loves to tell people that Darcy is her friend. 'Darcy had to stop coming,' she says, her smile fading. 'She almost ended up housebound, it got so bad. Such a pity. She was a really lovely girl. I miss her.'

'Sounds awful,' I say. I knew joining this class would be a great way to get some information about Darcy.

'It's so hard on her because she can't really be taking time off work. You've probably noticed she hardly ever posts on Instagram any more—'

I cut her off. 'No. Sorry. I don't use social media,' I say. 'Too many weirdos online.'

'Sure. Yeah.' She nods. 'You should have seen some of the nasty comments people were making after Darcy was on *Good Morning, Ireland*. I was praying she didn't see them.'

'People can be awful,' I say, caringly.

'Luckily her husband is amazing,' she continues. 'He has taken such good care of her. I wish I could find a man like that.' She stops to sigh and rub her tummy. 'But this little one's dad doesn't want to know. A total waste of space, he is.'

'I'm single too,' I say, not really sure why.

She smiles. 'I'm Polly by the way.'

'Tina,' I say, wondering what I'm doing. I never introduce myself to new people.

'Do you fancy a coffee, if you're not too busy, Tina?' she asks.

I'd literally rather do anything else than go to the local coffee shop with this pregnant airhead, but she obviously knows Darcy quite well and I'm sure the titbits of information about the Hogans that she could share would be worth the hell of sipping an Americano with her.

'Sure. I'd love to.'

Polly bends to pick up her mat. Her large pregnant stomach makes her awkward and I'm about to offer to do it for her when a woman from the opposite side of the room hurries over. Her hair is pulled into a ponytail so high and tight it strains her forehead taut. Her mat is crumpled under her arm and she's restlessly shifting from one leg to the other while she engages us in small talk.

'Did you hear about that body that they found in the Wicklow Mountains?'

Polly and I shake our heads. My interest is instantly piqued and I stand straighter. Listening.

'The man with no fingers,' she continues.

Fingertips. I want to correct her, irrationally irritated that the details are being skewed by this stupid woman.

'Well,' she says, taking a deep breath as if just a few words leave her puffed out. 'They think they know who he is.'

I gasp.

The breathless woman continues. 'They're searching for family first, obviously, but once they've been informed they'll release his name.'

Polly finally manages to retrieve her mat and she rolls it and slides it into a luminous pink sleeve, seemingly unfazed by the news. 'I hope they catch whoever did it,' she says.

The woman rolls her eyes. 'Trust all the good stuff to happen the minute I go on maternity leave.'

Polly laughs.

The woman laughs too and shrugs. 'Right. I've gotta pee. This child thinks my bladder is a trampoline.' She leaves without another word.

'That's Rose. She's a sergeant or a detective or something,' Polly explains. 'This is her fourth baby, she's on mat leave now, but I don't think she ever switches off being a cop, if you know what I mean.'

I swallow. I know exactly what Polly means. Suddenly this Pilates class is far less appealing.

'So – coffee,' Polly says.

I pull a face. 'You know, I'm not feeling very well. I think I'm just going to go home. I'm so sorry.'

Polly looks disappointed. 'Still sick?' she asks, placing her hand on my shoulder. 'You poor thing. I hope it eases off soon. Rain check, yeah?'

'Yeah,' I say. 'Another time.'

Chapter Sixteen

DARCY

Monday 24 June 2019

Luke holds my hair back as I throw up for a third time this morning. Dragging a shaky hand across my mouth, I flop on to my bathroom floor and whinge. 'I don't understand. I thought sickness was supposed to get better at the end, not bloody worse.'

'Maybe it was something you ate,' Luke says flushing the toilet for the umpteenth time. 'You haven't been this bad in a while.'

Before I have time to reply, my stomach rumbles again and fiery bile burns its way up the back of my throat as I lean over the loo once more to heave. Luke rubs my back and tells me it's okay.

'I'm so sick of this,' I say, catching my breath. My body aches all over with exhaustion. 'The last thing I actually enjoyed was a couple of Darcy's Dishes pastries at Gillian's house. Everything else has come back up since.'

'Who's Gillian?' Luke asks, passing me some tissue and flushing the toilet yet again.

I stand up and squeeze some toothpaste on to my toothbrush and shove it into my mouth, buying myself some time to think. I feel guilty for not telling Luke about Gillian before now. It wasn't as if it slipped my mind. I thought about my conversation with Gillian often over the weekend. I wonder if I said the right things to make sure she liked me. Liked Darcy's Dishes. She's so hard to figure out, and I hate to admit that. It's something else to add to a long list of can't dos right now. Can't manage my own business. Can't go to Pilates. Can't keep a simple meal down. But being nice to Gillian and word of my kindness getting back to Andrew is something I *can* do. I can help to close this deal.

I feel Luke watching me, waiting for an answer. I spit into the sink and rinse my mouth.

'She's our new neighbour,' I say, casually dropping my tooth-brush back into the holder. 'I told you someone moved into the house at the end of our road, remember?'

Luke's wearing a weird expression, one I'm not used to seeing. As if he's trying to read the thoughts between my words. 'Yeah, the removals van story. I remember. I didn't know you'd been talking to someone who lives there though.'

'Um. Just a quick chat, really. I wanted to welcome her to the neighbourhood.'

Luke tilts his head and smiles. 'Right.'

Luke knows me better than I know myself. He knows bringing baked goods around to a neighbour's house isn't exactly my style. I see the familiar twinkle of curiosity in his eye and I'm looking forward to the questions he's about to ask. I've been hoping for an opportunity to discuss the Buckley investment and my own part in helping it along by befriending Gillian, but any time I start to bring it up, Luke tells me not to worry about work stuff and just to concentrate on my health and the baby. He means well, of course, but it's slowly driving me mad. And now as I open my mouth his damn phone rings.

'Oh you have got to be kidding me,' I grumble under my breath.

'You okay here alone for a minute?' he asks, checking his screen.

'Who is it?' I ask.

Luke holds up a finger, and I wait as he says, 'Hello,' and backs out of the bathroom.

I roll my eyes as he closes the door behind him. I don't follow. My stomach is more settled after brushing my teeth and getting the taste of vomit out of my mouth, but I'm still afraid to leave the bathroom just yet. I sit on the edge of the bath and scroll through my phone. I've missed a couple of calls from the office landline, but no voicemails or texts. I call work back immediately.

It only rings twice before I hear a chirpy, 'Good morning. Darcy's Dishes. Mildred speaking. How may I help you?'

'Hi, Mildred. It's Darcy. Were you calling me earlier?'

'Oh my God, Darcy.' Mildred's tone changes completely. 'I've been trying to get hold of you. Are you at home? Is Luke there?'

'I'm at home. I'm not feeling very well. Luke hasn't left yet.'

I can hear Mildred gulping in air. 'Is your TV on?'

'No.' I shake my head as if she can see me. 'Mildred, what's wrong? What's going on? You sound freaked out.'

'Turn on the telly, Darcy. Quick.'

'*Good Morning, Ireland*?' I say, knowingly.

'There's some woman on the show. She says she knows you. She says she was at school with you.'

'Tina?' I ask, flinging open the bathroom door and hurrying downstairs. 'They must have tracked her down. Invited her on air.'

I turn on the television and sound encompasses the living room immediately. And Lindsay St Claire's face burns through the screen as if she's glaring directly at me.

'Take a moment. Compose yourself. I know this is hard but, please, just tell us what is in your heart,' Lindsay says, smiling

96

at the woman sitting opposite her. The woman has long blonde hair and thick-framed glasses and neither seem to sit naturally on her.

I shake my head. It's not Tina. In fact, I have no idea who the woman is sitting haggard on the couch where I sat just days ago. The on-screen text reads, 'Elizabeth Casey – school friend of Darcy Hogan'. But I don't recognise the name. I've never known an Elizabeth Casey. I do, however, recognise Lindsay's tone, the one I know she reserves for when she's live on air. And I can't tell if she cares about her guest or the story. Part of me suspects she cares about both.

Elizabeth Casey recounts episodes from my schooldays in front of the cameras as effortlessly as if it all happened yesterday. She tells the nation she was at school with me and Gillian and Tina. She was a couple of years below us, apparently. Her face is scrunched up and wrinkled and she looks years older, but it's the thin orange band stretching from one side of the screen to the other that I'm focused on. I notice now it's updated with incoming tweets and Facebook messages.

I went to St Peter's. I was very happy there. A great school.
Darcy and Gillian were in my year.
#StPeters

'What's happening?' I ask, barely able to breathe. 'What is Lindsay doing?'

Mildred doesn't reply.

'My schooldays were some of the happiest of my life,' the woman on the couch says. 'But then Darcy Hogan came to our school and ruined everything. She thought she was better than everyone else.'

'Maybe she found it hard to settle in. Sometimes shyness can be misconstrued,' Lindsay says.

'There was nothing shy about Darcy,' Elizabeth says. 'She fought with the chef. She made his life a misery until the canteen took meat off the menu almost completely. She encouraged the girls to start sneaking into the boys' dorms even though it was expressly forbidden—'

'Well now,' Lindsay cuts across her, shifting as if she's suddenly uncomfortable in her chair. 'Isn't that what teenagers do – push the boundaries? I doubt Darcy was the first girl at St Peter's to have a boyfriend.'

'Do you know this woman?' Mildred whispers, startling me. I forgot I was still holding the phone to my ear.

I shake my head.

'Darcy? Are you there?'

I take a breath. 'Yeah. Yeah, I'm here.'

'You okay?'

'I don't remember her,' I say.

'Is any of this true?' Mildred asks.

'Sort of,' I say, 'but she's twisting it. That's not how it happened. She's making me sound like a bitch.'

I take a deep breath as Elizabeth continues. 'The worst part was when Gillian went missing.'

'Gillian Buckley,' Lindsay says as she reaches out to place her hand on this stranger's knee. 'I can imagine. It must have been so hard for all the pupils at the time.'

Elizabeth scrunches her eyes and looks upset, but no tears fall as she says, 'No one said anything at the time, but we all knew what Darcy did—'

The screen goes blank and I find myself holding my breath. When colour returns it's a generic message about technical issues.

'They cut her off. Did you see that?' I ask, guzzling air as if my lungs are constricted and I can't fill them as much as I need to.

'What's going on?' Mildred asks. 'Should we be worried?'

'I'm not really sure,' I say, but I realise as the words tumble past my lips that I'm lying to myself as much as to Mildred, because I know who is hiding under Elizabeth Casey's fancy glasses, heavy make-up and glossy hair: Tina. And I *am* worried. I'm incredibly worried. I need to know what Tina was going to say. What was so terrible or slanderous that Lindsay cut her off air mid-sentence.

Lindsay appears on-screen again. She's smiling and apologising for technical problems but there's uncertainty in her eyes. When the camera zooms out it reveals that Elizabeth is gone and the text at the bottom of the screen has changed. It says:

Green fingers? Coming up next . . . how to keep your rose bushes in top shape this summer.

'Join us after the break when we'll be chatting to this year's winner of *Beautiful Gardens*,' Lindsay says, the apples of her cheeks rounder than usual as she tries hard to appear chipper. I turn off the television and I tell Mildred I won't be in the office today. And she's not surprised. She tells me to take it easy and not let all this media stuff get to me. I hang up and make my way slowly back upstairs.

'There you are,' I say, finding Luke sitting on the edge of our bed.

I want to tell him about Lindsay's show but I cut myself off before I begin. He looks worryingly washed out, and for someone who is usually so broad and strong he seems small and almost help-less suddenly.

'Who was on the phone?' I ask as Luke stares at his screen.

He looks up and exhales. 'Oh, eh, just Mildred.'

'Mildred?' I say, as I glare at my lying husband with narrow eyes.

'Um. Hmm,' he says, sitting on the edge of bed to slip his legs into his work trousers.

'Work Mildred?'

Luke stands up and shuffles his feet into his shoes, bending to tie the laces. 'Well, yeah, honey. How many Mildreds do we know?'

'Yeah,' I say. 'How many *do* we know?'

'Okay. I'm late for work,' he says, standing tall once again. 'See you later, honey. Rest up today, yeah?'

I swallow hard. 'Yeah. See you later.'

Chapter Seventeen

DARCY

Monday 7 September 1998

The wheels of my uncle's car rumble over the stony driveway. It's long and winding with tall birch trees lining each side. And it feels much more like driving into a fancy hotel than a secondary school. When we finally pull up outside the main door of St Peter's boarding school I instantly feel like I don't belong here. And I don't. I would still be at my old school if my parents hadn't died in a car crash during the summer. My dad, being a frugal restaurateur, had a trust fund set up in my name to take care of me in the event that anything ever happened to him or my mother. I can't help but feel he jinxed us with his over-planning. My sense of resentment is overwhelming. Irrational as I know it is, I can't forgive my parents for dying and leaving me alone with my only living relative. My father's older brother, Tommy – a bachelor and an asshole. Tommy has made no secret of how pissed off he is not to see a penny of my father's money.

The decision to enrol in St Peter's wasn't a mutual one. Joining a new school is never easy. But joining as a senior two years away from Leaving Cert. is unbearable and I just know I'll never make friends. Still, it's better than living in a rural cottage with my uncle, constantly reminded that my parents' death is an inconvenience he could do without.

'Here we are,' Tommy says, getting out and walking around the front of his car to open my door like a perfect gentleman. 'I hope you make lots of new friends, Darcy.'

I know the loving uncle act is for the principal's benefit, although I'm not sure why Tommy bothers – it's not as if he'll be back to visit. The principal stands in front of the main doors. I recognise him from the school brochure Tommy gave to me after the decision that I would attend St Peter's was made. And as the principal watches us with a strained smile, his arms folded across his chest, I get the impression he sees this kind of falsity a lot.

'Welcome to St Peter's, Darcy,' Mr McEvoy says. 'I know you will be very happy here.'

My smile is equally strained. Tommy takes my suitcase out of the boot, and my heart aches as I stare at the compact rectangular box on wheels that contains my entire life.

'Right. Good luck,' Tommy says, setting the case down at my feet.

'You're leaving,' Mr McEvoy says, walking down the intimidating granite steps to join us.

Tommy nods. 'Have to get back to work.'

His lie hangs in the air for a moment before the principal says to me, 'How about a tour of your new school?'

I look at my case which I know is heavy and I don't reply. Words seem hard to form, suddenly.

'Do you like tennis?' Principal McEvoy asks. 'We're hoping to have new tennis courts out the back – soon as we have the funding. In the meantime, there's a swimming pool in the basement, if you fancy a dip. And—'

My eyes glass over as the engine of Tommy's car starts and he drives away without looking back.

Principal McEvoy places his hand on my shoulder and says, 'Try not to worry, Darcy. Your experience here will change your life. I promise.'

'It really is a great school,' someone with an English accent says, and I look up to find a ridiculously handsome boy coming down the steps towards us.

His floppy blond hair bounces as he walks and he drags a hand through it, guiding it out of his eyes. His uniform is pristine and emphasises his height and broad shoulders. I guess he's about my age and I find myself hoping he's in my class.

'Luke Hogan,' Principal McEvoy says, his smile growing a fraction crooked. 'What are you doing out of class?'

Luke's emerald eyes gaze into mine and I wonder if my cheeks are as flushed as they feel.

'Where is Tina Summers?' Mr McEvoy asks. 'Have you seen her? I asked her to welcome Darcy in.'

'Darcy,' Luke says, raising a flirtatious eyebrow.

Principal McEvoy puts his hands on to his hips. 'Mr Hogan!'

'I have no idea where Tina is,' Luke says, and for a moment I believe him, before I see the naughty twinkle in his eye.

'Fine,' Mr McEvoy says, straightening. 'Since you're here perhaps you could show Darcy around, while I locate Miss Summers.'

'Sure.' Luke shrugs and his grin is so contagious I find myself smiling back.

'No getting any ideas, Mr Hogan,' the principal warns, wagging a finger.

Luke's shrug is followed by a nod.

'I'm sure you can understand the school has strict policies about boy and girl interaction, Darcy,' Mr McEvoy says, and I quickly realise this is a lecture. 'We encourage friendships, of course. But relationships? Absolutely not. And as for funny business?' He pauses to glare at me and then Luke. 'Well, I don't think I need to say much about that, do I?'

Luke smirks and it's hard to keep a straight face as I really, really hope Principal McEvoy doesn't elaborate.

'You'll be getting your timetable this afternoon,' Mr McEvoy says to me, 'and you will see that you and Tina have some overlapping classes. I'm sure she'll be a great guide, and friend to you here at St Peter's. Now, if you'll excuse me I must find out where she is.' He turns and heads off down the corridor.

'While Mr McEvoy is, eh, busy, I'll introduce you to some of the other girls,' Luke says, picking up my case as if it's not uncomfortably heavy. 'I mean girls you might actually want to be friends with,' he adds, whispering as his lips brush against my ear.

My eyes are wide.

'Well c'mon, then,' Luke says, making his way up the sweeping granite steps.

I follow like a loyal puppy.

'Don't look so scared,' he says, glancing over his shoulder to check that I'm tagging along. 'Most of us know what it's like to be dumped here by a relative.'

I stop walking. Insulted.

Luke shrugs. 'I saw your dad drive away. He couldn't get out of here fast enough.'

'He's not my father,' I say, folding my arms defensively.

'Orphan?' Luke says, and I know it's a statement, not a question.

I swallow hard and allow myself a brief moment to miss my parents. 'Yeah. You too?'

'I have parents.' Luke smiles, oddly brightly, considering. 'They're just *dead to me*.'

'Sorry?' I say, horrified that anyone would admit something like that out loud.

'They're not bad people. More the type of people who should never have had a kid. They dump me here for three quarters of the year while they travel the world, come back and wonder why we're not close.'

'Oh that's, erm . . . Well, I'm sorry.'

'Don't be.' Luke starts walking again. 'I'm not. I was serious when I said St Peter's is great. I love it here. You will too.'

Chapter Eighteen

GILLIAN

Friday 28 June 2019

It's all over the news today. The man found in the Wicklow Mountains has been identified. I can't scroll through my phone or flick on the TV without seeing his photo. Apparently, despite the body being purposely mutilated to make identification difficult, he had a distinctive birthmark on his wrist and one of his staff identified him. Although I don't remember ever seeing this mark. I like to think it's something I would have noticed. It's sad, really, that with all his success and power, in the end it was an employee who noticed he was gone.

Noise carries through the ceiling overhead. The people in the house above my flat are walking around. Laughing occasionally. They're simply being present, but right now I resent them. There's just already so much noise inside my head I wish they'd go to work and leave me in peace. Today will be hard enough without my mind aching too.

The kitchen countertops are littered with various newspapers, scrapbooks, scissors and glue. I gather everything up and stack it to one side. The mess reminds me of my schooldays and how hard I found it to never have any personal space. *I hated that place!* I don't bother to look at the newspaper cuttings. It's probably something about cold cases or CSI or something. It's creepy. *Sharing a house is so not me.*

I make some coffee and pour it into a takeaway paper cup that's showing clear signs of being reused too often. Glancing myself over in the mirror, I decide I look professional and not like I'm trying too hard, and I leave the flat. My timing is unfortunate and I open my flat door just as the couple who live overhead are descending the steps.

'Morning,' the guy says, his arm casually draped over his girl-friend's or wife's shoulders.

'Hope you're settling in well,' the girl says, reaching the bottom of the steps before him. She sidesteps out from under his arm.

I like her accent but I can't quite place it. Polish, maybe. Her platinum-blonde hair is scraped back in a high ponytail and her bright-blue eyes are striking. He reaches the bottom step immediately after and they stand side by side staring and smiling at me. He's decidedly average in comparison to her and I wonder if he knows he's punching well above his weight. I don't have time for small talk but they're clearly waiting for me to say something.

'Yes. Good. Thank you.'

'I'm Eddie.' He extends his hand and I shake it. 'This is Kimberly,' he adds, tilting his head towards her.

'Hello,' I say. 'I'm Gillian.'

'I'm sorry to rush,' Eddie says, clipped as he leans in to kiss Kimberly on the cheek. 'But I've only got three minutes to make my bus and what's the betting it will be early today. It was lovely to meet you.'

'Bye, baby,' Kimberly chirps as he dashes away.

'Are you on your way to work, Gillian?' she asks, her eyes dropping to my business suit.

I nod. 'Are you off to the gym?'

She runs her hands over her super-tight, fitted training top coupled with bright Lycra yoga pants. 'Sort of.' She smiles. 'I'm a gym instructor. But I do try to sneak in a cheeky workout when I can.'

'A multitasker,' I say, and she blushes. 'Well, it's been so lovely to meet you,' I continue. 'And, I hate to rush, but I'm afraid I really do need to be on my way. I have an important meeting this morning . . .'

'Say no more,' she says, beginning to jog on the spot. 'Eddie's always running late too.'

I'm not running late, I want to clarify. But I simply smile and accept the insult I know she didn't mean.

'Maybe you'll come by for dinner some evening. I do an amazing Mexican night. It would be lovely to get to know each other better.'

'Yeah. Definitely. That would be great,' I lie, knowing that will absolutely never happen. 'Anyway, best get off. Bye.'

'Bye.' Kimberly waves.

I begin walking faster than is comfortable, or my level of fitness allows, and coffee attempts to slosh out of the side of my cup as the slightly warped lid struggles to hold it back. I slow when Kimberly jogs past, waving at me. And I wait until she turns the corner at the end of the road before I switch direction and finally walk towards Darcy's house.

I slow my pace as I walk past lush green-leaved trees and count the colourful front doors of all the red-brick houses between Darcy's and mine.

'Thirteen blue . . . fifteen red . . . seventeen purple,' I say aloud as I sip a mouthful of coffee that is too hot and burns my lips.

Darcy opens her door before I even ring the bell. She's still in her pyjamas and her hair is piled high on her head in a messy bun. It's the first time I've ever seen her look less than perfect.

'Jinx? Here boy. Here, Jinx. Where are you?' she says, clicking her fingers as she stands at the top of the steps.

She stops when she notices me and stands a little straighter and I wonder if she knows she's rubbing her back.

'Gillian,' she says, surprised.

I want to say something but words won't come.

Darcy is staring at me with huge, round sympathetic eyes. 'I've just heard the news. I can't believe it. I'm so sorry about your father.'

I nod. 'Can I come in?'

'Yes. Of course. Absolutely.' Darcy pulls the bobbin out of her hair and her long, blonde curls flop around her shoulders, instantly reviving her appearance. 'Come on in. Please.'

Darcy steps aside and makes room for me to pass by when I reach the top step. She cranes her neck and looks around her garden one last time, shaking her head.

'Is something wrong?' I ask, knowing she can't find her puppy.

'No. Nothing,' she lies, closing the door behind us. 'You'll have to excuse the mess. I wasn't expecting company.'

Darcy's idea of mess is hilarious. Her huge, airy hall is gleaming. Porcelain tiles sparkle. And a bouquet of bright blue-and-purple oriental lilies perches on top of the sideboard just inside the door.

'They smell amazing,' I say, tilting my head towards the flowers and taking a deep breath.

'Thank you. They're from Luke.'

I grin. 'What a great husband you have.'

'He brings something small home after work most days recently. I think he's trying to take my mind off waiting for the baby to come.'

'And does it work?' I ask, following her as she leads the way into the kitchen.

She laughs and gestures towards the table and chairs, suggesting I have a seat. She waits until I'm sitting before she turns on the tap to fill the kettle. 'Tea or coffee?'

'Tea. Please,' I say as I place my empty paper cup on the table. I turn the grubby side, stained with brownish-grey streaks of old coffee, away and glance around. But both the cup and I seem out of place in Darcy's perfect home.

Admittedly, the kitchen is less pristine than the hall. It's not messy by any stretch. Just lived in. There are some envelopes on the countertop near the toaster. White ones with small plastic windows. Bills. There are quite a lot of them and some look as if they've sat there for a while.

'I'm afraid I don't have any biscuits,' Darcy says, flicking on the kettle. 'I'm waiting on a grocery delivery and I haven't managed to even pop as far as the local shop the last few days because I've been ill.'

'Oh,' I say, sounding surprised.

She shakes her head and rubs her stomach and I don't ask anything more. An awkward silence falls over us as Darcy pops a couple of teabags into cups and waits for the kettle to come to the boil.

'How do you like your tea?' she asks.

'Strong and black. Like my heart,' I joke.

Darcy swallows and I know I've shocked her.

'Here, let me get rid of that for you,' she says, reaching for the empty takeaway cup.

'Thanks.'

Darcy is smiling but it doesn't mask her wince of disgust as she tosses the cup into the nearby pedal bin and goes back to making tea. She fetches some sugar and milk and sets everything down at the table before she pulls out a chair and sits beside me.

'We weren't close, you know,' I finally say. 'I can't even say I'm upset he's gone.'

'But he was your father,' Darcy says, adding a large splash of milk into her cup.

I shake my head and point towards the milk. 'I thought you didn't use dairy?'

Darcy's smile becomes more natural and she says, 'It's almond. See.' She turns the milk around so the front label is facing me.

'Oh.'

Darcy raises the cup to her lips and savours a mouthful of tea. 'Your head must be spinning,' she says. 'Even if you weren't close, it's still a shock.'

I shake my head.

'But the way he died,' she says, her face growing paler as she thinks about it. 'It's just so . . .' She inhales sharply as she trails off.

I don't say anything but I can feel the hairs on the back of my neck standing on end as Darcy watches me, waiting for a reaction. Maybe she's expecting me to cry. Or have some sort of meltdown. And maybe I will. Maybe I will do both. But not right now.

I'm about to suggest we discuss Buckley & Co's investment in Darcy's Dishes and how the death of the CEO has complicated matters, but my phone begins ringing loudly and I'm furious that I forgot to turn the volume off.

Darcy stands up and says, 'I'll let you get that. I'll just be in the garden, if you need me.'

I watch as she walks out of the kitchen before I answer, 'Hello.'

'Hello. It's Lindsay. Lindsay St Claire.'

'Hello,' I repeat, standing so I can see Darcy through the kitchen window as she paces the garden.

'Hello. Hello. Can you hear me?' Lindsay raises her voice.

I watch Darcy. She's pale and desperately thin, despite her large bump. She is clicking her fingers and her lips are moving. Although I can't hear her through the glass, I know she's calling her dog.

'Hello,' Lindsay says. 'Hello. Are you there?'

'I can hear you.'

Lindsay takes a deep breath and says, 'Are you free to talk? I hope this isn't a bad time.'

I'm startled by a sudden scream in the garden. I hurry outside with the phone frozen against my ear. Darcy is on her knees at the end of the lawn near some tall, leafy trees. I can see from here that she's shaking.

'Help! Please. Someone help!' she shouts.

Lindsay's startled voice whispers in my ear. 'Is something wrong? I can hear screaming. Do you need help?'

I run towards Darcy, my work heels stabbing the grass, making it hard to pick up speed.

'I'm sorry. You must have the wrong number,' I say firmly, before I hang up.

Chapter Nineteen

DARCY

Saturday 29 June 2019

The waiting room in the veterinary practice is unusually quiet for a Saturday morning. An elderly woman sits with an overweight black cat across her knee, stroking him, and his sleepy purrs of satisfaction fill the air. There's a man with a leather jacket and a baseball cap sitting close to the woman. He has a cage at his feet. I can't see what animal is inside, but every now and then the cage rattles and he gives it a nudge with his foot and says, 'Shh.'

And then there is Luke and me. I'm sitting like a statue, exhausted, and Luke is pacing, with his phone held to his ear. He's been on the phone almost constantly since news about Andrew Buckley broke. Sometimes he's trying to reach someone in Buckley & Co who can tell us something about the status of the investment. Other times he's reaching out to other potential investors. There have been lots of promises of call backs and to look into it, but the silence is deafening and I'm struggling to keep it together. Most of the time he's simply on the phone to Mildred, checking in on stuff at work. Although I secretly call her later for updates. I tell Mildred that Luke and I are so busy we haven't had a chance to talk, but the truth is I'm so hurt that Luke lied to me. Why did he tell me Mildred was on the phone when she wasn't? We have so much more important stuff going on right now that picking an argument over a stupid phone call seems petty, but I can't seem to get it out of my goddamn mind.

Luke slides his phone into his pocket and flops into the seat next to me as he glances around the fancy waiting room. 'We need this like a hole in the head,' he says. 'This place costs an arm and a leg. Remember how expensive the vaccinations were. I can only imagine what they're going to try to squeeze out of us now.'

'Shh,' I say, as the man with the baseball cap glances at us. 'We'll figure this out. We'll figure it all out.' And I wish I felt remotely as confident as I sound.

Jinx was unconscious when I found him at the end of the garden. At first, I thought he was sleeping. He was lying on his side, panting. But when I touched him and he was cold and didn't budge I knew something was wrong. I thought an animal might have attacked him. Another larger dog perhaps. But there wasn't a mark on him. Suddenly he stopped panting and was very still. That's when I screamed.

Thank God Gillian was there. She helped me carry Jinx into the house. She calmed me down and made more tea. She waited with me as long as she could but she left just before Luke came home. And there has been lots of waiting since. Waiting to see if Jinx would make it through the night. Waiting to find out what the blood tests show. Waiting to hear if we can fix this.

The veterinary nurse appears from behind a frosted door. She smiles and I know she recognises us. She's seen Jinx a few times over the past few months. First for his vaccinations and more recently when he was neutered.

'Mr and Mrs Hogan,' she says, looking at me.

Luke is on his feet first and he helps me to stand. My back is aching from sitting in such a rigid chair for so long but I don't complain.

'Would you like to come through?' she asks.

I nod and Luke and I follow her through the frosted door.

'Is Jinx okay?' I ask, as she guides us into an office-like room with a low coffee table and some colourful chairs.

'He will be,' she says.

'What happened? Do you know what caused it yet?' Luke says, and he sounds as anxious as I feel.

'Rat poison most likely,' she says.

My eyes widen. 'What? A poison?'

'Or industrial-strength weedkiller. It's not unusual at this time of year. Have you had your garden sprayed recently?' she says, stopping to turn and look at Luke as if somehow he might be green fingered and inadvertently responsible.

'There's nothing like that in our garden,' I snap. 'It's safe for Jinx. Anyway, he's a house dog. He's not out much.'

She smiles. 'And he eats well normally? You haven't noticed a change in his appetite in recent days?'

'He was fine right up until yesterday,' I say. 'We had breakfast together. He loves scraps.'

'Hmm,' she says, tilting her head to one side and making a face as if she's disappointed. 'Scraps aren't ideal for a young dog's tummy. It might be best to stick to his regular food. Especially now that he's been so sick.'

My heart aches. Jinx loves climbing on to my lap for some treats from my plate.

'Okay.' She smiles, and I can tell she's managing the conversation and doesn't want to upset anyone or face any arguments. 'We've pumped his stomach and he has been given a strong sedative. He'll be very sleepy for the next twenty-four to forty-eight hours but he is ready to go home.'

'That's great news,' Luke says, subtly rubbing my back. 'Thank you.'

The veterinary nurse nods and smiles again. 'He's had a very lucky escape, but he should be fine.'

I choke back tears. 'Thank you. Thank you so much.'

Within minutes Luke and I are back in reception. Luke settles the bill at the desk while I cradle Jinx in my arms. He's wrapped in a chequered blanket and he's heavy, and it's uncomfortable to rest him on top of my bump. But I can feel the heat of his sleeping body radiating through my clothes, and I'm so relieved he's okay. I try not to think about my indigestion or the monster bill going on our credit card that I have no idea if we can pay.

'You'll have your hands full soon, love,' the old lady with the cat on her lap says. 'A baby and a puppy. Your house will be busy.'

I smile, but I don't say anything.

'Would you mind turning the telly up, my ears aren't as good as they used to be?' she asks, pointing to the small, wall-mounted television behind me.

'Sure,' I say, trying to manage holding Jinx in one hand while I find the button on the television that I can barely reach to raise the volume.

'That's lovely. Thanks,' she says, as sound fills the air.

I turn, about to walk towards Luke who looks as if he's getting annoyed at the desk, but the old woman continues talking to me.

'Have you seen this?' she asks, pointing at the screen.

I turned around to see a photo of Andrew Buckley on the TV. He's sitting on a boat, somewhere with blue-green waters, and although he's smiling with a glass of champagne in his hand there's an unmissable sadness in his eyes.

'Poor man has no one. Not a sinner to claim his body,' the woman says, stroking her cat. 'His family should be ashamed of themselves so they should.'

I open my mouth to explain that not everything you see on television is true. I've learned that the hard way, recently. I don't know Andrew Buckley, and I barely know his daughter. But somehow I feel compelled to defend her. To explain that not everything is always black and white and life is messy and complicated, and we should all have more respect than chatting about them in a vet's waiting room. Andrew isn't just some name on the news, or a body dumped in the mountains. He was a real person. A father, a friend, an employer . . . and an investor, and now he's gone.

'Wonder who he will leave all his money to?' she says, standing up as someone comes through the frosted door asking for Mr Whiskers.

As I watch her walk away, I wonder too. What will happen to all of Andrew Buckley's fortune? I assume Gillian will get it. She has been working with him, after all, and is the next of kin. At least he got to make peace with his daughter before the end. But who could have done such a thing? Such a horrible way to end up, left on a mountain somewhere.

I walk towards Luke, my back cracking audibly as I'm really starting to struggle with the weight of Jinx.

'What do you mean that card has been declined?' Luke is starting to shout, and the girl behind reception looks as uncomfortable as I feel.

She shrugs. 'It just won't go through. I had this problem before when I reached my limit.'

'Try another card,' I say gently, reaching Luke's side.

The girl on reception smiles, and it's all so awkward.

'I've tried them all,' Luke hisses.

'We have a payment plan,' the girl says. 'I can set one up for you, if you like. You can spread the cost over twelve months.'

'Yeah. Okay. Fine,' Luke grunts. 'But the problem is your stupid machine. The card is working just fine.'

'A payment plan would be good. Thank you,' I say, and the girl stands up to open the large filing cabinet behind her.

'Sorry,' she apologises as she roots around inside. 'We still do things the dinosaur way here. I'll have to get you to fill in a form and I'll scan it and get your account up on the system later.'

'That's fine,' I say, swaying. I'm light-headed and it's suddenly very, very warm in here. I had been enjoying the heat of Jinx's body, but now it's burning into my chest like a hot coal.

The girl lifts out a piece of blue paper from the cabinet and closes the drawer with a bang. Something falls off the top and tumbles on to the floor.

'Oh no, my lunch,' she says, bending to retrieve it.

I watch as she picks up a familiar light-brown box with an ivory label. It's Darcy's Dishes chilli con carne. I can see my silly, grinning face on the label. I hope she won't recognise me. But then she spins around with a toothy smile and a sparkle in her eyes and says, 'Oh. My God. It's you.'

I can't take the heat any more and my eyes roll before everything is suddenly black and I pass out.

Chapter Twenty

TINA

Tuesday 8 September 1998

I've been at St Peter's for four years. *She* has only been here four minutes and she's already caught the eye of every boy in school. That's impressive. Darcy Flynn with her long sandy-brown hair, straight white teeth and bright-blue eyes. She doesn't even have a freckle out of place. Darcy turns heads. So, it's no surprise that Luke Hogan's head is practically spinning.

Luke is the most popular boy in the school. He and I are in the same English class. I sit at the front. He sits at the back. I've said hello to him every morning since day one, but I'm not sure he even hears me because he's never once said hello back. It's not just Luke, of course, I'm invisible to most of the other kids here and I'm not sure why. At least the teachers see me. I can always be relied on to offer an intelligent answer to their questions, or engage in a healthy debate. Usually while the rest of the class chat among themselves. And as much as I enjoy the interactions with my teachers, I do get lonely.

When Mr McEvoy said a new girl was joining our class and he asked me to show her around, I was more than happy to oblige.

He said Darcy liked to cook, just like me, and I hoped, finally, I would have a best friend. I think Mr McEvoy hoped so too. I see the way he looks at me, his eyes full of sympathy – I hate it. Darcy only arrived yesterday, and, as per usual, I'm alone again already. Luke said he'd cover for me if I wanted to go to the hall for the chess team sign-ups, but I should have known he was just looking for an excuse to get out of class. He ended up showing Darcy around and already they are practically inseparable. They should be *my* best friend and *my* boyfriend. Not each other's. And I don't even like chess!

I'm not a nerd, although I am naturally academic. I've a photographic memory and that makes learning easy, and somewhat boring. My classmates don't know this, and it's certainly not the reason they exclude me. I'm not ugly. Okay, I'm not particularly attractive either, but there are plenty of other plain Janes here with lots of friends. Why not me? I play team sports. Though I'm not really sure why. No one ever picks me to be on their team. They just get stuck with me because I'm the only one left.

'Balanced teams always,' the teachers say.

The teachers mean an even number of boys and girls on each team. But the teams are never balanced. The popular kids choose each other first. Huddled in their groups as they laugh and giggle even when their team is losing. Life is all just a big game to them. And it's not that they don't want me to play. It's worse. They don't even notice if I play or not. I'd say it hurts my feelings, but that would be a lie. I stopped having feelings about most things a long time ago. These days, I exist only to observe. And to make collages. I love collaging. It's quite possibly my only joy and the one thing that keeps me sane.

Today, however, they've even ruined collaging for me. And I'll never be the same again.

I'm in the bathroom when the commotion starts. The shrieks and cackles from the dorm next door are so loud they make me jump out of my skin. I flush the loo, wash my hands and edge towards my dorm with caution. When I push open the door the noise inside is intense and overwhelming. Shrieks of laughter and someone shouting, 'Let me see! I want to see!'

Their shrill laughter claws at me. Then heads turn and they see me at the door. The girls nearest to me fall silent first. As if the sight of me has ripped their voices from their bodies. Some of them shake their heads, others stare at the ground. The silence seems to spread. The girls charging around in the middle of the room suddenly become statues. One after another they fall silent, until the only noise in the dorm is the squeak of the soles of my shoes as I enter.

The mass of girls in the stuffy dorm moves aside for me, clearing a path from the door to my bed – the second to last from the wall, and neatly made as always.

'Oh my God, she's pathetic,' a girl says. She is sitting on the edge of my bed swinging her legs.

I recognise her from my science class, although we've never spoken.

'Look! Look!' Gillian clambers on to my bed in her black leather shoes, stomping all over my bedsheets. And in her hand, I can see it now, she is holding my scrapbook. My secret, private scrapbook.

She opens it at the centre pages and the laughter starts again as everyone stares at the photo I've stuck there. It's Luke sitting on the shoulders of his rugby teammates after scoring the winning try in the biggest game of the year. I've dedicated countless pages to the rugby team. Their wins and their losses. But this page is different. Because around Luke's face I've drawn a bright-red love heart.

Next to his beautiful face I've written, in red marker and in capital letters: 'LUV U 4EVR'.

Gillian flicks through the pages and comes to a sudden stop. A sadistic grin lights up her freckled face and she squeals with satisfaction.

'Oh. My. God,' she says, as she raises the scrapbook higher so that everyone can see. 'Is that a wedding dress?'

Gillian points at the couple I have cut out from a magazine. It's a tall man in a black suit and a woman in a crisp white dress. It's Luke and me. I've stuck our faces on the models.

Stupid. Stupid. Stupid.

I've never seen them as a bride and groom. Ever. I'm not weird like that. They're just a couple. In love.

She's making this out to be something it's not. She's making it seem as if I have some strange obsession with Luke Hogan.

Then I'm aware of all these eyes shifting from the scrapbook to me, burning with intensity.

I want to move. I want to run and hide and never come back. But I'm frozen, like a deer in headlights.

'It's an actual bride and groom,' Gillian says. She's laughing so much she almost falls off the bed, which makes the other girls laugh even louder.

It's not! I want to shout but my chest is crushed by the weight of embarrassment.

She's not even showing them my other collages. The ones of sports day, for instance, or the time a well-being coach came to our school and told us about keeping a scrapbook of happy thoughts – that's where this whole idea came from.

Stupid bitch. This is all her fault. I feel the tears coming. I don't want to give them the satisfaction, but I'm going to cry.

'Hey, that's enough now,' a voice ripples from somewhere at the back of the dorm.

My feet are frozen to the spot, so I crane my neck to see who it is.

'Don't be such a dry shite,' Gillian says, finally jumping off my bed and closing the scrapbook. 'We're only having a laugh.'

Darcy Flynn steps forward through the sniggering girls until she's face to face with Gillian. 'Well, I don't think she finds it funny, do you?' she asks me.

I shake my head. It's no surprise that Darcy doesn't know my name, but I am surprised that she's taking my side.

Why is she helping me? I'm on my guard instantly.

'Fine. Whatever,' Gillian says, slamming my scrapbook into Darcy's chest. 'I'm bored now, anyway.'

Everything goes back to normal surprisingly quickly. The girls start chatting, breaking into their usual little cliques as they grab their bags and books and leave the dorm. The drama is over as quickly as it began. And if it wasn't for the stabbing pain in my chest, I could almost believe it had never happened.

Finally, it's just me and Darcy. I still haven't moved, so she walks over to me and hands me my scrapbook.

'You okay?' she asks.

'Yeah. I'm fine.'

Darcy looks at me with heartbreak-heavy eyes. And out of everything that just happened her sympathy makes me feel worst of all. That's why I couldn't bring myself to thank her.

'Who was that girl anyway?' Darcy asks.

I look at her wide-eyed. I'm surprised she doesn't know. 'No one,' I say, proudly. Besides, the way Darcy just pissed off Gillian, she's going to learn the hard way exactly who's who at St Peter's.

Gillian Buckley is popular. Although she has a complicated relationship with that status. As if being attractive and revered is too cliché for her taste. She has a particularly striking appearance. Her vibrant green eyes sparkle like emeralds and her hair is on the light-auburn side of red and long curls hang down her back. A smattering of freckles dust her nose, but she usually covers them with make-up. I often think if I dyed my red hair just a little darker and my hazel eyes were a fraction greener, people would think we are sisters. Maybe everyone would notice me then.

Chapter Twenty-One

TINA

Sunday 30 June 2019

I sit at the kitchen table with numerous windows open on my laptop. Andrew's photo is all over the internet – complete, of course, with eye-catching headlines:

> Business Tycoon Slaughtered
> Father and Entrepreneur Lost
> The Man. The Murder

The sensationalist words, chosen to tug at heartstrings, are bold and hackneyed. The spin to attract click bait has no shame. And, I won't lie, I've clicked through my fair share of articles this morning before breakfast. I've trawled the internet, searching for Andrew's name. I've read every article. And the comments. All of them. Every single stupid one! From the boring and pointless – *So sad. R.I.P.* – to the more self-centred – *I don't feel safe walking the streets any more* – right down to the utterly ridiculous – *I blame the government, there aren't enough guards on duty.*

The whole country is talking about Andrew's murder. But what nobody seems to know is who did it and why.

I print off the most interesting articles. Some with pictures. Some without. I like the ones with pictures best. And I cut and paste everything into my new scrapbook waiting on the kitchen table. I sip coffee that I made before I became distracted with the news. It's cold and scum has settled on the top. I spit it back into the cup and stand up to pour the whole thing into the sink.

It's only when I'm on my feet that I realise I'm shaking. My whole lower body is like jelly. I still can't quite believe what's happened. How it happened. Usually when I feel like this I replay the chain of events in my head that led me to this point – to the person I am today. But I don't have time this morning. I want to get my hands on the Sunday papers before they're all sold out. The traditionalist in me favours picking up a black-and-white broadsheet to truly understand the media's take on Andrew's death.

With the taste of bitter coffee still in my mouth, I slide my feet into some Uggs waiting by the door and throw a long coat on over my pyjamas before I leave the flat.

There are lots of people out walking. I get some funny looks as they pass by, glancing at my winter coat and boots on a sunny summer morning. I'm used to odd looks. It's the story of my life. I ignore them and march on towards the corner shop.

The small shop isn't busy. There are just a handful of people inside. And although none of them have bought a paper, they all seem to be talking about Andrew.

'Shocking what the country is coming to, isn't it?' the lady behind the counter says, as a man approaches to pay for some bread and a bottle of Coke.

'It is indeed,' he says, nodding.

'That's three sixty-five, love,' she says.

The man passes her a five-euro note and says, 'It's scary to think there's some psycho running around out there.'

'Evil. Pure evil,' she says, as she passes him back some coins.

I try to ignore her comment, but it's harder to ignore the way she stares at me.

'You all right there?' she asks, straightening so she seems a little less hidden behind the counter.

'Erm. I'm just looking for the newspapers,' I say.

'Right there. By the door.' She points and smiles, and when I turn around I find a shelf stacked with local as well as national papers.

I laugh, embarrassed, and I pick one up. 'Great. Thanks.'

Andrew's death – or as the cruder articles are reporting it, *murder* – is unsurprisingly front-page news.

'*Do we really know the man behind the facade?*' one bold journalist has dared to ask.

'*Man and mogul,*' someone else has printed. The paper in my hand promises to tell all inside. I flick through as quickly as I can, taking up too much space in the corner of the small shop with my arms wide as I hold the national broadsheet. My eyes can't take in the words fast enough.

> '*Let's rewind. How much do we really know about the man behind the empire?*'

The article sweeps over Andrew's present. His investments. Potential investments. Darcy's Dishes is among the mentions. And I try not to let my back teeth snap too hard as my eyes glide over her name. But, more interestingly, it dives into his past. The man he was.

'*Andrew was a keen nurturer of talent.*'

Was he? I think, my eyes rolling as I read the blatantly clichéd words. The article sweeps over his donations to St Peter's. Money for arts and sport and recreation. It rambles on at length about the fabulous tennis courts. There are even some photos interspersed among the gushing text.

'*Mr Buckley offered a bursary for the keenest entrepreneur at the school. A boy (or girl) after his own heart.*'

Boy. Or girl. My eyes ache as I stare at the bracketed text. I take a moment to remember that St Peter's was once an all-male school and the introduction of female pupils was a step forward. *A feather in their cap.* And I hate that some part of me acknowledges it.

'*The funeral is tomorrow. He was a good man. Lord, rest his soul.*'

Oh, Andrew.

The woman behind the counter clears her throat loudly, no doubt to command my attention. And it's only when I look up and find her eyes burning into me that I realise I've been holding my breath.

'Are you going to buy that?' she asks.

I fold the paper and gather up some more from the shelf. I'm not particularly paying attention to which ones, although I am careful to leave behind the trashy tabloids more concerned with Hollywood gossip than the hunt for a murderer.

'Yes,' I say, approaching the counter with a stack of papers in my arms. 'I'll take them all.'

The woman looks at me as if I'm crazy.

'Right,' she says, and she makes no effort to hide that I'm irritating her. 'That'll be twenty-seven euros and forty-six cents, please?'

I shove my hand into my pocket and realise I've left the house without my purse.

'Twenty-seven forty-six,' she repeats.

'I've forgotten—'

'Hello there,' someone says, and I turn my head over my shoulder to see who's talking.

'I'm so sorry,' the heavily pregnant woman behind me says, and I recognise her straight away. She's the cop from the Pilates class. She's shaking her head and stroking her chin as she adds, 'I'm really terrible with names. I've forgotten yours.'

I don't remind her that I never told her my name. Instead I smile and giggle and say, 'Me too. Dreadful. Sometimes I think I'd forget my own.'

'Rose,' she says. 'I'm Rose.'

'Ah. Yes. Rose. Of course. How are you?'

'Fed up,' she grunts. 'I just want to see my feet again.'

I look at the large tub of ice cream and the multipack of cheese-and-onion crisps she's holding.

'I'm not comfort eating, I swear.' She blushes. 'It's my eldest's birthday today. We're having a party. Ten eight-year-olds in the house. I must be mad.'

I don't have a reply for that and I can feel the eyes of the annoying woman behind the counter burn into me.

'Do you still want these, then?' the woman asks.

'Wow. That's some stack of papers,' Rose says.

I also don't know what to say to that. Rose makes me irrationally nervous. I wish Polly hadn't told me she is a cop.

'It reminds me of when I was pregnant with my second. I had this weird craving to eat paper. Used to give me the worst indigestion, but I just couldn't help myself. The doctors had to give me a stern talking-to and warn me it was dangerous. And even after that I struggled to stop. Thank God I don't have anything like that this time.'

Some more customers come into the shop. The small space is starting to feel overcrowded and I'm hot and clammy under my coat.

'Oh Lord, you're not going to eat them, are you?' Rose asks, pointing to the papers and then to me.

'No. God. No.'

Rose tilts her head, concerned. 'Why so many then?' Suddenly Rose doesn't feel like a fed-up pregnant woman. She sounds like a cop. And whether her tone and prying stare is intentional or a knee-jerk reaction from years spent on the force, the last thing I want is Rose thinking I'm someone to be suspicious of.

'I'm decorating,' I say, my mind racing to think of a plausible reason I'd be buying a mound of newspapers. 'I've just moved into a new flat and it's badly in need of some TLC. I want to put some papers down to protect the floor.'

'Love, I really am going to have to rush you,' the lady behind the counter says, and I'm actually grateful for her intrusion into the awkward conversation. 'There's a queue forming behind you.'

She's right. There are a handful of people lined up behind myself and Rose.

'I'm sorry,' I say. 'I've forgotten my wallet. Could you set the papers aside for me and I'll be back in a little while.'

'Oh, for—' The woman pastes on a smile and gathers the papers, moving them aside.

'My husband is a painter,' Rose says, stepping forward to put her crisps and ice cream on the counter space the woman has cleared.

'Four eighty,' the woman says, and I can tell Rose is trying her patience as much as I am.

Rose passes the woman some money and gathers up her goods. 'He has lots of dust sheets in the shed. I'd be more than happy to lend you some. Save you buying a tonne of papers that you're only going to end up throwing out.'

I wince. I can hear the woman behind the counter curse us under her breath as Rose walks towards the door, and I find myself being ushered along beside her.

'I have the party today,' Rose says, once we're outside. 'But why don't you give me your number and we can arrange something for tomorrow?'

The bright morning sun makes me squint, but I still see Rose pull her mobile out of her pocket. There's no way I'm giving her my number. Jesus.

'I'm not around tomorrow, I'm afraid,' I say, trying to keep the nervous wobble out of my voice.

Rose looks disappointed.

'Work,' I add, feeling an explanation is needed.

'Okay no problem. I'll drop them around to you in the evening.'

'No. No. I couldn't put you to the trouble,' I say, the mere idea of Rose coming to the flat makes me sweat. 'How about I get them off you after Pilates this week?' I suggest.

'Oh. Great idea,' Rose says, and I can hear tiredness in her voice. I hope she's going to say she needs to be on her way. 'And then maybe you'll come for coffee with me and Polly after? If you're new in the area you probably don't have any mammy friends here yet and we'd love to get to know you more.'

I smile way too widely. 'Absolutely.'

'Right. Sorry. I've gotta go,' Rose says, abruptly opening the door of the car parked on the road next to us. 'Need to pee.'

I don't actually have time to reply before she sits in the car, starts the engine and draws away with a wave.

I begin to walk home, disappointed not to have anything new for my scrapbook, but relieved that Rose still doesn't have my name or number, although now I have to go to bloody Pilates again so she doesn't come looking for me. Because I know she's the type of person who would come and find me.

Chapter Twenty-Two

DARCY

Monday 1 July 2019

'Can I get you anything?' Luke asks, sitting on the edge of our bed.

I'm tucked under the covers in my favourite pastel purple nightdress. It's silk and loose fitting and just about one of my only pre-pregnancy items of clothing that still fits me.

'Would you like some breakfast?' he asks. 'Something light might help settle your stomach.'

I shake my head and my brain feels like it might split in two. I wonder how long Luke has been sitting there, with his hand on my knee waiting for me to wake up. He's dressed for work. I can feel how torn he is between leaving me and heading to check on things at the factory. Time is passing in a blur. I don't remember getting home from the vet's and I've only got out of bed a handful of times since to use the bathroom, or to be sick. I haven't even been downstairs to check on Jinx once. And the guilt makes me feel even sicker than I do already.

'Jinx,' I croak, my throat dry and painful.

'He's fine, honey,' Luke says, squeezing my knee gently. 'He's asleep downstairs. It's you I'm worried about.'

'I'm sorry,' I say, trying to get comfortable. I'm lying too flat and the baby is putting pressure on my back.

Luke shakes his head. 'What are you talking about? You have nothing to apologise for. You can't help being sick. Any more than Jinx can.'

'He was poisoned, Luke. Poisoned. Who would do something like that?'

Luke takes a deep breath, as if my question exhausts him. 'You heard the vet, honey. It was weedkiller. You know what the neighbours around here are like. The Robinsons want their garden perfect.'

I try to sit up but I'm dizzy and the whole room seems to be spinning. I close my eyes and count backwards from five. Steadier, I try again.

'I think someone did this,' I say.

I hear Luke groan before he stands up.

'I'm serious,' I say, sternly. 'I told you someone was in the house. I think they've come back and hurt Jinx. What if they hurt you or me next?'

'Darcy, this is ridiculous. You're not well. You're not thinking straight.' I can hear the frustration in Luke's voice.

'Don't you think I know how crazy this sounds? But can't you see how strange everything is all of a sudden? I'm scared, Luke.'

'Look.' Luke exhales slowly. 'We've had a stressful few weeks. And now, with Buckley gone and the future of Darcy's Dishes up in the air, I think it's messing with your head. It's understandable. I'm worried too.'

'Really?' I ask, surprised to hear Luke finally admit that everything isn't, or might not be, okay.

'Of course,' he says, 'but at the end of the day it's just money.' He bends and places his hand on the duvet, covering my round bump. 'But once you and the baby are okay that's all that really matters.'

'Um,' I say, and I don't have the energy to feign positivity.

Luke sits beside me and takes my hand. 'Buckley had all the money in the world but he died a lonely man. I don't ever want to be in his shoes.'

'But Andrew Buckley didn't just die,' I say. 'He was murdered. Someone killed him, Luke. Every time I think about it I feel sick.'

'Darcy please,' Luke says. 'You'll drive yourself crazy thinking like this.' He lowers his voice and adds, 'You'll drive me crazy.'

'It can't all be coincidence. You said it yourself, Buckley had more money than he knew what to do with. Someone clearly wants it. Or doesn't want us to have it. You have to at least see that, don't you?'

'I see that you're exhausted, heavily pregnant and stressed out . . .' Luke repeats the same tired mantra.

You're pregnant, Darcy. You're tired, Darcy. That's been my husband's answer to everything for the last seven and a half months.

'Can you hear how patronising you're being?' I ask, rolling my eyes.

Luke begins to pace the floor, his hands on his head. 'And can you hear how insane you sound?'

I swallow hard and try not to let my husband see how much what he just said has hurt me. Luke is my best friend. He has been for twenty-one years. He's the person I confide in about everything. About anything. It's breaking my heart that confiding in him about this is so hard. He actually pities me. I can see it in his eyes.

'You were fine until we had trouble with the credit card,' Luke reminds me. 'You got completely stressed out. Money trouble is weighing heavily on you. Especially with the baby coming. And I get it. I do. I'm not expecting you not to worry. But I think you need to realise that it's pressure making you paranoid. That's all. Pressure.'

I take a deep breath. Just thinking about money makes my chest feel tight. I'd be lying if I said I wasn't worried about the future. Luke and I both know that Darcy's Dishes barely has enough funds to survive for another six months. I think about giving Gillian a call. I'm desperate for an update about Buckley & Co's commitment. But Gillian has lost her father in the most horrific of ways. No matter how much I crave financial reassurance, I have to respect that.

The microwave dings downstairs and startles me.

Luke smiles. 'I made you some scrambled eggs,' he says. 'I wanted to make sure you've eaten before I go.'

'You're leaving?'

'I have to check on things at work,' Luke says.

I don't have time to reply before he adds, 'Toast too, yeah? I'll make you some before I go, if you're up for eating.'

I throw back the duvet and try to slide my legs out over the edge of the bed, but they're heavy and like jelly all at the same time.

'Hey. Hey. What are you doing?' Luke asks, placing his hand on my shoulder and steadying me.

'Wait for me. I'll grab a quick shower and I'll be ready in ten minutes.'

Luke shakes his head. 'Ready for work? Oh c'mon, Darcy. You can barely move. Why won't you just take it easy?'

'I don't want to be here on my own,' I admit, hating myself for the juvenile statement.

'Oh, honey.' Luke smiles, tucking me back in as if I really am a child. 'I'll try to get home early. How does that sound?'

There's a sudden sharp clatter downstairs and I yelp and bolt upright in bed with energy that wasn't there a moment ago.

'What was that?' Luke says, walking towards our bedroom door. 'Bloody dog. I better let him out for a wee.'

'I think it came from the kitchen,' I say.

'A chair probably. I hope he hasn't broken something.'

My heart is racing. Jinx isn't strong enough to knock one of the heavy kitchen chairs over, and if he did he'd get a fright and be yelping and scratching at the door to come up to us.

'Luke,' I say, calling him as his fingers curl around the door handle. I catch my breath and whisper. 'What if someone is downstairs?'

Luke throws his hands in the air and says, 'Oh, for God's sake. I can't talk to you when you're like this,' before he walks out of our bedroom.

I drift in and out of restless sleep as I listen to Luke pottering about in the kitchen. I can hear voices. Mumbles, really. As if whoever's there is making a conscious effort to keep their voice down.

I'm more groggy than ever when Luke returns with a plate of piping-hot scrambled eggs and some toast. Luke places the plate on the bedside table and leans over me to kiss my forehead.

'Eat up. It's the only way you're going to feel better,' he says, fetching his suit jacket from the wardrobe.

'Who were you talking to?' I ask, pulling myself to sit up, and I try to ignore how the smell of eggs makes me feel.

Luke shakes his head and his brow wrinkles as if I've asked a stupid question.

'Just now. Who were you talking to? I could hear voices.'

'Jinx, of course.'

'No.' I shake my head. 'Someone was talking back to you.'

I expect Luke to tell me I was dreaming or something, but he doesn't.

'Oh,' he says. 'I was on the phone. There's a botched order. I'm dreading the paperwork already.'

'But I could hear someone. I mean, I could hear voices here. In the house.'

'Eh, my phone was on loudspeaker,' Luke says, sliding his arms into his suit jacket, instantly making himself look more dapper. 'I needed my hands free to make your breakfast. Now please *do* eat it, honey. For your own sake, and for the baby.'

'Of course,' I say, nodding. 'Loudspeaker.'

Luke smiles. 'Right. I have to go. I'm so late already I can't leave Mildred on her own much longer sorting this mess out.'

I smile back and watch as Luke hurries out of the door. I lean to the side and push the plate of stinking eggs away from me. I wait until I hear the front door close before I dial Mildred's number and I wait even longer, until I hear Luke's car pull out of the drive, before I hit call.

It rings for a long time and I'm just about to hang up when a groggy voice says, 'Hello?'

'Mildred. Hi.'

'Darcy?' Mildred sounds surprised to hear me. 'Is everything okay?'

'I was just about to ask you the same question.'

'Hmm.'

Mildred sounds sleepy so I have to ask, 'Did I wake you?'

'Yes, sorry,' Mildred says. 'It's the middle of the night here.'

'Here?' I echo.

'In Los Angeles.'

'Oh God, yes, of course. I'm so sorry. I forgot you're on holiday for the next week. I'm so sorry.'

'Darcy, is everything okay? You don't sound like yourself. Is something wrong at work?'

'Everything is fine, honestly. I'm just silly. Let's blame baby brain, eh?'

Mildred laughs.

'Anyway, go back to sleep,' I say. 'And I'm so sorry again. Please enjoy the rest of your holiday.'

I hang up with shaking fingers as I wonder why the hell Luke is lying to me.

Chapter Twenty-Three

GILLIAN

Tuesday 2 July 2019

It's cooler today than it has been for a while and I'm not sure if it's me or the weather. I pop back into the flat to find a light jacket before I leave. The kitchen is a mess. There are more scrapbooks than ever scattered around the countertops. Some of them look as if they're years old, with yellowing covers and dog-eared pages. There's a bottle of glue that's fallen on its side. There's no lid, and half the glue has dripped all over the countertop and on to the floor, creating a sticky mess. I try to ignore it as I search for my jacket. I spot it draped over the back of a chair and I slide my arms in before I take one last look around at the clutter. Collaging seems to be less of a hobby and more of an obsession. It's beyond frustrating. This place needs a good tidy. I'm going to have to put my foot down.

I leave the flat, and try not to think about the mess.

'Morning.' A voice overhead grabs my attention as I close the door behind me.

'Good morning,' I call back without needing to look up to know that it's my gym bunny neighbour out on her balcony the way, I've noticed, she is every morning, eating breakfast.

'Lovely day, isn't it?' Kimberly says.

I nod, but I wrap my arms around myself as a gentle summer breeze flutters by. I'm about to wave and be on my way when she asks, 'Did you have a nice weekend?'

I pause and I realise I have no memory of the weekend. It's as if it never happened. I bought some vodka on my way home from Darcy's on Friday night. I drank it neat, with a takeaway pizza. I've no doubt I repeated the process on Saturday and Sunday and I spent most of yesterday in bed sick as a dog with a horrible hangover.

'I tried knocking on your door yesterday,' she says, 'but there was no answer.'

I tilt my head back so I can make eye contact with her. 'Sorry I missed you.'

'I was wondering if you'd like to come around this evening for a chat to get to know one another better.' I don't have time to answer before she explains further. 'Eddie is away for the week and I hate being home alone. I'd really love the company if you're not busy.'

I make a face.

'I know it's midweek, but I'd love an excuse to open a bottle of wine. And what better way than toasting new neighbours.'

'Sounds good,' I say. And I mean it. I could use something to occupy my evening.

'Super.' She smiles. 'How does 8 p.m. sound?'

'Perfect,' I say, walking away. 'It sounds perfect.'

I'm at Darcy's front door in less than five minutes on foot. I take a moment that I've never allowed myself before to notice the sparkling white stone that glistens in Darcy's granite doorstep. The stone is quite obviously bespoke. Steps this fancy weren't around in the nineteenth century when this house was built. I can only imagine how much something like this must have cost, and I wonder if they used company money. Darcy and Luke definitely enjoy treating themselves to the finer things in life. Neither of them have changed since school in that regard.

I try to push the memories of twenty years ago out of my head and ring the bell. The dog starts barking straight away and I'm surprised to discover he's still alive. Nothing else happens, so I ring the bell again. It takes a while, but finally I see Darcy's silhouette coming towards the door through the colourful glass pane. The dog reaches the door first and bares his teeth.

Darcy reluctantly opens the door and the dog bounds outside yapping at my ankles.

'Jinx, stop that,' Darcy commands, clicking her fingers.

The dog ignores her and I take a step back, worried he's going to nip me.

'I'm so sorry,' she says, 'he's usually so friendly. I don't know what's gotten into him.'

I take another step back, stepping out of the porch.

'Jinx, come here right now,' Darcy hisses through clenched teeth.

Finally, the dog obeys and goes back inside to stand beside his master, but his tail is pointed straight as he glares at me.

Darcy seems surprised to see me, but she hides it well while scolding her pet. 'Silly boy. Silly, silly Jinx.' She turns her attention towards me. 'Are you all right? I hope he didn't scare you.'

I force a smile and say, 'It's fine. I'm just glad he's okay.'

Darcy bends awkwardly and gathers Jinx into her arms. She looks as if her back might snap in half as she cuddles him. 'Me too. I got such a fright. I love this furry little guy.' She drags her fingers through the short fur on the top of his head and he closes his eyes, clearly enjoying it and forgetting his disapproval of my arrival. 'The vet thinks it was weedkiller,' she explains. 'People really need to be more careful.'

My eyes widen. 'Weedkiller. Wow. I never knew it could be so dangerous.'

'Me neither.'

Darcy bends a fraction and opens her arms to let Jinx jump down. No doubt a move they've perfected in recent weeks.

In Darcy's surprise to see me, she forgets to ask me inside and it's only when an uncomfortable silence descends that she stands a little straighter and chirps, 'Come in. Come in.'

I step inside and she closes the door behind me, but everything seems to be moving in slow motion. Darcy's movements are slow and jerky as if she has to concentrate hard on even the simplest task. She's also alarmingly thin. Her belly is round and full but her arms and legs are like sticks that could easily snap, and her cheekbones look as if they might protrude through the layer of greyish skin covering them. Darcy has always been slim. I used to envy her long legs and high cheekbones. But there is nothing to envy now. She looks frail. Like a dying woman fifty years her senior.

'Can I get you some tea? Or coffee.'

I shake my head.

'Water perhaps,' she adds, unsure and definitely uncomfortable.

'Is Luke here?' I ask, casually.

'No. He's gone to the funeral—' Darcy cuts herself off mid breath and I wonder what she's thinking.

Maybe it's the first time she's thought of the funeral and realised that's where I should be. Or maybe she's been thinking about it since she opened the door and has been trying to avoid putting her foot in it.

Either way, I ignore the mention and carry on. 'Okay,' I say. 'It was you I was hoping to chat to anyway.'

'Oh,' Darcy says. 'Okay. Are you sure I can't get you something? I'm making a cup of tea for myself.'

I don't want to drink anything. But Darcy is so on edge I can tell she needs something to do with her hands.

'You know what, tea does sound good. Thank you.'

Darcy seems lighter instantly and she leads the way to the kitchen, and I follow.

She doesn't invite me to sit, but I do anyway. And when she notices she winces, and I can tell she prides herself on being an impeccable host and failing is embarrassing her. I try to lighten the mood with small talk as she walks around her stunning kitchen with its high-gloss, cream cupboards and ebony, granite work-tops. Every inch of Darcy's world oozes elegance and taste. And, of course, money.

'Tea,' she says, after a while, when she places two cups on the table in front of me.

'Thank you,' I say, waiting for her to sit down, and déjà vu washes over me. 'I'm sure you're wondering why I'm here.'

'Perhaps a little,' Darcy says, sitting.

She sips tea that I know must be too hot, but she doesn't so much as flinch. She dabs the corner of her lips with a tissue she pulls from her sleeve. 'It's just a little surprising, considering the day it is.'

'The day it is, is the exact reason I've come.'

Darcy lowers the cup with steam still swirling out the top away from her lips, and looks at me as if I'm babbling nonsense.

'I know what you must be thinking,' I say, 'but I haven't been his daughter in a long time. And he's certainly no father. I said goodbye a long time ago.'

'But his funeral. Surely—'

I cut across her, my voice shriller and more frustrated than I intend it to be. 'It's just business. I will honour his legacy and see

143

through his investments as planned. Anything more, I can't be a part of. And that includes the man's funeral. Especially his funeral.'

A tear trickles down Darcy's pale cheek as she softly whispers, 'But he has no one.'

'He has Luke,' I say, and I hope I don't sound bitter. 'And all his staff.'

Darcy nods.

'And you have me,' I say.

She dries her eyes and looks at me. I wish I knew what she was thinking.

'I mean it,' I say. 'Everything is going to change from this point, Darcy. Just you wait and see.'

Fresh tears trickle down Darcy's cheeks. Heavier, fatter tears, the tears of relief, and she sobs. 'Thank you. Thank you so much. I wasn't sure . . . We weren't sure . . .' Darcy runs a shaking hand through her hair and catches her breath. 'Luke and I didn't know if the investment would still go ahead. Under the circumstances.'

I smile.

'This really means so much to us. Thank you.'

My smile grows wider. 'I know.'

'I can't wait for Luke to hear the good news.' Darcy's pale skin and sunken eyes contradict her excitement. 'You must stay and tell him yourself.'

'Oh, I really don't think—'

Suddenly Darcy begins shaking. Her eyes roll and she tumbles off the chair, her head hitting the ground with a loud thud before I have time to catch her.

Chapter Twenty-Four

DARCY

Wednesday 9 September 1998

The school infirmary is depressing, especially compared to the rest of the elegant building. There are two beds, pushed up against opposing walls and with mismatched duvets. One floral. One striped. I'm lying on the striped bed and it smells funny. Like anti-bacterial spray and lemons. The walls are a bright orange and the paint is flaking away in patches where the wall joins the ceiling. There's nothing particularly medical about the room. It could easily be a badly decorated bedroom, or a spare room in an old house. There isn't a nurse or anything, but one of the teachers asks for a volunteer to sit with me. Tina seemed eager to oblige. Although I don't know why. We barely know each other and the conversation is so awkward. I'd much rather just be alone and actually get some rest. One of the younger teachers ducks her head around the door every now and then and asks, 'Are you all right?'

Tina answers for me. 'She's fine, miss,' she says, placing the back of her hand against my forehead to check for a fever. It's super weird and I hope Tina notices me cringe so she won't do it again.

'All right. Try to get some rest. I'll check on you again in a little while.'

When the teacher leaves, Tina hops on to the edge of my bed, bouncing on it. I move over and she smiles, probably thinking I'm making room for her, and I guess I am. But I'm also making room so we're not touching.

'Want one?' Tina asks, pulling out a bag of Skittles she had hidden up her sleeve. She opens it and shoves the bag towards me, shaking it.

I really don't feel like eating but I reach into the bag and pull out a green one. 'Thanks.'

Tina tosses a handful of multi-coloured Skittles into her mouth and between chews, she says, 'This is nice, isn't it?'

'Yeah. I like Skittles,' I say.

Tina laughs. 'You're so funny. I meant chatting is good.'

'Oh.'

'But, I love Skittles too,' she says. 'Yellow is my favourite.'

I hate the yellow ones, I think. But I don't say anything.

'We like lots of the same things,' Tina says.

I wonder how Tina could possibly know that, but I don't ask. My head is pounding and I think I might actually have a fever.

Tina shuffles back to sit more comfortably. Her back is against the headboard and only her shoes drape over the edge of the bed. I hope a teacher comes back soon. Tina is scrunching up the empty pack of Skittles when the principal knocks gently on the already-open door and comes into the room.

'How are you feeling?' he asks.

Tina hops off the bed and I wonder if she's embarrassed.

'I'm okay,' I say.

He tilts his head and looks at me with round eyes that say, *I don't believe you*. And he'd be right. I'm not fine at all. I feel as if

I've been hit in the back of the head with something hard, and the pulsing inside my skull makes me feel as if my brain might explode.

'You hit the canteen floor with quite a bang,' Principal McEvoy tells me. 'Gave your head a right knock, so you did.'

I blush as the memory of lunchtime plays over in my mind. I'd just had a great chat with the chef about introducing a veggie option. He even asked if he could use one of my dad's recipes. He said he'd have to clear it with the principal and probably the board and it could take a few weeks, so I'd have to make do with meat in the meantime. I didn't want to argue when he'd been so understanding, so I took a plate of lamb stew and looked around for somewhere to sit. I was so relieved when Luke waved to me and beckoned to me to join his table. I walked through the canteen with a huge smile on my face, but I knew the eyes of some of the girls were burning into me. But at that moment I felt so special, I didn't really care.

I joined Luke and his friends. They all seemed really nice and made me feel very welcome. I couldn't bring myself to eat the meat on my plate and the vegetables were swimming in meat gravy, so even though I was starving I couldn't touch them. Nonetheless I was enjoying chatting until I suddenly became horribly dizzy and weak. My palms were sweating, and beads of perspiration gathered on my hairline and trickled down my forehead and into my eyes. I think someone asked me if I was okay. It was hard to tell because of the loud ringing that had started in my ears.

And the next thing I remembered was the orange walls and ugly duvets of sick bay. I don't know how I got here. But I can only imagine the whole school is laughing at me. *I'm never going to settle in now.*

Mr McEvoy comes a little further into the room, looking at me as if he's sad or worried or something.

'Miss Arlington thinks you should see a doctor,' he says. 'There's a nasty flu doing the rounds. One of the first years fainted earlier too.'

I scrunch my nose. Miss Arlington must be the teacher who's been checking on me. I still don't know all the teachers' names and I'm not in her class for anything.

'I think she's right, Darcy,' Tina says. 'I'll come with you.'

'I really don't think that's necessary, Tina,' Mr McEvoy says.

'Sir,' Tina says, sounding offended. 'Darcy is new here. She needs me.'

I'm lost for words and I hold my breath, waiting for Mr McEvoy to tell Tina to get back to class.

But instead he says, 'I've called your uncle . . .'

'. . . but he didn't answer,' I finish his sentence for him.

Mr McEvoy smiles kindly, and I can tell he feels sorry for me. 'No. No, he didn't. I'm sorry, Darcy. But Miss Arlington said she is happy to take you to the local doctor and I'm sure you'd much rather a female teacher than—'

'Can I come in?' A voice at the door follows a gentle knock.

I smile, seeing Luke's head pop around the corner.

'I just wanted to check Darcy is okay,' he says.

'Mr Hogan,' Mr McEvoy says, and he's clearly unimpressed that Luke is here and not in class.

'You all right?' Luke asks, his round eyes locked on mine. 'You hit the ground with a massive bang.'

'Is everyone laughing at me?' I ask, cringing.

'Nah.' Luke shrugs and I know he's lying.

My cheeks are stinging and I've no doubt they're bright red. 'Oh, great.'

'They're really not,' Luke says. 'Gillian and that gang are the only ones laughing. Typical bitches.'

'Mr Hogan,' Mr McEvoy says, more sternly than ever.

'Sorry, sir,' Luke says, sheepishly. 'Everyone else is just worried about you, Darcy. Hoping you're okay.'

'She's fine,' Tina says.

Luke ignores her and keeps his eyes on me.

'Shouldn't you be in class?' Tina says, sounding like a teacher.

'Shouldn't you!' Luke snaps back, finally looking at her.

Tina tilts her head. 'Actually, I'm going to the doctor with Darcy. She needs a friend to take care of her.'

'A friend,' Luke says, and the look on his face is priceless. It falls somewhere between confusion and disgust at Tina deciding for us both that we are *friends*.

'It has to be a female friend,' Tina says quickly. 'Mr McEvoy said so.'

'Actually, Tina. That's not exactly what I said,' Mr McEvoy says, and he turns from Tina towards me to add, 'but if you would really like a friend with you, maybe Tina could—'

'Can Luke come?' I ask before he finishes.

'Well, eh . . .'

'Please,' I say.

'Sir,' Tina says, her eyes wide and pleading. 'I really don't think that's appropriate, do you?'

Tina's teacher act is weird and annoying and I get the impression that even Mr McEvoy finds it strange.

His brow is wrinkled as he says, 'Thank you for your concerns, Miss Summers.'

Luke smirks as Mr McEvoy quickly adds, 'But I think you're right. Darcy, if you would like a friend, Tina has my permission to go with you. Otherwise, I think you'll be fine on your own.'

'Sir,' I say.

Mr McEvoy ignores me and says, 'Back to class please, Mr Hogan.'

Luke opens his mouth to protest but I shake my head. Mr McEvoy is losing patience. Any arguing is only going to get Luke in trouble.

'Class, Mr Hogan,' Mr McEvoy repeats.

Luke's frustration is palpable as he glares at Tina. 'I'll catch you later, Darcy, yeah,' he says.

'Yeah, later.'

Miss Arlington walks in as Luke walks out and the room begins to feel claustrophobic and stuffy.

'Are you ready?' she asks.

'We are,' Tina says.

'Actually,' I say, sliding to the edge of the bed and trying to catch Miss Arlington's eye, 'I think I'm okay going on my own.'

Miss Arlington nods. 'I think so too.'

'Right. Grand,' Mr McEvoy says, marking the end of the discussion with a single, loud clap of his hands.

'But sir,' Tina says.

'You can go back to class now, Tina, thank you,' he says. 'And could you let Darcy's teachers know where she is, please?'

Tina lowers her head and walks out of the door without saying goodbye, and I guess this means we aren't *friends* after all.

Chapter Twenty-Five

DARCY

Wednesday 3 July 2019

Light shines through the window of our bedroom but my eyes are firmly shut, reluctant to open. Nonetheless I can tell that another day has come around and I've slept the evening and night away. I sink deeper into the mound of pillows under my head and I think about how much I can't wait to have my body, and my mind, back. *Damn this pregnancy.*

Disorientated, it takes me a moment to realise that I'm not lying down, I'm propped up. And there are voices in the room; they're both male. Luke is one, I know that straight away, but I have no idea who the other is.

I open my eyes slightly and it takes a while to adjust to the light. Luke is pacing with his hands on his head. It worries me. The other man is tall, even taller than Luke, and he's wearing a pin-stripe shirt and tailored navy trousers. And when he turns around, I realise he's our GP.

'Here's my referral,' Dr Whelan says. I watch as he passes Luke a piece of paper. 'She'll be fine. Not long to go. I've no doubt they'll admit her from now until the end of term, just to keep an eye on things.'

'Thank you,' Luke says, and both men shake hands. 'I'll talk to Darcy when she wakes up. I think she'll understand.'

When Luke leaves the room to escort the doctor downstairs, I drag myself out of bed and potter into the bathroom. I want to brush my teeth, craving the feeling of fresh breath to start the day, but the tube of toothpaste is empty. I search the overhead cabinet and find a new box. Sliding the tube out, I press my foot on the pedal of the bin and toss the box inside. It's such a swift motion it's surprising that the contents catch my attention, but they do. Shards of broken soap tray are hidden among cotton buds and dental floss. It catches me by surprise and I step back, crashing into Luke who's suddenly behind me. His arms are strong and calming.

'You're awake,' he says, dotting a kiss on the top of my head. 'Are you okay?'

'Yeah. Yes. Course,' I say.

Luke hums. It's deep and vibrates in his chest. 'You sure? You're shaking.'

'I'm sure,' I say, making an effort to sound chipper. Luke is asking me how I am, but he sounds like the one who needs reassurance, the one who's a little off.

'Okay,' he says as he walks back into our bedroom, and I'm glad of some space.

I take my time brushing my teeth and I wash my face, more than once, before I follow Luke into our bedroom. Finally feeling human, I walk into our bedroom to find Luke sitting on the edge of our bed with his elbows on his knees and his head in his hands.

'Hey,' I say, edging close to him. 'You okay?'

He doesn't budge or make a sound. I sit beside him.

'Luke?'

Nothing.

'Hey, Luke. What's wrong? What's going on? I heard the doctor here.'

Luke is still painfully silent. My heart is racing.

'Who was here last night, Darcy?' Luke finally asks, raising his head for a brief moment to make eye contact with me before dropping it again.

'What?' I ask, so confused.

'There was a woman in the house,' Luke explains. 'She was with you. Here in our bedroom. She was watching you while you slept. She told me you'd fainted. And then she left. Suddenly. She just sort of disappeared before I had a chance to ask her what happened or who she was.'

'Oh,' I say, and I cringe as I remember passing out and needing a future business partner to put me to bed as if I were a child, but I'm glad Gillian was here. If she hadn't been here, I'd probably still be lying in a heap on the kitchen floor.

'She didn't even introduce herself,' Luke says. 'I checked you were okay and when I turned around, she was gone.'

'That was Gillian,' I say, trying to sound normal, but the whole situation is making me twitchy.

'Gillian?' Luke says, chewing on her name as if he needs time to digest it.

'Mm-hmm,' I say.

I put my hand on Luke's leg, trying to ease the tension, and I keep my voice steady as I say, 'I told you we had new neighbours.'

Luke nods. 'You did.'

There's a strange silence that consumes us. It's so unlike Luke and me. We're normally so in tune, but right now I've no idea what he's thinking.

'The doctor was here,' I say, desperate to break the tension.

'Yeah. *Gillian* called him.' Luke says her name with such distaste, it makes me uneasy and I pull my hand from his knee and shuffle a little further away from him on the bed.

'How did she do that?' I say.

'You must have given her his number. Or his name at least.'

'I don't remember.'

'Well, she called him last night and this morning was the earliest he could come,' Luke says. 'And now he wants you to go to the hospital so they can keep an eye on you.'

'But I don't want to be admitted,' I say, standing up. 'I've told you that.'

'The doctor thinks it's best,' Luke says, looking at me with bloodshot eyes. 'And to be honest, at this stage I think he's right. I can't keep leaving you alone.'

'I'm pregnant, Luke. Not dying or helpless. Just pregnant.'

'C'mon,' Luke encourages. 'You should pack a bag. Will I help you?'

'I'm not going,' I hiss like a stroppy teenager.

'Darcy—'

'No,' I snap, stomping my foot. 'Gillian shouldn't have called Dr Whelan. She was out of line.'

'Mmm,' Luke says, frustration scribbled into the wrinkled lines of his forehead, which makes him look years older than usual. I can tell he's decided Gillian is a nosey neighbour and he's taken an instant dislike to her. And although the timing is all wrong I know I have to explain.

'I can't go to hospital right now . . .' I begin.

Luke folds his arms and says, 'Really?'

'Yes really,' I say. 'Because we have paperwork.'

'Darcy,' Luke says, and I can hear the mix of worry and frustration in his clipped tone.

'We do.' I'm smiling as if I've won the Lotto. On some level it feels as if I have.

Luke is shaking his head and he looks so sad, and I wish I'd told him sooner.

'Gillian isn't just a new neighbour,' I admit at last. 'She wasn't popping in for a cup of tea. She came by to tell us she is going to invest.'

Luke drops his head down until he has three chins and I quickly realise that I've made no bloody sense.

'Sorry. Let me try that again. Gillian Buckley would like to honour her father's faith in us.'

Luke's eyebrows are pinched as he frowns and shakes his head. 'That was Gillian Buckley?' he says, pointing towards the door as if Gillian is still standing there.

'Yes,' I say, disappointed that Luke isn't more excited.

'Really?'

'I'm surprised you didn't recognise her from school,' I say. 'You're so good with names and faces. Mildred says you have a memory like an elephant. She calls you the walking spreadsheet.'

Luke laughs.

'I'm useless with names, aren't I?' I admit.

Luke laughs louder. 'You really are. You called the new girl at work Linda for at least a month.'

'It is Linda, isn't it?'

'It's Lisa.'

Luke's laughter fills the whole room. It makes me giggle too. Luke and I used to make each other laugh all the time, and my heart hurts when I realise exactly how long it's been since we were like this.

'Andrew Buckley's daughter,' Luke says. 'My God.'

'I know.'

'Andrew Buckley's daughter is our new neighbour,' Luke says. 'And she wants to give us lots of money.'

'It's crazy, isn't it?' I say.

'It really is.'

'I thought you'd be more excited.'

'Our new neighbour is our new investor,' Luke says. 'Don't you think that's all a little coincidental?'

'Yes. Definitely. And maybe it's not ideal that we're neighbours now. Living so close to a new business partner could get awkward. But we need this money, Luke. It's going to save us. Everything is going to be okay now. It really, really is.'

Luke stands up and begins pacing again, a habit he's picked up recently. Every now and then he stops and looks at me as if words are on the tip of his tongue, but he doesn't let them spill. Finally, he sits down again and takes my hand in his. He takes a deep breath and I can feel something huge coming – he's going to explode with excitement. My heart is racing.

'Gillian Buckley. My God,' he says. Luke's expression is surprised as he remembers her. 'The years have not been kind to her. But . . .' he pauses, mulling it all over. 'I guess she hasn't had the easiest life.'

'Did you know her well at school?' I ask.

'Nah,' Luke says. 'A few of the lads said she acted like she owned the place. Probably because her dad was throwing money around for the science lab and new tennis courts. And I wasn't complaining. I liked tennis.'

'We're so lucky the Buckleys are still so keen to support alumni,' I say.

'Remember when she ran away?' Luke asks.

I nod.

'I wonder what changed. Over the years, I mean. Why did she come back?' Luke asks, more thinking out loud than really posing a question.

'Dunno.' I shrug. 'Time, maybe. People change a lot over the years, don't they? I've had a nose job for a start and you're not as fit as you were in school.'

Luke glares at me.

'What?' I shrug. 'You're not.'

'Ouch.' Luke's shoulders slouch and he half smiles. 'Twenty years! Can you really believe it's been so long?'

'We'll never change, will we?' I say, pausing when I realise I'm contradicting myself. 'On the inside, I mean. We'll always love each other, won't we?'

Luke nods.

I rub my belly as the baby kicks hard, reminding me that everything is already changing. 'Even when the baby comes. We won't let it change us, will we?'

'I promise I am the same guy now that you met in school. Even if my six-pack isn't quite what it used to be.'

I smile.

'You know what?' Luke asks.

And I look at him with an expression that asks, *What?*

'You never wanted anyone to take care of you. Even when we were in school. Once your parents were gone and your Uncle Tommy turned out to be such a dick, you knew you had to go it alone, didn't you?'

I feel the familiar pinch of heartache, remembering.

'But I wasn't really alone,' I say, my hands cradling my bump, and I still can't quite believe that Luke and I will be parents ourselves so soon. 'I had you.'

Luke takes a deep breath and I think I can see his eyes glistening.

'I'm kinda glad Tommy is an arsehole,' I say. 'We'd never have met otherwise.'

Luke's crooked smile grows into a toothy grin. 'Right,' he says, pulling himself straighter and taller. 'I'm going to call Dr Whelan and let him know that we won't be going to the hospital today. But any more—'

'Any more,' I cut him off. 'I know. But before you get too comfortable, Dr Hogan, do you think you should call around to Gillian? Introduce yourself properly at last.'

Luke presses a kiss on my forehead. 'And this is why I love you,' he says, 'because you're full of good ideas.'

Chapter Twenty-Six

TINA

Thursday 4 July 2019

I've never enjoyed change, but I am slowly beginning to enjoy this apartment. Mostly, I like the privacy. The whole house is set back from the road with a larger front lawn than back garden. It's a bit overgrown and I wonder if someone will cut it. The people upstairs, perhaps. It's one of the few houses on the road with foliage around the perimeter – green prickly stuff that looks as if it should flower at some stage but just hasn't.

Most of the other houses are surrounded by a low wall with ebony wrought-iron bars on top. Each one identical to the next, their only individual feature is the colour of their front door. And the houses almost all stand closer to the road. As if trying to catch the eye of passers-by so they can stop to admire how grand and beautiful the old, red-brick buildings are. And they are grand and beautiful. Just like the people inside. No wonder Luke and Darcy live here. They fit right in.

This house is bigger than the rest. Although, with my scrapbooks scattered around the kitchen most days, it does make the space feel cluttered, and I tell myself today is the day I will tidy up.

But I'm reluctant in case another juicy news story breaks and I have to find my glue and scissors again. Maybe I'll just move everything into the bedroom – out of sight. Because, not for the first time, I remind myself that collaging cold cases is a slightly unusual hobby and I probably shouldn't leave bits and pieces lying around.

I gather a handful of newspaper clippings and tube of glue with a wonky lid into my arms and walk towards my bedroom, thinking about what key words I can google today to bring up the best articles about Andrew. I hope there's something about his funeral. If I'm really lucky there might even be photos. Not any of those distasteful ones of upset mourners. I'm not that sick. Just maybe something with the hearse and coffin pulling up outside the church. I hope there are flowers. The pages of my scrapbook could definitely use some colour. All these black-and-white articles can be very draining on the eye.

I tumble everything out of my arms on to my bed and I'm about to flick on my laptop when I hear the crunch of pebbles underfoot outside. It sounds worryingly close to my window and I listen carefully. I spin around and stare outside at the silent garden: there's not so much as a breeze ruffling the trees. I squint as bright sunshine streams into the house, shining off the walls, like a radiant spotlight ready to share my beautiful papered room with whoever comes around the corner. I dart across my room, grab a curtain in each hand and shut them quickly, almost ripping the flimsy satin from its hooks and eyelets.

It's not dark. Light still shines in through the porous material of cheap curtains, but I suddenly feel blind, not knowing who is outside. I'm not expecting anyone. At first, I think it's someone to visit that gym bunny who lives upstairs. But her door is to the front and up the steps. No one would come around the back looking for her, would they? The footsteps grow closer to the window, stopping right outside. There's just a pane of glass and some floral curtains between me and whoever is out there. It could be that busybody cop with her damn dust sheets, but I quickly remind myself that she still doesn't know where I live.

There's a knock on the window and I freeze. Seconds tick by in painful slow motion before there is another knock. Louder this time, with enough force to rattle the glass. I don't budge. The third knock is more of a thump and warns me of growing impatience. But I won't open the curtains. I can't.

I can hear the swish of my blood coursing through my veins. It's loud and furious inside my head, like a tiny hammer tapping on the inside of my skull.

'Hello?' A deep male voice rattles through the glass, and an unmistakable sound of confidence clings to every syllable. 'Are you there?'

He clearly knows I'm here. He must have seen the curtains snap shut as he rounded the corner. I hold my breath and wait for him to leave. His politeness should compel him to feel awkward and move on soon. But, there's more knocking. It's strong and determined. Each knock is a fraction more assertive than the last, and I'm reminded that Luke and Darcy are two very different individuals. He's a little rougher around the edges than his wife. A little cockier too. It's as attractive as hell, but nonetheless it's terribly inconvenient. At best, he's a beautiful distraction. At worst, he's a very real problem.

The banging stops. And a calmer and somewhat concerned Luke says, 'Is everything all right in there?'

He's so charming I have to restrain myself from throwing back the curtains and smiling brightly at him. But alluring as his gruff voice is, I remain steady with my feet cemented on the spot.

Luke begins walking again. I can hear him move to the next window. The kitchen. There are no curtains in the kitchen, just a blind that I don't think even rolls down. I hurry towards my bedroom door and open it slowly, as if the gentle creak of hinges that need oiling could be heard from outside. Silly, really. But that's the effect Luke Hogan has on me. I can't think straight when he's around. I never could.

When my bedroom door is open enough to pop my head through, I peek out. It's just my eye and nose, really. And I'm careful Luke can't see me as he cups his face with his hands and presses his nose close to the window for an uninterrupted view inside. I'm suddenly so glad I tidied up my scrapbook and papers. The kitchen now just looks like any other. A mundane place to cook and clean and certainly not somewhere to plan a murder.

'Hello?' Luke says, his voice sing-song now.

I reach into my pocket and curl my fingers around the key of my bedroom. If I lock the door behind me, then perhaps I could let Luke in. I'm not sure he'll go away otherwise. Determination was always his middle name.

I'm slowly pulling the key out of my pocket when I hear another set of footsteps outside and voices. They're muffled and clipped. I've no idea what's being said, but I can tell it's an awkward exchange. I duck back into my room, afraid I'll be spotted. But I keep as much within earshot as I possibly can.

'Excuse me. This is private property,' a female voice says. I recognise her slightly squeaky pitch from conversations that rain through my ceiling from the apartment overhead. 'I mean it, mate. You need to go.' I've no doubt she's trying to be assertive, but the subtle tremble in her tone tells me that she's unsure and afraid. She should be. But not of Luke.

'This isn't what it looks like,' Luke says.

A third voice joins the conversation and there are lots of footsteps. I can't tell how many people are out there, although I imagine it's just the couple overhead and Luke. The exchange grows more heated. There are raised voices, shouting, more footsteps. I

162

can't make out who's saying what. It goes on for several minutes. It ranges from loud to calm to loud again, and finally I hear the rapid crunch as someone walks away, followed by slower, calmer footsteps as the couple overhead don't bother to give chase.

'You okay?' I hear the guy ask his girlfriend.

I don't hear a reply and I wonder if she nods or simply cuddles him.

'Who the hell was that?' the guys asks.

'No idea,' she says. 'But he looked familiar.'

'Creep,' he says. 'Do you think she's okay?'

The footsteps stop right outside my window and for a moment I expect to hear a knock, as if they know I'm hiding in here.

'He's obviously some guy from her past,' she says. 'Poor girl.'

I sigh. Luke isn't just *some guy* from the past. He's so much more than that.

Chapter Twenty-Seven

TINA

Wednesday 1 September 1999

The first day back in school after the summer is hard for most students. There's lots of hugging of parents and long drawn-out farewells as kids don't want to say goodbye after a summer spent catching up with family. It's hardest of all on first years. Twelve-year-olds being dropped into a new world of timetables and dorms, and for most of them it's their first time away from home. There are almost always tears. Usually from the kids. Sometimes from the parents. Occasionally from both. And then there are the kids whose parents just don't give a crap. The parents who drop you on the steps and you're not even sure if they'll come back. You don't have to look very hard to spot these parents. They're visible a mile away. The clue isn't in the way they dress. They're not always in stilettos or a fancy suit – too busy with some high-flying job to have time for children. Neither are they a picture-perfect Disney villain wearing a fur coat on a warm autumn day. The hint is in their eyes – in their vacant expression. The way they hold their noses high, as if St Peter's reeks of adolescence and innocence and the smell upsets their stomach. But in spite of their flaws at least they're here.

There aren't many of us with no parents at all. Kids whose parents are dead, or might as well be. There's no first day back in school for us because we never leave. But I like St Peter's best during summer time – when being invisible feels like a choice and not some too-tight cloak that I can't shake off.

The dorms feel different when they're not littered with a swarm of teenage bodies. It's just like having a huge bedroom all to yourself. It's probably one of the few times all year when I can really enjoy collaging without feeling beady eyes peering over my shoulder ready to make fun of me.

This morning, I'm standing just outside the main doors. I've a headache from not sleeping well last night. The thought of everyone returning today and the dorm once again becoming a hive of activity with gossiping teenage girls makes me sick to my stomach. In spite of my dread, I stand straight and wave encouragingly at parents dropping kids off, just as Principal McEvoy asked me to. And from the bright smile on my face you'd never guess how I'm really feeling inside as another academic year at St Peter's begins.

Darcy Flynn should be standing next to me. I overheard Mr McEvoy asking her to welcome new students.

'You remember what it's like to be the new girl,' he said. 'And you've settled in so well. I'm sure it would really help uneasy parents and new students to see how happy you are here.'

'Sure. Of course. Happy to help,' Darcy said with such enthusiasm it excited me too.

But she's not here now. I am, as always, alone.

Darcy spent her summer at St Peter's too. She should have spent warm nights sleeping three beds down from me under a duvet clearly designed for winter. But her covers were barely touched. At first I thought she'd gone home for the summer. But then I saw her a couple of times helping out with sports activities. St Peter's is open for camps during the holidays. Local kids sign up on a week-by-week basis and enjoy the sports facilities the school has to offer. They're here only during the day. Office hours, mostly 9–5. Or even shorter for the younger ones.

Mr McEvoy asked if I'd like to help with the arts-and-crafts camp for the under-tens group this year.

'You like crafting, don't you?' he said, and I know rumours of my scrapbook have made it all the way to the principal's office. 'Helping pays, of course, not huge bucks but enough for some trips to the cinema or a day out shopping.'

I appreciate the freedom we're allowed during the summer months with no classes to worry about missing. We can come and go as we please, leaving the grounds completely, if we like. There's a bus stop at the top of the road and I know some of the girls in the year below go into town regularly. The only rule is we must be back by 7 p.m. for supper. Despite only a skeleton staff working during summer, the cook is here and the canteen keeps the usual hours, much to the delight of the local kids who enjoy the gourmet food.

The camps are run, mostly, by young straight-out-of-college teachers who obviously need the overtime. And they all seem to enjoy bitching and sympathising with each other about how badly they need a break from this place, and this is not how they want to spend their summer.

'Are you sure you don't want the job?' Principal McEvoy pressed me when I pulled a face at his offer. 'I could really do with someone reliable. Someone I can trust.'

'No thank you,' I said. 'Not this year.'

'Okay,' he said, and I could hear his disappointment. 'But you'll be sorry when everyone is off to the cinema with their hard-earned cash and you're stuck here with me.' He added a little forced laughter so I knew it was a joke, and I laughed back so he didn't feel uncomfortable.

He's right. I was upset when everyone went to town without me. But I know, money or not, I wouldn't have been going with them.

Days blurred into weeks, with nothing to differentiate one day from the next. Evenings and weekends were punctuated by silence without the noise of excited local kids running around playing football or tennis. Occasionally laughter would carry through the halls after supper. Someone would be back from town and have snuck alcohol into a dorm and everyone would gather to drink it neat. I'd tell myself it was a foolish act of teenage rebellion, pointless and messy. But sometimes the feeling of missing out was overbearing.

I'm drawn back to the here and now by someone crashing into my shoulder. I rub my arm as if they've hurt me and look up to find Luke Hogan standing next to me. He doesn't notice that he's almost knocked me over as he tucks his shirt into his trousers and adjusts his tie. His usually pristine uniform is sloppy and he looks unsteady on his feet.

'You okay?' I find myself saying, almost subconsciously.

Luke finishes adjusting his uniform, and, more composed, he says, 'Yeah. Yeah. Good, thanks.'

'Is Darcy coming?' I ask.

'Erm . . .' Luke sounds unsure, but I can see the naughty smirk twitching in the corners of his lips. 'Maybe in a while.'

I look at my watch. It's after 8.30. Assembly is at 9 a.m. If Darcy arrives on the steps at 8.55, all smiles for Mr McEvoy's benefit, I swear I'm going to scream.

'She's not feeling great,' Luke says.

'Did she have too much to drink?' I ask, and it comes out all snappy and as jealous as I feel.

Luke laughs sheepishly and runs a shaky hand through his hair, and I realise he looks so awful because he's epically hungover.

'A party the night before school starts?' I say, and I concentrate, so the feeling of missing out isn't written all over my face. 'If Mr McEvoy finds out he'll go ballistic.'

'Who's going to tell him?' Luke asks, and I wonder if it's a threat. 'Anyway, even if he does find out it'll be worth it. Best. Night. Ever.'

I close my eyes. *Best night ever*, I think silently, my heart aching. Well, the joke is on them. I had a fun night of my own – collaging with no one to disturb me. And I'm not the one with so much alcohol still in my system that my breath smells like the bottom of a beer barrel.

I want to tell Luke to close his mouth, or at least to take a step back, but instead a dig at Darcy slips out. 'Well, just be glad she didn't puke in your bed.'

Luke looks at me with unsure eyes.

And I stare back with a confidence I don't really feel as I say, 'Oh c'mon, I'm not blind. Her bed is three down from mine and she hasn't been in it all summer. It doesn't take a genius to work out she's been sleeping with you.'

'You're not going to tell anyone, are you?' Luke asks, and I think it's the first time I've ever seen him act like the schoolboy, worried and afraid he'll get in trouble.

I think about it for a moment. If I tell Mr McEvoy he'll expel Darcy and Luke for sure and they'll probably never see each other again. But then I won't see Luke either, and how is he going to fall in love with me then?

'Don't worry,' I say, and I've never felt so empowered. 'I know how to keep a secret.'

'You're the best,' Luke says, and my heart actually skips a beat. I can feel my cheeks blush and I try to shrug it off, saying, 'Yeah, well, you might want to brush your teeth.'

Luke slaps a hand over his mouth and I'm not the only one with red cheeks.

'Smells like you had a good night,' I add, on a roll. 'Just don't breathe on any of the first years, the fumes could kill them.'

Luke can't hide his smirk any longer. 'Oh, don't make me laugh. It hurts my head.' He closes his eyes and massages his temples with his fingertips.

I smile at Luke and he smiles back at me, and we share this wonderful moment when I think we might actually be becoming friends.

'Right,' he says, straightening his tie. 'You're okay on your own here, aren't you? This is boring as hell.'

I stop smiling, but Luke doesn't notice as he turns to walk away and I wonder if he's even going to bother saying goodbye.

Mr McEvoy appears on the steps behind us, suddenly. 'Tina. There you are,' he says, placing his hand on my shoulder.

Luke's mouth snaps closed and I wonder if he's holding his breath, afraid to give Mr McEvoy any clues about what he was up to last night. Luke's eyes search for mine, and I know he's silently checking that I'll keep my word and keep his secret.

I move my head up and down. Nodding so subtly that if Luke wasn't watching for it he'd miss it. He smiles and his tense shoulders drop. He knows his secret is safe with me. *For now.*

'I've been looking for you,' Mr McEvoy says, and I know for certain now that Luke is barely breathing.

'Is everything all right, sir?' I ask.

'Darcy isn't feeling very well. A dizzy spell.' Mr McEvoy sighs. 'She's in sick bay. Would you sit with her, please?'

'Yes. Of course.' My whole face smiles.

'Dizzy again,' Luke says, finally opening his mouth. 'Is she okay?'

'She's fine,' Mr McEvoy adds. 'But I think she could use some company while I try to get hold of this uncle of hers. I'm not having much luck, as per usual.'

I study Luke. His smile is crooked and his shoulders are tense. I thought he'd be more relieved that I'm keeping secrets for him. Or more grateful, at least. But he's not even looking at me. He's too busy thinking about Darcy and her self-inflicted starvation because she's too good for the canteen food unlike the rest of us.

'Don't worry, Mr McEvoy. I'll take care of her,' I say.

'But Tina already has a job – welcoming the incoming first years,' Luke reminds our principal. 'I can sit with Darcy, sir. If it helps.'

Mr McEvoy nods, making a face that falls somewhere between concerned and impressed. 'You've a way with words, Mr Hogan. Hold on to that as you get older and you'll go far someday.'

I'm about to protest, knowing where this is going, but Mr McEvoy doesn't give me a chance.

'Right, Tina. You stay here. Keep smiling and waving and doing a great job. Remember St Peter's is a home away from home.' Mr McEvoy gives my shoulder an encouraging squeeze before he claps his hands and adds, 'Luke, hop along to sick bay. Quick march. I'll try calling Darcy's uncle again soon, but I really must get to assembly now.'

Luke and Mr McEvoy hurry away without looking at me, and I stand alone waving to strangers who pass by without waving back.

Chapter Twenty-Eight

GILLIAN

Friday 5 July 2019

The doorbell rings and I ignore it. It's early, not long after 8 a.m., and I'm not fully dressed. I want to curl my hair and pop on some make-up before I leave to walk around to Darcy's. I have big news for the Hogans today, and I really would like to look my best when I deliver it.

The doorbell rings again. It irks me that someone thinks it's okay to call unannounced at this hour of the morning, and I assume they're actually looking for Kimberly or Eddie. When the bell-ringing stops and knocking starts instead it grows a little harder to ignore. And when it escalates to the door rattling on its hinges as someone actually pounds their fist against it, I slam down my foundation brush on my bedside table in frustration.

'Helllllloooo,' a female voice calls. 'Hello, Gillian, are you in there? Please open the door.'

I roll my eyes as I recognise Kimberly's voice and I can sense her strange determination to find me. I march through my apartment, the stomp of my feet echoing the pounding on the door.

I creak the door open slowly and Kimberly almost knocks on my face as she has her fist raised and ready to pound some more.

'Oh,' she says, as if she wasn't really expecting to see me, and I'm suddenly sorry I answered after all. 'You're okay.'

'Sorry,' I say, running my hand through my hair that's frizzy and that I won't have time to curl if I have to stand chatting for long.

Kimberly stares at me. Her eyes are washing over me as if she's searching for something. It makes me instantly uncomfortable and I don't understand.

'I was in the shower,' I lie, wondering if she's searching for an explanation as to why I took so long to answer the door.

'Thank God, you're okay,' she says again, and I realise she's somewhat breathless. It can't simply be from knocking with such vigour. Kimberly's toned arms and slim legs, emphasised by the neon yoga pants and Lycra top she's wearing leave no question about her fitness. Kimberly is frightened, I decide. I'm just not sure of what. *Me?*

'Can I come in?' she asks, looking all around as if someone is watching.

I glance over my shoulder. Both bedroom doors are closed.

'Please,' she adds, as I look back at her and make eye contact.

I nod and step back so she can walk past. I close the door behind us with some reluctance, and I can't seem to take my eyes off the bedroom doors.

'I just wanted to check you're okay,' Kimberly says, looking all around.

'Of course, I'm okay.' I smile. 'Are you?' I want to add that Kimberly is acting so oddly it's making me uncomfortable, but I barely know her and I've no idea if this isn't simply what she's always like. And I find myself momentarily regretting the decision to move into such a domestic community where people all seem to know each other's business – or at least want to know it.

'I was so worried about you,' Kimberly says, flopping on to one of the kitchen stools without my inviting her to. She eyes up a half-full cup of coffee that I left on the shelf earlier, and despite the less-than-subtle hint, I don't offer to make us some.

I want to tell Kimberly I'm running late, and I won't have time to curl my frizzy hair now. But damn curiosity forces me to ask, 'Why were you worried about me?'

'Because of that guy that was here,' she says. 'Sorry, could I get some water? My heart is racing.'

'Yeah. Sure,' I say, taking a glass from the cupboard and running the tap. 'What guy?'

'Tall. Broad shoulders. Dark hair. Very good-looking, especially for a psycho.'

Luke.

I almost drop the glass, and water splashes out over the edge.

Kimberly notices and with concern she says, 'You know him.'

I shake my head, desperate to sidestep anything and everything about my complicated past.

'Really?'

I can tell she doesn't believe me.

'I could swear he lives at the end of our road,' Kimberly continues. 'Gimme a second, his name is on the tip of my tongue. It's eh . . . it's eh . . .'

'I haven't had a chance to meet any of the neighbours yet,' I say, cutting her off. 'Except you and Eddie, of course.'

Her smile is false and she says, 'He's married. You haven't got yourself mixed up with him, have you?' I can feel Kimberly looking at me, but I don't meet her gaze. I suspect any reaction I give will only fuel this silly theory. 'Not that I'm judging, I swear. I mean he is absolutely gorgeous,' she says. 'But if it's the man I'm thinking of his wife *is* pregnant . . .' She clicks her fingers and suddenly smiles brightly. 'Luke. That's his name. Luke something-or-other.'

I turn off the tap and place the glass of water on the countertop next to her. 'I'm not really one for relationships,' I say. 'I don't have the time.'

Kimberly guzzles a large mouthful of water, but she seems more on edge than before. 'Oh.'

'Did he say who he was looking for, or why he was here?'

Kimberly shakes her head.

'I've ordered some new bits and pieces for the apartment,' I say, glancing around, as if I'm envisaging where cushions and throws might go. 'You know, put my own stamp on the place. Maybe one of my boxes was delivered to his house by mistake and he was dropping it off.'

Kimberly is wide-eyed as she sips more water. 'Are you sure everything is all right? You can tell me, you know. I'm a good secret keeper.'

'Everything is fine,' I say, thinking of my stupid frizzy hair and how, if I want to catch Darcy and Luke before Luke leaves for work, I really need to be on my way. 'Or maybe he was looking for whoever lived here before me.'

Kimberly shakes her head. 'Your apartment has been vacant for ages. Eddie and I were beginning to wonder if anyone would ever move in.'

I sigh. This is going nowhere and I really need to go. I look at my watch hoping she'll take the hint. She does. She drains her glass and stands up.

'Look,' she says, placing the glass on the table. 'If you ever need to talk . . .'

I pick up the glass, rinse it and turn it upside down on the draining board to dry.

'Thanks,' I say as I guide Kimberly to the door. 'You're so good to call in this morning.'

Kimberly has worry etched across her wrinkled brow. 'Just please be careful. Call Eddie if he comes around again giving you hassle, okay. I have a bad feeling about all this.'

I nod. There's no point arguing.

'Or the cops. Call the cops. It's trespassing or something, after all.'

'Kimberly.' I say her name in a sing-song voice, trying to tell her that this is all far too dramatic.

'I'm serious,' she says, stepping outside, and turning to hug me. She catches me unawares and I baulk. I haven't been hugged in so long I've actually forgotten what it feels like to have someone's arms around me, or to have someone care about me. Kimberly may have made a mess of my morning but she's sweet, and I know she wants to be friends. I like her.

'I know trouble when I see it,' Kimberly says.

I nod. Kimberly has her mind made up.

'I really don't think he'll be calling around again,' I say.

Kimberly's eyebrows narrow and she opens her mouth but I cut her off, telling her what she wants to hear. 'I'll be careful,' I say.

Kimberly looks at me with an expression that asks if she should stay.

And I stare back with determination. 'I promise.'

I watch as Kimberly walks away, turning when she's halfway down the driveway to blow me a kiss and a wink. I close the door and smile.

Kimberly is right, Luke really can't come here again. I decide my frizzy hair doesn't matter after all, and today is not the day to speak to Luke and Darcy. I need to have patience. Soon I'll make them an offer they can't refuse.

Chapter Twenty-Nine

DARCY

Saturday 6 July 2019

Morning light shines through my open bedroom curtains. I'm getting used to Luke being up before me, and sometimes he's left for work before I even wake up. I sit up in bed. The baby kicks and my ribs ache, reminding me of how big I'm getting and how close my due date is now. As usual my mind wanders to work. I hope we can have all the investment paperwork signed before I go on maternity leave. Obviously, I know Luke can take care of everything if the negotiations drag on and the baby arrives in the meantime, but I'd rather have it all sorted out as soon as possible.

I check the bedside table for a note from Luke. He's taken to leaving notes to say good morning if he has to leave while I'm still asleep. Yesterday's one was particularly sweet and left me smiling all day, even when I was too sick to get out of bed. I read it so many times, when I close my eyes now I can still see the words.

> *Good morning, honey.*
> *I watched you sleeping for a while. You're so beauti-*
> *ful. I hope our baby is a girl and looks just like you.*

I'm going to the office now, but I'm just a text or a call away, if you need me. I will always take care of everything.

Love you so much,

Luke xx

I folded it and put it in my underwear drawer with all the others. I don't tell Luke I'm keeping his notes. I want it to be a surprise after the baby is born. I plan to buy him something lovely as soon as this is all over and I'm back driving. I'll go into town and get him that expensive watch he's had his eye on for a couple of years. I'll give him the watch and the notes together, to say thank you for all the time he's spent taking care of me. And not just during this pregnancy from hell. He's taken care of me always from my very first day at St Peter's, and I grow to love him more and more with the years.

I'm still swooning over thoughts of my husband when I hear the wind catch the back door downstairs and it slams with a bang. It gives me a fright and I find myself on my feet surprisingly quickly, considering how long it usually takes me to pull myself out of bed.

'Everything all right down there,' I shout as I reach the bedroom door.

But there's no answer.

'Luke?' I say again.

Nothing.

I shuffle on to the landing. The house is silent and still and I wonder if Luke has left for work after all. Maybe he was in a hurry this morning and didn't have time to leave me a note. Leaning over the banister on the balcony outside my room, I stare into the hall below. All the doors downstairs are open. I've spent the last couple of days in bed, too poorly to go downstairs even for meal times. Luke has brought me everything I need. I call Jinx quickly.

'Here, boy. Here, Jinx, Jinx, Jinx.'

I wait and listen, hoping to hear the scramble of his little paws on the kitchen tiles. But Jinx doesn't come, and my heart sinks. I really thought he'd have bounced back to good health by now. I miss my full-of-energy puppy. And the vet promised it would just be a couple of days before he was as good as new. But Luke says Jinx has been sleeping a lot and he didn't want to bring him upstairs in case he was sick in our bedroom. I said I didn't mind, we could clean it up. But Luke wouldn't hear of it. Deep down I know Luke is right. The smell of dog puke would set me off and I could be sick for days. The thought of spending any more time leaning over the loo is torture.

Feeling less shaky than I have for days, I venture down the stairs.

'Luke? Jinx?' I call, after another door bangs and I stall on a step.

Damn this creepy old house, I think, hating how nervous I feel in my own home. I know it's ridiculous, but my heart races nonetheless.

I take the remainder of the stairs at a faster pace, ignoring the banging, which I suspect is Jinx trapped in the utility room. I hurry into the kitchen and I'm surprised to find the window above the sink wide open and swaying in the wind. It explains the banging, but I wonder why Luke left in such a hurry he forgot to close it. I lean over the sink and try to grab the window handle, but my enormous belly is in the way and I can't get close enough to the countertop to reach it. A strong gust of wind whips by and catches the window, slamming it against the wall outside.

I unlock the back door and hurry out, crossing my fingers that the glass isn't broken. Surprisingly the window is intact and I push it closed from this side. Letting it go, I know I'll need to be quick getting back into the house before the wind catches it again, and the window and I are trapped in an endless game of cat and mouse. I turn, ready to run back inside, when a mound in the corner of the garden catches my eye. I forget about the window and take reluctant steps forward to investigate, my heart racing faster than ever. Moist, dark-brown earth is heaped next to the hedging that separates our house from the next. It's round and fresh.

I can barely breathe as I scurry back into the house.

'Jinx. Here, boy. Oh Jinx, please,' I shout, rushing into the utility room to check his bedding.

My heart squeezes and I hate that I'm not surprised when I don't find him there. I know. I hate that I know. But still, I keep searching.

'Jinx. Jinx. Jinx.'

I click my tongue against the roof of my mouth over and over, making the clicking sound that always catches his attention, and I hope that my fluffy little puppy will come bounding through one of the open doors. But he doesn't.

I've no idea how long I spend running from one room to the next, throwing cushions and throws off furniture. When I struggle to catch my breath and I'm beyond exhausted I finally give up. I know where Jinx is. Deep down I know.

It's hard to drag myself back into the garden. And the damn window has started banging again, but I don't care if the glass breaks or not. My legs and arms are weak and ache and I know I'll need to lie down soon. My heart is pounding as I choke back tears and slowly approach the mound of disturbed earth. I flop on to my knees next to it and I barely make a sound as fat, salty tears trickle down my cheeks.

'I'm sorry, boy. I'm so sorry.'

I cried for months after my parents died. For days on end at first. And, in the months and even years that followed, every now and then something would remind me of them and my heart would break all over again. My mother's favourite song would come on the radio and I would break down, because I could remember how she loved to sing, but it was becoming harder and harder to remember the sound of her voice. When I was little I wanted to be a dancer, the type onstage, flipping and doing the splits in the background as a superstar wowed the crowd with their latest track. But my father always warned me that I'd never have money working for someone else. I know I have him to thank for my drive and determination, and if Darcy's Dishes becomes a global success with Gillian's investment, I know I have my parents to thank. I often think about how much they would love Luke and I really wish they'd had a chance to meet him.

That's what makes crying so hard now. I'm so consumed with anger, and it's directed at Luke. *How could he let this happen to Jinx? How could he? He promised he'd take care of him. He promised.*

I must have spent hours in the garden. And I've definitely fallen asleep, because when I look up the sun is shining blisteringly bright overhead in a cloudless sky, and my arms and shins are red and stinging where my fair skin has been exposed to the July sun. I know I should go inside out of the heat. But before I do, I pick some of the wild white flowers that bloom in our hedging in the summer and press them into the freshly turned soil. They look almost withered straight away, but it's the best I can do for now. I'll go to the shop later, when I'm steadier on my feet, and buy some roses for my puppy's grave.

Time seems to pass in slow motion, and it doesn't help that Luke is late home from work. I meet him at the front door, hearing the sound of his key turning slowly in our stubborn lock.

'When were you going to tell me?' I snap, as soon as the door creaks open.

Luke stares at me with surprise. 'You're downstairs.'

'He's gone, Luke. Jinx is gone.'

I hear Luke exhale as he steps inside and closes the door behind him. 'He is.'

The sobs that I held back earlier begin and Luke wraps his arms around me.

'Why didn't you tell me?' I say.

Luke gives me a moment to cry, before he guides me towards the kitchen with one arm still draped over my shoulder.

'He didn't feel any pain, honey. If that helps.'

'If that helps?' I hiss.

Luke pulls out a chair from the table and I'm glad. My legs are really wobbling now and for some reason I don't want him to notice. I sit. Luke doesn't speak as he fills the kettle with water and flicks it on.

'Tea?' he asks.

I shake my head.

'Darcy, you need to have something. Look at you. You're shaking like a leaf.'

My eyes narrow and I glare at my husband.

'You're in shock,' Luke says, calmer. 'You need some food and something to drink.'

'I need Jinx.'

'I know. I know,' Luke says, edging closer to me and gently stroking my hair.

'Why didn't you take him back to the vet?' I ask, struggling to keep the resentment out of my voice. If I wasn't pregnant, if Luke hadn't accidently got me pregnant when I was always honest about not wanting kids, then none of this would have happened. I wouldn't be confined to my goddamn bed so often and I'd have been downstairs taking care of Jinx.

Luke makes tea and I hear him sigh often over the stirring of the spoon and the pouring of almond milk. I don't usually take milk in my tea but the doctor freaked out when he heard I was vegan, suggested all these supplements, and Luke has made it his mission to balance my diet with all these new dairy substitutes that taste gross, if I'm honest. But he's trying hard and I've just sort of gone along with it to appease him.

Luke places a cup of tea in front of me, and I realise he hasn't made one for himself.

'C'mon,' he says, trying to smile. 'Drink up. It'll help.'

I take a reluctant sip and it tastes worse than usual. Horribly sour as if the milk is gone off. I put the cup down and pull a face and Luke seems instantly offended. But right now I don't care. I direct the conversation back to Jinx.

'You didn't answer my question,' I say. 'Why didn't you take him back to the vet?'

'I did.'

'Then why didn't you tell me?'

'I didn't want to worry you.'

'Didn't you think I'd want to spend time with him? Hold him, at the very least.'

Luke shakes his head and sighs. 'Darcy, drink some more. You're very pale. You're worrying me.'

'No,' I snap, pushing the hot cup further away from me. 'I can't believe you let this happen.'

Luke drops his head and stares at the table. 'There was nothing they could do,' he says. 'He was just too sick. They had to put him to sleep.'

'What?' The pounding in my temples is intense. 'You had no right to make that decision without me. No goddamn right, Luke.'

Luke looks up and my heart aches when I see fear in his eyes. 'You were so sick. The stress of going to the vet's made you bed-bound, for goodness' sake. I didn't know what would happen if I told you this. What if something happened to the baby because of it?'

I don't have anything to say.

'I thought I was doing the right thing. I know how much you loved him.'

I nod. 'I did. I really did.'

'I know. I know,' Luke says. 'I did too.'

Luke's words jolt me. 'But you didn't,' I say. 'You said he was a little fur ball. You made it blatantly obvious you didn't like him.'

Luke shuffles in his seat and I can't read his expression. I'm not sure I've seen him make this face before. 'Ah, but they were teething problems. He was just a puppy. He just needed to be house-trained.'

'He's not the only one,' I say, and my tone is clipped and bitchy but I don't regret it.

I'm irked even more when Luke stares back at me with a clueless expression.

'The kitchen window,' I say, pointing. 'You left it open.'

Luke taps his chest with his finger. 'Me?'

'The wind caught it and it was banging like crazy. Imagine if the glass broke. We'd have had to call someone to fix it. More money.' I pause and roll my eyes. 'Money we can't afford to spend.'

Luke folds his arms and raises his voice. 'I didn't leave the window open.'

He's both defensive and pissed off as he glares at me and I know he's preparing for me to yell back, but I don't. The tiny hairs at the nape of my neck are tingling – because I believe him.

And with a shaky whisper I ask, 'If you didn't open it, who did?'

Luke groans. 'Oh, not this again.'

I ignore him and say, 'Well it didn't open itself. I knew I could hear someone downstairs. Someone was here.'

Luke holds his hands above his head in mock surrender. 'You know what? It was me. I left it open. Happy now?'

'No.' I make a face. 'Because you're lying.'

'I can't win,' Luke says, exhausted. 'You're upset about Jinx and looking for an argument. But I'm not going to have one. End of story.'

I inhale sharply through my nose and hold it for a second before I puff it back out through a barely open mouth. Luke and I have faced a lot of change since I've been pregnant. And although I've been frustrated with the new direction many times, I've never felt like we were growing apart. Now, I'm not so sure.

Luke stands up and walks over to me, picking up the cup of steaming tea by the handle. 'C'mon,' he says, still trying to smile like normal. 'Let's get you back to bed. It's been quite the day.'

'Yeah okay,' I say cocking my ear to listen for a stranger's footsteps in the house, because I'm convinced that an argument is the least of our problems.

Chapter Thirty

Tina

Sunday 7 July 2019

It's much too hot for bloody Pilates today. It's the hottest day of the year by far and much, much hotter than usual for an Irish summer. My fair skin can't cope with the humidity. Sweaty bodies are lying on multicoloured floor mats and the studio at the gym seems smaller today than it did before, as if the humid conditions are sucking all the air out and shrinking it.

'Breathe in, two, three. And hold. Hold. Hold.'

Everyone does as they are told, including me. But it doesn't feel any less stuffy and I wonder who will be the first pregnant woman to faint.

'And out, two, three.'

There's lots of sighing and humming before instruction continues. 'Good. Great, everyone,' she says. 'Let's take five. Grab some water.'

People slowly begin to stand up and I crane my neck to look around. It's easier to take in faces when we're all upright. There's no sign of Rose the cop today. In fact, a few of the women with the largest bumps last time are missing, and I can only assume they've had their babies.

Polly crosses the studio to come chat with me. 'Teacher's pet,' she teases, giggling as she nods at the instructor who's smiling and waving at me, uncomfortably enthused. I glance over my shoulder hoping it's directed at someone else, but the girl behind me is still lying on her side with her eyes closed.

'Do you always impress the instructors this quickly? I bet you were a real gym person before you got pregnant. Sure, look at you, there isn't a pick on you. Hard to believe you even have a little one in there,' Polly says, and I jump away just in time to dodge her hand that she tries to place on my stomach.

'Where's Rose?' I ask, desperate to change the subject. 'Did she have her baby?'

Polly shakes her head. 'Not last I heard. Poor thing. Can only imagine how fed up she is. She probably has a doctor's appointment or something, she'd definitely be here otherwise. She's a machine. Never misses class.'

'Um,' I say, as if I understand pregnancy ailments.

Polly nods and we share this weird silent exchange where I think we are expressing sympathy for Rose. Really, I'm wondering if I can leave mid class without drawing too much attention to myself. There is no point my being here if Rose isn't.

'You know, I'm not really feeling great,' I say.

'Oh?' Polly's eyes round. 'Morning sickness still getting to you?'

'Yeah. I guess.'

'It's a nightmare.'

'I think I'm just going to go. I'm not as strong as Rose.'

'None of us are,' Polly says. 'But I think you're doing great. You haven't failed until you've thrown up in class.' She nods and points to herself.

Ew.

'Are you sure you won't stay?' Polly says. 'No one is judging you and sometimes the stretching helps.'

I shake my head. 'No. Not today. I really only came because Rose had some dust sheets for me.' I gasp, wondering why I said that.

'Oh, you're decorating,' Polly says.

'Okay everyone, how are we all feeling?' A voice of authority fills the studio, drawing everyone's attention.

There's a chorus of enthusiastic women expressing how great they feel, eager to get back to exercise. In sync, our attention turns towards clapping our hands and jogging on the spot. Everyone seems to know the drill.

'Let's get back to it, ladies. Arms out and knees up. You can do this.'

Cheers echo around the hall. 'Whoop. Whoop.'

It's exhausting even if you're not pregnant.

'Oh Christ,' Polly says, as we fail to join in. 'I don't have the energy for that.'

I begin to laugh, but Polly is looking at me very seriously and she gestures towards my mat. 'Right, grab that and let's get going. Something like a milkshake or smoothie sounds a lot better than exercise right now, you and me?'

I pick up my mat and try to think of a reasonable way to blow her off. 'You know, I really would but—'

Polly's hands are on her hips and she carries an air of curiosity that makes me uncomfortable.

'Ah, c'mon,' she says, smiling. 'I could really use a pick-me-up. And we never got around to it last time.'

'I know, but . . .'

Polly's seriousness turns to sadness. 'Please? My last Pilates friend ditched me when her pregnancy became kind of compli-cated and I don't have any other pregnant mates. Well, except for

Rose and she's going to pop soon. I just want someone to moan and complain to who really gets it.'

'And kick, two, three. Again, two, three.'

Both Polly and I look at the top of the room, knowing we're disrupting class.

'Everything okay, ladies?' the instructor asks.

'Morning sickness,' Polly answers for us both.

The instructor nods knowingly. 'I've class again tonight, so if you're feeling better later pop back then instead.'

'Cool. Ta,' Polly says, and she hurries over to her side of the room and grabs her mat impressively quickly, considering how much most of the women seem to struggle with bending down and getting up. She crosses back to me, rolling her mat as she walks.

'Right, c'mon. Smoothie, my treat,' she says, linking her free arm around mine with the vigour of a teenager who's determined to make a new best friend. She turns her head over her shoulder as we walk, linked uncomfortably together. 'See you later, Kim.'

The instructor doesn't reply. She's counting backwards from ten and encouraging everyone to breathe slowly and deeply. But she waves and smiles and I've no doubt Polly will be as good as her word and come back later.

Outside, I unlink our arms and I'm about to make my excuses and leave, but Polly keeps talking.

'Rose, Darcy and me started Pilates together. You should have seen us in the beginning – so enthusiastic and full of beans.' Polly stares into the distance, smiling as she reminisces. I don't interrupt and she continues. 'Rose is the furthest along and she already has a tonne of kids at home so she gives the best advice. But it didn't matter that Darcy and I were first timers and Rose wasn't. We all just clicked. I was really looking forward to us all being good friends but Darcy was just too sick. The poor girl. I haven't heard from her in a while, actually. I must give her a text.'

'Ah Darcy Hogan,' I say, her name stinging as much as ever as it passes my lips.

'Yes.' Polly's face brightens at the mention of Darcy's full name. 'Did you check her out online?'

'No. Like I said – I don't like social media.'

'You really are a curious one, aren't ya?' Polly begins to laugh. 'Judy's Juices is just around the corner. You'll have to tell me all about how you know Darcy there.'

'There's not much to tell,' I say, taking a step to the side to avoid her linking my arm again. 'We were in school together. But I haven't seen her in years.'

Polly's eyes widen. 'No bloody way.' She throws her head back for a second, and gasps. 'I can't believe you didn't mention this before. Small world, eh?'

'Yeah. Very small,' I say. 'Maybe you could tell me all about what Darcy is like now. I'd love to hear what she's like as an adult.'

Polly's eyes twinkle. 'Definitely. I'd love to. You'd like her. Everyone does.'

'Oh, it sounds like she hasn't changed a bit,' I say, having to make a conscious effort not to grind my teeth.

'I'll have to put the two of you back in touch,' she says. 'Wouldn't it be wonderful to reconnect after all these years?'

Wonderful indeed.

'C'mon,' I say, walking in the direction I hope is right for Judy's Juices. 'I'm parched.'

Chapter Thirty-One

DARCY

Monday 8 July 2019

Luke seems to want me confined to bed for the remainder of this damn pregnancy as if I'm made of papier mâché and he has to be extra careful with my fragile body.

'And we can put a telly up here,' Luke says, drawing a rectangle in the air with his fingers as he stands next to my dressing table. 'There's a sale on at Electro World this week, I'll pop in after work and get one. What will we say? A 32 inch? That's probably big enough.'

I ignore him and stare into space. My body is aching, my joints especially. It feels a bit like the flu, except without the bunged-up nose or sore throat – at least that's something to be grateful for, I try to remind myself, when all I want to do is curl up in a ball and cry because I miss Jinx so much. The guilt at not being there when he needed me most is almost too much to bear. Damn this pregnancy. *Damn it.*

'Darcy,' Luke says, sternly, and I realise he continued talking while I zoned out. 'I'm trying here. I really am trying to make this easier for you. But I can't help you, unless you help yourself.'

'I don't care about a damn TV,' I snap. I haven't been able to watch television since Tina's appearance on Lindsay's show. I've avoided social media since then, too. I've no doubt a storm is waiting for me online, but with Andrew Buckley's murder and then losing Jinx I'm not strong enough to face any of it. I haven't even been able to bring myself to talk to Luke about it.

Luke's gaze falls on to the bedside table. I haven't touched my breakfast. He's made granola with summer berries sprinkled with icing sugar and there's freshly squeezed orange juice, and I can tell from just looking at the glass that there's no pulp – just the way I like it.

Luke tilts his head to one side and says, 'Won't you even taste a little bit? I don't want to leave for work until I know you've eaten at least something. I'll be worried all day otherwise.'

My stomach rumbles, thankfully not loud enough for Luke to hear from the far side of the room. But it's uncomfortable and it reminds me that I'm starving. But I just don't feel like putting a morsel past my lips. All I can think about is Jinx. And even though I know it's not Luke's fault, it's not anyone's fault – except maybe a neighbour's with their overzealous use of weedkiller – I'm still filled with anger and resentment.

'How about a nibble?' Luke says, pointing at the dark flakes of nuts and seeds smothered in bright berries.

My stomach rumbles again, louder this time, drawing Luke's attention, and I hear him exaggerate a sigh.

'I'm not hungry,' I reiterate for what seems like the umpteenth time this morning.

'Darcy,' Luke says, and I hate it when he says my name like this, as if it's too much effort to get the syllables past his lips. 'Please, Darcy,' he says, his eyes round with concern.

Finally, I pick a large, juicy strawberry from the top of the bowl. There's lots of sugar on this one. I take a bite and flavour bursts in my mouth. It's delicious. I reach for another. Before I know it I'm munching into the whole thing. I'm just too hungry to stop, despite knowing I'll pay for it later with my head over the toilet bowl. Some days I feel good for the first half an hour or so and I enjoy an initial energy burst. I might have time to grab a shower, or pop downstairs to stretch my legs. Other times I'm too exhausted to get up at all. It's completely unpredictable and out of my control. But one thing that never changes is my desire to get back to normal.

I can see the relief wash over Luke. I suspect he's counting down the days until the baby is born as much as I am. I'm sure he'd like his wife back too.

'Right,' Luke says, watching as I wash down the last mouthful of granola with refreshing orange juice. 'I better get to work.'

'Call me if there's any news on the contracts with Buckley & Co, won't you?' I say, dabbing the corners of my lips with my fingertips to wipe away some sticky sugar.

Luke nods and starts explaining how accountants and solicitors on both sides are holding things up. I'm well used to the never-ending paper trail and how sluggish these things can be. But that's not why I stop listening. My concentration has moved to my tingling fingertips and the sensation travelling up my hands and into my wrists. It happens a lot recently straight after I eat. I haven't told Luke, or my doctor. I know it will only give Luke something more to worry about, and my doctor will no doubt suggest hospital admission yet again. That seems to be his answer to all my unorthodox pregnancy ailments. Thank God I have Luke here to take care of me, or I'd have ended up in hospital long ago.

The sudden ring of the doorbell is loud and almost obnoxious as it bursts through the whole house without warning.

'Jesus,' I say, clutching my chest.

Luke laughs. 'It's just the door, Darcy.'

My cheeks flush.

'I'll get it,' Luke says, walking towards our bedroom door.

It's a redundant comment, but it pinches more than it should. I'm in no fit state to answer the door even if I wanted to. Luke pauses to turn his head and passes me a look that says, *Sorry*, as if he can read my mind. Sometimes I think he can. I smile as the doorbell rings again, impatiently.

Luke walks out of our room and I hear his tired footsteps on the stairs. I crane my neck to better hear the chatting that follows. Luke's deep tone drifts towards me, followed by a female voice. But when the words reach me, they're nothing more than indecipherable mumbles.

The talking continues for quite some time and then I hear the closing of the front door. There's a moment of silence before voices continue and the sound shifts, and I know Luke has invited someone in and they're walking towards the sitting room or kitchen. An internal door closes, shutting the voices out.

My eyes are sleepy and my body is heavy. An all-too-familiar pang settles in my chest – today is going to be a bad day. But I'm determined not to succumb. Deciding that looking at some photos of Jinx will cheer me up, I stretch my arm out and pat my hand around on the bedside table searching for my phone. I knock against the glass of orange juice and it falls to the floor with a bang. I exhale, frustrated, and open my eyes, sliding myself to the edge of the bed. I look over to find the glass hasn't broken, but there's a small puddle of orange juice and it's gradually seeping between the floorboards. *Dammit.*

With limited energy I stand up and drag myself to the bathroom to fetch some tissue. By the time I get back, most of the orange juice has soaked through the crack. I bend as best I can and begin to dry up the rest. I notice the gap between this floorboard and the next is wider than any other in the whole floor. It's not hugely noticeable, but now that I've seen it I know it will grate on my nerves as a glaring imperfection for ever more. When I scrub hard on the floorboard it slides a little from left to right as if it's loose and could easily be lifted. I wonder if there's something wrong underneath. This floor must be pretty old. These boards were in the house when we bought it. We had them sanded and re-polished until they sparkled. But the builder couldn't give us a guarantee on the work because he couldn't say how old the boards were exactly, or how they'd cope with the new varnish. I wanted to replace the floor entirely but Luke pushed to keep it. He was really rather adamant. He'd left all the other decorating to me so I didn't feel I could argue about this one insignificant detail. But I'm wondering now if we shouldn't just replace the whole floor – perhaps there's woodworm or rot or something separating the boards. No doubt it will be expensive and something we could do without.

I decide to investigate a little further. I reach for my phone and use the torch app to shine between the boards. I'm not sure what I'm looking for, really. Dark spots, cracks maybe. Any signs of mould or extensive wear and tear. I'm not expecting to find something white or cream. Paper, perhaps. I try to adjust the angle of my phone so the light shines on whatever is down there, but the narrow gap offers a limited view. Finally, I bend as low as I physically can and squint above the gap. I'm certain now that I can see a small mound of stacked paper. There's something printed on the top page. Numbers and letters. I nudge closer. My back aches, pleading with me to straighten up, but I ignore the twinges and squint. I can just about make out the bottom line of letters and I'm slowly sounding out *F.I.N.A.L. N.O . . .* when there's a squeak and something grey and furry scrambles across the paper.

'Rat. Oh God a rat.' I shriek and kick the rug over the hole in the floor before I straighten up and my back cracks audibly.

My hands seem to instinctively cradle my bump and my head is spinning as Luke hurries into our room. He catches me just as I'm about to fall and I find myself floppy and helpless in his strong arms.

He helps me to sit on the bed, before he asks, 'What's wrong? What happened?'

'I . . . I . . .' My heart is racing and I place my hands on each side of my head to steady myself and stop the room from spinning.

I can't tell Luke about the rat without him knowing I was peering through the floorboards. Luke has clearly been hiding paperwork from me and I want to see for myself what it says. I decide the best thing right now is to swallow my pride and play my part as the damsel in distress that my husband seems to think I am.

'I had a cramp,' I lie, rubbing my thigh for effect. 'I needed to stretch my legs.'

'Oh you poor thing,' Luke says, taking over rubbing my leg for me. But I want to push him away because I'm beyond hurt that he's been hiding bills from me.

'That explains the screaming,' he says, his hands stroking me. 'I thought you'd seen a ghost.'

It's so hard to force a smile and I can feel the pounding of frustration in my temple.

'You should have called me,' Luke says. 'I heard a bang. I thought you'd fallen.'

'I dropped a glass,' I say, pointing to the semi-cleaned-up orange spill and the glass lying on its side next to Luke's foot.

Luke shakes his head as he bends to pick up the glass. I hold my breath and wonder if he'll notice the gap in the floorboards. It seems so glaringly obvious now that I know it's there. But he stands up without a word. He takes the glass into the bathroom and I hear him running the taps before he returns with a damp cloth. At first I think he's going to finish cleaning up the mess, but he presses the cool cloth against my forehead and reiterates, 'You should have called me.'

He sounds exhausted or exasperated – both, maybe.

I wince, and not just because the cloth is cold and uncomfortable against my skin.

'You're sweating up a storm,' Luke says, shaking his head as I try to wriggle away from the cloth and his hand holding it in place.

My skin is hot and clammy under my nightdress but I feel cold and shaky. Luke dabs my forehead with the cloth.

'Were you coming to see who was downstairs?' Luke asks, his words accusatory. As if I'm a small child disobeying a parent.

I take exception to his passive-aggressive tone and push his hand away from me.

'No. I told you. I was stretching my legs,' I snap, standing up despite very much wanting to stay sitting down. 'But now that you bring it up, who was at the door?'

Luke exhales and shakes his head. 'No one.'

'No one,' I echo, as my eyes narrow and I stare at Luke with a face that says, *So you were downstairs chatting to no one for the past twenty minutes?*

Luke sighs. 'It was Gillian, actually. She's a bit odd, isn't she? I think she'll take a lot of warming to.'

'Is everything okay? Did she mention the deal?' I ask.

Luke shakes his head and I inhale sharply and am reminded that my back hurts.

'Should we be worried?'

'I knew you would worry,' Luke says. 'This is why I didn't want to tell you she was here. But everything is fine, honey. Please don't stress.'

Luke seems to have picked up a bad habit of lying to me since I've been pregnant. I wonder if he even knows he's doing it. Any time he seems to think I'll worry or be upset about something he

196

alters the facts, or hides them completely. I know he's doing it to protect me. He's trying to take all the worry on his shoulders to spare me, but I wonder when he will realise that keeping secrets is what worries me the most.

Luke pushes his shirtsleeves back and checks his watch. 'Christ I'm late,' he says. 'Will you be okay here on your own while I'm gone?'

'Of course,' I say, already planning all the phone calls I'm going to make today from the comfort of my bed. First Gillian, then our solicitor, then some sort of vermin exterminator. 'Have a good day, honey. I'll see you later.' Because I have a horrible feeling the furry creatures under the floor aren't the only rats in my life.

Chapter Thirty-Two

DARCY

Thursday 16 December 1999

The smell of pine cones and cinnamon dances in the air at the annual school pre-Christmas dinner. Every student, from every year, is crammed into the canteen, along with all our teachers. The windows are wide open. And despite it being minus two degrees outside, the canteen is unbearably stuffy, complete with thick condensation on the skylights in the roof. Every now and then an unsuspecting student shrieks or laughs when a droplet of moisture falls on their head.

The long, rectangular canteen tables are laid with red, plastic cloths embellished with green holly leaves in a distinctive design that repeats on a loop. There's non-alcoholic punch that tastes as bad as it smells, but the food is fantastic. Baked ham, roast turkey with pine-nut stuffing and all the trimmings. For most of the kids, today's celebration marks the start of the holiday period and excitement clings to the air as they can't wait to get home to spend quality time with their families. For others it's the nearest thing to a family dinner we will see this Christmas, and each of us treasures the evening for our own personal reasons.

The chatter is noisy and the laughter is even louder and the roof feels as if it might lift off, but the teachers never once encourage us to quieten down as they usually would when we're overly boisterous or excited. Christmas spirit is high and it's the most content I've been since I lost my parents. I really have found my happy place. St Peter's is more than just my school. It's my home. It's where I belong now.

Luke is sitting beside me. Every now and then I'll feel his hand on my knee or the warmth of his shoulder against mine as we both enjoy the banter at our table. But when he taps me on the shoulder I stop talking to the girl beside me to turn around to face the boy I'm falling in love with. He passes me a cracker which he holds firmly at the other end.

'Pull,' he says, smiling as brightly as I do.

We both tug and there's a quick snap and something falls on to the table between us as Luke clings to the larger piece of the broken cracker.

'You won,' I say, picking up the silver key ring and bottle-green paper hat that have dropped out of the centre of the cracker and landed next to my plate. 'Here you go.'

I pass Luke the silly trinket and he tilts his head towards me so I can pop the hat on his hair.

'It suits you.' I giggle as he straightens up, proudly wearing his floppy paper crown that is much too big for his head and is just about held in place by his ears.

Luke's face is serious as his eyes lock on to mine. 'I know we said no gifts,' he says unexpectedly, as he leans a little awkwardly to one side so he can slide his hand into his trouser pocket.

I hold my breath. We did say no gifts. Well, *I* said it, actually. I thought it would make everything easier and not put pressure on us to put a title on our relationship. Exchanging presents feels very much like something a boyfriend and girlfriend would do. And although Luke and I spend almost every waking moment together, we've never actually said what our relationship is. Of course, the rest of the school enjoys gossiping and mumbling behind our backs. And although I pretend not to notice, I quite like it when someone says something like, 'Oh, they make a cute couple', or, 'I can totally see them staying together when we finish school'.

'It's just something small,' Luke assures me, obviously noticing the embarrassment written all over my face.

I try to hide it, but I can feel the heat in my cheeks and I've no doubt they're glowing as brightly as the crimson bauble hanging on the beautifully decorated Christmas tree close to us.

Luke produces a small box wrapped in shiny silver paper that catches the light. But before he can pass it to me there's a sudden wave of shushing and everyone turns towards the top table where all our teachers are sitting. The teachers' table is incredibly long and it sits at the top of the canteen, perpendicular to the rest of the tables. The teachers all sit on one side, facing into the canteen. The rest of the tables are stacked up like dominoes with students sitting on both sides. We're squashed so close to the person next to us that there's barely room for our plate and glass in front of us.

The shushing grows louder and more insistent until all chatter stops. I look at Luke and he places his hand on my knee and smiles at me with gentle eyes that tell me we'll pick our conversation up exactly where it left off as soon as we can. I smile back in excited anticipation.

The vice-principal clinks her spoon off the edge of her glass with such animation I'm surprised it doesn't break. And when the large canteen crammed with giddy students and equally excited adults is completely silent, apart from the odd cough or the squeak of a shoe rubbing against a chair leg, Principal McEvoy stands up.

It's no surprise to find him in the centre of the teachers' table. 'Good afternoon everyone. I hope you're having a lovely time.'

Loud applause erupts. There's foot-stomping too, so enthused the floor vibrates below us. I toss my head back and gasp, guzzling in the joy.

'Okay. Okay,' Principal McEvoy says. His cheeks are hot after too much wine and his eyes are glistening with happiness. 'Are you all ready for Kris Kindle?'

The noise in the canteen is deafening. Joyous whooping rings in my ears and the stomping is more ecstatic than ever.

'On the count of three,' Principal McEvoy says, and I look around as heads duck under tables, hands slide into pockets and arms reach under chairs. Gifts seem to appear out of thin air and are placed on top of all the tables. Silver, red, green and gold wrapping paper explodes over every table like a stunning Christmas-coloured rainbow. The wrapped gifts are all shapes and sizes and it's anyone's guess what's inside.

'Well, what are you waiting for?' our principal says, his gaze concentrated on the teachers' table like an eager child, because there's no doubt a gift is waiting for him too. 'Tuck in.'

Luke and I smile at one another before rummaging around the table to find the presents with our names on the label. I find mine first. It's a small box: matt gold wrapping with a not-so-neatly tied bright-red bow. It takes Luke a little longer to seek out his, and there's an awkward mix-up between Luke and one of the other Lukes in the year below us. It's easily sorted out and once everyone is in possession of their present, frenzied unwrapping begins. The excitement is palpable and my heart beats fast as Luke looks at me and says, 'On the count of three.'

I tug on the red bow around my box as Luke tries to peel back stubborn sticky tape on the odd-shaped gift in his hand. I don't know what draws my attention to the girl at the end of the table. Her fiery red hair frames her face and her eyes glisten with what looks like tears. Her name is on the tip of my tongue. I'd noticed her watching Luke and me earlier, but I'd ignored how she stared. People often stare at us. Or, more accurately, girls always stare at Luke and his toned athletic body with his broad shoulders and chiselled jawline.

Luke finally releases the sticky tape and the wrapping falls off a gaudy key ring that spells out *SEX GOD* in chunky, bright letters. Luke shoves the key ring into his pocket and tries to act as if he's not embarrassed as some of his friends notice the key ring and begin to tease and laugh.

'Don't look now,' Luke tells me. 'But that Tina has been staring at us all night.'

'Tina. That's her name. I knew it. She's in my dorm,' I say.

'What's her problem?' Luke asks.

'What?'

Luke shrugs. 'Her staring freaks me out.'

'She just fancies you, that's all,' I say, knocking my shoulder gently against his. 'That key ring is probably from her. No wonder she's staring. She wanted to see your reaction.'

Luke rolls his eyes. 'That's even weirder.'

I can't hold in a snorty laugh and I feel bad as Tina looks away with her head hanging low, and she's as still as a statue. Her stillness stands out as awkward and odd among the excitement buzzing all around her. And I wonder if she's realised we're talking about her. I look at the table in front of her. There's a near-full plate of food she hasn't touched and although there is wrapping paper scattered all around, there's none in front of her.

Suddenly my happiness is pushed aside and replaced by the sting of sadness. I watch her for a little while, but she doesn't move or look up. The people around her laugh and enjoy themselves and they don't seem to even notice she's there.

Luke has returned to laughing and joking with his friends too. I tug on his arm to get his attention and I whisper, 'She doesn't have a gift.'

'Hmm.' Luke turns towards me, still sniggering after a crude joke made by one of his friends about his new key ring.

'Tina. She didn't get a Kris Kindle present,' I say, a little louder. 'I think she's been forgotten.'

'Forgotten?' Someone laughs. 'You have to know someone exists before you can forget them.'

I glare at the guy sitting on the far side of Luke. His gummy smile is stretched wide as he belly laughs.

Luke looks as if he's thinking about giggling too, but I shake my head and he straightens up and becomes serious. 'Maybe we should tell Principal McEvoy.'

'Oh for God's sake,' the guy beside Luke says, before he turns his back on Luke to joke some more with the people at the other end of the table.

'No. No, don't do that,' I say, glancing at Tina, and my heart aches for her. 'Mr McEvoy will make a big deal out of it and that would only embarrass her.'

I look at the present in my hand. I've taken the ribbon off and the paper is torn on one side where I've been subconsciously picking at it. I can't very well give Tina a gift that I've half opened. As if Luke has read my mind, he slides his hand into his pocket and pulls out the present he was going to give me earlier.

'This?' he says.

I swallow hard. I really want the present Luke has bought for me. I want to open it slowly and savour the moment, before I throw my arms around his neck and tell him that I love it, no matter what's inside.

Luke sighs, clasping the box with both hands as if it's terribly delicate and he might drop it if he doesn't concentrate. 'It's a bracelet. As soon as I saw it, I thought of you. I ducked into the shop last week when you were in the loo after the cinema.'

'Oh, Luke.' I can feel my pulse coursing in my veins. 'Thank you. Thank you so much. And thank you even more for knowing that giving it to Tina is the right thing to do.'

Luke's forehead wrinkles which makes him seem more mature. I've never been more attracted to him.

'Tell her it's from you,' I suggest. 'Tell her that you're her Kris Kindle.'

'Darcy.' Luke says my name in a way that tells me he really, really doesn't want to tell her that.

'Please,' I say. 'I don't want her to feel any worse than she already does. She can't know this is a sympathy present. Please?'

'I dunno,' Luke says, reluctantly. 'She'll think we're friends or something.'

'Would that be so bad?' I ask.

Luke takes a deep breath and shakes his head. 'If it'll make you happy . . .' He pushes his chair back, ready to stand up. 'But I'm not making friends with her.'

'I love you,' I say.

'What?' Luke's eyes widen and I cringe instantly. I can't believe I just said that.

My cheeks are on fire. 'I . . . I . . .' I mumble.

'I love you too.'

Luke kisses me, hard and passionately, and then he stands up and walks around to the far side of the table to give an unsuspecting Tina my bracelet.

I watch as she's unsure at first. But as her slender fingers tug at the ribbon, her face lights up. She's open-mouthed when she discovers the bracelet inside and she takes a moment to stroke the silver almost possessively.

Luke begins to walk away, his eyes on mine with a gaze that asks, *Happy now?* I'm nodding when Tina grabs his arm and pulls him back. He wobbles, thrown off balance by the sudden tugging. Tina stands and brushes her fingers against his cheek and I shift in my chair, suddenly uncomfortable as I look on. She leans closer to Luke and whispers something in his ear. I imagine it's simply 'Thank you', but I'll ask Luke for certain in a moment. Luke pulls away while dragging a hand through his floppy hair, the way he always does when he's embarrassed or nervous. Before he has time to take a step away, Tina drapes her arms around his neck and hugs him. Luke's body stiffens and I can tell he wasn't expecting that. Neither was I. She kisses his cheek and her lips linger much longer than appropriate. Luke finally breaks free, quite roughly, and hurries back to me.

'What the hell was that?' he asks, flopping back into his seat. 'See, I told you she was bonkers.'

Tina glares at me with wicked eyes as she sits back down and strokes the bracelet some more. A sense of malaise settles into the pit of my stomach and I think Luke might be right. Luke has made Tina's day, and I can't help feeling that we might regret it.

Chapter Thirty-Three

DARCY

Tuesday 9 July 2019

The whole country seems to be on holiday at the moment. I've called my solicitor a couple of times hoping for a quick update on the Buckley contract, but his secretary told me he's off the grid in the Maldives for the next two weeks. And I haven't had much luck getting hold of an exterminator either. A quick Google search brought up plenty of websites, but most of the numbers rang out. The one or two who did answer couldn't get to me before next week, and I'll go crazy if I have to wait that long to fish out Luke's secret papers.

One guy, who seemed to take great pleasure in telling me that he was answering his phone from the comfort of a poolside sun lounger in the Costa del Sol, made some suggestions.

'My best advice, love, would be to get yourself a few traps,' he said in a thick inner-city Dublin accent. 'Shove them up in the attic and forget about it. Or, if you're very worried, throw down some poison. That should sort the feckers out. But be careful. Don't want to get that stuff on your hands. It's lethal.'

I wondered, if taking care of a vermin issue is so easy, how this guy had a job, but I didn't say anything. I thanked him for his advice and asked him to call me back when he got home from holiday. 'Just in case I'm still having a problem,' I said.

I lay in bed awake for most of last night. My tummy was rumbling with hunger. Luke made a really nice butternut-squash curry with jasmine rice, my favourite recipe, and one that I included in my cookbook that was published a couple of years ago. And although it smelt so good my mouth watered, I couldn't bring myself to actually eat any. I threw it in the bin when Luke left to take another secret call with *nobody important*.

I've spent the morning napping, drifting in and out of light sleep. Luke left for work hours ago. By early afternoon I can't stay in bed any longer. It's no surprise to find a bowl of muesli and a jug of milk left on the bedside table. There's a yellow Post-it stuck to a glass of juice. I squint to read Luke's handwriting.

> *Eat and drink me, please.*
> *Love you.*
> *Luke xx*

I pour some milk over the flakes and carry the bowl into the bathroom and flush it down the toilet. I get dressed and go downstairs. My legs are a little shaky on the steps so I hold the banister extra tight and take my time.

In the kitchen I pour a glass of water and sip slowly as I stare into the garden on a beautiful, cloudless day. I look at the mound where Jinx is buried. The delicate flowers I placed on top have blown away and the mound is flattening as the soil settles, and it blends in with the lawn as if it's always been there.

Abruptly I drop the glass into the sink and dash outside and towards the garden shed. Luke loves this shed – his mancave, I've teased him several times. But I find the clunky, metal shed ugly and think it spoils our pretty garden.

The handle is rusty and difficult to open. It takes several rough tugs to finally get it to budge, and the heavy door is even less inclined to shift. Finally, when I lean my back against it and force with my full weight, it slowly creaks open and the musty smell of old, rotting grass rushes out. It's dark inside as the light creeping in the door can only stretch so far. Luke wanted to buy a shed with a large window on one side but it was expensive and we settled on the cheaper windowless option. Thankfully Luke's toolbox is just inside the door. I duck my head inside, holding my breath and open the box. I pull out a screwdriver, chisel and wrench. I don't bother to close the shed door behind me as I hurry back inside and up the stairs.

It's not easy to get comfortable with my knees on the floor in my bedroom as I lean over the loose floorboard. I tilt my ear towards the floor and listen. I don't hear any squeaking or scurrying but my heart is still pounding as I slide various tools in the narrow gap between the boards. The screwdriver is useless – too round and bulky. But I make headway with the chisel. I'm damaging the corner of the board but I'm definitely widening the gap on one side. Finally, the board pops up and I screech, jump back and clutch my chest, as I expect a rat to come hurtling at me with its claws poised, ready to rip my flesh off.

I pant loudly as I catch my breath. After a couple of seconds I begin to laugh at my dramatics before I set the board to the side and lean over the hole in the floor to look. My laughter stops as I stare at the mound of paper. It's bowed in the middle with its edges curled up like a canoe, and I wonder how long it has spent stuffed in this small space. I lower myself on to my hunkers, hold my breath and reach my hand into the gap. My fingers have barely grazed the paper when I hear the sudden onset of footsteps creeping up the stairs.

I'm quickly upright. Inside my head is noisy as pounding blood races through my veins. My panicked fingers tremble, and I almost drop the board when I try to put it back, as the footsteps draw closer. Finally, my hands cooperate and the board settles into place like the lid of a treasure box.

'Hello. Hello,' a female voice calls.

Gillian? I think, and suddenly feel exposed and vulnerable. I was expecting it to be Luke. I kick off my shoes as quickly as I can and jump into bed.

There's a gentle knock on the ajar bedroom door. 'Hello, Darcy. Are you in here?'

I think about pretending to be asleep. There's something deeply disturbing about Gillian lurking in the house, just outside my bedroom.

'Are you okay?' she asks, knocking once more. 'The back door was wide open and . . .'

'I'm fine, Gillian,' I reply, my voice more clipped than I would like it to be, and I hope she doesn't pick up on my anxiety.

Gillian's head slowly appears in the doorway followed uncertainly by the rest of her. 'I hope you don't mind me letting myself in. But when the door was open and there was no answer—'

'It's fine, honestly,' I lie. 'You're very thoughtful to check on me. But I was just letting in some fresh air. I have a headache.'

'It's very warm today.' Gillian states the obvious. 'Maybe you need some water?'

I don't reply. I'm not sure what Gillian expects will happen here. I'm not comfortable getting out of bed with her standing watching me, despite being fully dressed under the covers.

'I had some, thanks. I think I just need some sleep now,' I say, dropping a not-so-subtle hint.

'I wish I could say this was just a friendly neighbourly visit,' Gillian begins, and I notice her eyes drop to the tools I've left scattered on the floor next to the wonky floorboard.

'But it's not,' I finish for her, anxious to bring her attention back to me and away from Luke's tools.

'Unfortunately not.'

'The investment,' I say, my heart sinking.

Gillian nods. 'It's more about Luke, actually.'

'Is something wrong?' I ask. My heart is beating so furiously it feels as if it might burst through my chest. 'Luke's not here. He's not here.'

'I know.' Gillian nods with calm certainty.

My palms are clammy and beginning to sweat. This is too bizarre.

'I thought maybe you and I could talk,' Gillian says. 'Just one woman to another.'

I clench the duvet, drying my palms. 'Okay,' I say.

'Maybe I could make us some tea,' Gillian suggests. 'You look like you could use a cuppa. If you're okay with me in your kitchen, that is.'

Of course I'm not okay with that but I swallow hard, and, taking a deep breath I say, 'Yeah. Sure. I'll be down in a minute.'

Gillian backs out of the room and I hear her footfall on the stairs, descending much quicker and with more confidence than when she came up.

I hop up and gather all of Luke's tools. I stuff them into my underwear drawer. I take off my comfortable tracksuit and pull on a green dress with cream polka dots. It's not maternity wear but it's oversize and slides on effortlessly over my bump. I find a pair of open-toe wedges with a low heel and slide my feet in. They pinch and are uncomfortable on my swollen feet, but, glancing in the mirror, I feel more respectable and polished than I have in weeks.

I brush my hair and I don't have time for make-up, but this small effort has helped me feel more confident going downstairs to speak with Gillian. Whatever her concerns are about Luke, I feel better capable of ironing them out now than I did ten minutes ago.

There are two cups of tea waiting on the table when I come into the kitchen. Gillian has brought cake too. It's in a box in the centre of the table with the lid open.

'I hope you like carrot cake,' she says. 'It's my favourite.'

'I love it,' I say.

'Well, don't you look lovely,' Gillian says, opening a drawer and pulling out a knife. She moves to a cupboard and takes out a couple of small plates, seemingly familiar with where Luke and I keep our crockery.

'Wow. You certainly know your way around a kitchen,' I say as she places the plates on the table and slices into the cake.

Gillian stops cutting and looks at me to giggle. 'Ah, all these old houses are the same, aren't they?'

'Um,' I say, as I think about the old kitchen that was ripped out and replaced by this bespoke design shortly after we moved in. 'What's going on, Gillian?' I say, firmly. 'There's clearly something amiss. Luke reassured me these things take time, but—'

'Has he given you the old "it's the paperwork" problem?' she asks, placing a slice of cake on a plate and passing it to me.

I grimace.

'Ah, well, that answers that question.' She cuts another slice of cake for herself. 'The paperwork is tedious and boring but that's not exactly the problem.'

'Right,' I say, accepting what I've known all along. I get the distinct impression that Gillian has an issue with my husband.

Darcy's Dishes is a brand primarily directed at women, but that doesn't mean we can't have clever, efficient men working behind the scenes. It's hard not to take offence and keep my professional hat on.

'I'll be back at work as soon as this baby is born,' I say. 'I have no intention of taking a long maternity leave. I've built Darcy's Dishes from the ground up. I'm always going to be involved and present wherever possible.'

'Good. I'm glad to hear that,' Gillian says, digging her fork into her cake.

'Saying that,' I add, quickly, 'Luke and I are a partnership and we work best together.'

Gillian lowers her fork and runs her tongue across her teeth as if what I've just said is so difficult to digest it's put her off her cake.

'I know it may not seem like it right now, but don't lose faith in us,' I say. 'Luke and I are a powerful team, honestly. Since I've been sick, he's done an amazing job of stepping into my shoes, and as soon as I'm well again—'

'Darcy, I know how hard both you and Luke work. And I know you've had some health issues recently. That's why I've tried to be so understanding about Luke's reluctance to accept this posting, but really—'

'A posting?'

'In Ohio. We need a Darcy's Dishes face in the office there. If we want to expand throughout the US over the next few months, they need to know how serious we are.'

I feel like a deer in headlights. I hate that I'm so stunned and have no words.

Gillian's face pinches. 'Luke spoke to you about this, didn't he?'

I shove some cake into my mouth as frustration boils my blood.

'Not yet,' I say, my mouth half full. 'I guess it must have slipped his mind.'

'Hmm,' Gillian says, unconvinced. 'He's worried about you. I can completely understand. I know his reservations are because his

212

focus is on you and the baby right now. As they should be. But it's only for a couple of weeks in the States. Three weeks max. He'd be home before the baby is born, obviously.'

I nod, processing, and I hope my face doesn't appear as blank as my mind feels.

'Look, I've caught you off guard. I can see that,' Gillian says, stroking two fingers across her forehead as if she's appeasing a headache. 'And the last thing I want is to cause any upset for you. Or for Luke. Why don't you two have a little chat this evening? And I'll chase up this damn paperwork. Just send me a text when you've made your decision.'

'Yeah. Yes, of course.' I puff out, short of breath. The baby has decided that now is a good time to lean on my lungs.

'You're an amazing businesswoman, Darcy. And I can see you want this to work as much as I do. I know I can count on you to make the right decisions, can't I?'

Gillian's request is both inconsiderate and unnecessary. But I've played enough hardball in my time to know her threat is far from subtle. Either Luke goes to Ohio or we can kiss her money goodbye. Luke's presence in a stateside office will make no difference to growing our brand. We've been dipping our toe in international waters for a while now and I've learned it will all boil down to the right packaging and a colossal marketing budget. Gillian is that budget and I'm not about to piss her off. I'll have plenty of time to be assertive when the funds are secure.

Gillian smiles at me, warning me to get this sorted, and I smile back with a growing distaste for her which I hope I'm hiding.

She clears my empty plate from the table to the sink and the gesture feels less considerate and more dominating.

'Don't worry about that,' I say, glancing at her plate and the slice of cake she hasn't touched. 'I'll clean up later.'

Gillian moves her plate to the sink anyway. She closes the cake box and pats the lid saying, 'I'll leave this here for you. I'm so glad you enjoyed it.'

'Thank you,' I say.

I walk Gillian to the door and it takes all my self-control not to slam it behind her. I wait until she walks out of view before I close it and race to the downstairs bathroom to throw my guts up.

Christ, I hate carrot cake.

Chapter Thirty-Four

GILLIAN

Wednesday 10 July 2019

It's harder than usual to get out of bed this morning. I've picked my phone up, glanced at the screen with no notifications, and put my phone back down countless times. I thought I'd have heard from Darcy by now. She seemed so confident she could sway Luke's decision. I fully expected a confirmation text or call shortly after he got in from work, but there hasn't been a peep from her.

There's a knock on the door just as I'm about to get into the shower and I roll my eyes at the terrible timing.

'Just a minute,' I shout, hoping my voice will carry far enough.

Another knock sounds louder than the first and the light front door rattles on its hinges.

I slip on my dressing gown and push my feet into slippers.

There's more knocking and I can hear a deep male voice outside.

'She's not here,' he says.

'Give it a minute,' a female voice quickly retorts.

I recognise his voice first. Luke has never lost his English twang.

'I told you we should have called first,' Luke says.

'Knock again,' Darcy insists. 'One last try.'

Luke does as his wife asks and there's another loud pounding on the door. I hurry into the hall. I'm reaching for the door handle when I realise both bedroom doors are wide open behind me. I double back to shut them both quickly.

Finally, I open the front door and unsurprisingly find Darcy and Luke outside. Luke is wearing a smart, tailored navy suit with a crisp blue shirt and a white-and-navy pinstripe tie. His brown shoes are polished to perfection. He oozes charisma. And after all these years my heart still flutters like a silly schoolgirl's when his eyes meet mine. Darcy is draped on his arm – a flawless accessory completing his look. Her long, floral dress is colourful and I can only imagine it swishes when she walks. Weeks away from giving birth, she's more stunning than any average woman on an average day. Nearly twenty years may have passed but Darcy and Luke are still the same beautiful couple they were in school. The type you expect to see on the covers of magazines and in movies.

'I hope you don't mind us stopping by unannounced,' Darcy says, smiling as she strokes Luke's arm up and down, and I can't tell if it's a subconscious endearment or a subtle reminder that Luke is hers.

'Of course I don't mind. We're neighbours, aren't we?' I say, ignoring Darcy's dig at me for not calling before I dropped by her place yesterday.

I shift my eyes from Darcy's wide smile and blisteringly white teeth and on to Luke. He's holding a pretty box: pink-and-white candy stripes with some cream twine wrapped around to secure it.

'You brought cake,' I say, knowingly.

Darcy's smile widens even more.

'It's a Victoria sponge. I hope that's okay,' Darcy says.

'She made it herself,' Luke adds. 'I keep telling her she needs to put the recipe in her next book. It's delicious.'

'I haven't even had breakfast yet,' I say, glancing towards the kitchen. 'But what the heck, how can I turn down cake?'

I turn my head over my shoulder and double-check that the bedroom doors have remained firmly closed behind me. Satisfied, I step to one side and say, 'Come on in.'

Darcy and Luke walk past me and I close the door behind us, as the fine hairs on the back of my neck twitch and warn me that this is not a good idea. They don't belong in my space. Alarm bells are ringing in my head. Really, I know it's tinnitus. I also know stress triggers it. As hard as I try to hide it, Darcy and Luke – together – intimidate me. I think about making up a reason they'll need to leave. I look at my phone, about to spit some excuses about having to dash to work. Darcy will understand, surely. The words are literally forming in my mouth when I look at Luke who is staring me down with wide, confident eyes. His arm is around Darcy's shoulders and he holds her close to him. The way he always has. And I remember. I remember exactly why I'm doing everything I'm doing. And I can't stop now!

'We won't keep you long,' Luke says, as he unwraps himself from his wife and walks towards the open kitchen area to place the cake box on the nearest countertop.

I should probably offer them tea or coffee. But I don't. 'You'll have to excuse my appearance,' I say, hating how Darcy's beauty makes me feel about myself.

'This is a little unexpected, I know. Sorry,' Darcy says. 'You did say to text, but Luke really, really felt we needed to discuss this further. All three of us.'

'Right,' I say, as I smile at Luke.

'I hope you don't mind,' Luke says, glancing over his shoulder at the couch in the compact living area, and I know he wants me to invite them to sit.

I tilt my head towards the couch and exhale as I glide my arm through the air and say, 'Please.'

Darcy and Luke sit down. I stay standing.

'So,' I begin, keeping my tone welcoming and warm. 'How can I help? Ask anything you need to.'

Neither of them speaks and the only sound in the flat is the low hum of the fridge in the kitchen.

'Guys, please. Don't be shy. Let me set your worries at ease.'

Darcy is smiling, but Luke's face is blank and hard to read. I have a headache. Luke Hogan hasn't changed in twenty years, I decide.

'The doctor wants Darcy to spend the remainder of the pregnancy in hospital, but I've promised to take care of her,' Luke says, as he places his hand on Darcy's knee and squeezes gently, but his eyes are locked on mine. 'I promised to take care of her, you see. To take care of everything. But I can't do that from Ohio.'

'Oh gosh, I didn't realise,' I say, shaking my head. 'I do hate that I've put you in this position, but the US office are adamant they want you present as all this kicks off. If we don't give this a shot, I'm concerned our aims for expansion will go under.'

'We *do* understand,' Darcy says, her lip twitching nervously. 'This has to happen, it's just—'

'The baby,' I cut across her.

Darcy nods and her eyes gloss over. 'We've wanted this for years. Haven't we, Luke?'

'Yeah,' Luke says, shaking his head and flicking his tongue against the roof of his mouth. 'But—'

'But not like this,' Darcy interrupts, taking a deep breath, and her shoulders rise and fall dramatically. 'I'll just have to go into hospital.'

'Oh honey,' Luke says.

'I've made my decision, Luke,' Darcy says firmly. 'We can call the doctor this afternoon and make all the arrangements.'

Luke's head is low, and his voice is too. 'This isn't what you want.'

'It is,' Darcy says, sliding her finger under his chin and tilting his head up until he has to look at her. 'It's our future.'

'You know, maybe I could help,' I say, and both their heads turn towards me as if they've almost forgotten I'm here. 'I could stay with Darcy while you're away, Luke.'

Darcy's eyes widen.

'Oh,' Luke says.

'It's no problem. It's short term. Just a change of bed, really,' I say.

'Really? Would you? Could you?' Luke seems lighter already.

'Absolutely. I mean, I'll have a few things to organise but it should be all fine. And it will give Darcy and me a chance to get to know each other even better. Won't it?' I say, turning towards her.

Darcy is fidgeting as she says, 'We couldn't ask you to do that, Gillian.'

'You're not asking. I'm offering.'

'What do you say?' Luke asks, looking at Darcy with worried eyes. 'It's not really a good idea for you to be on your own right now, honey?'

'Um . . .' Darcy muses and I wish I could tell what she's thinking. Although I'm confident I know what is in Luke's head. *This is perfect.*

'Darcy.' Luke calls for his wife's attention as she seems uncharacteristically lost. 'Is this happening? Am I going to Ohio?'

'Mm-hmm,' Darcy says, but I don't miss how forced her smile is as she slides closer to the edge of the couch, and I wonder if she's as uncomfortable as she appears. 'Go over there and impress the hell out of 'em.'

Luke leans forward and kisses Darcy's forehead. His tone is heavy with trepidation as he says, 'I'll do us proud.'

'I know you will,' Darcy says, standing up slowly with her hand supporting her lower back. 'This will be good.' And it's obvious that it's herself she's trying to convince.

I already know it will be good. *It will be great.*

Chapter Thirty-Five

GILLIAN

Thursday 11 July 2019

My fingertips are numb and my body trembles with cold. A gentle wind whips past me, pinching at my arms and legs. The ground is cool and damp beneath me and I can feel blades of long grass tickling my neck as they blow in a gentle breeze. I can't tell if my eyes are open or closed. I rub them and finally pick some stars out from around dark, thick clouds. The moon is hidden and the night is eerie and silent. The realisation that I have no idea where I am dawns on me slowly.

My dressing gown is twisted and uncomfortable. The belt is tangled too tightly around my chest, making deep breaths difficult, and the collar is trying to choke me. I stumble to my feet, shivering as the damp from the grass clings to the fluffy material of my dressing gown. I gasp when I find myself in a misshapen circle of paper and scrapbooks. It's too dark to read the words on the pages. But I know what they say. I know they're newspaper articles. And I know they're about some gruesome murder of a missing person. They always are.

Clouds part and moonlight dances across the grass, illuminating everything in shades of shimmering silver. The hedge. The patio. The back of the house. I'm in the back garden, I realise. A sense of relief washes over me that I haven't woken up miles from home in a random field just like before. But worry quickly follows. *What if someone sees me? They'll think I'm mad.* I bend and gather up the scrapbook and papers as quickly as I can. There's more than an armful. My haste affects my coordination and I'm dropping clippings almost as quickly as I'm gathering them up.

A light flicks on in an upstairs bedroom, casting a yellowish square on to the grass. I hurry more, constantly switching my gaze from the papers to the window and back again. I pick up the last page and jump out of the light just as the curtain twitches and the window opens.

'Oi, who's out there?' Eddie says, his voice groggy and laced with sleep.

I stand like a statue and wait, my heart beating furiously against my chest.

'Don't make me come out there,' Eddie says, sounding more assertive and more alert.

An owl hoots and flies overhead, startling me. I drop a couple of papers and the wind catches them and blows them right across the garden.

'Right. That's it,' Eddie bellows, furious now. 'I'm coming down. You better start running.'

The moment the window closes I dash across the garden, grab the paper and sprint towards the patio door of my flat. Being able to access my flat from the back of the house is one of the few things I like about a ground-floor apartment. I'm fumbling with the key when I hear racing footsteps crunch across the stony driveway. I expect Eddie to turn the corner at the side of the house and appear in the garden at any second.

'Whoever you are, you're going to be sorry you tried to break into my house. Do you hear me?' Eddie's voice is loud and threatening as he veers closer.

'Be careful, Eddie.' Kimberly's distinctive accent follows. 'Oh my God. Be careful.'

'I'm not the one who needs to be careful,' Eddie is shouting, but there's a contradictory wobble in his tone.

The door unlocks and I slide it back just as I hear Kimberly say, 'Gillian. Gillian, is that you?'

I freeze.

Kimberly is edging closer to me, unsure, in the darkness. I tumble the articles and scrapbooks out of my arms and on to the floor just inside the open door. I kick them further back with my foot and close the door as quickly as I can before Kimberly reaches me.

I turn around and step forward as if I've just come outside rather than trying desperately to get inside. I rub my eyes and sleepily I ask, 'What's going on?'

'Didn't you hear?' Kimberly asks, as Eddie scours the garden with a raised golf club.

I shake my head.

Kimberly seems confused. 'All the shouting, didn't you hear?'

'Shouting out here?' I point to where Eddie is poking the hedge with his putter.

Kimberly nods enthusiastically and she seems less nervous now. 'It was crazy. We didn't know what it was at first. We thought it might have been cats fighting or something. The noises were so strange. But then we could make out voices. Eddie thinks it was two women arguing.'

'What?' I shake my head. 'What would two women be doing in our garden in the middle of the night?'

'That's what I said,' Kimberly says. 'I thought it might be the neighbours.'

'Well that explains it, then,' I say. 'We should all go back to bed.'

'No. No. Eddie said the voices were too close. They had to be in the garden. We should get to the bottom of this. You know, in case they come back.'

'Okay, well, I'm going to leave you to it,' I say, hoping they'll tire themselves out and give up soon.

'Eddie thinks we should call the guards,' Kimberly says, reaching into her pocket for her phone.

'No. God. No. Don't do that!' My voice comes out much squeakier and higher pitched than I mean it to.

'Gillian, are you okay?' Kimberly asks.

'Look, this is actually really embarrassing but . . .' I pause as if the next words are difficult to find or even harder to say. 'It was me. I was shouting.'

'Oh,' Kimberly says, and I can tell I've made her uncomfortable.

'So, there's no need to call the cops,' I say.

'No. No, of course not.'

'And I'm sorry,' I add. 'I didn't mean to wake you.'

'Are you okay?' Kimberly asks, softly and genuinely concerned, and I know I'm not getting out of this without an explanation.

'It was a heated work call,' I lie, beginning to twitch. 'I stepped outside to get better reception. I honestly didn't realise I was being too loud.'

Kimberly tilts her head slightly. 'A work call in the middle of the night?'

'It's business hours internationally,' I say.

'Oh yes. Of course,' Kimberly says, noticeably relaxing. 'Do you often have to take late-night calls?'

'Don't worry,' I say, throwing in a girly giggle. 'I promise I'll be quieter next time. I really am so sorry for waking you.'

'No, it's not that. I just mean it must be exhausting having to deal with work stuff when you should be sleeping. No wonder you were frustrated.'

I take a deep breath. Kimberly is kind and caring. And in another set of circumstances I think we could be friends. I muse for a moment about how lovely that would be. About how we could go for coffee and walks and enjoy girls' nights out in fancy cocktail bars.

'Right! There's no one here,' Eddie says as he crosses the garden with the golf club by his side now. 'Whoever it was is long gone. Cheeky bastards. I'd say it was a drunken row. We'll probably get more of that sort of thing now that the pub down the road has reopened after refurbishment.'

'Oh, I forgot about that,' Kimberly says, her usual bubbly self once again. 'We should go there for a drink this weekend?'

'Yeah, maybe.' Eddie nods.

'You should come too, Gillian,' Kimberly says.

Eddie doesn't comment, clearly unimpressed by the idea.

'We should get back inside,' Eddie says. 'Whoever that was, I don't think they'll be back.'

'It's a pity you didn't get to use some of your killer tae kwon do moves on that hedge,' Kimberly teases, high-kicking her leg while slicing the air with her arms.

'Ah, Kim, leave it out,' Eddie grumbles.

Kimberly may only be messing around, but I've no doubt she could kick arse if she really needed to. I decide to bear that in mind, moving forward.

'Right. C'mon, let's get back to bed,' Eddie says. 'I'm wrecked.'

I feel my racing pulse ease.

'Yeah. Me too,' Kimberly says, linking her arm around Eddie's and dropping her head on to his shoulder as if he's her hero. 'Na'night, Gillian.'

'Goodnight,' I say, reaching for the handle of my patio door, but I don't go inside. I wait and listen.

'What was she doing out here?' Eddie whispers after they turn away.

I strain my neck trying to hear as much as I can before they walk out of earshot.

'Long story. I'll tell you about it in bed,' Kimberly says.

Eddie groans. 'Don't get too friendly with her, eh, Kim. There's something off about her. I don't trust her.'

'Don't be silly. She's lovely,' Kimberly says with a sigh as they turn the corner.

Chapter Thirty-Six

GILLIAN

Thursday 11 July 2019

Inside, I press my back against the patio door and slide to the floor. I'm shivering and my teeth chatter. Drawing my knees close to my chest and tucking myself into a ball helps. I've no way of knowing how much time has passed before I'm calmer and warmer, but it's dawn outside when I finally look up. I groan inwardly and close my eyes again when my messy flat greets me. It almost looks as if the place has been burgled, except, of course, the furniture hasn't budged. Sheets of paper are strewn everywhere – on the floor, the couch, the kitchen countertop. It's as if giant pieces of confetti have rained from the ceiling. They are in fact pages of old newspapers, crisp and yellowed with age. Some are large pages ripped from broadsheets and discarded on the floor. There are tabloid pages too, some ripped in half, some crumbled into misshapen crinkly balls, and some don't seem to have been touched in years. I pick up the page nearest to me and check the date. 1999. I do the maths in my head. I would have been eighteen then and in my final year in school. There's an article circled in red pen and the heading catches my attention immediately.

Extension Approved For Exclusive Private School in Dublin

Minister for Education Frances Black has today said she is delighted to announce the expansion of a science and enterprise wing at St Peter's, the already large school in west County Dublin. Speaking from her office she said, 'St Peter's is a fantastic school which up until now has been private. However, from next September St Peter's are proud to announce a scholarship for a number of children to attend without paying fees thanks to the generosity of businessman Andrew Buckley. The Buckley Bursary will be open for applications to children from any county and is based on academic achievement.

Mr Buckley is out of the country on business and unavailable to comment. However Mr Martin McEvoy, principal at St Peter's, said he was confident speaking for both men when he said, 'Andrew Buckley has long been a friend of St Peter's. He is a man who places great emphasis on academic achievement. He is beyond pleased to offer this opportunity to deserving young people. And I very much look forward to welcoming Buckley Bursary students to our school in the coming academic year.'

Neither the school nor Buckley & Co would answer speculation that a large sum of money was offered to the council in order to obtain the necessary planning permission. They also refused to confirm if Buckley & Co are funding the new build.

One thing is for certain: some very lucky children will be crossing the steps of St Peter's next autumn without paying a penny.

'Bullshit,' I hiss, as if anyone is listening. 'Utter bullshit.' Andrew Buckley firmly believed in class. People had boxes and they should stay in them. Private education was for the wealthy. The special. I heard him say it with my own ears. This article makes him out to be something he wasn't. He wasn't understanding, that's for sure.

I rip the paper in half and a long-overdue sense of relief washes over me. I tear again. Quarters. The sound of ripping paper hangs in the air for a moment like a glorious melody. I tear again and again, shrieking loudly with each satisfied rip.

When the pieces of paper are too small and finicky to tear any more, I flop out flat on the floor, exhausted. I'm about to close my eyes, content to drift to sleep on this very spot, when I notice something pinned to the fridge door. I pull myself up and drag myself over. I pull off the huge magnet that says 'I Love Guinness', and my hands are trembling as I catch the page underneath. It's yellowish and somewhat crinkly, but I can tell it was once white. There are faint blue lines running horizontally across it. They're so faded they're hard to see, but I know this is a page once torn from a school exercise book. In the centre of the page is a large, red love heart. It's hand drawn and bigger on one side than the other and inside are the words 'Luke n Tina 4EVR'. I drop the page.

Chapter Thirty-Seven

TINA

Friday 14 April 2000

Today is usually my least-favourite day of the year. Awards day. We're all crammed into the sports hall. The hum of a few hundred teenage voices whispering is low and deep and vibrates in my chest. There are medals for the sports teams and they all whoop and cheer each other like hooligans. Usually several students are singled out as sports stars of the year. Someone who scored the winning goal at the football final, or the captain of the hurling team. They still get a medal but a little something extra too, perhaps a book token that will inevitably land in the bin because heaven forbid they might be seen reading a book, they'd never live down the reputational damage.

There's acknowledgment for academic achievements too. An English essay so well written the teacher just has to read it out onstage. Or the science geek who has been getting straight As all year. In my time at St Peter's I've never once been invited onstage or received a medal or a voucher. I usually sit through the entire boring ceremony without talking to or cheering for a single person.

But this year is different.

A few months ago, when one of the girls from my English class said, 'Oi, you're that one who likes scrapbooks, aren't you?' I held my breath and waited for the inevitable teasing to follow, just like that last time she embarrassed me for collaging.

But when I didn't reply, Gillian glared at me and said, 'Well are ya?'

Realising it wasn't just a rhetorical question I cleared my throat and said, 'Erm. Yeah. I do like them. Yeah.'

'Right,' she said, her bright smile and straight teeth too close to my face. 'Miss Arlington has asked us to put together a yearbook.' She points to herself and then to some of her friends who have come to stand beside her and stare at me.

'Oh.' I smiled, thinking how exciting that task must be.

'But,' she said, scrunching her nose. 'We'd rather boil our heads.'

My excitement plummeted and I wondered why she was telling me all this.

'You like all that kind of crap though, dontcha?'

'I've never made a yearbook before,' I admitted, sensing where this was going.

'Well, do you want to do it or not?'

'Yeah. Yes. I'd love to.'

'Jesus, relax,' she said, and she turned to face her friends as they shared a giggle.

I took a deep breath and tried to curb my enthusiasm.

'Right, so. You've agreed to it. You can't back out now,' she said.

'I won't. I'll do a great job. It will be really good, I promise.'

'Yeah. Okay. Whatever. But this means we don't have to do anything, right? I mean, you're taking all the responsibility and you can't change your mind.'

I nodded so enthusiastically my neck hurt and they all walked away laughing.

So, when the moment finally comes at the end of the long ceremony to hand out the yearbooks, I can barely contain my excitement. I haven't been able to eat all morning. Bubbles of nervous energy pop in my stomach and my knees bob up and down, and I can tell I'm shaking the whole bench, as every now and then someone from the other end will stare at me with an angry scowl.

'I must say this year's yearbook has exceeded all expectations,' Principal McEvoy says as he stands centre stage with a freshly printed yearbook clutched close to his chest.

It's thick and glossy and it looks better than I even hoped.

'Could the team behind this clever masterpiece please stand up,' Mr McEvoy asks.

My smile is so big my jaw aches. I think about how surprised our principal and teachers will be to discover I single-handedly put the book together. They'll be more impressed than ever, no doubt.

I'm just about to get to my feet when loud cheering and clapping erupts, and I look behind me to see Gillian and her friends standing up behind me.

'Come up here girls,' Mr McEvoy says, beckoning to them. 'Not only have you done yourselves proud, you've done the whole school proud.'

I shake my head as the girls shuffle out from their position on the bench and begin walking towards the stage. A couple of them snigger as they pass me. Someone taps my shoulder and tears gather in the corners of my eyes as they pass me a yearbook. I turn it over and read the names printed on the back. Gillian Buckley is printed in cheery comic sans. There are several others below. The names of all the girls currently walking up onstage are there. But my name is missing.

I flick through the pages, stopping to sniffle back tears or to drag the sleeve of my jumper across my eyes to catch the ones I hold back. All my work is here. The articles I wrote about the hurling team. The collage of science equipment and experiments spans a double page. I've done my best to make sure every single student is mentioned at least once. I flick right to the back page as the girls reach the stage and the principal and vice-principal pass them a huge bouquet of colourful flowers each and sing their praises.

I shake my head and look away, my eyes dropping to the final page in the yearbook. My name *is* here after all. Gillian must have added this part at the last minute. It's only a single page, but she hasn't forgotten me, after all. It's such a lovely surprise and I can feel excitement return. There's a photo of me that I think was taken when I started in the first year. I'm young and innocent and smiling as I faced an unknown future. There's a subheading under my name in brackets. It says 'Most Likely To Be Alone' in a large, bold font. And there is an unmissable black arrow pointing towards my photo. Underneath my smiling face is a hand-drawn love heart with the words 'Luke n Tina 4EVR' scribbled inside. My heart flinches as I recognise it. It's one of the doodles from my scrapbook.

I'm surrounded by laughter. Loud, throaty guffaws ring in my ears as other students discover the back page. Some of them point and stare, others don't even care. But everyone has seen it. *Everyone.* My cheeks are on fire and I feel as if Gillian's hands are curled tightly around my neck. I can't breathe. I glance over my shoulder at the door of the gym. It seems miles away through a sea of laughing kids. But I'm about to stand up and make a run for it, when I feel a hand on my shoulder.

My heart sinks lower when I discover it's Darcy Flynn. No doubt she wants to have a go at me over the stupid Luke and Tina doodle. *God, why am I so pathetic?*

'Are you okay?' Darcy asks.

Her simple question rattles me.

'Don't let them get to you. They're just bullies.'

My mouth is open but no words are coming out. I can't understand why Darcy isn't annoyed. I would be. She must be embarrassed at the very least. I can hear whispering about her and Luke too.

'We only have another couple of months left in school and then you never have to see or think about them ever again,' Darcy says.

I clutch the yearbook close to my chest, Darcy's words hurting more than anything Gillian has done. She's right. I don't have long left at St Peter's and what am I supposed to do then? *Oh God.*

'You're better than them,' she says. 'The yearbook is lovely. The best one yet.'

'You know I did this?'

Darcy nods. 'Yeah. Course. I remember you like collaging and I saw you working on something most nights recently. It's great, Tina. You should be proud.'

Luke catches Darcy and me talking from the corner of his eye and slight horror flashes across his face. 'Darcy, c'mere,' he calls to her as if I'm a bacterium and getting too close to me might make her ill.

'Coming,' Darcy chirps. 'See ya round, Tee,' she adds, patting my arm fondly with the back of her hand.

Tee, I think. Tee. I've never had a nickname before. I like it.

The ceremony seems to come to a sudden, abrupt end and everyone stands up. It's noisy and crowded as people push and shove their way towards the door. Gillian is swallowed into the crowd and soon all I can see is the back of her head as she chats with friends. I wait for the familiar, empty feeling of loneliness to encompass me, the one that holds me tightly in its clutches, some-times for days. But it doesn't come. Instead a warm, satisfied feeling fizzes in my veins and I stare at Gillian, so glad her back is turned. I hope she keeps it that way because then she won't see me coming.

Chapter Thirty-Eight

DARCY

Friday 12 July 2019

Luke's suitcase is open on the bed. I said I thought he needed a bigger one if he's going to be away for a couple of weeks, but he didn't take my advice. There's no method to his packing. He has several shirts in an array of colours folded and placed to one side, but he hasn't decided what suits to bring or what ties. I've tried making suggestions about which tie is best with which shirt but Luke grunts and turns his back, and I can tell he's flustered and doesn't want to be going.

I try to make it easier for him, telling him how excited I am that Gillian will be staying while he's away, but he can see through my lies as if I am made of glass.

'How many pairs of socks do you think I'll need?' Luke asks, as he opens his underwear drawer.

I laugh at the mundane question. 'Seven,' I suggest.

'Seven?' Luke squeaks as if I'm mad. 'For a fortnight.'

I laugh louder. 'I'm sure they have washing machines in Ohio, Luke.'

Luke scowls, clearly not finding me funny. 'I suppose I can pick up anything I need in the shops when I get there.'

'Exactly,' I say.

Luke opens the top drawer of the chest of drawers. It's my underwear drawer, not his.

'Oops,' he says, closing it again. 'Wrong drawer.'

But before he walks away he opens it again and pulls out a screwdriver, asking, 'What's this?'

'It's a screwdriver,' I say.

I completely forgot they were there, I think, hating that Luke has found them at the worst possible time with his flight in just a few hours. I don't want to get into a conversation about money and bills today. A shiver runs down my spine as I'm reminded of the rat problem too. I haven't heard from the exterminator. He was supposed to be back from his holidays by now. I must give him another call.

'I know what it is, Darcy,' Luke says, pointing the silver end of the tool towards me. 'But I don't know why it's hiding among your thongs.'

'Oh, erm . . . ' I can't seem to think quickly. *Damn baby brain.* 'I was measuring up for the new television.'

'Really?' Luke raises a single eyebrow.

'Mm-hmm,' I say.

'Measuring for the new television you said you didn't want and asked me not to buy.'

'Well, maybe I changed my mind.'

'And you were measuring with a screwdriver.'

I shrug as Luke stares at me, waiting for a better explanation. 'I just grabbed whatever tools were nearest. That place gives me the creeps – it's so dark. And what's that smell? Do you know it smells rank in there?'

'This is why we should have bought the shed with the window,' Luke says. 'I told you.'

I feel awful for lying but I'll open up the floor again, and while Luke's away I'll go through all the bills he has stashed down there. Hopefully they won't even be an issue by the time he gets back. Gillian's funds should be transferred soon and then I can get us back in the black. It will be a nice surprise for Luke to come home to and it will help me to feel useful again. I'm so excited thinking about the company being solvent again.

Luke pulls out the chisel and wrench. He tuts and shakes his head. 'Right, I'll put these back so you don't have to go in the shed again.'

'Your taxi will be here soon,' I say. 'Why don't you leave the tools there?' I point to the top of the dresser. 'You need to finish packing. Do you have your passport and tickets?'

Luke places the tools down and walks towards the wardrobe. 'Passport in my suit pocket. Tickets on my phone. And Gillian says a driver is picking me up at the airport when I arrive so I won't have any trouble finding the hotel.'

'Sounds good,' I say, my eyes dropping to the wonky floorboard that bounces every time Luke steps on it. He doesn't seem to notice.

'Speaking of Gillian, I thought she'd be here by now,' Luke says. 'Did she say what time she was coming?'

'Stop worrying,' I say, wishing I could take my own advice. 'Gillian knows your flight is today. She'll be here.'

'Yeah,' Luke says, as he glances restlessly at his watch. 'I just don't want you to be on your own.'

'I know. But I still wish Gillian wasn't coming to babysit me.'

Luke stops packing to look at me. 'I know you don't like to hear it, Darcy. But you need taking care of, and Gillian knows we have no family. Besides, she offered. We couldn't exactly say no and offend her.'

'Yeah.' I shrug. 'She's just hard to make conversation with.'

'Talk about Darcy's Dishes. Fill her in on all your great ideas and plans for the future. Use this time to really show her how awesome you are.'

I smile, and getting as close to my husband as my bump will allow, I wrap my arms around him. 'This will all be worth it, won't it, Luke?'

'I hope so,' Luke says, dotting a kiss on my forehead before he slips away from me and finishes packing.

It takes a lot of effort to lower myself into the corner armchair where I sit and watch my husband get ready to leave. I have a sinking feeling I wish I could shake off. I usually tell Luke everything. I have for twenty-one years, but I don't think I can tell him how I feel now. I can't tell him I'm scared that if he leaves, he'll miss the birth, or that Gillian kind of creeps me out, or that we have rats in our house and I can't get anyone to help me.

I must have fallen asleep because I'm groggy when Luke kisses my cheek, and when I open my eyes I find him standing beside me wearing his powder-grey suit. My favourite. His case is packed and standing upright beside him and he says, 'It's time to go.'

I rub my eyes and Luke helps me to my feet.

'What? Already?' I say.

Luke smiles and kisses me. 'Gillian is downstairs,' he says. 'She arrived a few minutes ago.'

'Oh.'

'She says she'll move in gradually over the weekend and she'll be here full-time from Monday or Tuesday.'

'Really. Living here from Monday. Wow.'

Luke tilts his head and half smiles. 'You don't want to be alone for long.'

'You don't want me to be alone for long,' I correct.

Luke's smile widens. 'Well, yes. That's true. Not this close to the baby coming.'

I sigh.

'My taxi is outside, honey,' he says.

My stomach somersaults. 'So soon?'

Luke nods.

'Okay,' I say, trying to seem confident. 'I'll miss you.'

'I'll miss you too. I'll call you as soon as I land.'

'Do. Definitely do,' I say.

'And I'll tell you all about the office.'

'Tell me everything.'

'I will. Of course, I will. I'll be calling so often you'll get sick of the sound of my voice.'

'I could never get tired of your voice,' I say.

Luke and I walk hand in hand down the stairs. A delicious smell wafts from the kitchen and greets us in the hall.

'Three-bean risotto,' I say, recognising the distinctive scent.

'Gillian is making dinner,' Luke says, as if the smell isn't hint enough. 'Another recipe from your cookbook.'

I stare at the barely ajar kitchen door and wonder why the hell Gillian is cooking dinner in *my* kitchen.

'She asked me what you liked to eat. I didn't know what to say so I directed her towards your cookbook,' Luke says.

I can understand Luke not knowing what to say because I'm completely lost for words right now.

Luke winces and I can tell he feels uncomfortable too.

'She's really planning to make herself at home, isn't she?' I say.

'Seems so.' Luke pulls a face.

'Oh, Luke. What are we getting ourselves into?'

He gathers me into his arms and we sway together on the spot. A boat adrift at sea, weathering an unexpected storm.

The taxi driver honks his horn impatiently.

'I have to go,' Luke says, slackening his arms around me, but I cling on tight. I'm not ready to let go.

He kisses the top of my head that sits, as always, just under his chin. 'Think of how different everything will be a month from now.'

'Yeah,' I say, snuggling closer to him. 'Everything will be fine.'

The horn honks again.

'Oh for goodness' sake,' Luke grunts, letting me go to pick up his suitcase. 'I'm coming. Okay. I'm coming.'

The kitchen door swings open and Gillian comes into the hall. She's wearing the apron that I bought Luke a couple of Christmases ago. At least she has it turned back to front so the cheeky 'Naked Chef' lettering isn't visible. But I cringe nonetheless as she's suddenly privy to our private joke.

'You're off, then?' she says.

Luke nods.

The damn horn honks for a third time.

'Good luck,' Gillian says. 'You'll do great. And I'll be speaking to you on the conference call first thing on Monday.'

'Monday.' Luke nods.

Gillian copies the nod, smiles and turns back to the kitchen.

'Take the weekend to explore the city. Find your feet,' I suggest.

'Yeah. Yeah I will,' Luke says.

'I love you.'

Luke hugs me tightly and says, 'I love you too, honey. Bye.'

'Bye.'

I stand in the doorway, watching and waving, as Luke gets into the taxi and they drive away. But I don't close the door. Even when it turns the corner and he's out of view. Instead, I stand and watch life on our street. Our beautiful street that looks as if someone cropped it from the pages of a magazine. Outside is awash with vibrant colours. The sky is clear and baby blue, the row of red-brick houses across the street that mirror ours seem to stand taller and more attractive than ever. And leaves dance in the air when a summer breeze whips by, rustling the trees. Suddenly I feel as if it's been a long, long time since I've belonged in that outside world. I long to walk down the street and inhale the smell of summer. I long to walk. To stretch my legs and wander far. And as Gillian comes out of the kitchen again with a wooden spoon in her hand, I expect her to ask if I'm hungry, but instead she says, 'You're not going to believe this but I've forgotten my phone. It's like my arm. I can't function without it.'

Gillian doesn't have to explain. My phone was like a body part for me too until recently. We diverted all Darcy's Dishes' calls to Luke's phone to give me some rest. But I miss the buzz terribly; now the only notifications I get on my phone are Facebook ads or the odd text from a friend.

'Go. Go get it,' I say.

'I won't be long,' Gillian says, taking off the apron and dropping it and the greasy wooden spoon on to the hall table. 'Dinner is ready, help yourself.'

Chapter Thirty-Nine

TINA

Saturday 13 July 2019

'Hello. Hello.'

The female voice outside the door of my flat is so faint and unsure that if I wasn't just about to open the door and head outside, I'd certainly have missed it.

'Is anyone there?'

I don't recognise the voice. I take a step back from the door and glance around the flat. It's gleaming. I spent hours tidying up. All my scrapbooks are neatly stacked on my dresser in my bedroom. I've shredded and recycled newspapers, cropping anything of interest first and adding them to a clear folder that I'm keeping in the top drawer next to the glue and scissors.

'Hello,' the voice says again, more assertive this time as she finally knocks on the door.

I check that both bedroom doors are closed behind me, and, content that the flat seems relatively normal, boring even, I decide to answer the door. I'm reaching for the handle when there's another louder knock and the voice calls, 'I've brought you those dust sheets I told you about. Sorry it's taken so long.'

I jerk my hand back and freeze, finally placing the voice. Rose, the pregnant cop from that damn Pilates class, knows where I live. *Great. Just great.*

'Tina. Are you there? I can see a car in the drive.'

I sigh, knowing that her inquisitive nature means she's not likely to give up until I answer.

'I missed you at class. And Billy, my other half, says he'll need the sheets back by next week for a job he's got on, so I thought I'd call round this morning.'

She's much louder and more confident now and I can't be sure, but I pick up on an air of irritation. As if she knows I'm in here and ignoring her.

She knocks again and quite firmly says, 'Look, the sheets are just an excuse. Polly thought you might be sick or something and I just want to check in.'

I think about wrapping my hair in a towel and pretending I've just got out of the shower, but I'm worried she'll expect me to invite her in. There's a cake box on the shelf and I could probably distract her with a slice of whatever's inside and a cup of tea, but there's always the worry that she'll start snooping – even just with her eyes. And with that monster baby bump it's practically a guarantee that she'd need to use the loo at some stage. It would only take her opening the wrong door, even accidently, for everything to come crashing down. *No.* I can't let a cop into my flat. Not ever.

'Well, hello. This is a lovely surprise,' a second female voice carries through the door. I recognise her accent immediately. It's my upstairs neighbour. *Dammit.*

'Kim,' Rose says, sounding genuinely shocked. 'This really is a surprise. How are you?'

Nervously, I tiptoe closer to the door and squint through the peephole. Kimberly and Rose are standing face to face and smiling.

While my view is limited, the flat door is flimsy and old and is no barrier to my effort to listen in. There are two large shopping bags at Rose's feet, no doubt full of these treasured old sheets for painting. The bags look bulky and awkward, and certainly not ideal for a heavily pregnant woman to horse around town with. Kimberly, as always, is wearing tight gym gear that fits her like a second skin and leaves nothing to the imagination as it flaunts her slender body shamelessly.

'I'm good, thanks,' Kimberly says. 'Did you enjoy class today?'

'Loved it,' Rose says. 'And I'm definitely going to try all those suggestions you mentioned to bring labour on. I just want to meet this baby, already.'

'They're old wives' tales, really,' Kimberly says. 'But worth a try. I'll keep my fingers crossed it happens soon.'

There's a brief silence, and not being able to see their expressions clearly is making the conversation hard to follow, but I can tell they're both feeling awkward. I decide it's probably the first time they've bumped into each other outside of the gym.

'I didn't know you did one-to-one classes,' Rose says, edging closer to my door and pointing at my flat.

'Oh no. I don't,' Kimberly says. 'Although maybe it's something I should look into. I'm just getting home from work. I live upstairs, actually.'

'No way,' Rose says. 'I didn't know you and Tina were neighbours.'

'Tina?' Kimberly shakes her head.

'I've got some dust sheets for her,' Rose says. 'They're heavy auld things, so maybe I could just leave them here and you could let her know I stopped by when you see her? She's planning to redecorate for the baby. She has ages yet, but she's so excited, bless her.'

'Tina,' Kimberly repeats, as if she doesn't like the taste of my name in her mouth.

'Tina. Tina, oh gosh this is embarrassing, I've just realised I don't know her last name,' Rose says. 'The wee red-haired girl from class.'

'Oh, Gillian,' Kimberly says.

Oh shit!

My eye is watering as I press it ridiculously close to the peep-hole, as if that will give me a better view. I wish I could see their faces more clearly. I need to read them. I need to see their reaction.

'No. No. It's definitely Tina I'm looking for,' Rose says. 'Gimme a minute. God, I'm just dreadful with names.'

'Gosh, I don't think I know any Tinas.' Kimberly sounds confused.

'Ah, don't feel bad. She only joined two or three weeks ago,' Rose explains. 'She's very quiet. Keeps to herself, really. Polly said you waved to her last week. I'm sure that made her feel welcome.'

'Did I?' Kimberly asks, and I don't need to see her clearly to know her cheeks are red, because I can hear the embarrassment in her voice. 'I can't say I remember. But I've been teaching a lot of extra classes recently – my boyfriend and I are trying to save for a deposit on a house.'

'Lots of new faces to keep track of, so.' Rose laughs. And I never understand why people do that, laugh when something isn't funny as if it makes them feel better to pretend it is. 'And don't worry. Tina isn't the type to take offence if you don't know her name,' Rose says as if she knows me well, or knows me at all, really. 'Sure, you're neighbours after all, I'm sure you'll get to know each other soon.'

'Hmm.' Kimberly's confusion is almost tangible. 'This is Gillian's flat.'

'Summers,' Rose says suddenly. 'That's it. Tina Summers.'

'Okay,' Kimberly says, patiently. 'But the girl who lives in this flat . . .' she points at the door, 'is Gillian. Gillian Buckley.'

'Oh. A female couple. I didn't realise,' Rose says.

'No. Just Gillian,' Kimberly says. 'Gillian lives on her own.'

'Really?' Rose backs away from the door and almost out of my view completely. 'I could have sworn Tina said she's not long moved in. And 106A was the only flat around here I could find that was recently to let. I must be losing my touch,' Rose says, and I can hear doubt creep into her tone.

Thank God!

'Addresses around here are so confusing,' Kimberly says. 'They're always changing when more old houses are split into flats. It's so easy to get mixed up.'

'Oh, this is a bit embarrassing, isn't it?' Rose says, picking up the two heavy bags effortlessly. 'Bloody baby brain. It has my senses all over the place.'

'Well, I won't tell anyone if you don't,' Kimberly says, and they both laugh again.

'Right, I better get out of your hair,' Rose says.

'Why don't you get one of your colleagues to double-check the address for you? There has to be some perks to being a garda, even if you are on maternity leave, right?' Kimberly says, as they begin to walk away and the sound of the driveway stones crunching under their feet makes their voices harder to hear.

Rose says something about wanting to catch up with everyone before the baby arrives and she adds more that I can't quite make out about stopping by the station.

Not if I stop by her first, I think. I fling open my bedroom door and grab the scissors from the top drawer of my dresser and race back into the hall, almost slipping on the tiles in my haste. My long, black coat is hanging by the door. It's my favourite, even in summer. It covers me from head to toe, zipping all the way up the front, complete with a floppy hood that hides my face perfectly. I slip it on, instantly too warm, and return to spying through the peephole. I wait until Rose walks out of the gate, yielding to the weight of her stupid bags, and Kimberly is safely behind her own front door before I hurry outside.

Chapter Forty

DARCY

Sunday 14 July 2019

There's a gentle knock on my bedroom door and before I answer, Gillian pops her head in and gingerly says, 'Oh good, you're awake.'

I don't tell her I've been awake for ages. I've so much on my mind. I'm waiting on a call or text from Luke to let me know he's arrived safely. And of course, the worry that seems to consume most of my waking moments is weighing on me. Money. Mainly, Gillian's money – and I wonder when is a good time to bring up the investment. For a busy woman she doesn't spend as much time on her phone as I used to. I know she's been dropped in at the deep end after her father's death, but I'm concerned that she's not chasing this much harder than she is. But I don't know how to bring it up without coming off as if I don't care about her dad. Because I do. I know how very hard it is to lose a parent. And I imagine that feeling is just as raw, estranged or not.

'I made you a little something,' Gillian says, pushing back the door and walking towards my bed with a tray in her hands.

I blush. 'Oh, you really shouldn't have gone to all that trouble.'

'It's no trouble.' She smiles. 'I know Luke makes you breakfast in bed every morning.'

I pull myself up, embarrassed. I'm surprised Luke shared something like that with her. He's usually so reserved. Sometimes painfully so.

'I love to cook and your kitchen is just fabulous,' Gillian says, hovering with the tray above the bedside table.

I set my sights on the glass of orange juice wobbling on the tray. I wait for Gillian to step away before I reach for the juice and drain the glass.

'Thirsty,' she laughs.

I nod.

'Do you mind if I join you?' she asks, pointing at the pair of matching bowls on the tray.

I wonder if Gillian is asking to sit on the edge of my bed the way Luke does some mornings, and I find myself losing my appetite. But feeling I can't exactly refuse, I shuffle a little closer to Luke's side of the bed and a little further away from Gillian as I say, 'Sure.'

Gillian passes me a bowl and I look inside.

'Thank you. I love granola,' I say, and it's hard to keep the tremble out of my voice.

'I know,' she replies, reaching for the second bowl before perching herself on the edge of my bed in Luke's usual spot.

God, I miss him already.

'Berries,' I say, looking at the colour of the mouth-watering summer fruits against the cool beiges of nuts and flakes.

Gillian has dusted the berries with a heavy helping of icing sugar. It's even more than Luke usually uses. I force myself to tuck in and I'm pleasantly surprised when amazing flavours burst in my mouth.

'Yum,' I say, feeling Gillian needs to hear my approval.

I wonder when she's going to eat hers. I don't want this to be another situation when I've munched away and she hasn't taken a bite. That was horribly uncomfortable last time. But who am I kidding? Whether Gillian eats her breakfast or not, this is all excruciatingly awkward. And I wonder how on earth I'm going to cope with this for a couple of weeks.

'This reminds me of school,' Gillian says, suddenly.

'Really?' I say, between mouthfuls. 'In what way?'

'You know. Sitting on each other's beds. Gossiping the way friends do.'

I don't say anything. Not least because Gillian and I were never friends in school. I don't remember her. I mean, certainly her name is familiar, being Mr Buckley's daughter, but it was a huge school and our paths never really seemed to cross. Once or twice maybe in all my years there.

'Good times,' Gillian muses. 'Such good times.'

I almost choke on a raspberry as I wonder if Gillian really remembers school that way. I can't say I ever sat on any other girl's bed gossiping. And I don't remember inviting anyone to sit on mine. Maybe the other girls did but I never noticed. I had Luke. His was the only bed I ever wanted to be in.

'Do you ever miss it?' Gillian asks.

'School?'

'St Peter's,' she says, and her nostalgic tone catches me by surprise. I thought Gillian ran away because she hated the place. I guess there must have been another reason. And I suddenly find myself curious to know why Gillian disappeared and where she was for the last nineteen years. And the slow, uncomfortable realisation that Luke and I have welcomed a stranger into our home hits me.

'Can you really believe it's almost been twenty years?' Gillian asks.

I can. My time in St Peter's feels like a lifetime ago and I never think about my schooldays. Not until recently when Tina rang in to *Good Morning, Ireland*. Luke never mentions school either. But I get the distinct impression that Gillian is the opposite. She almost seems to be pining for a time gone by.

'Twenty years. Gosh, makes you feel old when you think about it like that, doesn't it?' I laugh, hoping to move on from this conversation.

'Um,' Gillian says, and she almost seems irritated by my laughter. As if a giggle to lighten the toll of ageing has offended her. *She is so strange*, I think, as I remember an expression my mother was rather fond of. *If you want to know me, come to live with me.* She used to say it all the time when I was little. Always accompanied by a shake of her head and a bright smile. My father was a brilliant chef but he was also insanely messy. The kitchen would be a blitz of pots and pans when he worked. My mother said if they'd lived together before they were married, she'd have learned of his bad habits and would have run for the hills. She was joking, of course. My parents made an amazing team. He was messy, she was anally retentive. They were good for each other. They were great for me.

But the expression is apt here. A business partnership is a lot like a marriage, and I do wonder if Gillian and I can make this work. Maybe *I* should consider running for the hills now?

Gillian shifts granola around her bowl with the back of her spoon. And there's something poignant about how she sits with her shoulders slouched forward as if the weight of unhappiness is dragging them down. *All that money and she's still so miserable*, I think. And yet again I wonder if Luke and I are making a mistake. He should be here. For me and for our baby. Our family should come first. I hate myself for thinking it, but I don't want to end up like Gillian and her father. All the money in the world couldn't bring their family back together and now it's too late.

It doesn't take a rocket scientist to work out that Andrew Buckley's death has affected Gillian more deeply than she's letting on. Maybe she has regrets that they were still estranged, feels that she should have gone to his funeral after all. I know I would.

I'm about to tell Gillian that we need to reconsider Luke's stay in Ohio when her phone rings.

She reaches into her pocket and, glaring at the screen, she says, 'Sorry, I've got to take this.'

Gillian stands up and presses the phone to her ear, but she waits until she walks out of my bedroom, closing the door behind her, before she says, 'Hello. Gillian Buckley speaking.'

I set my bowl down on the tray and check my phone. There's still no word from Luke. I type a simple *I love you* and hit send. I've already asked how his flight was, if landing was okay and if he caught his connecting flight. I try not to read too much into his silence. I know better than most how exhausting travelling can be and I assume he's tucked up in a fancy Ohio hotel snoring his head off. I expect his first text will be long and grovelling and I'm lighter just thinking about it.

My attention is drawn towards my bedroom door. Gillian's anxious vibrato piques my concern.

'Stop calling me,' she shouts. 'Don't ever call this number again. I have nothing to say.'

I clutch my phone, my knuckles whitening and my hand trembling slightly as I dial Luke's number.

'Pick up. Oh please, please pick up,' I whisper as it rings and rings.

Chapter Forty-One

DARCY

Monday 15 July 2019

Morning light streams past the curtains that I forgot to close last night. I rub my eyes and start to wake up. The two half-eaten bowls of granola and empty glass are still on the tray beside my bed. The glass is grubby with a scattering of dried pulp stuck around the rim. I drag myself out of bed determined to make it downstairs today.

Gillian never came back upstairs after breakfast and now when I appear in the kitchen behind her, my legs shaky and my arms aching from the weight of the flimsy tray, she seems surprised to see me.

'I thought you were sleeping,' she says, setting down a cup with steam swirling from the top to hurry over and take the tray from me.

'I was,' I admit. I smile as if I have more energy than I do and, noticing Gillian's chalk-grey pencil skirt and lemon blouse, I ask, 'Are you going into work?'

'I have to,' she says, tumbling everything off the tray into the sink. 'But I've made you coffee. I was just about to bring it up to you, actually.'

'Oh,' I say, glancing at the countertop. There's a lonely cup waiting by the sink. There's no steam and I wonder how long it has sat there.

I must have made a face because Gillian says, 'I wasn't sure how you like it.'

'Black is good. Thanks,' I say.

Gillian folds her arms, saying, 'Go back up to bed; I'll bring it up to you.'

It sounds very much like an order, and I shake my head. 'Actually, I think I'll stay down here for a while. Maybe watch some TV or something.'

Gillian's eyes thin and I can tell she's irked, almost as if I'm the one intruding in her space.

'But we don't want you overdoing it,' she says. 'Luke will never forgive me if I don't take care of you.'

Her words are coated in a thick layer of familiarity, as if she knows my husband like the back of her hand.

'I'll take it easy.'

'Speaking of Luke . . .' she continues while pottering about in the kitchen, overly comfortable. 'How is he? Settling in all right?'

'It's early days yet,' I say, my tone laying claim to my husband.

'Does he like the hotel?' she asks.

'He, eh . . .' I tug at the collar of my T-shirt that suddenly feels too tight. 'He erm . . . he didn't actually say.'

'I hope he likes it. It's my favourite.'

I smile. I'm not sure what else to do.

'Right,' Gillian says, turning her wrist to glance at her watch. 'I've got to go. Get yourself back to bed, eh?'

'Mm-hmm,' I say as she leaves the room. I glance inside the cup of coffee waiting on the countertop. As I expected, a cold scum floats on top. *Gross.* I toss it into the sink and flick the kettle on to make a fresh cup.

'I'm serious,' Gillian says, and I feel her hand on my shoulder. I thought she had gone. Is she pinching the fleshy part between my neck and collarbone on purpose, or am I imagining it? 'I'm not leaving until I know you're tucked up, resting.'

I pull away from her and glare, waiting for her to realise she's way out of line.

'Bed,' Gillian reiterates with a click of her fingers.

A string of profanities is on the tip of my tongue. I'm aching to tell Gillian to get the hell out of my house. No amount of money is worth this! But then I remember how bad our finances are. Gillian has us over a barrel. I can't risk ruining the deal. I have to play nice. I need to speak to Luke. I'm more desperate than ever to reach him. He needs to come home.

'Bed.' I nod, feigning obedience as I forget about coffee and hurry back upstairs to grab my phone.

I dial Luke's number but there's no answer. Instead, I email him. Because even if he's lost his phone, if his baggage has gone awry, whatever the hell has gone wrong, he can always find his way to an online cafe and contact me from there. I discard my phone on the bedside table just as it begins to ring. I fumble to grab it again, praying it's Luke.

'Everything all right up there?' Gillian shouts from downstairs.

'All good!' I shout back. 'I'm just getting into bed now.'

Gillian doesn't say anything more and I hear the kitchen door close with a sudden bang.

My phone continues to ring and when I look at the screen I see Mildred's name flashing up.

'Hey there,' I answer. 'How are you?'

'Darcy, where are you?' Mildred asks.

I pause. I could swear I hear footsteps on the stairs again. I pull the phone away from my ear and jam it against my chest.

'Gillian?' I whisper, and wait.

Silence.

I wait. And wait.

Nothing.

'Darcy. Darcy, you there? Where are you?' Mildred's voice carries over the distant line.

I shake my head and drag my phone back to my ear. 'Sorry. So sorry, Mildred. I'm at home. Why? What's wrong?'

'I'm really sorry to bother you at home, but I've been trying to get hold of Luke all morning. His phone keeps ringing out. And he's not replying to emails, either.'

'He must have lost his phone,' I say.

'Erm, oh, okay . . .' Mildred says.

'Is something wrong?' I ask.

'I . . . eh . . .' Mildred is a stuttering mess.

'Look,' I say, sharply. 'I know I'm on sick leave but if something is wrong at work I need to know.'

'It's just . . .' Mildred takes a deep breath before she races on. 'I've been on the phone all morning trying to calm down most of our suppliers.'

'Mildred slow down,' I say. 'I didn't catch all that.'

'No one has been paid, Darcy. That's what's wrong. No one. Not the staff. Not the suppliers. Not a single soul.'

'That's crazy.' I shake my head as if she can see me. 'That can't be right. Luke took care of everything for the weeks ahead before he left. He was buried in paperwork. I practically had to beg him to come to bed the other night, he was so tired. There has to be some sort of a mistake. Have you spoken to the bank?'

'Yes. Of course,' Mildred snaps, as if that is a stupid question.

'And?' I snap back, equally as frustrated, worry mounting in the pit of my stomach.

'There's no money there. It's heavily overdrawn,' Mildred says.

My mind races. I don't understand. I thought we had more credit. Luke and I went over the books just a few weeks ago. We had months before we faced foreclosure. And that was without Gillian's investment coming in.

Mildred exhales, and I can hear her exhaustion. 'I'm sorry, Darcy. I know you're not well and stress like this is the last thing you need but—'

'You did the right thing calling me,' I say, cutting across her. 'We'll get to the bottom of this, try not to worry. Just don't take any more calls for now, the less people who know the better. I bet this is all a big mix-up and we'll have everything figured out by evening.'

'Okay. Okay,' Mildred says, and I can sense she's already reassured. I just wish I felt as confident as I sounded.

I'm breathless as I bend and reach under my bed for my laptop bag. I'm normally on my laptop all the time. I could lie in bed with it on my bump and still work on things. But I've been so ill recently I haven't used it in ages. I brush off the dust that has accumulated on top and by the time I crawl on to the bed, my heart is racing with a mix of worry and exhaustion.

Trying to log into my online account is a nightmare and an error message in stubborn red font appears on the screen every time I click ENTER on my password. I try manually answering the security questions.

What was your mother's maiden name?

Kinsella, I type confidently, but nothing happens.

Next I opt to reset the password, but the system informs me that my email is not the correct email associated with the account. It takes me a while to realise that I've been blocked from the account. The shock of it makes me numb for a moment.

Then I slam my laptop shut and hurry to the wonky floorboard as fast as I can. The gap between it and the next board is wider now and I slide my finger between them and pop the board. My nail snaps. I ignore the stinging and my bleeding finger and drag out the bundle of bills. I flick through them, smearing them with my blood. They're mostly household bills. Electricity. Phones. Heating. They're all overdue notices. Some of them are dated weeks ago, even months. I concentrate on the letter from the electricity company. Skim reading, I discover they've been in touch several times and this is the end of the line. If they don't receive payment within days they're cutting us off. There are handwritten sums on the bottom of some of the pages. I recognise Luke's writing as he tries to balance large numbers. There's a letter from the bank too. It's punctuated with capital letters and formal language adduces that we haven't paid our mortgage and the bank is preparing to repossess our house. I drop the letter and clutch my chest. What the hell is Luke trying to do? Destroy us? How could he possibly think he could hide something like this from me? We could lose our home before the baby is born. I tear off the end of one bill and wrap it around my pulsing finger. I stuff the rest of the paper back in the hole and slide the floorboard into place again.

Physically shaking, I grab my phone and call Luke again. I fully expect the phone to ring out. When I hear Luke's raspy voice say, 'Hello', I choke back emotion.

'Oh God you're there,' I say. 'What's going on? Why haven't I heard from you? We really need to talk.'

I expect Luke to pick up on my anger but he's silent apart from heavy breathing. As if he's been submerged under water and he's just come to the surface, catching his breath.

'Are you okay?' I ask.

There's a pause and the line cracks. I hear a throaty grunt like an animal in pain before Luke says, 'Yes.'

'Then why haven't you called? I've been worried,' I say.

Luke doesn't reply and the only sound on the line is his laboured breathing. I've never heard him so exhausted.

'Listen, Luke, I know it's still early over there and I'm sorry for waking you but there's something important I need to talk to you about. Okay?'

There's more deep breathing and Luke puffs out. 'Is it the baby?'

I sigh. 'The baby is fine. I'm fine.'

Luke's breathing lightens and I can sense his relief.

'But we do have a big problem,' I say. 'We have no money.'

'Okay,' Luke whispers, and I think I can hear a voice in the background.

'Okay?' I snap. 'No. Not okay. Didn't you hear me? We're broke. Mildred is going crazy; she's had staff and clients chewing her up and spitting her out. People haven't been paid.'

There's a guttural gurgle and I could swear Luke is drifting in and out of sleep. And I'm almost certain someone is talking to him. I can hear muffled mumbles followed by heavy breathing as if someone is there with him, telling him what to say. *Christ, I'm losing my mind.*

'I can't log into the account,' I say, becoming ever more paranoid as if someone is listening in or looking over my shoulder. It must be the stress. 'All the settings have changed,' I continue. 'The passwords, the security. All of it. I can't even get in to see what's happened. Did you do this?'

Luke doesn't reply.

'Our mortgage, Luke. You haven't paid our mortgage. I'm scared.'

'Gillian is taking care of everything,' Luke says, almost robotically.

'What?' I say, palpitations making it hard to breathe. 'This doesn't sound like you. Where are you? Are you alone?'

'Gillian is taking care of everything,' he repeats.

'I heard you,' I snap again, struggling not to shout. 'I just don't understand what the hell you're talking about. Gillian has no access to our accounts. She can't authorise payments. She can't save the roof over our head.'

'Gillian is taking care of everything.'

'Luke, I swear . . .' I grit my teeth. 'If you say that one more time . . .'

There's no reply.

'Look,' I say, taking a calming breath. 'I'll get on to the bank and get this sorted, but Luke . . .' A sadness washes over me and it's not money worries, or even panic, that Darcy's Dishes could be in real trouble. It's something else. Something I don't quite understand. 'You need to come home. Please. I need you here. Just come home.'

Luke doesn't speak. The line crackles.

'I'm serious, baby,' I say. 'Book a flight. Book it now. We'll face everything together when you get here. Just come home.'

There's silence on the line. Not even the sound of breathing.

'Luke?'

Nothing.

'Luke are you there?'

More silence.

'Luke, you're really freaking me out. Talk to me.'

There's a sudden inhale and Luke races to whisper, 'Darcy, run.'

A gasp. A muffled grunt. A loud bang. The line goes dead.

Chapter Forty-Two

TINA

Monday 8 May 2000

Gillian Buckley is pretty, I think, as I sit behind her in assembly twirling a strand of my hair around my finger. Her sand-red hair swirls around her shoulders in large, loose curls like beautiful leaves blowing in an autumn storm. My poker-straight, much-too-bright ginger hair is cropped and sits on my head like a bowler hat. A smattering of faint freckles dusts the bridge of Gillian's nose and spills across her cheeks. I wish I had freckles. Sometimes I think about drawing them on with pencil, but it wouldn't be the same.

But regardless of our differences, every now and then someone will mistake me for her. They tap me on the shoulder and say, 'Hey Gillian.' And when I turn and they realise their mistake, they walk away as if I'm infected with some sort of disease that they might catch if they stand too close.

I often wonder what it would be like to be even more like her. *Maybe if I let my hair grow*, I think. And if I stayed out of the sun, perhaps my skin would lighten until my face was as perfect as a china doll's too. People might think we are sisters. Twins, even. But I guess there can be only one Gillian Buckley.

Just as there is only one Darcy Flynn. And she has only one best friend. Me.

I've decided Darcy and I are best friends now. Lucky Darcy.

We've been practically inseparable since the yearbook fiasco.

Just last week, for example, Darcy said, 'Good morning', when we happened to be at our lockers at the same time.

And I said, 'Hello.'

It was fabulous.

And then a few days ago at lunch I asked if the seat beside her was taken and she quickly replied, 'No. You can take it.'

So, I sat down. Unfortunately, Darcy had to leave a couple of minutes later. It must have been something to do with class, because everyone else at the table left too, when I sat down. Darcy was in such a rush she didn't even get a chance to say where she was going or why she took her lunch tray with her.

I asked her about it later of course. 'What happened at lunch-time?' I said.

'What?'

'You were in a hurry,' I explained.

'Oh.'

'Is everything okay?' I said.

She shrugged and replied, 'Eh, yeah. Sure.'

I thought she seemed a bit stressed so I made her a cup of tea and snuck some biscuits out of the canteen into our dorm. She was so impressed, she smiled and said, 'Thanks, Tee.'

I've brought Darcy tea and biscuits every night before bed since. Most of the time she shares them with some of the other girls, the ones who expect it. But every now and then they fall asleep before I sneak back from the canteen, and Darcy is free to share them with me. Once we even sat on her bed and chatted the way the others do, because I know Darcy hates being alone as much as I do.

She told me all about hair and make-up and clothes. It's our little secret. Our conversation. *Our time.* The moment we shared is so special we pretend like it never happened, and none of the other girls know that Darcy and I have become best friends.

I'm late for this morning's assembly and when I try to slide into the seat next to Darcy she says, 'Sorry, Tee. Luke is sitting there.'

'Oh. Okay. I'll sit in the next row,' I say as I shuffle into the seats in front, but I don't think Darcy hears or sees me once Luke arrives. He's all red-faced and still in his rugby gear – a beautiful mess. He flops into the seat Darcy has saved for him and drapes his arm over her.

'Ah here,' she says, squirming away and laughing. 'You're all sweaty and gross.'

I can't believe Darcy spoke to Luke that way. I would never hurt him like that. Darcy doesn't deserve him. No one deserves him except me.

'Ew, did I just see that ginger nut try to sit here?' Gillian, the yearbook-credit-stealing bitch leans forward from the row behind Darcy.

'Tina?' Luke whispers, and I don't like the sound of his voice. 'Ah Darcy, c'mon. I thought you were going to stay away from her.'

Darcy says as I strain to hear, 'I'm not friends with her or anything. I'm just being polite really.'

'Well when your picture starts appearing in her creepy scrapbook, you'll be sorry,' Luke murmurs and the whole row erupts with laughter.

Darcy doesn't laugh. It so happens I do have a picture of her in my scrapbook. It's a beautiful one taken on sports day last year. The sun is shining right above her and her hair is all shimmering and glossy. It wasn't easy to snatch it from the noticeboard outside the sports hall without getting caught. I decide I'm going to rip it out and burn it.

'Enough. That's enough talking.' The vice-principal's squeaky voice carries over the speakers, and although she's probably onstage she's so short she's lost behind the podium and not visible to any of us. I laugh.

'I said, that. Is. Enough,' she snaps again, and the chatter slowly fades away until there is nothing more than the odd cough or loud sigh.

'Mr McEvoy is indisposed,' the vice-principal begins, pausing as one of the other teachers carries over a step and places it next to the podium. She climbs up and her flushed cheeks and round glasses come into view.

'Good morning, Mrs Purcell,' everyone chimes.

'Ah yes, that's better,' she says. 'Good morning, everyone. As I said, Mr McEvoy can't be here this morning. So, I'll be speaking to you in his place.'

A dull groan ripples across the hall like a Mexican wave. Mrs Purcell either doesn't hear it or she is so used to ignoring teenage opposition that it rolls off her like water dripping down shiny wax.

'I don't say this lightly, boys and girls,' Mrs Purcell continues, her lips barely parting. 'But it has come to our attention, Mr McEvoy and me, that we have a bullying problem in this school.'

Gasps and sniggers divide the hall. The bullied and the bullies. I glance around as quickly as I can, taking in as many indignant and scared faces as I can register.

'And worst of all, it's our senior year where the problem is most rampant. I must say I'm ashamed. What a terrible example you are setting for younger children here at St Peter's.'

The groaning among bored students gains traction, once again.

Mrs Purcell is quick to continue. 'Mr McEvoy and I will be calling each of you out of class this morning to speak to you about it. Everything you say will be held in the strictest confidence.'

'Ugh, God. Would you listen to her,' Gillian whispers. I can only imagine the rolling eyes that accompany her droll moan. 'She sounds like a bloody detective. *Everything you say will be held in confidence, blah bloody blah,*' she mimics, and I have to press my lips firmly together to hold in a laugh. 'I bet it's the yearbook that's the problem,' Gillian says. 'Ugh, trust Tina to not take a joke.'

'Shh,' Darcy whispers. 'I think that's Tina in front.' And I can only imagine she's pointing at the back of my head. I'm not brave enough to turn around.

'So,' Gillian says, even louder. 'She's obviously the snitch. She deserves everything that's coming to her, if you ask me.'

'Do you want me to beat some sense into her?' someone asks, and I hold my breath as I try to figure out who. I hope it's not Flabby Gabby. She's about three times as wide as I am and at least a foot taller.

'Nah,' Gillian says. 'The snitch isn't worth it.'

'I was the one who told actually,' Darcy says.

'Oh, you have got to be kidding me.' Luke sighs. 'Darcy, Jesus. What were you thinking? Are you trying to make sure everyone at school hates you?'

'The yearbook stunt was a dick move and you know it,' Darcy says. 'I didn't mention names. To be honest I don't even know the names. I just told Mr McEvoy that Tina was really upset.'

My cheeks flush and fire burns in the pit of my stomach. I can't believe Darcy did this. *How could she embarrass me like this? What a bitch.*

'Excuse me!' Mrs Purcell bellows, startling everyone, including me. 'What is all this mumbling about?' She points, but really her finger could be directed at anyone.

Darcy freezes.

And Gillian stupidly says, 'Nothing, miss.' As if butter wouldn't melt on her notoriously fiery tongue.

Mrs Purcell pulls herself especially tall, and, looking down on the entire hall, she says, 'Well, nothing certainly seems to be very interesting. My office. After assembly, Gillian. Let's see if you're as chatty then.'

Whispering and giggling start at the back.

'Enough!' Mrs Purcell roars, and for a petite woman her voice is incredibly large. 'Unless, of course, more of you would like to join Gillian in my office.'

An instant hush follows.

Mrs Purcell cocks her head to one side. Satisfied, she says, 'No. I didn't think so.'

Chatter begins again as assembly ends and teachers and pupils disburse to their respective classrooms. I'm swallowed in a group of boys roughhousing as they laugh their way out of the double doors of the hall. It takes me a while to shuffle free and I instantly search for Darcy. I see her chatting with a group of girls from our dorm, but I keep my distance.

'She's so weird,' I hear one of the girls say.

'Who?' someone else pipes up.

'Your one, the scrapbook freak. You know, what's-her-name.'

A deep and angry voice that I instantly recognise as Gillian's cuts across both girls. 'Why the hell are we talking about that ginger freak?'

'Exactly. Why are we talking about her?' says a softer, calmer voice that I also recognise.

It's *Darcy*.

'She's obsessed with you, Darcy,' Gillian says, exaggerating an exhausted sigh.

'Yeah, she really is,' one of the other girls says. 'It's kinda creepy. I think she wishes she could magically become you, or something.'

'Well, yeah.' Gillian laughs. 'Then she'd be the one sleeping with Luke Hogan, wouldn't she?'

'That's not funny,' Darcy says, securing a flyaway strand of hair behind her ear. And she's instantly perfect again. 'Luke can't stand her.'

'Yeah c'mon girls, be nice.' Gillian laughs again. 'That's no way to talk about Darcy's best friend.'

'She's not my best friend,' Darcy says.

'That's not what she's been telling people.'

There's a flash of disgust in Darcy's eyes and she scrunches her nose and says, 'What?'

'She's been telling everyone stories about tea and biscuits and chats,' someone else says.

'Ugh, God.' Darcy drops her head. 'I was just trying to be nice. She's lonely.'

'See. Bet the yearbook doesn't seem so bad now,' Gillian says.

Darcy doesn't reply.

'Tina Summers is a freak,' Gillian says, jamming her hands on to her hips. 'And I'm not going to rest until the whole school knows it. Hell, why stop there? I should probably do the world a favour and tell everyone.'

'Bit far maybe.' Darcy smiles. 'But yeah, something about her makes me uncomfortable no matter how nice I try to be.'

'Freak. Freak. Freak,' Gillian chants, seeing me by the lockers.

'Freak. Freak. Freak,' chorus other kids, joining in.

It's loud and scary and I run. I'm outside and all the way down by the construction area for the new tennis courts when the ringing in my ears finally stops. I look up to find birds flying overhead. I envy their simple life. A life without judgement. Or bullies. Or Gillian Buckley.

Chapter Forty-Three

DARCY

Monday 15 July 2019

I'm standing in my bedroom with my phone in my shaking hand. I've tried calling Luke back but his phone goes straight to voice-mail. I have to figure out what he means. *Run.* But from whom? Gillian? Surely not. I'd be running away from her money and towards bankruptcy.

The doorbell rings as I'm pulling on an oversized tracksuit. Good. This will distract Gillian while I slip out the back. I've no idea where I'll go – I can't get far in my condition – but the fresh air will clear my head. I need to think. I creep out of my bedroom and on to the landing as Gillian opens the front door.

'Thank you,' she says.

And a man's voice I don't recognise says, 'Should we carry this into the sitting room or where would you like it?'

'Upstairs,' Gillian says confidently as if it's her house. I gasp when she adds, 'Please put the new TV in the master bedroom. Second door on the right.'

'Upstairs, Mick,' the man shouts, beckoning his colleague to assist.

A skinny man with a goatee appears under the door arch. He stubs a cigarette out on the porch before walking into my house. 'All the way up the bleedin' stairs,' he grumbles.

'Second door on the right,' the original man says.

My heart is beating quickly as I skulk backwards.

Despite their complaining, the men are at the top of the stairs before I've made it back as far as the bed.

'Oh hello,' the clean-shaven man says, clearly surprised to notice me. 'Where do you want this, love?' he asks.

'Is it heavy?' Gillian asks, appearing behind them.

'Well, it's not light.' The skinny man snorts as they shuffle into my bedroom.

'You can just leave it there,' I say, pointing to an open space near the door with no furniture. I eye up the door, ready to slip downstairs as soon as Gillian and the men are out of the way, but Gillian's eyes are on me as she positions herself in the centre of the doorway.

Gillian twirls a strand of hair around her finger and she juts a provocative hip towards the nicer of the two men. 'Would you mind lifting it up here for us?' she asks, pointing at the dresser.

The skinny man looks as if he's about to protest when the other man says, 'Sure thing, love, we'd be happy to help.'

'You're a star.' Gillian giggles like a schoolgirl.

I swallow my disgust and watch as the men carefully slip a shiny television from the box, fiddle around to attach the stand, and position it on the dresser. The whole process is messy but Gillian showers the gullible man with praise.

'Excuse me,' I say, approaching Gillian in the doorway.

She ignores me and continues talking to the man. 'You're so strong,' she says, shamelessly. 'Do you work out?'

'Excuse me,' I repeat.

Gillian drapes her arm over my shoulder and spins me around to face the men. 'They're doing a great job, aren't they?' she says. 'A great team. It's so important that when people work together, they make a good team. Don't you think so?'

I know Gillian is referring to me and her and the investment. But right now, we couldn't possibly feel like less of a team. Especially as Luke's words ring in my ears. *Run. Run. Run!*

As soon as the television is safely in place, Gillian straightens up and says, 'Right, I'll see you out.'

The man's eyes cloud over with disappointment and his cheeks flush as he realises he's been played.

'I'll see you out,' Gillian repeats, firmly.

The men walk towards the door, one behind the other. Gillian guides me aside, her arm still across my shoulders, weighing heavily.

'Eh, you're not leaving that there, are you?' Gillian says, pointing towards the large cardboard box.

'We don't take recycling,' the skinny man says, and Gillian's nostrils flare as she glares at him.

'Fine,' she hisses.

'Ah c'mon, Mick,' the nicer man says, 'we can make an exception today, can't we?'

Mick picks up the box. 'Happy?' he says, as he marches past us.

'Very.' She shrugs.

The nice man doesn't say another word as he walks out of the bedroom behind his colleague. I slide away from Gillian and hurry into the hall after them.

'Wait?' I say.

He turns and smiles. 'Yes?'

'Could I get a lift with you? Into town please.'

'Sorry, love,' he says. 'We can't have more than two in the van at any time. Insurance.'

I swallow, catching Gillian looking at me. There's the glint of something unsettling deep in her hooded eyes.

'Goodbye,' she says to the men.

Gillian stands statue-like beside me until the sound of the front door closing behind the delivery men is long gone. But Gillian doesn't move.

Finally, I say, 'Won't you be late for work?'

'I'm not going to work today.'

'But earlier you said—'

'I've changed my mind. I'm going to spend all day here. Right beside you.'

'There's really no need. I'm probably just going to spend most of my day napping,' I say.

'I insist.' Gillian places her hand on my shoulder again, and this time she pinches so hard I yelp and squirm away.

'Get into bed,' Gillian says. 'I'm going to make us tea and toast and we are going to eat it and watch *Good Morning, Ireland*. Together. The way friends do. You like *Good Morning, Ireland*, don't you?'

I nod timorously. If Gillian is trying to intimidate me it's working.

I climb into bed as Gillian watches and I pull the covers up to my neck. She nods her approval.

'I won't be long. Don't move,' she warns, and she flicks on the new television.

The moment she's gone I mute the television. I turn away and stare out of the window. Seconds tick by in exaggerated slow motion as I sit, still and afraid, in a place I once felt the safest in the world.

It isn't long before my attention is drawn to an intermittent banging that seems to resonate in the belly of my old house. Gillian's bustling in the kitchen mostly overrides the sound. But it's there when she stops making a noise. I hear it again now and it's not just the rattle of rusty old hot-water pipes. This sound is new and different. I've never heard it in the house before. When a distinctive clawing strikes my ear, I immediately think of the rats. I drag my knees up and cradle my bump as if they can scurry through the floorboards and reach us. My baby and me.

Another bang follows. Louder this time, and I cover my lips with my hand to stop myself from screaming. I could swear the sound I hear next is a human tone.

I want to run. I want to run out of this goddamn house. But Gillian is all over the kitchen. I hear her beneath me, loud and present. So present. She'd hear me come down the stairs and would see me open the front door. I'm so weak I couldn't put up much resistance. And even if I managed to get away from her, if I could leave, where would I go? And why? Maybe I'm going crazy. What's that expression? *Cabin fever?*

I hear voices. The sound of a person, or people, trying to keep quiet but just not managing it. The oddest sound follows. It's distinctive and shrill and intermittent and someone is trying to hold it in, but every so often a cry escapes.

I need air. *Oh my God I need air.* I fling open the bedroom window and stick my head through the gap. Inhaling sharply, I glance all around my back garden.

'Oh Jinx,' I whisper as I see the mound on the grass. Then I cast my eyes all the way to the end of the garden and the shed.

It's still and silent outside and not so much as a summer breeze rustles leaves on the trees. Looking over the hedge I can see Mr Robinson, my elderly neighbour, bent over his vegetable garden. I can just about make out the green leafy tops of carrots protruding above freshly watered soil. I realise he's singing as a sweet sound carries in the air. He stands up and stretches as he notices me at the upstairs window. Tilting his cap away from his eyes, he shouts up, 'Veg love music, Darcy. It helps them grow!'

'They look lovely!' I shout back.

Mr Robinson cups his ear and shouts, 'What was that?'

'They're lovely,' I shout a little louder, remembering that he's hard of hearing.

'Ballads for the carrots, a little jazz for the spuds. I know all the tricks,' he says, proudly.

I smile. Mr Robinson always makes me smile.

'It's good to see you up and about,' he says. 'Luke told us how poorly you are. My Mary was on bed rest with all of ours. Will be worth it in the end. You'll see.'

Mr and Mrs Robinson have seven grown-up children and many, many grandchildren. But as much as I envy their large family, I can't possibly imagine doing this more than once.

'Have you heard anything strange recently?' I ask.

He smiles up at me. 'Stranger than an old man singing to his spuds, you mean?'

I nod. 'Banging? Have you heard anything unusual? It's not too loud, like a ringing that hangs in the walls.'

Mr Robinson shakes his head. 'Can't say I have, Darcy love.'

'Have you heard crying at all?' I add, becoming light-headed, my voice scratchy from shouting so he can hear me.

'There'll be plenty of crying soon enough,' he says.

'Paddy. Tea's ready, love,' I hear Mrs Robinson call without coming into view.

Mr Robinson stands his spade in the soil and shouts, 'Coming, love', as he waves goodbye to me.

'Wait! Wait, please?' I say, but his back is turned and I know he can't hear me as he walks away.

I close the window. My eyelids are heavy but I'm too afraid to sleep. I lower myself on to the bed and reach for the remote control

273

to unmute the TV. I'm about to turn the television off when I'm jolted awake by a familiar name. It's *Good Morning, Ireland*. It's Lindsay St Claire talking.

'Rose Callahan is missing,' she says.

Within a second I'm on my feet and alert, every muscle in my body burning and objecting to the sudden change of position, but I ignore the pain and concentrate on the screen. Lindsay St Claire's voice fills the room as a photo of Rose in her Gardaí uniform burns into the screen.

'Rose Callahan is thirty-six and she has been missing for two days,' Lindsay says. 'Rose is five-foot seven with blue eyes and dark-brown, shoulder-length hair. Rose is currently on maternity leave from her position as Sergeant at Cherryway Garda station. She is heavily pregnant and her husband is deeply concerned for her wellbeing. Anyone with information is being asked to contact Cherryway Garda station on 01 7857363. Rose was last seen in the local Cherryway corner shop wearing leggings and a sports top. I am joined on the line now by Rose's Pilates instructor and one of the last people to see her before her disappearance. Kimberly Kowalski. Hello Kimberly . . .'

'Oh God. Oh God,' I say, as tears stream down my face.

'What? What is it?' Gillian says, arriving into the room without tea or toast.

I didn't hear her come up the stairs. 'Do you know her?' Gillian asks, cupping my elbow and guiding me to sit on the edge of the bed.

I nod. I'm about to explain how we met when I clamp my top teeth on to my bottom lip. I've said enough.

'Gosh, look at her. She looks about ready to burst,' Gillian says, pointing to the screen at a new photo of Rose that has just appeared. Her face is round and her cheeks are pink. Flushed. She's wearing a bright cerise top and I know the photo has been taken just after a Pilates class. This week's class maybe.

'Your babies must be due around the same time,' Gillian says.

I don't say anything.

'You're as pale as a ghost,' Gillian says. 'Can I get you something? A cup of tea maybe.'

'Weren't you making tea and toast?'

Gillian glances at me blankly for a second before she says, 'Of course. Tea and toast.'

It's obvious I've jogged Gillian's memory. Tea and toast were never on the horizon. What was all the noise in the kitchen, then?

Gillian helps me to lie back against a mound of pillows and says, 'Shh. Shh. Shh.'

And I lie back and close my eyes, sleepily. Knowing I'll open them again the moment she's gone.

Chapter Forty-Four

TINA

Tuesday 16 July 2019

Rose's picture is unsurprisingly on the front page of every news-paper in the country today and I can't scroll through Facebook or Instagram without seeing an article about her, with that same unflattering photo of her in her work uniform before she was preg-nant. Her husband must have given the cops more photos, because the papers are sharing shots of her with her children too. Rose is pictured with her arms around a floppy-haired toddler, or hugging a brood of ice-cream-licking children. Tugging on the heartstrings of the nation, I decide. It's good journalism, if nothing else. But it won't help them to find her.

I cut out some of my favourite headlines from the papers.

> Pregnant Garda missing from Dublin
> Mother. Garda. Missing
> Gardaí 'extremely concerned' for missing colleague

The last one is my favourite. I enjoy the sense of camaraderie, some-thing I long for so much in my life, and I dedicate an entire page of my scrapbook to this headline alone. As usual, I highlight my favourite passages in the article and add some photos. Although I don't include any of Rose in her uniform. I don't want to ruin my pretty collage with a stern cop outfit and an ugly hat.

Satisfied with my handiwork, I close my scrapbook and resist the temptation to flick back to previous pages to make fun comparisons. I tidy up and place everything into the top drawer of my dresser and potter into the kitchen to make something to eat. Collaging always makes me hungry.

I take a Darcy's Dishes lemon cheesecake out of the fridge and open the packet. As always the little, round tray of pale-yellow curd on a biscuit base doesn't look very appetising. I reach for some sugar and sprinkle a healthy helping on top. I dig a spoon into the side of the cake and I'm opening my mouth ready to gobble a heaped spoonful when my phone rings. Furious, I slam my hand down on it, rejecting the call. The television studio's number quickly disappears from the screen. The studio has been relentlessly attempting to reach out. I even had Lindsay St Claire try to call personally. I'd feel special if it wasn't so damn inconvenient.

My fingers tremble and the lump of cheesecake slides off the spoon and splashes on to the floor at my feet. *Another problem caused by Lindsay St Claire*, I think. The woman just will not go away. I'm starting to think I'm going to have to do something about that. I decide to flick on the television and check out what nonsense she broadcast today. I flop on to the couch and point the remote control.

There's a movie I've seen before on the first channel. Some ads on the next. And so many reality TV shows I lose track. I start flicking until I find a station showing a repeat of Lindsay's show. A banner stretches across the bottom of the screen with text that moves from left to right, clearly warning viewers not to call now as lines are not live but they may still be charged.

The camera is focused on a panel of three guests. Lindsay doesn't introduce them; I've obviously missed that part of the show. But I recognise the lady sitting in the middle from magazines and TV ads, a model-turned-businesswoman who has her own range of tanning products and make-up. And she is by far the most vocal on the otherwise reserved panel.

'I mean, I just can't help but feel this country is gone to the dogs. Y'know what I'm sayin'?' she says, turning to her fellow panellists who are evidently thrown by her conviction. 'A missing cop. That's just crazy. As if someone is trying to give two fingers to the law.'

'I think it's important not to speculate,' Lindsay says, pressing her finger to her ear. 'Let's try to remember that Rose Callahan is a missing mother with a desperately worried family.'

'Yeah. Absolutely,' the ex-model nods, and quickly adds, 'but it isn't long since the guards found a body in the mountains.' She looks into the camera forlornly and melodramatically as she says, 'Rich old men don't usually end an evening in a body bag. Do they?'

I gasp – suddenly realising that Ms Vocal is the blonde woman irritatingly perched at the bar the night I met Andrew. She's not pining for the state of the country's moral compass, she's bitter and dejected. Perhaps when Andrew died so too did her chance at climbing the social ladder.

Lindsay is adept at finding these people. The rich and the soon-to-be. An exclusive circle with near-impenetrable walls. The rest of us aren't welcome. Never were. Never will be.

Another panellist, an older gentleman, agrees, reminding viewers of how tragic Andrew's loss is. Not only for those who loved him but for his staff and everyone whose shoulder he brushed. *A little dramatic*, I think. But noble nonetheless.

'Mr Buckley's death is undeniably tragic, but surely we're not drawing parallels?' Lindsay asks.

The final panellist is happy to share what she's obviously read in the papers or drummed up in an extensive internet search. 'Didn't his daughter go missing years ago and—'

I flick off the television and throw the remote across the room. It smacks against the wall and the back falls off, spitting out batteries. I watch them as they roll around, my head spinning.

'Oh God. Oh God!'

Chapter Forty-Five

DARCY

Wednesday 17 July 2019

'You can't live on fresh air,' Gillian complains.

I don't bother with a reply as she stands at the end of my bed with another tray of bloody granola and orange juice.

I shake my head. 'I'm not hungry.'

Uninvited, Gillian marches across my bedroom floor, leaves the tray next to my bed and says, 'Eat your breakfast.'

I'm pissed off already, but when she adds 'Or I'm telling Luke', the flash of anger heats my whole body. I've tried calling Luke countless times since we last spoke. His phone is switched off and going straight to voicemail. Logically the person I should tell is Gillian. She could reach out to her people over in Ohio and check what's going on. But my gut is warning me not to. I've always trusted my gut.

'I have to go to work,' Gillian announces as if it's somehow unexpected.

'Okay.'

Gillian stomps down the stairs and into the kitchen. I listen for a long time and I wait for the sound of her leaving the house so I can too. In the meantime, I stare past the open curtains at life on our street. Neighbours hurry to work. Teenagers ride their bikes. People walk their dog. Everyone is simply getting out and about. I don't know them by name, but I recognise their faces, the same faces I used to see at the same time every morning as I went to work, and I wonder if anyone has noticed my face is missing.

Thirsty, I hate myself as I guzzle the glass of orange juice Gillian has left. I'm setting the empty glass down on the tray when I hear my phone ringing. The upbeat tones of 'I Will Survive' are cumbersome in the air. Luke changed my ringtone before he left. He thought it would be funny and cheer me up, and it did at first. Now the catchy lyrics mock me. The melody continues blaring loudly because I can't find my phone. The noise is blistering in the otherwise painfully silent house, and I know the sound will drag a curious Gillian back upstairs. The slightest sound seems to pique her interest lately. And if it's Luke calling, I need to speak to him in private. I dive on to the bed and tumble the sheets and pillows on to the floor. My back creaks from the weight of my bump but I'm near euphoric when I find my phone.

'Hello,' I say, snapping it to my ear.

'Darcy?' Mildred says, clipped and anxious.

My ears are on her voice. 'Everything okay?'

'So, you spoke to Luke?' she says, and I know Mildred well enough to know when she's pissed off about something.

'Yes. But only briefly. I'm working on getting things under control. I'm planning to call into the bank today in person, actually.'

Mildred exhales and it's loud and uncomfortable so close to my ear. 'Well then, why the hell do I have your husband calling me, after work hours, I might add, bitching at me? Telling me I need to keep things under control?'

I take a deep breath and shake my head. 'What? Luke said that? That's so unlike him—'

'He barely gave me time to say hello,' Mildred cuts across me. I know it's more hurt than anger that has her acting this way. 'He told me to keep my shit together and not to contact you again. And then he hung up. He was crazy, Darcy. He scared me. He really, really scared me. What the hell is going on?'

'Listen,' I say, calmly, in spite of how short of breath I am. 'Luke is just freaking out about finances. This isn't him. You know that.'

'I'll quit, Darcy,' she says. 'I mean it. If he ever speaks to me like that again I'll walk straight out that door.'

'No. No, don't do that. We'd never cope without you. I'll speak to Luke,' I say, feeling hypocritical. 'I'll make sure he apologises.'

'I've had it, Darcy,' Mildred says. 'I've really, truly had it. I love you. You know I do. But I hardly see you any longer. The staff are all twitchy. And then your husband comes on the phone telling me I can't be troubling you with business stuff any more.'

'He shouldn't have said that.'

Mildred is short of breath; I can hear her smoker's wheeze down the line. 'It's a step too far, Darcy. Too far.'

'Yes. It is. Luke knows how heavily I rely on you. I just don't understand . . .'

I hear the click of a lighter as Mildred lights up a cigarette and takes a calming puff. 'I just thought you'd want to know what's going on. I know you're not well, Darcy. I do. But it's your company at the end of the day, isn't it?'

'I'm glad you said that, Mildred. Because it is my company, isn't it? Listen Mildred, can you do me a favour?'

'Yeah,' she says.

'Can you get me contact details for Luke in the Ohio office? I doubt he'll have his own phone line so his email is preferable.'

'He hasn't given me them yet. Can't you just use his personal email?'

I don't tell Mildred that I've tried, and when I let silence hang in the air she reads me the way old friends often do and says, 'I'll get you an email, Darcy. Don't worry.'

'Hey. Hey,' Gillian says, bursting into my bedroom without a knock. 'Everything okay in here? Who are you talking to?'

Fortuitously kneeling on my hunkers, I say, 'Myself. I'm practising hypno-breathing for the birth.'

'Hmm,' Gillian says in a tone that tells me she doesn't believe me.

'I was just watching some videos on YouTube,' I say, sitting back on to crossed legs and waving my phone.

'You're not hungry,' she says.

I glance at the granola and my stomach turns. 'I got distracted online. I'll probably have some in a little while.'

'Hmm.'

We make eye contact for a few moments and finally Gillian falters and glances at my phone in my hand.

'Luke called,' she says.

'Oh,' I say, and it's my turn to not believe her.

'He's so happy I'm taking care of you.'

'Hm-hmm.'

'He says it's just like old times. The three of us together as best friends again.'

Gillian glances at the bedsheets and pillows tossed around the floor and before she says anything I say, 'I was too hot.'

She puffs out and bends down to gather up the bedclothes.

'Get into bed,' she orders, standing up with the sheets balled up under one arm and the pillows stuffed under the other.

I lie down and Gillian tucks me in.

'You'll catch your death with no covers,' she says, pulling them right up to my chin and wrapping them so tightly around me I'm worried she's crushing the baby. 'And we wouldn't want that, would we?'

Chapter Forty-Six

DARCY

Thursday 18 July 2019

I call Luke. His phone rings out. I try again but it goes straight to voicemail. I try over and over, but all I hear is his familiar voice saying, 'Hello. You've reached Luke Hogan, CEO of Darcy's Dishes. I'm sorry I missed your call. Leave a message after the tone and I'll get back to you as soon as possible.'

'I'm scared,' I whisper, desperately fearing that I'm whispering into the wind.

I think about Rose. Poor, poor Rose. I wonder about where she could be or what could have possibly happened to her between the corner shop and her home. Most of all, I wonder when her husband started to panic. Was it after a couple of hours, after a whole night, the next morning? When? When did he realise something was very, very wrong? When was the moment of realisation that Rose was gone?

The digital clock in the corner of the television says it's almost midday. I'm not watching telly. It's just on. It's almost always on. Gillian seems to like it that way. As if the low mumbles of chat shows drown out the noise of her walking around my house. As if

I'll get so lost in a cookery programme I'll forget she's ever present in my home. I never forget. And I never don't hear her. Even now, as the afternoon approaches and Gillian should have left for work long ago, I hear her talking and fidgeting.

My phone vibrates on the bed next to me and a number I don't recognise flashes up on-screen. I don't usually answer unknown numbers, it's often someone begging for sponsorship for a race or walk or something similar in the name of their chosen charity. As much as I'd like to, Darcy's Dishes simply can't support them all. And people's reactions range from heartbroken to furious when I explain. But I have no hesitation answering today, as I cling to the possibility it could be Luke. Maybe he really has lost his phone. Maybe this is his new number. Maybe everything is okay. Maybe. *Please God, maybe.*

'Hello. Hello,' I gasp, pressing my phone to my ear.

'Is that Darcy Hogan?'

My heart sinks and slowly I say, 'Yes.'

'Ah. Good. It's Hugh here, you called about a problem with some rats.'

'Oh.'

'Is this a bad time?' he asks.

'Erm . . .' I swallow, struggling to get my thoughts straight. 'I'm not sure there is a problem, after all. I thought I saw something. Heard something, actually. But, eh, I'm not so sure any more. It's an old house and . . .' I trail off.

'And it sounds like a problem to me,' he says. 'Rats don't stay still for long. If you saw one, I'm sure there's a few you didn't see. Old houses are the worst for it. Lots of cracks and such. The little buggers can get into the slightest of gaps. You'd be surprised.'

'Oh.'

'Will I come round later and take a look?'

My head hurts and the sound from the television is blurring with the sound of his voice.

'No rat. No fee,' he adds. 'You're there on Cherryway Road, you said?'

'Did I?'

'I remember because that's where that cop went missing, isn't it?'

I swallow. *Oh, Rose.*

'Ah, feck. Sorry,' he says. 'You probably knew her. I can be an awful insensitive eejit sometimes, I can. Me wife says me gob is the biggest part of me.'

I don't have words for a moment.

'It's okay,' I say. 'You didn't know.'

'Right, I'll be round later to sort this out for ya. I've a job on the north side first. I'm on me way there now. No telling what time I'll finish, but I won't leave ya stuck. I'll sort these buggers out for ya. And I'll keep me rate low, love. Least I can do after opening me big mouth. I'm about to drive through a tunnel here, so I'll see ya later.'

I don't have time to reply before the line dies. I listen for the sound of creatures scurrying through the wall or under the floor. I try so hard to pinpoint the strange sounds of recent days. But the house is blissfully silent. There's no eerie scratching, no muffled tone that seems to resonate in the walls. And, most important, there is no hint of Gillian in the house. Maybe she has *finally* gone to work. If I grab a shower and get dressed I might make it to and from the bank before she gets back. I can't remember the account number off by heart but I'm sure they're in my emails somewhere. I try searching but I can't connect to the internet. My phone has no service. I can only imagine I've been cut off because the bill hasn't been paid. It could also explain why I can't reach Luke. It's the weirdest thing to be almost relieved that an unpaid bill could explain so much.

I bend over the usual floorboard. It gets a little easier to lift each time. I shine the torch on my phone into the hole. The paper is gone. My heart races as I fetch Luke's tools and try to loosen the next floorboard. It's harder than it looks and I'm working up a sweat, but I finally pop it. Still no paper. I pop the next one. And another. But there's nothing here except some thick underlay and a cobweb.

I look at the mess I've made. The hole is four boards wide and I've taken a chunk out of the side of one of the boards and scratched a couple of others. *And for what?* To find a spider that's been dead for goodness knows how long. I put the boards back in place as best I can, but they bounce and creak when you step on them and the damaged one stands out like a bloody beacon. There are only two people in this house. If I haven't touched the bills then Gillian has. But I can't figure out why.

The doorbell rings. Quickly, I drag the heavy shag rug that resides at the end of the bed to the side and cover everything up. The exterminator must have decided to call on me before his other job. *Dammit.*

I pull on a hoodie and a pair of Luke's tracksuit pants over my pyjamas. I can't find my flip-flops and my feet are too swollen to shove into anything else.

The doorbell rings again.

'I'm coming!' I shout.

Another ring. *Jesus.*

I finally find my flip-flops behind the door, shuffle in and waddle downstairs, clinging tightly to the banister.

The doorbell rings twice more before I reach it.

'Hello,' I say, pulling back the door that feels insanely heavy today. I gasp when I see who's on the other side.

'Darcy,' Polly says, standing in front of me. She has a neat, noticeable bump now. Her stomach was washboard flat the last time I saw her. Her beautiful, long shiny hair is scraped off her face in a much-too-tight bun and the bags under her eye are fierce.

'Can I come in?' she asks.

'Gosh. Yes. Of course,' I say. 'Sorry. Sorry. Come in. Come in.'

'I don't mean to drop by unannounced like this. I know it's been months. It's just . . .'

I nod, and Polly nods, and I know we're both thinking the same thing. *Rose.*

I close the door behind us and give Polly a moment to catch her breath. I guide us towards the kitchen. My mind is on fire as I shuffle slowly forward. Polly doesn't seem to mind how slowly we move, as she keeps her head low and her shoulders round.

In the kitchen I offer to make us tea and she nods and takes a seat.

'Have you seen the news?' she asks.

'Yeah,' I say, pouring some water in the kettle. 'Have you heard anything? Any updates? Her poor husband.'

I flick the kettle on and sit at the table opposite Polly.

'I just can't believe it.' Polly sighs, dropping her head into her hands, and I realise Polly and Rose have become very close while I've been missing from Pilates class.

'She's overdue, you know, by a few days now,' Polly says.

I didn't know. Rose and I are due around the same time, but I didn't know she was there already. Instinctively, I hold my large bump. Even beneath clothes I can feel my skin taut and stretched, and I realise how soon this will all be over.

Polly's hands touch her face, and I watch with a breaking heart as her fingers tremble. She says, 'Rose didn't turn up for her last hospital appointment. Her phone is turned off. Her phone is never off. Her family are sick with worry.'

Luke's phone is turned off too, I think, my heart racing. I wonder if I should tell someone. But not Polly. I can't burden her with my worries now.

The kettle bubbles loudly behind us and the noise almost feels inappropriate somehow.

'Where do you think she is?' I ask, and I know as soon as the redundant words tumble past my lips that I've upset Polly even more.

She shrugs.

'Sorry,' I say, standing up to make tea I know neither of us wants to drink as the kettle flicks off.

'Look,' Polly says, the leg of her chair squeaking when she turns to watch me. 'As I said, I know this is a bit weird, me turning up out of the blue after months. We don't even know each other that well, but . . .'

She pauses and she's obviously waiting for me to say something. But I'm lost for words. I pop a teabag into each cup and add some water, glad to have a distraction.

'Sugar?' I ask, the weight of awkward silence crushing me.

Polly nods.

'Milk too?'

'I need a favour,' Polly says.

Listening, I fetch some milk, assuming she'll want some. I don't. Polly watches me with heavy eyes as I move the cups to the table and place down the milk and sugar too.

'You need a favour?' I say, sitting.

Polly curls her hand around one of the cups and drags it close to her as she puffs out heavily. 'You know Lindsay St Claire, don't you?'

'Well not—'

'It's just, everyone watches her show,' Polly cuts across me. 'And if we could get Rose's family on the air, to raise awareness . . .'

'Yeah. Erm . . .' I spoon some sugar into my cup, noticing how my hands are shaking. I spill a little on the table, but Polly doesn't seem to notice, or care. 'I think it's a great idea to raise awareness,' I say. 'I'm just not sure how much help I could be.'

'Could you ask, at least?' Polly's eyes are glistening and I can hear her choking back tears. 'They'd only need a quick slot. Even ten minutes would do.'

The desperation in Polly's voice is heartbreaking. And I want to help, I'm just not sure I have the influence Polly so desperately hopes I have.

I try to be optimistic as I stir my tea and say, 'Rose's name is in all the papers. And I've seen her picture on social media. Facebook mostly. But Instagram too. People know she's missing. Hopefully someone will come forward with a sighting soon. I can only imagine how hard this must be for her husband. And her kids. She has quite a few little ones, doesn't she?'

Polly nods. 'The youngest is only two. He doesn't understand and just wants his mammy.'

Tears cloud my eyes.

'It all helps.' Polly sips some tea that must still be too hot, but she doesn't flinch. 'If people don't see Rose's face online, they'll see her on the telly. If they don't read about her in the paper they'll hear about it on the radio. I mean, I don't know how effective it *really* is. But it's helping her husband and kids to know people are doing all they can.'

I nod. I can imagine. If it was me and Luke . . . I freeze as a shiver runs down my spine. I can't bear to think about it.

I place my hand over Polly's and I say, 'I'm not really that friendly with Lindsay, but—'

'But you will ask . . .' Polly cuts me off, guessing. Hoping.

'Of course. If it helps. I'll try my best to get Rose's family on the show.'

'It will. It really will.' Polly sips more tea. 'This is nice. Thanks.'

I'm sipping tea too, when we're both startled by banging that seems to be coming from somewhere within the house.

'What was that?' Polly asks, sloshing some tea over the edge of her cup. It trickles towards the loose grains of sugar I spilt earlier, creating a sticky mess.

'I don't know,' I say, and I can tell from Polly's face that she thinks the noise is as unusual and weird as I do.

The noise stops as suddenly as it began. And Polly stands up, straightens her clothes over her growing bump, and says, 'Thank you so much, Darcy. We'll find Rose, won't we?'

I'm nodding when I remember I have no phone service. I'm about to ask Polly if I can borrow hers when the kitchen door swings open roughly and Gillian appears in the gap.

'Oh,' she says, her eyes wide as she ducks back out.

Pretending this whole situation is not peculiar, for my own sake as much as Polly's, I say, 'S'okay. Come on in. Polly is a friend from Pilates.'

I wait for Gillian to open the door wider and enter. But after a couple of silent seconds I realise she's not coming back.

Polly squints and scrunches her nose, staring at the door, as if she can see through to the other side. 'I didn't realise you two were friends.'

'Sort of. She's looking after me while my husband is away with work,' I say. I can't understand why Gillian ducked out so quickly. It was almost as if she got a fright seeing Polly. Surely she can't be that shocked that someone has called around to visit me in my own house?

The banging and scratching starts again. It's quieter this time, you have to really concentrate to hear it. But I can't concentrate on anything other than where Gillian has gone. No doubt the creepy noise is coming from her. It's only here when she's here. *What the hell is she doing to my house?*

'That was the new girl from Pilates, right?' Polly says, pointing towards the kitchen door.

I'm so confused. My mind races. The noise. Gillian. Polly. Rose. Pilates. Lindsay. And Luke. Oh, Luke.

'She's new, so . . .' Polly tilts her head towards the sounds from deep within the house, distracted for a moment by how dramatic and freakish it is. So am I. 'She started after you left,' Polly continues. 'I didn't realise you two knew each other.'

The house is suddenly silent again, apart from the sound of our breathing in the kitchen. I shake my head and say, 'She's a new neighbour.'

'Oh right, okay.' Polly shrugs, but I get the impression she thinks I'm lying. Why on earth would I lie about something like that?

Polly and I finish our tea and we try to chat and act normal, but her mind is on Rose and mine is on every damn thing. We seem to naturally drift towards the door when we've run out of tea and conversation. We hug and Polly wipes tears from her eyes before she mouths, 'Thank you', and slowly walks away. I close the front door and take some much-needed deep breaths. It's less than a couple of minutes before I remember I still have no way of making a call. I'm about to race after Polly when I feel the weight of Gillian's hand on my shoulder.

'Sorry about earlier,' she says. 'I didn't realise you had company.'

I don't say anything.

'I wanted to talk to you about the investment and some serious financial concerns.'

'Oh.'

'We'll discuss it now?'

I nod. It's probably too late to catch Polly anyway, and I can borrow Gillian's phone to call Lindsay. Gillian has already helped herself to our private bills, she knows we're broke. And when I'm finished on the phone, I can tell the nosey bitch to get the hell out of my house. Enough is enough.

Chapter Forty-Seven

DARCY

Friday 19 July 2019

I tolerate Gillian's bullshit for at least half an hour as we sit side by side at the kitchen table. She presented reams and reams of paper. Legal documents that I'm almost certain she printed off the internet.

'Shouldn't our solicitors be dealing with this?' I ask.

'Bloody solicitors.' She rolls her eyes. 'Expensive idiots in suits. We can handle this ourselves. We're all friends after all.'

'I really think we need to sign stuff like this in the presence of our respective solicitors. And Luke needs to be here.'

'Don't you trust me?' she says, flicking to the next page.

'Of course I do,' I lie. 'As you say. We're old friends.'

Gillian never once mentions the bills she stole from under our floor and neither do I. And as I sit and listen to her lies and rambling, I realise Gillian Buckley hasn't the faintest idea about running a business.

'Excuse me,' I say, standing up.

Gillian glares at me as if I'm interrupting an important meeting. Her reaction would be laughable if it wasn't for her warped belief that this impromptu kitchen-table nonsense is actually of significance.

'Bathroom,' I say, pointing to my bump.

Gillian grimaces but she nods. 'I'll be reading over this while you're gone.'

'Sure,' I say, keeping my tone as interested as I can fake.

I hurry upstairs and search for my handbag. It's at times like this I wish I could drive. It's a long walk to the factory but I have to reach Mildred before she finishes work for the day.

As always, the television is on in my bedroom. The sound is off and I'm surprised to find Lindsay St Claire on the screen at this time of day. I instantly feel a pang of guilt that I've promised Polly I'd call Lindsay with a phone that can't make calls. Thankfully I can borrow Mildred's when I make it to the factory.

It takes me a moment to realise that Lindsay is the interviewee and not the host. She's sitting centre screen, radiant and dressed to perfection as always, but her face is serious and stern and she's not her usual bubbly self.

Lindsay and the host are talking about Rose and sharing her photo again. My heart soars, assuming Polly found her own way to get in touch. I find my bag resting beside my dressing table. I sling it over my shoulder and I'm ready to make a dash for the front door when I'm startled by a photo flashing up on-screen.

'A MISSING WOMAN', it says, in giant bold letters that jump out at me from the bottom of the screen. But this isn't Rose. She's years younger. A teenager, in her school uniform. And I remember her. Or the uniform, at least.

I turn up the sound. I recognise her cherry lips, which curl at one edge into a slightly crooked smile. Her long, strawberry-blonde hair has a natural curl and her eyes glisten turquoise like the Caribbean Sea on a sunny day. This is the photo that was splashed all over the newspapers when Gillian ran away. It was taken from our yearbook and it's shocking to see how much she's changed. The Gillian on-screen takes my breath away, with her ivory skin like a porcelain doll's and freckles that sprinkle the bridge of her nose and spill on to her cheeks. Gillian's skin has darkened with age and she doesn't have freckles any more and I think what a pity it was she had them removed. She really was beautiful. Much more so than now.

'Ladies and gentlemen, you may remember the twisted web of deceit Lindsay introduced you to recently on her morning show?' The presenter's voice sounds before the photo of Gillian fades and Lindsay appears on-screen, sitting cross-legged and nodding. 'Why don't you tell us what you've found, Lindsay?'

'Thank you, Frank,' she says, and her usual charm for the camera is effervescent. 'Folks, I'm sure most of you will remember the lovely Darcy Hogan whom I had on my show not too long ago. Poor Darcy had every guest's worst nightmare live on air. A disgruntled someone from her past calling mid show.'

I can't breathe. It's as if Lindsay is reaching her hands through the screen and wrapping them tightly around my neck with every word.

'What you don't know is who this caller was, and what on God's green earth she wanted, am I right? Well, try as I might, I couldn't get hold of the mysterious Tina. But as some of you may know I started my career as an investigative journalist and I know alarms bells when I hear them. And my goodness, folks, were they chiming.'

Oh my God. Oh my God. I grab my chest.

Lindsay continues and I could swear she's staring right at me. 'It seems that Tina Summers and Darcy Hogan were at school together. The exclusive St Peter's – recently privately sold and commissioned for apartments, but that's another story.'

297

'Maybe we'll cover that soon. You heard it here first, folks,' the male presenter sitting opposite Lindsay interjects, breaking the flow.

Lindsay visibly inhales and quickly smiles and nods. 'Good idea, Frank.'

There's a pause as Lindsay gathers her thoughts. And I find my eyes wide open and my fingers tugging on the strap of my bag as I will Lindsay to hurry up and finish the story.

'Further research led me to Andrew Buckley,' Lindsay continues.

There's a collective intake of breath and it's only then I realise there's a studio audience.

Lindsay appears saddened and she sinks lower into her chair as she says, 'As we're all too aware Mr Buckley was recently laid to rest after his body was found in the Wicklow Mountains.'

'God rest his soul,' Frank says.

The flash of irritation that sweeps across Lindsay's face might not be noticeable to the audience and certainly not to Frank, but I recognise it. It's that sudden look of *what the hell* that your face registers before your mind has a chance to catch up. Of course, you wipe it quickly once your brain catches up, but it doesn't mean you didn't wear it for the briefest of moments. I've no doubt I wore this look the morning I was on Lindsay's show and Tina caught me off guard. And I'm certain I sported it again just now when Gillian tried to spin some generic internet crap off as legal documents. I think I'm still making this exact face.

'Andrew Buckley, himself once a pupil at St Peter's, was a keen investor in alumni. He had recently shown an interest in Darcy's Dishes. A wise decision, no doubt. Have you tried their plant-based cheesecake, folks? Absolutely a-mazing!'

'I haven't actually tasted it, but I hear great things,' Frank says, just about remaining in shot on his own show.

'It's great, Frank. You'd love it,' Lindsay says, and the camera once again zooms in on her, cutting Frank out. 'But Andrew Buckley wasn't just a clever and successful businessman,' Lindsay continues, bringing the tone right back as if Frank never spoke. 'He was also a loving father. Behind the suits and cars and mansion was a broken man.'

The audience gasps again and it's no doubt directed but it doesn't lose the effect.

Lindsay's eyes shine and I believe her empathy as she continues. 'His only daughter, Gillian, whose photo you saw just moments ago, was also a pupil at St Peter's. Kind. Clever and popular. An integral cog in the school.'

Lindsay pauses. Maybe to let the audience catch up with a story I'm so familiar with. Maybe to catch her own breath.

Lindsay doesn't have to say the next sentence. I know what comes next. But my heart still skips a beat when she says, 'Gillian has been missing for nineteen years.'

'What are you watching?' Gillian barges into my room without knocking. The door is flung back and hits the wall behind with a loud thud, the handle, no doubt, taking a chunk out of the wall as I quickly switch off the television.

'Nothing,' I say. 'Just the news.'

Goosebumps pucker my skin as Gillian's eyes crawl all over me and I wait to see if she will flick the television back on.

'Global warming,' I say, pointing towards the blank screen. 'There was a really interesting piece on it.' There's a quiver in my voice but I think I'm passing it off as tiredness. 'Methane. It's a huge problem, as we know. Plant-based foods are the way forward. Darcy's Dishes is the way forward, isn't it?'

Gillian ignores me as she shuffles her hip between the dresser and the wall. She grunts as she pushes hard and the dresser and wall separate.

'What are you doing?' I ask.

'Got it,' she says, pulling a cable out from behind the television.

She shoves the dresser back, straightens up and dusts her hands off.

I begin to sweat as I wonder when Gillian will notice my handbag slung over my shoulder.

'You need rest,' Gillian says, spinning the cable around her hand until it's a neat loop, then she slides it off and tucks it under her arm.

'Okay,' I say, afraid to move.

'You moved the rug,' she says, pointing.

'I, eh . . . I thought it looked nicer here.'

Gillian makes a face. 'I'll get you something to eat. You haven't eaten in a while.'

'Yeah, that would be great. Thanks.'

Gillian places the cable on the rug. A simple gesture to warn me she's always been one step ahead.

Chapter Forty-Eight

DARCY

Saturday 20 July 2019

I roll over and wrap my arms around Luke ready to snuggle for another few minutes before the day begins. My eyes flicker open when I don't find my husband next to me and reality dawns quickly. I find myself in bed with my eyes closed and I have the worst headache ever. Every now and then I hear noises downstairs. It's bright outside but I don't know if it's late evening or early morning. I'm not sure it matters. Gillian locked my bedroom from the outside and after I fought against it for too long and lost too much energy, I realised it was pointless. I think that's when I crawled into bed. I can't really remember.

Warm summer light shines through the window kissing my face, and I remember how I love this feeling. The way the bedroom window captures the light is one of the reasons I suggested to Luke that we buy this place. It's beautifully bright. Or at least it was. The window is open and a gentle breeze rustles in every so often as the sound of carefree children playing in the distance carries on the wind.

When my stomach heaves, reminding me that mornings often start this way, I crawl my way towards the en suite on all fours. Surprisingly Gillian hasn't locked that door too. I flush the loo, but the smell of vomit clings to the air and I fetch some air freshener from the cabinet above the sink. It's empty and I drop it into the bin. The broken shards of soap tray stare at me. I fish them out piece by piece, pricking myself a couple of times and sucking on my fingers.

Back in the bedroom I arrange the pieces on my dressing table, trying as best I can to recreate the original shape. It's tricky and I'm missing a few pieces that were, no doubt, lost between empty aerosol canisters and dirty cotton buds.

My ringing phone startles me and I jump, jumbling the pieces all over again. I hurry towards the bed where the ringing is muffled by the haphazard bedclothes it's got tangled up in. I'm relieved I can still receive calls even if I can't make any.

'Hello?' I say, and I can't believe how I sound. As if I'm underwater. Luke sounded just like this the last time we spoke.

'Darcy.' The voice on the other end sounds noticeably shocked.

I try again. 'Hi. Hello.'

'Darcy, it's Mildred.'

'Millirred. I'm stuck,' I say.

'You're drunk?' Mildred replies, baffled.

'Stuck,' I repeat.

'Drunk? Darcy I can't understand what you're saying.'

'S'locked me in. S'not real. It's not real. You have to help.'

There's heavy sighing.

'Darcy, if it wasn't early morning and you weren't heavily pregnant, I'd honestly believe you're high as a kite right now.'

'S'bad, Millirid. She's bad.'

'Take some deep breaths, okay?' Mildred says.

'Okay.'

'You have to listen. Are you listening?'

I *am* listening.

'Darcy?'

My eyes close without me telling them to, but I keep the phone pressed against my ear. I'm past words but I'm desperate for Mildred to keep talking.

'Darcy. Darcy, are you there?'

I'm here. Oh God, I'm here.

'There's no office in Ohio, Darcy,' Mildred says. 'Or certainly none that I can find. There's no email. No phone numbers. No goddamn building.'

Mildred pauses and I try so hard to ask her to keep going, but I can't speak.

'Look,' she says, 'I have no idea what's going on but I know you need this information. You also need to know Gillian Buckley isn't a partner at Buckley & Co. From what I can find there is no mention of her anywhere in the company at all.'

I want to thank Mildred. I want to tell her that the woman in my house isn't Gillian Buckley and that I think whoever she is has hurt Luke and she wants to hurt me, but all that comes out is a tepid grunt.

'Darcy, I'm worried about you,' Mildred says. 'If Luke is having an affair, drink isn't the answer. Especially not now. We can trace accounts. We can always find money. He can't bleed you dry.'

It's not Luke, I want to scream, but I merely manage an animal cry.

'Maybe you could come stay with me for a bit?' Mildred suggests. 'We can figure this out together. A break up is hard, trust me, I know.'

I swallow again; this lump is larger and more cumbersome to force down. I often think Mildred knows me so well that if anything were to happen to me she could keep Darcy's Dishes. But it breaks my heart that she doesn't seem to know Luke.

'Look, I'll be home in forty minutes,' Mildred says. 'Go to my place? Let yourself in. There's a key under the mat.'

I can't make words.

'I really hope I see you soon,' Mildred says, and then she hangs up.

And I'm suddenly plunged into silence, loneliness and fear.

I cling to my phone and dial 999. Thankfully, even with an unpaid bill, emergency numbers still connect.

'Hello emergency services, which service do you require?'

A throaty gargle is all I can manage.

'Emergency services,' the male voice repeats. 'Which service can I put you through to?'

The key rattles in the lock and the bedroom door creaks open.

'Hello. Hello,' the voice echoes in my ear.

I hang up and lower the phone, defeated, as Gillian walks into the room.

'How are you feeling?' she asks.

I can feel the beads of sweat on my forehead, but I can't quite manage to raise my arm to wipe them away.

Gillian leans past me and reaches for the window, closing it.

I inhale deeply, desperate to breathe. Just breathe.

'Just needed some fresh air, eh?'

I wonder if I opened it. Maybe I could shout for help if I could find my voice.

Gillian takes my hand in hers and squeezes gently. 'I can only imagine how you must be feeling.'

My eyes can't seem to focus on her but my mind still drinks in her sadistic smirk.

'Can I get you anything? Tea? Water? Your husband?'

Chapter Forty-Nine

DARCY

Sunday 21 July 2019

I can't see. I can't tell if my eyes are open or closed as I try to work out where the hell I am. It's cold too, the floor beneath me. And moist. The smell is familiar, like the garden. Soil and earth. Musty and damp. But there are smells of the house too. Toast and coffee. The smells of morning. And the odd rattling and banging is louder than it has ever been.

'You're awake,' a voice whispers.

I rub my eyes.

'Who's there?' I say. I think I'm on my feet. My legs are shaking and I stretch my hands out in front of me, feeling my way around in the darkness.

'Darcy?' the voice whimpers.

'Rose?' I gasp.

'It's me. Are you okay? You've been out of it for a while.'

'Oh my God you're alive,' I say.

'Do you know where we are?' Rose asks.

I shake my head, and slowly realise that I haven't found Rose. I've joined her. In that place where the missing go. *Where is that place?*

'You don't remember what happened, do you?' Rose asks.

I shake my head again, before realising she can't see me. I'm engulfed by anger and fear and confusion and words are hard. But I say, 'No. I have no idea what the hell is going on. Do you?'

'Not really,' Rose says. 'I mean, I know Tina is nuts, but that's all.'

'Tina?' I echo. 'Oh God. Oh God.'

'Yeah,' Rose says, sounding ecstatic that I seem to have some idea of what she's talking about. 'She's new. I just wanted to be her friend and this . . .'

There's a long pause, but its meaning seems to get lost in this void of darkness.

'What does she want?' Rose begins to cry. 'I don't know how long I've been here.'

'Have you had any food? Some water?' I ask.

'Yeah. Yeah. She brings some. On a tray. Orange juice and granola, mostly. And there's light sometimes too. There's a crack in the wall over there.' I can only imagine Rose is pointing. 'There must be clouds tonight because the moon isn't shining. This is the darkest it's been. You'll see in the morning. There *is* light.'

'What time is it?' I ask.

There's a pause and I imagine Rose is shrugging. 'I don't know. I'm not sure what day it is either, but you've been here for a while. Hours, I'm guessing. A day or so. I was beginning to worry you would never wake up.'

Suddenly there's a creak and a door opens. There's a burst of light too. It's subtle and obviously night light, but it's a dramatic contrast to the darkness my eyes are struggling with. I can see shapes at the very least.

'Hey. Hey. I've brought some treats,' Gillian says.

I can hear Rose crying. Her whimpers are subtle, but mirror mine.

'Come on now,' Gillian chirps like a cheerleader trying to rally the crowd. 'It's a favourite. Smoothies and granola. I've even added berries. Don't say I don't spoil you.'

'Where are we?' I step forward, but as soon as I do my legs give way and I fall, barely managing to position my hip to the ground first, saving my enormous belly from the impact.

'Cherryway, Darcy,' Gillian says, half laughing. 'Where else would we be?'

'No. You've taken me somewhere. Taken us, somewhere.'

Gillian sets a tray down next to me and Rose. I gag when I recognise the bowl. It sat on my bedside table for two days last week before Gillian took it away. Rose lunges forward. She wolfs down the granola and guzzles back a full glass of smoothie. 'Sorry. I'm sorry,' she says to Gillian, retreating just as quickly.

This isn't Rose, I think. This isn't the feisty, fit cop who could plank for three minutes while pregnant. *What has Gillian done to her?*

'Luke asked me to take care of you,' Gillian says to me, 'and I'm never, ever, ever going to break that promise. Because Luke is special. But, hey. Who am I telling? You already know how amazing he is, right?'

'Where's Luke?' I ask. 'What have you done with my husband?'

Gillian laughs, and it's dark again as soon as she closes the door. I hear rattling and clanking. And I know wherever Rose and I are, we're locked in.

Oh Luke. What has she done?

'I told you Tina is crazy,' Rose says.

'Tina.' I say aloud the name that has been plaguing me since the day she called *Good Morning, Ireland* and told the world my company was in trouble. 'Who was that? Just now, with the food?' I ask the question I already know the answer to.

'Tina,' Rose says with certainty.

'Yeah.' I swallow. 'That's what I thought.'

'You should eat,' Rose says. 'I left you some. It could be a few days before she's back.'

'She doesn't bring food every day?' I ask.

Rose makes a noise and I can't tell if it's a laugh or a cry. 'No. She doesn't come every day. I think that's the thing she loves the most, my excitement when I do see her. Like I said—'

'She's crazy.' I finish Rose's sentence for her. 'Believe me I know. I just wish it hadn't taken me nearly twenty years to figure it out.'

Chapter Fifty

Tina

Monday 22 July 2019

I stare at my reflection in the bedroom mirror. My hair is slowly darkening at the roots, more brick red than strawberry blonde now, and I know it's time to dye it again. My skin breathes for the first time in months without make-up. A clear, slightly jaded complexion stares back at me.

I can see the reflection of Darcy's and Luke's bed behind me. The bed they've spent countless nights together in. No doubt holding each other, caressing each other, making love. Making a baby. Every time I push the jealousy into the pit of my stomach it bubbles up at the back of my throat. I throw the hairbrush. It clanks against the mirror, not breaking it, but it does cause a large crack to trickle down the centre, splitting the mirror in two. I toss my head back and laugh at the irony. A mirror, mirroring me so well.

I stand up and, pouting, I place my hands firmly on my hips. I stare at my reflection in one side of the damaged glass. I am sophisticated. Elegant. An achiever.

I shift my weight on to the opposite foot, my reflection following. My image switches to the other side of the hairline fracture in the glass. On this side is an exhausted, broken woman. Slouching, and sad and real.

I snort and look away, hating to be reminded of the two halves of me that still don't make me whole. I pick up the hairbrush and drag it through my hair. It's knotty and dry, exhausted from having its natural limpness constantly manipulated into curls.

The house is painfully silent. I actually miss the sound of Darcy's movements. Luke has stopped making noise too and I haven't bothered to check on him in a while. I wonder if Darcy will see the irony when she realises she's been searching under the wrong floorboards all this time. If only she'd popped the heavy old boards in the sitting room, she'd have discovered her darling husband.

Inspired by Darcy's obsession with her bedroom floor I decided to do a little digging of my own. It's rather fortuitous that Darcy and Luke spent a fortune on insulation and underfloor heating to warm up their old house. When you dig it all out there's quite a bit of space down there. Admittedly it's a little snug for a grown man, but I still managed to make it work. I had to tie Luke's hands by his sides rather than behind his back, and he's turned slightly on his side because I just couldn't stuff him in any other way. It's not exactly the photo I wanted for my scrapbook – Luke bloodied and bruised with thick black masking tape across his beautiful lips and fear in his eyes. But it will do. He was heavy too, but that didn't surprise me. I worked up quite a sweat managing to get him in, in a race against the clock. I only had enough Xanax to knock Darcy out for a couple of hours. I wasn't even sure if she was going to drink the damn orange juice. And the pills are long out of date. I've had them for years. I tried getting more but the GP wouldn't prescribe them. He wanted me to see a counsellor and talk about my issues instead. As if that was going to help. *Useless idiot.* I get annoyed now just thinking about it.

I turn the radio on. Low in the background, a white noise to drown out the overbearing noise in my head. Unsurprisingly, they're talking about that missing cop. Lindsay's interview seems to have set off a tsunami of interest from every presenter and DJ in the country. Rose's face is everywhere. TV and newspapers. I can't even look at my phone without her face staring back at me online. She's dominating all channels as if she's more special than all the other missing people. She's pictured in her uniform. With her kids. On holiday with her husband. How can the media expect people to feel sorry for her when she's led such a damn charmed life? It's not fair.

Lindsay St Claire has appointed herself chair of this story. It's hers now. And all the other presenters and DJs seem to concede that. It's strange how that happens. How one person, with a burning confidence, can dominate and command, and others accept and follow like sheep. I used to think it was behaviour confined within the walls of an exclusive school, but I've since learned it follows into adult life. There's no real way to ever escape it other than to take charge for yourself. That's what I'm doing. It's what I've always done. Albeit in my own, unique way.

I scrape my hair into a neat ponytail, pop on some fancy clothes that I take from Darcy's wardrobe, and relish the fact that they're a little too big and oh so expensive, before I make my way into the kitchen. I pour granola into two bowls. Equal portions, of course. I wash strawberries, raspberries and blueberries and add them on top. I'm making my way towards the shed when I turn back and detour by the sitting room. I set the bowls down on the coffee table and laugh as I pick up the chisel I found on Darcy's dresser. It's almost as if she wanted to make this too easy for me. I pop the floorboard and Luke's eyes are closed and he doesn't seem to be breathing. I crouch, hovering over him. I hold my breath so I can listen for his. He's still breathing. Although just about. I snap off the masking tape and he screams.

'Darcy get out. Get out now.'

I roll my eyes and wait for him to realise he's wasting his breath.

'Two things,' I say tilting my head and raising a couple of fingers. 'One. It's rude to shout. Especially indoors. And two. She's not here. Not any more.'

'Darcy! Darcy!' he shouts.

'Now. Now. What did we talk about?' I say. 'If you're going to kick up a fuss I'm going to stop visiting.'

'Let me talk to her,' he begs, tears in the corners of his sleepy eyes.

'I already let you talk to her,' I remind him as I lean over his almost-lifeless body. 'On the phone, remember? And you told her to run.' I take a deep breath and sigh. 'I don't think we can let that happen again, do you?'

'What have you done?' There's terror sticking to his words and there's even more fear in his eyes now than when I tied him to a chair in the shed and we had a little fun with his tool box. He's afraid I've buried her, shoved her underground. Next to that yappy little dog of hers, perhaps.

'Where is she?' he begs.

'She's fine, but you should see your face.' Luke's relief is short-lived when I say, 'She's in the shed.'

'The shed?' he gasps as his eyes roll, and I wonder if he's going to pass out on me.

This is no fun.

'Yeah.' I make a face. 'Big metal structure. End of the garden. You know the one?'

'The baby?' he asks, opening his eyes again.

'The babies,' I correct. 'Rose is pregnant too.'

Luke doesn't reply. His eyes are closed again and his bloody lips have stopped quivering.

'Ugh,' I groan, wondering where I'll get rid of his body later. He's so much heavier than Andrew.

I pick up the bowls and walk away, making my way to the end of the stupidly large garden.

I shove my hand into my pocket and fish out the key. My fingers tremble and my hand shakes as I try to guide the key into the lock as if I'm opening a secret diary. It's rusty and weather-beaten and it always takes some patience to prise it open. Finally, it clicks and I unravel the chunky metal chains from the door, enjoying their clanging melody.

As always Rose scampers back as soon as the light slices into the confined space. I'm not sure if it's because she's a cop and she's always on guard or because she's watched one too many thrillers at the cinema. Maybe she's just genuinely terrified of me. She gave up trying to engage in psychobabble cop talk after the first night, when I knocked her sideways across the shed. She didn't wake up again until the next morning. Darcy, on the other hand, doesn't move. She's curled in a ball to one side, her hands covering her face, and if it wasn't for the noisy rattle when I open the door, I could believe she's asleep. I wait for her to look up but she doesn't. I'm dying for her to ask about Luke.

'Did you bring some food?' Rose asks, desperate.

I smile and I wait for her eyes to adjust to the light so she can see the bowls. Soon she notices and creeps forwards, on all fours like an animal.

I raise my leg to kick her away. She scurries back before I make contact.

'Are you hungry too, Darcy?' I ask, taking a single step forward but keeping the door right behind me.

There's no reply.

'Are you?' I raise my voice.

'Who *are* you?' Darcy asks, finally lifting her head.

I don't bother to reply to that redundant question.

'Where's Luke?' she asks, her tear-smeared eyes glistening in the moonlight.

I laugh, stepping closer still.

'Where is he?' Darcy raises her voice, and her body rises too, albeit exhausted and not very intimidating. 'If you've hurt him, so help me God . . .'

'You'll do what, Darcy? Get your solicitor to send me a strongly worded letter?' I snort. 'You're pathetic. All the money in the world can't buy you a backbone. Any guts and you'd have kicked me out of your house before my feet got too comfortable on your coffee table.'

'I'm going to kill you.' Darcy lunges forward with a burst of energy I didn't see coming. With a fervent slap I swat her away as if she's an irritating fly. She hits the ground with a loud thud.

'Careful!' Rose shouts, and my temper flashes for a moment before I realise she's warning Darcy and not me. 'Don't antagonise her,' Rose adds.

I like Rose. She's sensible.

'Now. Now. Now,' I say. 'Who said anything about killing anyone . . . yet.'

There's silence. Except for deep breathing, of course. Amplified by the stillness of the night. I reach my hand outside the door and fetch the shovel I've left leaning against the outside wall. It took me ages to clear out the tools. I really don't think Darcy appreciates my efforts. The shed has never been so tidy.

Rose looks at me, her neck long and curious. I place my finger over my lips and curl my fingers a fraction tighter around the handle. She nods with understanding, her body shaking as she takes in the cruel, sharp edges of a garden spade – she knows from past experience the damage it can do. Darcy might be thinking about

314

running but Rose knows they won't get far with cool metal to the back of the head.

I reach my other hand into my pocket and pull out my phone. Silent and still, Rose watches.

'Hello. Hello. The Gardaí please?' I say. I am quite the actress, and a slight quiver appears in my voice that wasn't there before. 'I want to report a missing person.'

'Help us!' Darcy bellows, but Rose charges forward shoving her hand over Darcy's mouth. Rose understands. Rose knows the consequences.

Tears trickle down Darcy's cheeks and over Rose's fingers.

'She's pregnant,' I say, choking back impressive fake tears. 'She's very poorly. I'm so worried something has happened to her. I think . . .' I pause and sob. 'I think she might be dead.'

Darcy shakes her head, and finally I sense it – her fear. It grips her tighter than my fingers around the spade. Realisation is painful, I know from experience.

'Please don't kill us,' Darcy says, cowering away from me.

I snort as I slide my phone back into my pocket. 'Don't be so dramatic, Darcy. I told you. Nobody is killing anybody.'

'Then why are we here?' she whimpers, crying so hard she can barely draw her breath.

'Because you have something I want.'

'You can have Darcy's Dishes,' she says. 'It won't cost a penny. I can just sign it over to you. And I won't tell anyone about this. If you let us go. I promise I won't.'

'That's a lie and you know it.' I scowl. 'Rose, will you tell her? She's making this harder by upsetting me with nasty lies.'

'Darcy,' Rose whispers and places her finger on her lips.

'Anyway,' I continue. 'I don't want your stupid Darcy's Dishes. Vegans save the planet crap. All I ever wanted was Luke, but you just couldn't let me have him. You're so bloody selfish. You brought this on yourself, you know.' I shrug as if I'm over it. 'But it doesn't matter because now I have something even better.'

Darcy stares at me blankly and I take some deep breaths to restrain myself from kicking her in her petrified face.

I point towards her round belly and say, 'Luke's baby, silly. I'm going to be a great mam.'

Chapter Fifty-One

DARCY

Tuesday 23 July 2019

Rain pelts the roof of the shed. The pitter-patter of large drops that I usually love to listen to from the comfort of my warm bed are loud and hostile, refusing to allow us to sleep. Time is losing all meaning and I can't tell if it's morning, evening or some time in between. The rain has dragged with it a cooler temperature, unseasonably low for July.

'Leave it, Darcy,' Rose says, as I rummage around for something to help get us the hell out of here. 'I've tried everything. There's no escaping. There are chains on the door and it's reinforced steel. Two pregnant women can't knock it down from this side.'

I rummage more and my wedding ring clinks against something glass. I slide my hands around its unusual shape and I recognise it instantly. It's my Businesswoman of the Year crystal award. Luke wanted to display it on the mantel but the idea made me uncomfortable. My parents always taught me to be modest. They said humility is our greatest gift. And so my awards over the years have ended up in the shed.

'Darcy, please?' Rose says. 'We need to be smart. And conserve energy. Sit down. You're exhausted.'

Rose is right. Deep down I know that trying to get out is futile. I just about have enough energy to lift my arms. And I can't even see what I'm searching for. I don't stand a chance of breaking the door down.

Defeated, I follow Rose's voice to the back of the shed and find her somewhere between the lawnmower and what I think are old tins of paint. I set the trophy down on the lid of a tin and sink on to the floor. We cling to each other. The hunger makes the cold in our bones even harder to bear. A wind whistles outside, trying desperately to shake the sturdy shed, but failing miserably.

Rose and I huddle at the back of the shed, waiting for the night to end.

'Who the hell is she?' Rose asks as we sit in the blackness.

'Honestly?' I pause for thought, wondering how I could have been so stupid. 'I'm not sure. All I know now is who she isn't.'

'How do you know her?' Rose asks. 'It's not from Pilates, that's for sure.'

I swallow hard. 'We were at school together.'

Rose is quiet for a moment, then says, 'Go on.'

'I didn't *really* know her. Not well, anyway. She was always kind of odd and no matter how nice I tried to be she just . . .' I sigh, thinking back. 'I dunno. Luke warned me never to get close to her.'

'But you ignored him,' Rose says.

'No. No. I took his advice. I stayed away from her. Then we left school and grew up. I never really thought about her again. She could have passed me on the street and I wouldn't have recognised her.'

'I couldn't name half the people I went to school with either,' Rose says. Another pause follows before she asks: 'Was she always a narcissist?'

'Yeah,' I say realising, possibly for the first time, that she was.

◆ ◆ ◆

Time loses all meaning in the darkness, and when Rose goes into labour there's no way of telling how long it's been. But her breathing is gradually becoming heavier and she's increasingly exhausted so I'm guessing it's been at least a few hours. She's trying so hard to be calm, dragging mostly controlled breaths in and out with the experience of someone who has given birth before. But every now and then it all becomes too much and a groan of pain will burst past her lips.

'You're doing great, Rose,' I say, tearing the hem of my T-shirt to create a makeshift cloth to dab against her forehead.

Rose pants and shakes in distress.

'They'll come,' I say, taking her hand and squeezing it gently. 'Someone will find us.' I try not to cry for Rose's sake. 'Help!' I shout as loud as I can. 'Help us please! Help us!'

Rose and I both know I'm wasting my breath. The shed walls are thick and insulated, and my nearest neighbours, the Robinsons, are elderly and hard of hearing. Everyone else in Cherryway is so concerned with privacy that their walls and hedges are high and their gardens large. My exhausted shouts can't scale that far.

Rose clutches her stomach and grits her teeth. It's terrifying to watch her in so much pain.

'What can I do?' I ask her. 'Is there anything I can do?'

Rose ignores me and concentrates on breathing. I try to move some stuff around to give Rose space to lie down. Feeling my way in the dark I shove some boxes of old books out of the way. I shriek as something crawls over my hand. It's just a spider, but a big one. I hate spiders but I don't have time to give it a second thought.

When the pain stops and Rose is calmer, I help her move into a half-sitting, half-lying position. I'm not sure it will help, but we always sit like this in antenatal classes. Rose closes her eyes and concentrates on her breathing. In, out. In, out.

'You're doing great,' I say, by way of encouragement.

Rose groans, suddenly gripping my hand, crushing my fingers as another contraction engulfs her. I want to help her get through the pain, so we breathe through it together – in, out. It helps us both. I'm less dizzy when I'm calm. The last thing I want to tell Rose is that I'm feeling faint. I can't pass out on her, she's scared enough already. I plead with myself to keep it together.

We fall into a pattern of Rose humming and rocking and managing her pain. I rock with her and hold her hand and I push my fear deep down. I try not to think about all the potential complications that I'd stupidly googled after my first antenatal class. I try not to think about the darkness and how I'm possibly supposed to help if I can't see what I'm doing.

'Rose,' I whimper, breaking the silence. 'Do you think Luke is dead?'

'I don't know.' Rose gasps. 'But it's really important we stay positive and focused.'

My heart breaks, because I think Rose does know. Ever professional and ever a trained Garda, Rose knows.

Chapter Fifty-Two

DARCY

Tuesday 23 July 2019

Rose grunts. It's sudden and animalistic and it scares me. I don't know what to do. The pain is getting worse. She twists and turns as if somehow she can escape it. 'It's coming, Darcy,' she puffs. 'I can feel it!'

'No. No. Not yet. It can't.' I'm trying so hard to hide my fear, but I'm not sure I can keep it up without Rose seeing through me or worse still, me scaring her even more. 'Oh Rose please try to hold on.'

A key rattles and chains clank and finally the shed door opens and light dazzles us. I cover my eyes, as the sudden brightness burns. Gillian takes one look at Rose and shakes her head. 'Now?' she says. 'You're having the baby now?'

'Do something!' I shout. 'Let us out of here!'

Gillian shakes her head.

'Call an ambulance,' I beg. 'We need paramedics.'

'Please help me!' Rose cries, squirming.

Gillian considers for a moment, then closes the door and locks it again, plunging us into a darkness that seems so much blacker than before.

'Darcy. Darcy are you there?' Rose says, and her voice is worryingly faint. She's not screaming any more either and she's suddenly oddly still.

'I'm here,' I say, taking her hand in mine and stroking my thumb over and back across her clammy palm.

'Don't leave me,' she whispers. 'Please don't leave me.'

I make the redundant promise. 'I'm not going anywhere.'

Rose is drifting in and out of consciousness and when I feel something warm and wet trickle past my knees, I suspect it's blood.

Oh Christ.

I hold my breath as the key rattles in the lock. No chains this time. And the door opens.

'They're here, Rose,' I say. 'They're going to help.'

I really hope they're going to help.

But it isn't paramedics, it's Gillian. She's carrying the large halogen torch that Luke uses when he's fishing the Christmas tree out of the attic. The torch lights up the whole shed. Gillian locks the door from the inside and puts the key in her coat pocket. My jaw drops as I stare at the puddle of blood that Rose is sitting in. It's a bright red and there's more of it than I was expecting.

'Is she still alive?' Gillian asks, and I can see lines of worry etched into her brow.

'I'm fine,' Rose answers.

'Don't fuck this up,' Gillian warns her. 'There's only one practice run.'

'Practice run?' I echo. *Oh God.* I begin to shake harder than I ever have before. 'So Rose is your guinea pig. This is your practice delivery and I'm next.'

'Rose is my patient,' Gillian snaps, genuinely offended.

In my panic I didn't notice the stethoscope that dangles around Gillian's neck before now. It's short, barely sitting on her shoulders on both sides, and I'm not sure but I think it's made of plastic. *A toy*, I think, horrified. If this is Gillian's idea of a joke it's bloody sick. And if it's not, then that's even more worrying.

Gillian places a baking tray on the ground next to Rose and me. There's a towel, scissors and tongs on it. Rose is ghostly pale and she's not moving. She's losing a lot of blood. I wish I knew how much is too much. My heart is beating out of my chest.

I look at Gillian, hoping she will suddenly realise how insane this is and do something to help. She can't seriously deliver Rose's baby with a child's-play toy and some kitchen equipment.

Rose screams, and I'm so relieved to hear her, despite her agony. 'It's coming! The baby is coming!'

'Gillian please,' I cry. 'It's not too late. Call an ambulance.'

'It's natural, Darcy,' Gillian says. 'Having a baby is the most natural thing in the world. You'll see. Soon it will be you.' She points towards my stomach.

'It's not natural to have a baby in a shed,' I say. 'Look around us. This is dangerous. Anything could go wrong.'

'I can see the head,' Gillian says, giddily.

'Breathe, Rose. Just breathe,' I encourage.

Gillian stands up and pulls her phone out of her pocket. But she isn't making a call for an ambulance. She's taking a picture.

'What are you doing?' I say.

'What?' Gillian shrugs. 'It's for my scrapbook.'

'You're still collaging,' I say, remembering.

'It's an underappreciated art,' Gillian says, snapping shots on her phone before putting it back in her pocket.

Rose howls and strains with all her strength. Her screams ring in my ears and Gillian, dropping to her knees, catches a tiny, blood-ied baby. Shock cuts through the air, chopping out any sound, and there is a moment of disbelief and reverence, before a tiny newborn's cries fill the air.

'Huh, a little girl,' Gillian says.

She reaches for some scissors and I gasp as she holds the scissors above the baby. Her hands shake as she cuts the cord and she turns towards me with round, softening eyes. And I know she's thinking about my baby. I glare back, determined not to let her see how petrified I am. She wraps the baby in the towel and it settles, crying less. Rose stretches her arms out waiting for Gillian to pass her the infant, but Gillian turns away and places the baby in the baking tray. She whips the towel off the infant and uses it to wipe the floor. 'You made a mess, Rose,' she scolds.

'She's cold,' I say, my eyes on the tiny baby girl whose spindly arms and legs squirm about as she shivers. 'Can't you see? The baby is freezing. She needs a blanket.'

Gillian continues to mop the floor.

'Please,' I shout. 'Listen to me.'

Rose's eyes roll back and the pool of blood beneath her swells. I shake her and call her name but she's unconscious.

'Help her!' I scream. 'Please, help her—'

'I knew I could do it,' Gillian says, cutting across me with a giddy sense of achievement.

'She's dying.' I'm hysterical as I alternate between shaking Rose and casting an eye on her shivering little girl.

'I know.' Gillian shrugs as she grabs the shovel that she left resting against the side of the shed. 'I'll need to get digging. Hopefully this won't take long. There's a repeat of *Good Morning, Ireland* in twenty minutes and I don't want to miss it.'

Rose is deathly pale and she's not moving and I can just about make out her chest rising and falling. The baby has stopped crying. The only sound is my hurried breathing.

'You can't leave us here,' I say as I crawl closer to Rose, placing my hand on her chest, desperate to feel her breathing. Fat, salty tears trickle down my cheeks when I feel her chest rise, pause and slowly fall as she clings to life.

'Stay with me Rose,' I beg. 'Please.'

I pull off my top and turn towards the baby, wrapping her up in it. She's cold to touch and she's so tiny my shirt can double fold over her.

'What are you doing?' Gillian snaps, catching my shoulder and jerking me away. 'Don't touch her!'

I wrap my arms around myself, shivering in just my bra. 'Gillian please. She's cold.'

'Stop calling me that!' Gillian screeches, raising the shovel above her head.

I scream and dive over the baby.

'I'm not Gillian.' She stands up, the shovel still held high. 'I'm not Gillian.'

'You're not Gillian,' I say, hoping that's what she wants me to say.

I reach my hand out for the baby but keep my eyes on Gillian's.

'I'm not Gillian,' she repeats.

I rub the baby's belly gently, hoping to warm or rouse her. It's only when a subtle cry follows that I realise I'm holding my breath.

The baby's crying grows louder.

Thank God.

Gillian twitches and snaps out of her daze. She lowers the shovel and points the sharp metal edge towards the baby. 'Shut that thing up!'

I grab the baby as quickly as my exhausted arms can and cradle her wrinkled, new skin close to my chest. I can feel her warm up instantly and she's moving again, all uncoordinated and helpless.

'You can't keep her,' Gillian says.

'I know,' I say, kissing her little head. 'She has a family.'

Gillian laughs. 'No. Not that. Bloody hell, Darcy. You can't keep her because I need rid. Rid of them both.'

I glance over my shoulder at Rose. The puddle on the floor isn't any bigger than the last time I checked and I can hear her laboured breaths – just about, but she's still here.

'You wouldn't do something like that,' I say, a part of me still believing that she isn't capable of such darkness.

'It wouldn't be the first time.'

It's hard to breathe. Fear is a heavy thing. It can crush a person. Realisation is even heavier.

'What have you done?' I gasp.

Gillian smirks, but there's an unmissable sadness in her eyes. A hint of regret.

'Andrew Buckley?' I ask, knowingly.

Gillian shrugs.

'And Gillian. The real Gillian.'

'She thought she was better than me.' Gillian exhales.

Rose groans, rousing to consciousness.

'Right. Gimme her,' Gillian says, reaching her arms out to me.

'What?' My eyes drop to the baby. 'No.'

Gillian, exhales, losing patience. 'I said give her to me.'

I clutch the baby tighter, turning her away. 'Gillian please,' I beg.

'Gillian is dead!' she hisses, spraying saliva into the air. 'I'm Tina. And you fucking know it!'

'Okay. Okay,' I say. 'You're Tina.'

I turn towards Rose and press the baby against her chest. I fold her arms around her daughter, securing them both together.

'Get up,' Tina hisses.

'Okay. Okay,' I say as I drop my hands by my sides and I slide the scissors from the baking tray between my fingers. My whole body is shaking, but I remind myself that Tina doesn't know that.

Tina bends and reaches for the baby and I raise my arm and lunge. The scissors swipe her face, dragging a chunk from her chin. She presses her hand to her face, blood trickling past her knuckles, and she tumbles and bangs against the lawnmower knocking my clunky Businesswoman of the Year trophy on to my foot. Pain surges through my bones but I don't make a sound as I bend down and pick it up. Gillian drags herself to her feet, furious and bloodied. My teeth are chattering. I was cold in my bra before but now my body is on fire.

She glares at me. I can't take my eyes off the blood trickling down her fingers. I didn't mean to hurt her, just frighten her. But she's not scared.

Tina raises the shovel above her head. The baby cries and I scream, and as she jerks forward I kick the halogen lamp. She trips and flaps her arms to keep her balance. Her spade falls, but she doesn't. And when she bends to pick it up again, I scream, loud and petrified and powerful, as I raise the trophy above my head and bring it crashing down.

This is it.

Chapter Fifty-Three

GILLIAN

I don't see her face as her hands curl around my neck, her fingers overlapping when she squeezes. Her chest is hot against my back as she works up a sweat when I buck and twist. My mouth gapes, searching for air, and my lungs burn when I can't find it. Pointing my tiptoes, I can just about manage to sweep the blades of freshly cut grass as I dangle from her strong hold.

I hear her scream. Above the racing squish of my blood coursing through my veins, above the high-pitched ringing in my ears, I can hear her scream as she realises she's gone too far. Too crazy. She's killing me. And she knows it.

When her grip loosens and she tosses me to the ground, for a fleeting second I think it's over.

I guzzle air. The smell of soil and summer as I lie face down in the grass. Pain explodes in my lower back and something snaps under the weight of her boot stomping me into the earth. When her hand fans my hair, shoving my face into the soil, I know this is it. I taste blood and muck as I drink in my final moments. The crack of the rock as it slams into my skull is loud and sudden. It takes my breath away as the noise hangs in the air. And then. I'm gone.

TINA

Stars twinkle in a cloudless sky. Moonlight shines through the branches of huge old trees casting creepy shapes and shadows on the ground. I stand under the tallest one and cross my arms, and then I rub my hands up and down my arms trying to keep myself warm while I breathe in the enormity of what I've just done. Exhausted and blood spattered, I scorch the grass so it's like the stamp of a half-arsed bonfire. I fetch the cans of cheap cider from my school bag. The smell turns my stomach as soon as I open them and spill each one on to the ground, tossing the empty cans on to the grass in the notorious binge-drinking spot. Satisfied I'm leaving the remains of a good party behind, I roll Gillian down the hill. It's much harder work than I thought and beads of nervous perspiration trickle down my spine. Finally, I dump her into the shallow grave I've dug in the foundations for the wall around the new tennis court. I overheard Mr Buckley telling Mr McEvoy that the cement trucks are arriving first thing in the morning. Gillian will be under three feet of concrete before anyone notices she's missing.

I take one last look at her beautiful face before I cover it in clay. As I walk away, leaving Gillian's mutilated body under cold soil, I whisper aloud, 'I don't like it when people think they're better than me,' and I watch my foggy breath dance across the night air as I skip back to the dorm.

Chapter Fifty-Four

Darcy

Wednesday 24 July 2019

The sound of my screams is ringing in my ears and the pain in my foot is almost unbearable. I look down. Tina is face down on the ground with my blood-spattered trophy beside her. Crimson blood trickles past her red hair and pools around her.

The baby stirs, but I'm paralysed. My chest is constricted and I can't breathe. I can't believe what I've done. I've killed her.

The crying grows louder and I know we have to get out of here. I crouch over Tina's body and yelp as searing pain shoots from my foot all the way up my leg, and I'm desperate to stand and take the weight off my foot, but I don't. Not until I reach into Tina's pocket and fish out the key. Euphoric, I pull myself up and hop on my good leg towards the lock. The key slides into it with ease and I turn it, waiting for the blissful clink of it opening. But it doesn't unlock. I turn the key back. And forward again. And back. Nothing. And finally when I turn the lock over I discover a combination is needed too. My heart breaks as I look around at the carnage in the shed and realise it was all for nothing.

I drag myself back to the crying baby as she tries to suckle.

'Rose?' I whisper as I bend and place my hand on her shoulder. 'Rose, are you awake?'

Rose groans and tries to lift her head.

'Can you feed the baby?' I ask, wondering if that's the right thing to do. Rose is so weak. What if I make her sicker? I'm so scared.

Rose's eyes flicker open and she nods.

'Shh,' I encourage. 'Shh. It's okay.'

I lift Rose's shirt and guide the baby to her breast. Rose rouses enough to smile, thanking me without words, but she can't muster enough energy to completely open her eyes.

'She's feeding,' I say, as the baby cuddles close to her mother. And my hands cradle my bump, as I fear we might all die in this shed.

Rose and I fall into a pattern of feeding and sleeping. When the baby cries, I help her to her mother's breast. When she's content I place her in the baking tray and clean what I can. I took my trousers off – my leg is badly swollen and I needed the relief – and ripped the material into cloths. They clean the baby up when she wees or poos. I hang the damp ones over the handle of the lawnmower so I can use them again when they're dry.

The pain is intense, and I'm not sure if I'm passing out or sleeping, but it grows increasingly harder for me to wake when the baby cries, and I wonder if she's been crying for a while before I heard her this time. I lift her and press her against Rose but she continues crying and nuzzles away from her mother. I try again but she's becoming distressed. Rose too. Rose is hot. Too hot. I place my hand against her chest and her skin sears like hot coal. *A fever*, I think. And it doesn't take a genius to work out Rose has an infection. She's barely had more than a few lucid seconds since the baby arrived, hours ago now. I want to ask her where it hurts – if it hurts – but I know she's not strong enough to offer a response.

A film of dust clings to the back of my throat. I've never been so thirsty. And Rose must need water too, especially as she's feeding the baby. The smell of bodily fluid and dried blood mixing with old grass is rancid, and if I leave this place I swear to never take fresh air for granted ever again.

Time passes in a blur. Hours are punctuated only by the baby sleeping or crying. Rose doesn't wake any more. And the baby seems to cry and cry now. I wish I could pace to soothe her in my arms, but I'm weary and broken. I sit next to Rose and the baby and I close our eyes.

I hear a distant voice call my name. 'Darcy!' someone shouts. 'Darcy, I'm here.'

I smile, thinking I'm dreaming, but the door rattles and rattles and then a voice says, 'Step back' and there's a crashing sound and with my eyes closed I feel a burst of light against my face.

'Oh thank God. Oh thank you Jesus.' I recognise Mildred's voice. I try to open my eyes but the light is too bright.

'I have it. I have a pulse,' someone else says, and I feel fingers on my wrist.

'It's Rose Callahan, Sarge,' a voice I don't recognise says. My eyes flick open and I see a woman in Gardaí uniform standing over me. 'Rose? Is that you?' I ask.

'You're safe now, Darcy,' the woman whispers. 'Everything is okay. We have you.'

There's commotion all around me. The baby crying. Voices. Someone is lifting me. I feel fresh air on my skin. I'm outside. *They came. They really, really came.*

'Luke,' I whisper. 'Find Luke.'

Someone is holding my hand. Sunlight shines on my face. I'm lying down and I feel slow and steady waves of movement beneath.

My eyes flicker open and I see blue sky and fluffy clouds overhead as I'm carried across my lawn on a stretcher.

We pass by a low hum of voices.

'Unresponsive male in the sitting room, Sarge,' someone says.

'And the kidnapper?' a man asks.

'Female. Late thirties. Bled out in the shed.'

Epilogue

There's a guy doing my hair. He pulls and tugs.

'Post-baby hair,' he complains. 'We can never get it right.'

I glance at my daughter, nursing on my lap. It's hard to believe she's two months old already. Her hand is curled around my finger, a habit she's had since the day she was born, and her knees are tucked into her chest. Mildred says it's because my bump was so small it'll take her a while to unravel. As if she's a ball of beautiful twine that has changed my life.

The doctors couldn't believe she survived. She was delivered by emergency C-section shortly after my arrival in hospital, but I was so dehydrated and malnourished that she was massively underweight on her arrival.

We spent the first week of her life apart. Me in one hospital, Rosie in another.

'She's a little fighter,' the doctor said when I was finally strong enough to visit.

'Just like her mother,' the nurse said, and then she asked me for a selfie because she couldn't wait to tell her friends she'd met me and cared for my baby.

In the here and now, someone from make-up tells me to shut my eyes as she brushes shadow over my lids.

'Hello, hello, hello,' Lindsay St Claire says at the door. 'Welcome back, Darcy. We're so excited to have you.'

'Thank you,' I say.

'Don't forget to leave your phone here. No more calls on air this time.' She winks.

I laugh. But what Lindsay probably doesn't know is that my phone is hopping. Every big-name entrepreneur in the country wants a slice of Darcy's Dishes. When the story of my kidnapping broke, sales went through the roof. The factory can barely keep up with demand. And the banks are throwing money at us.

I do still wonder if things would be different if Luke had been more honest with me instead of hiding mounting bills and lying to me about panicked phone calls to the bank. But, on reflection, I understand why he did it. He was trying to protect his family. It was misguided and foolish but it was also kind and caring, and so typically Luke.

Lindsay places her hand on my shoulder and says, 'We're on air in five, are you ready?'

'So ready.'

'And we're live in three . . . two . . . one . . .' the man with the headset says, and I smile and face the camera as I open the door of Luke's hospital bedroom and walk inside, just as we rehearsed. I have my baby in one arm and a crutch in the other and Lindsay said it's TV gold.

The camera rolls as I approach Luke's bed and he smiles.

This isn't the first time I've walked into Luke's room. The first time, I sat in a wheelchair crying in the hallway before I even got near the door. And I was a hysterical mess when I saw him lying in bed for the first time draped in wires, as machines did the work for him that his body simply could not. Luke saved my life when he managed to free himself enough to raise the alarm, but the worry that he wouldn't pull through was too hard to bear. I sat beside his bed for hours every day. Often the nurses from my ward would have to come and drag me unwillingly back to my bed. And when I was discharged, I divided my time evenly between Rosie and Luke, bouncing from one hospital to another. Rosie and I were discharged weeks ago, me first and Rosie three days later. We've been crashing at Mildred's since – not quite ready to face our house. And especially not without Luke.

Today isn't the first time Luke, Rosie and I have been together as a family. I've brought our little girl to the hospital often to see her dad. But today is the first day we tell our story, in our own words, to the whole country.

After the regular theme tune to *Good Morning, Ireland* and the usual light introduction from Lindsay, the camera focuses on Luke's bed. I'm sitting perched on the edge with my beautiful baby in my arms. Lindsay sits in a navy plastic chair next to us.

And she says, 'Folks. You'll notice we're on location today. And what a special place it is. Thank you to the doctors and nurses and all the staff at Beaconfield for all the amazing work they do. And thank you to the Hogan family for welcoming us with open arms today. This is their story.'

The interview doesn't run over but the segment feels long as I answer kindly worded questions.

'The real Gillian Buckley has been exhumed and buried with her father,' I say. 'It's been nearly twenty years but they're together again.'

'And Rose Callahan, the Garda who was also kidnapped?' Lyndsey asks.

'Writing a book,' I say, beaming proudly. 'An autobiography about balancing life on the force with being a mother of four.'

'Remarkable. And, you're a remarkable woman too, Darcy. You really are.'

As the interview continues Rosie cries a couple of times and I rock her patiently. Luke wilts on occasion too, as he describes his ordeal under the floor of the house, and how his chance to escape finally came when Tina, after telling him about the impending arrival of Rose's baby, had dashed away to play midwife without properly securing the floorboards.

And when Lindsay says, 'Just one last question', I'm light with happiness.

I just want to sit beside my husband and feed my daughter. Like any regular family.

'What is the first thing you're going to do when you get home?' Lindsay asks.

Luke places his hand on my knee and I know he's got this.

He says, 'We're having carpet fitted. No more floorboards.'

ACKNOWLEDGMENTS

Some books are effortless to write. Fingers bang keys furiously until all the characters, feelings and crescendos of action come together in a beautiful symphony of black and white. This was not one of those books! *Keep Your Friends Close* challenged me every step of the way. But, it also reminded me that writing is a team effort. And I am so grateful for all the other players.

Hayley Steed – you are a trailblazer. You're also kind, funny, encouraging and most importantly Westlife-loving! I'm so lucky to have an agent like you at my side.

Sammia Hamer – thank you for giving me, and this story, the time needed. It's made a world of difference to me and the characters. Ian Pindar – for pushing for the best. Always. From me. And from the story. And mostly, thank you so much for doing it all with a sense of humour intact. And thank you to Sadie Mayne and Swati Gamble for your eagle eyes and attention to detail.

To my fellow writer and dear friend Caroline Finnerty – thank you for your ever kind and encouraging words. For understanding the ups and downs. And for being the sounding board that I so badly need.

To my family – I love you. But, if it's 7.30 p.m. and I'm still in my pyjamas at my desk with four empty coffee cups next to me, the answer to, 'What's for dinner?' is probably takeaway, or pizza – if you can find some in the freezer.

Finally, Dear Reader – thank you very much for reading this book. I will forever remain blown away that people choose to spend their precious time reading my words. I so hope you enjoyed this story.

ABOUT THE AUTHOR

Photo © 2019 Steve Langan

Janelle Harris penned her first story on scented, unicorn-shaped paper. She was nine. A couple of decades, one husband, five children, two cats and a dog later she wrote another story. Unfortunately the paper lacked any fragrance but that didn't hinder *No Kiss Goodbye* from becoming an international bestseller. Janelle now writes psychological suspense for Lake Union and women's fiction for Bookouture. She is always on the lookout for aromatic notepads.